Arnie Carver

AND THE PLAGUE OF DEMEVERDE

Arnie Carver

AND THE PLAGUE OF DEMEVERDE

KENNETH R. BESSER

FOR ZVUL, YITZCHAK, GITTEL, SHMUEL, TZIPPORAH, AND BINYAMIN,
THE MOST PRACTICALLY PERFECT CHILDREN IN THE WORLD
AND
SUSAN, THEIR MOTHER, WHO LOVES US ALL BY READING TO US

THANKS TO ETHAN FRIER, SETH GREENBAUM, KAILA HOUGH, DAVID
HOWARTH, JENNIFER KLUPT, ORI LEIBERMAN, MAX MEIZLISH, AND
MATTHEW TETTELBACH, ALL OF WHOM SHARED MUCH WITH US

© 2007 Kenneth R. Besser
Illustrations by Darren W. Cranford © by Kenneth R. Besser
All rights reserved. Published by RTMC Organization, LLC

No part of this book may be reproduced or transmitted in any form or by any means, electronic or mechanical including photocopying, recording, or by an information storage and retrieval system – except by a reviewer who may quote brief passages in a review to be printed in a magazine, newspaper, television or radio program, or on the World Wide Web – without the publisher's written permission. For information, please contact: Permissions Department, RTMC Organization, LLC, Post Office Box 15105, Baltimore, Maryland 21282-5105, permissions@RTMC.org Telephone: 410-900-7834

Although the author and publisher have made every effort to ensure the accuracy and completeness of information contained in this book we assume no responsibility for errors, inaccuracies, omissions, or any inconsistency herein. Any slights of people, places or organizations are unintentional. This is a work of fiction, Any similarity to real people or events is purely coincidental.

McDonald's and BigMac are trademarks of McDonald's Corporation, Oak Brook, IL, USA

Library of Congress Cataloging-in-Publication Data
Besser, Kenneth R.
Arnie Carver and the plague of Demeverde / Kenneth R. Besser.
p. cm.
Summary: After his billionaire parents are murdered in 2024, thirteen-year-old Thayne, a sheltered child prodigy, sets out to find their killer, first by replacing himself with a life-like robot and then by adopting an alter ego and attending the Global Optimum Development Academy, an international high school for physically, intellectually, and sensorially gifted students.
ISBN 978-1-934316-02-3
[1. Orphans--Fiction. 2. Identity--Fiction. 3. Gifted children--Fiction. 4. High schools--Fiction. 5. Schools--Fiction. 6. Science fiction.] I. Title.
PZ7.B46547Ar 2007
[Fic]--dc22
2007001090
Printed and bound in the United States of America.
March 2007

CONTENTS

Arnie Carver

AND THE PLAGUE OF DEMEVERDE

THAYNE DAVIDSON MILLER III

Like most children his age, Thayne Davidson Miller, III, often said he hated his very existence. He didn't really hate it, but he didn't love it either. Thayne enjoyed some big advantages in life. Huge ones, actually; but everything always costs something and, in Thayne's case, the costs of his huge pluses were some even bigger minuses.

As a childhood prodigy who could speed-read two pages per second, Thayne found learning almost anything very easy. Going to school like regular kids would have been no problem at all, if only he would have ever had the chance. Nonetheless, being the only child of two of the richest people in the world meant that Thayne never got the opportunity to have an ordinary school experience or any of the other parts of a normal childhood either.

Waking up to the smell and sound of his butler preparing his favorite breakfast in a closeted kitchenette, halfway across his enormous bedroom, Thayne sat up in his king-sized bed and looked at the calendar on the far wall to be sure he wasn't still dreaming. It was, in fact, his thirteenth birthday, June 1, 2024. He adjusted his silk pajamas and satin-covered comforter and waited for the kindly, but short, fat, balding, and bespectacled Jacques Marquis to feed him. The scrambled eggs with American cheese, rye toast with butter, and an ice-cold glass of milk were his standard morning fare.

"Thanks," Thayne said, taking the first bite of the creamy eggs, while Jacques stood beside the bed. He nodded his approval of the repast to his grandfatherly companion, who then walked to the closet cabinets lining the wall beside Thayne's slumber palace. "Where are we going today?" Thayne asked.

Jacques took a navy blue pinstripe coat and pants from the rack full of suits and matched it with a light blue shirt and a tie with a touch of red. "Well, today, in honor of your birthday, we have a special surprise for you. Then, tonight, we have to go to TDM Textiles in Chapel Hill, North Carolina, and after that on to Color Week in Paris, France."

"Great," Thayne moaned, in a voice absolutely devoid of enthusiasm. "Another tour of the mills followed by a week locked in a suite in Paris, while Mom and Dad go decide what colors the world's clothes will be next year." He followed the last of the eggs with a final gulp of milk and a sigh. "I hate my life."

"*Les pauvres sont l'enfant riche,*" Jacques said. Poor little rich kid.

Thayne was one of what most everyone else called "those fortunate few." The key word being "fortunate" because his parents were loaded. Not just loaded mind you, but pretty much filthy rich. And not just filthy rich, but absolutely obscenely wealthy. In fact, Thayne's father, Thayne Davidson Miller, II, was one of the top ten wealthiest people in the world.

Being so rich, however, was no bed of roses. Most children of the obscenely wealthy had a nanny to stay home and take care of them as they grew up, while their parents flew around the world doing whatever it was that they did. Those children often grew up hating their parents for never being around.

Thayne's parents told him they had both had nannies and they had hated having them because they felt that neither their parents nor their nannies seemed to want them. That was why they never used a nanny or ever left Thayne at home. "We're smarter and more loving than our parents were," they explained. "Plus, we worked so hard for so many years to have you and we're so worried that something might happen to you while we might be away. So that's why we take you with us everywhere we go."

Still, even smart and loving parents need a little help every now and then; and for that they had Jacques Marquis. Thayne pushed his breakfast tray aside and walked into the bathroom just off the sleeping corner of his bedroom. By the time that he came back with his very curly hair slicked straight with gel, Jacques had finished laying out his clothes and was about to carry the breakfast tray back to the kitchenette.

Thayne looked at the outfit that Jacques had selected

and moved the shirt and tie to a table beside his bed, so he could replace them with his own choices. As he put on his fresh underwear, Thayne said, "You know, I am about to be thirteen years old and I've been able to dress myself for years now. So you don't have to pick my clothes for me anymore."

Jacques put the tray down in the kitchenette, walked back to the table, and placed the shirt and tie back on the bed with the suit. He picked up the pants and held them ready for Thayne to get in them. "I dressed your grandfather as his gentleman's gentleman from the day that he hired me until the day we buried him." Thayne begrudgingly stepped into the pants. "I dressed your father as his gentleman's gentleman from the day he was born until the day he married your mother." Jacques shook out the folds of the starched shirt and held it up for Thayne to put on. "And I will continue to dress you as your gentleman's gentleman until the first of us either marries or dies."

Jacques, too, often glibly complained that he hated his very existence, but he did love his current responsibility. Having to raise a child was not the position for which Jacques had applied or been hired. He was sixty-five years old when Thayne was born, and though he was still pretty healthy, for a seventy-eight year old man, he was ready to retire as his fourth gentleman's gentleman.

"Piff! You're not really a gentleman's gentleman after all, are you, Jacques?"

"Most assuredly I am, young sir." Jacques picked up the socks.

"You are not," Thayne smiled. "Mom and Dad found you out long ago and told me."

"Really?" Jacques replied, with feigned indifference,

bending over and holding the first sock open for Thayne to step into.

"Yes," Thayne explained. "You have always called yourself a gentleman's gentleman, but you aren't a typical gentleman's gentleman."

"I'm not?" Jacques asked incredulously.

"No. You were born to French parents in upstate New York and you lived your late teenaged years in England. There, you learned how a butler acted by watching the neighbors' servants. You left your parents in London and moved back to the states, seeking to make your own way to California; but you ran out of money here in Philmont, Wyoming."

"Whatever you say, young sir," Jacques deadpanned again, holding the second sock open.

"You convinced Grandpa T.D. that you were a gentleman's gentleman when you found yourself out of work forty-nine years ago. Grandpa T.D. needed a gentleman's gentleman and you needed a job."

"Oh, really?"

"Yes," Thayne continued, relaying the story his parents had told him. "Grandpa T.D. had just become really rich, nouveau riche the rest of American society called them."

"I see," Jacques replied, in a dignified, but bored, kind of way.

"Yes. Just like me, he was an only child. He had invested the Miller family's mining fortune in several other companies and became a centimillionaire in just a few more years."

"I see," Jacques repeated.

"Not just the mere multimillionaires that his parents and grandparents had been."

"If you say so, young sir." Jacques placed a shoehorn in

one shoe.

"Did Grandpa really ask you 'What is a centimillionaire gentleman without a gentleman's gentleman?' like Dad says he did?"

"A gentleman's gentleman never repeats anything that his gentleman might have ever said," Jacques coldly replied.

"And did you really answer, 'Nothing, why nothing at all' like Dad says you did?"

"Your father always speaks too much of foolish things," Jacques said through a tight hidden smile, moving the shoehorn to the second shoe.

"He also said that he inherited you when Grandpa T.D. and Grandma Essie, suddenly died in the train crash in Japan. Were you really handed down to Dad as part of the estate?"

"People are not chattel, young sir."

"Dad says you stood as the best man at his wedding to Mom."

"I did."

"And that you've taken care of me ever since I was born."

"Have you ever noticed anyone else accompanying you since your first day?" Jacques inquired.

Thayne hesitated uncomfortably. "No."

"Then learn from that what you will," Jacques smiled, putting the tie through the collar of Thayne's shirt.

Thayne craned his neck and groaned as Jacques made the perfect knot. "I hate my life," he repeated.

Jacques groaned sympathetically and asked, "What exactly is the source of your discontent today?"

"Well, first of all, no offense intended, you are the only person other than my parents who I have ever been allowed to really know in the whole wide world."

"That is true," Jacques confessed. "But don't blame me. Your parents are just very particular about your safety."

"Yeah, but they go way too far with it," Thayne explained. "You were the only person present, besides my parents, if you don't count the jet pilot flying somewhere over France, when I supposedly 'graduated' kindergarten."

"Yes."

"If that's what you'd call it when they declared I was able to read and count to a hundred at age two."

"I know, young sir."

"And you were also the only other person present for my high school 'graduation,' somewhere over China, when I was barely eight."

"I know, again."

"Ditto for every other one as well," Thayne added.

"Ditto," Jacque agreed with him.

Thayne's parents gave him a bachelors of liberal arts when he was only ten. His father, a lawyer by degree, but just another family centimillionaire by inheritance, presented Thayne his juris doctorate somewhere over Spain when he was eleven. Thayne's mother, a doctor, declared him more knowledgeable than she was about medicine somewhere over India the week before, on the way home for his thirteenth birthday.

Thayne gave Jacques a frustrated look. "I mean, I understand they don't want anything bad ever to happen to me, but they have made my life horrible. Not only does nothing bad ever happen to me, but also nothing at all ever happens to me either; except getting to read and learn and travel around the world with them. And even then, all I end up doing is sitting in one apartment or office or another."

"You know they are just trying to protect you," Jacques

said, seeking to console him again in what was a regularly recurring argument. "They would simply die a thousand deaths if anything ever happened to you. And in these days and times, you are one of the most likely targets in the world for a kidnapping."

"Kidnapping, shmidnapping." Thayne slid into the jacket that Jacques held out for him. "In five more years, I'm going to be old enough to live on my own, and mark it to the day, Jacques, in five years and a day, I will be." Thayne sat down in a winged-back chair, picked up a VirtuComp palm game, and turned it on. "So, Jacques, Mom and Dad told me all the stories about you. What dirt do you have on them?"

"We haven't the time for such foolishness today," Jacques answered him, watching the boy play a noisy, explosive war on the screen.

"Sure we do," Thayne said, thumbing the buttons with both hands.

"You already know your parents' life stories," Jacques replied. "They say they were meant for each other from the time they were born. Both of them were the only children of doting parents, who spared no expense of time or money to constantly prepare them to move up in the world. Just like they are doing for you."

"Yeah, right," Thayne mocked, as one commando slaughtered another.

Jacques continued. "Both of them made a perfect score on the tests they took to get into their university, where they met shortly after your Grandpa T.D. and Grandma Essie died, when I became your father's gentleman's gentleman."

"Yeah, I know all that," Thayne egged him to go on and pushed the restart button. "What about the dirt, though?"

"None to be found," Jacques assured him.

"Sure there is. There has to be."

"No, I'm sorry. There isn't. Your parents were sweethearts at first sight and got married in the university chapel, while your dad studied law and your mom studied medicine, though neither one of them would ever have to really work a day in their life."

"'A useless life of leisure,' Dad says." New warriors appeared on the VirtuComp's screen.

"Quite," Jacques agreed. "Your dad's businesses were well run for him by the same people that had worked for T.D., while he studied whatever he wanted merely for the sake of learning something new to keep from being bored."

"Where do I come into the action?" Thayne prodded both Jacques and the killer in camouflage between his thumbs.

"You know very well where," Jacques replied. "Why are we wasting this time going down memory lane again?"

"Because it's my birthday, and it has now become our own private ritual for you to tell me the story of my life each birthday," Thayne informed him.

"Our ritual, eh?"

"Yes, our ritual of passing each year," Thayne said.

"Since when do we have this ritual?" Jacques asked.

"Since now," Thayne advised him. He paused a second from his game and motioned toward Jacques. "So, go on."

"If you wish," Jacques replied, sitting on the chair opposite the boy playing general. "Where were we? Oh, yes, your parents had it all, almost. The one thing they really wanted, however, no amount of knowledge or money was able to give them."

"And what was that?"

"They wanted to have a baby, a child of their own, and for whatever reason, whoever or whatever controlled such things was keeping it from happening for them." Jacques sighed. "Not having a child made them very distraught and they began to lose interest in anything else going on in their world, except for being parents of their very own child."

"Sounds sad," Thayne quipped. "I hope they get to do it soon."

"Quite," Jacques grimaced. "I tried to help them, of course, but there was not much I could do."

"What did you do, Jacques?"

"I suggested they adopt a child. There were plenty of beautiful little kids out there who would have loved to have them as parents, but they didn't want someone else's child. They wanted their own. And they grew sadder and more despondent with every day they remained childless."

"Get to the trip to Demeverde already," Thayne hurried him on with both hands on his game.

"If you know the story so well, then why don't you tell it," Jacques rejoined.

"Nope, you have to tell it. That's part of our ritual."

"Then be patient."

"Okay."

"One day they decided to go on a second honeymoon and try to find a little happiness on the tropical island paradise of Demeverde."

"Just out of the blue?" Thayne twisted the palm game, squeezing the buttons firmly.

"No." Jacques sighed. "As you know, your parents talked about wanting to be beachcombing vagabonds many times." Jacques imitated Thayne's mother's high-pitched voice. "'It looks so beautiful,' your mom said, as she showed your dad the travel brochure." Jacques switched to a deep husky voice. "'And it sounds it, too.' your dad agreed. He'd recited the first paragraph of the brochure to her so many times that he could do it from memory as he acted out holding it up."

Jacques held an imaginary brochure up in the air and pretended to read from it.

"'Whether you come to Demeverde to explore the land or just to discover yourself, you will surely join the many who have found shelter and renewal in this Atlantic tropical paradise's fair shores, lush mountains, and fertile valleys.'"

"Why Demeverde?" Thayne asked, making one player cause another to disappear in a puff of acrid, greasy, black smoke.

"You already know why," Jacques said with a sigh, lowering his arm again. "They wanted to get away from everything for a while. Just to relax and be romantic."

"Tell me about the virmail messages," Thayne implored.

"You already know about the messages," Jacques complained and then teased. "You know, for a kid with a photographic memory, you don't seem to retain much of what you hear."

"I know I know it," Thayne said. "And you know I know it, but just do it anyway for our ritual's sake."

"Fine then," Jacques acquiesced, "for our ritual." He shook his head in a sham of displeasure. "Your parents sent me several virmail messages about the vacation, which kept getting longer and longer than the initial two weeks. Two weeks became four, which then became two months, which again became four. After the first two weeks your dad sent a virtual mail message. I remember his torso popping up out of the virtual reality display.

"'Having a wonderful time sharing life with the locals. Staying another two weeks.'

"After two more weeks, your dad sent me another message by virmail.

"'Having a really great time! Signed up for sharing sessions at a local university. Still working on the problem. Staying another month.'

"After the end of the second month, another message came.

"'Think that we may be onto something big here. Local experts are sharing their solutions with us. Very advanced technology. Still working on the problem. Staying another month.'

"After the end of the third month, still another message came.

"'Jacques! Eureka! We are going to have a baby! Staying another month to make sure it sticks. Plus, making great business contact with the local leader. Will be home in another month.'"

Thayne put down the VirtuComp game, picked up a wireless controller for a small Intellitron lifelike doll, and began making the miniature likeness of himself march around the chair where Jacques was sitting. "So how did I get to be born so smart?" he asked.

"Now, you are really pushing it!" Jacques complained. "Retelling the story of your life as a birthday ritual is one thing, but doing so conceitedly is totally unacceptable."

Thayne held the Intellitron's control up to his mouth and made the doll say in his own voice, "Come on, I need the boost."

"Fine, then," Jacques relented with a heavy sigh. "We will continue with the story only."

"Good," the Thayne doll said.

"Even before you arrived, your parents thought you

would be the cutest and smartest child ever born on earth. They started reading to you all of the time they were with you, even while you were still in your mother."

Thayne began making the doll do calisthenics. "Did you ever ask them what they were doing?"

"Sure," Jacques said. Then he inhaled and strained to get out Thayne's mother's voice. "'It has been proven that children who are shared with in the womb are significantly smarter in kindergarten than children who are not. So I've been reading him the entire Children's Encyclopedia from cover to cover, all twenty-six volumes, as soon as I found out that I was going to have him.' They had worked so hard to get you, she said, that she did not want to do anything other than what the most noted experts in Demeverde said was best for a child."

"What did Dad say about that?" the doll asked in between counting pushups.

"You already know what your father said."

"I know," Thayne smiled. "But it's for our ritual. Remember?"

"If you insist. Your father said, 'The boy doesn't need to hear dry facts and figures all the time. He also needs to hear literature and music.' So he took his turn reading you The Classic Books of the World, when your mother's voice failed."

"What did you think about all of that?" Thayne asked by himself, turning the doll off and then spinning a virtual globe projecting from a stand nearby.

"You already know I always thought your parents were overdoing it, trying to push so much knowledge into a baby boy before he was even born. But it was not the place of a gentleman and gentle lady's gentleman to say such things.

So, I would just whisper to myself--"

"I know," Thayne cut him off, "*Les pauvres sont l'enfant riche.*"

"Exactly," Jacques said, before he dozed off in the chair for a second.

Thayne didn't wake him. He just sat and watched the only friend he had ever had and started to look at a virtual scrapbook sitting on the table between them.

Reading was pretty much the only thing that Thayne ever got to do growing up. His mom and dad never gave him a chance to do much else, except when he got to play with gadgets being made at his parents' various companies. Owning and running an international conglomerate of fifty companies around the world did not leave much time for his parents to play much with Thayne. He looked at a virtual projection of all of them getting on a plane and made the images come to life as it flashed back to the day.

Thayne asked, at age six, "Why do we have to constantly keep flying around the world to take care of all of your businesses, Dad?"

The image of Thayne's father replied, "Maintenance is the price we pay for ownership, son."

The smaller Thayne looked up at a younger Jacques with a puzzled face. The image of Jacques explained, "If you own it, then you have to take care of it." Jacques would often make sense of Thayne's parents' sayings for him early on in life. Never in front of them, mind you, but just as soon as his parents had turned their attention to something else besides Thayne.

The family businesses weren't the only thing that always cloistered Thayne and his parents in their own little world. Security was another obsession that kept him alone. When he was less than one, someone made a threat to kidnap him and hold him for ransom. So Thayne's parents hired a lot of bodyguards and started traveling only on the family jet.

Thayne looked at the ubiquitous security guards in the background of the virtual image and then flipped it to another scene. As he grew up, Thayne's mom and dad would always warn him that everyone would always be jealous of him. He was the only child who would some day inherit their fifty billion dollar family fortune, which was growing every minute. "Trust no one out there," an image of his mother told him. "Everyone else will always try to hurt you, any time they have a chance." So Thayne was never allowed to go out in the world and see how real people lived. His world was a house, a jet plane, and fifty companies spread out around the world.

He played some virtual movies on the scrapbook. The family plane would take off from the private airport on the secluded family ranch in Wyoming and land at the private airport at each of the fifty companies, to which Thayne's parents traveled once every two months. Thayne would putter around each company's plant, usually under the watchful eye of Jacques, while his parents met with the executives and boards of directors running each place. Almost every employee of every plant would try to play with Thayne whenever he was around. Who wouldn't like to play with a cute, little, dark-haired, brown-eyed boy who looked like a movie star, talked like a professor, and was the heir to one of the largest industrial fortunes in the world?

But Thayne's life wasn't all that bad. He watched some more of the virtual scrapbook and smiled at a few other memories. No other kid that he had heard of was allowed to blast space junk with orbital satellite lasers. Or mine minerals from an ocean floor using an unmanned submarine via remote control. Sometimes, Thayne would even solve problems for the higher level researchers while he walked around the companies. Passing the doors to their laboratories, Thayne would often see a group of them standing around a computer wall screen trying to figure out an equation. He would walk over and put a symbol here or a number there and the word "Error" would disappear from the bottom corner of the display.

All of his parents' employees let Thayne do whatever he wanted. They knew that the owners' son would someday be their boss and each of them tried to become his favorite employee whenever they could. But no one would be a more favorite or more trusted employee than Jacques Marquis, who was just waking from his catnap.

"Well," Jacques said, rousing himself and rising out of the chair. "We need to get going."

"Why can't we really be related?" Thayne asked Jacques, turning off the virtual scrapbook.

The two of them left his bedroom and began the long trip of walking through the family mansion to the library, where his parents should have been working like they normally did every morning.

"Because there is no place on a chart of consanguinity for a Dutch great-uncle," Jacques answered, turning the two of them down a long hallway.

A 'Dutch great-uncle' was how they had long ago agreed that Thayne would consider Jacques. He was more of a grandfatherly member of the family than a gentleman's gentleman.

Most thirteen-year-olds could not even say consanguinity, much less know that a chart of it showed all of a person's direct blood relatives. Lawyers used it to figure out which of the person's heirs would inherit what part of their fortune, if they died without a will.

"You've been reading my law books too much," Thayne joked.

"I have to keep up with the local 'know-it-almost-all,'" Jacque replied.

Thayne stopped, as did Jacques, and asked, "What's a 'know-it-almost-all'?"

"You know almost all there is to be learned from a book," Jacques answered. "But what you need to know most, your parents have yet to let you begin to learn."

"What's that?" Thayne asked, beganning the trek again.

"You have to learn to become a part of the world, young sir, instead of apart from it," Jacques explained. "And you cannot learn that at all from a book."

"Where do you learn it?"

"You learn it from your friends."

"But I don't have any friends other than you and Chopsie."

"Your Lhasa Apso and I don't count," Jacques told him. "Your parents are going to have to let you have some real friends sometime."

"I hope they do it soon." Thayne sighed.

"Maybe today, for your thirteenth birthday," Jacques said with a knowing smile. He turned and continued leading his charge down the hall toward the library.

"What do you mean?" Thayne asked, with a sound of excited anticipation in his voice.

Jacques knocked on the door to the library. After he heard nothing but silence on the other side, he opened the sliding wood paneled doors. Thayne and Jacques both looked all around the two-story library, which was as big as a basketball court and lined with all of the books that Thayne had read, at one second per turn of two facing pages, for almost all of his lifetime.

Thayne walked behind his father's desk and saw a note flashing on his father's computer screen. It read:

Thayne,

> Your mom and I have gone out for a ride. You should head on to your party with Jacques. We will catch up with you in a little while.

Happy Birthday,

Mom and Dad

"What party?" Thayne asked.

Jacques walked up to stand in front of the desk and looked at Thayne. "Well, I guess I may as well tell you, now that your father has let the cat out of the bag. I finally convinced them to let me find you some friends and have a genuine birthday party that will include something different than another degree presented by them at forty thousand feet in the air."

"Jacques," Thayne asked, "you did that for me?"

"Like I said, you need to learn how to be a part of the world and I thought this would be a good way to start."

"Jacques," Thayne said, walking around and hugging his Dutch great-uncle, "that's the best present I ever could have wanted."

A few minutes later, Thayne, Jacques, and four security guards were driving across the family ranch in an armored car, which Thayne always called a "tank".

The tank was one of Thayne's family's cars. It wasn't really a car though. It was much more like an armored truck. It had a bulletproof and bomb-resistant body that could stop almost anything. The inch-thick bulletproof windows could never be opened. The vehicle had six doors -- two in the front for two security men, one of whom would drive; two in the back for two more security men; and two larger ones in the middle for entering the family riding compartment of four seats. Thayne's Mom and Dad always sat in the two seats facing forward. Jacques and Thayne always sat in the two facing back.

"Who's coming to my party?" Thayne asked, in a giddy way, which belied his usually mature manner.

"I've arranged a completely secure birthday party with a dozen other children about your age. They're the grandchildren of some friends I made, who live at a home on the other side of the canyon. All of their grandchildren come to visit for two weeks starting June first every summer. Because all of their birthdays are in other months of the year, the grandparents start each visit by throwing one big non-birthday party, with all the works, for all of them as soon as they arrive. When they told me the story and the date, I told them that it was your real birthday that day and I asked them if we could have your birthday party with their celebration this year."

Thayne developed an ear-to-ear grin and hugged Jacques a second time, in a rare display of affection. "That's the best thing anyone has ever done for me, Jacques."

The combination non-birthday and birthday party was a huge success. Jacques had completely outdone himself with the arrangements. He had arranged some spectacular business parties for Thayne's parents, but this was even better. The tank pulled up in front of a complete carnival company, which Jacques had rented for the day. As he hopped out of the tank, Thayne heard a calliope playing somewhere. He quickly led Jacques around, looking at the more than twenty rides and amusement games set up on the host's front lawn. He found the musicians playing as some festooned clowns entertained the other children in a three-ring circus under a big tent set up in the back garden. After Thayne was introduced to his new friends, they all sat down at a package-laden table. Every one of the neighbor's grandchildren had a non-birthday cake of their own and Thayne had a huge real birthday cake as well. Each child spent a long time opening many very novel presents, which Jacques had obtained from the Millers' various companies around the world.

Jacques even did some of his tricks. He was very good at sleight of hand and misdirection and he could make you believe that he was pulling a coin out of your ear or make a fountain of them pour out of your nose. He even once before made Chopsie disappear in a black bag somehow.

The only thing missing from making it a perfect birthday party, however, was Thayne's parents. They still had not shown up by the time the circus master started the noisy animal show. Still, Thayne didn't really mind much. He was getting to do something new for the first time in his life, which was play with friends his own age. Sure, they weren't real friends. He had never met them before and, if his parents had anything to say about it, he would probably never see them again, until maybe next summer. But, for now, they were his friends. His only friends. His lifelong friends as far as he was concerned and he was enjoying himself for all it was worth.

And then, all of the fun was suddenly interrupted; during

the trapeze act, about halfway through the circus show. Thayne noticed Jacques walking towards his seat from the entrance of the circus tent with his finger in his ear. "This can only be trouble," Thayne thought. Jacques' finger in his ear always meant that Jacques was talking to Thayne's dad's head of security, Phineas Rubino.

"Come on, kid," Jacques said, halfway paying attention to what was going on in his ear. "We have to go."

"But the circus isn't over yet!" Thayne complained.

"I know. I'm sorry, but Phineas says we have to go."

"Why?"

"I don't know yet. Phineas won't tell me anything, except that he wants you back in the tank and heading home A-S-A-P."

"It's a false alarm again," Thayne said, sighing and looking around for the security guards, who had thankfully been keeping a very low profile so far during his party.

"Phineas has already said it isn't. He says it's a bona fide threat."

"He always says that." Thayne looked around and saw two security guys at the front of the bleachers. He figured the another one was on the ground at the back of the stands, watching whatever there was to watch back there.

Jacques moved his finger out of his ear and used it to cover the microphone hanging on the wire about two inches below it. "Phineas says he heard that and that you should do what he says and get in the tank and get home before he has the guys put you in there."

Thayne noticed the security guy on the left front of the bleacher take his hand from inside his coat, put his finger in his ear, nod his head, and start walking toward Thayne. "Looks like he already has," he said standing up. "Let's go if we have to."

"Good idea," Jacques agreed, hurrying Thayne ahead of him to block off the guard coming with his finger still in his ear.

After all of the security guards converged around Thayne and Jacques as they got off the bleachers, the five of them walked quickly to the tank as it screeched to a dusty stop, right outside the door of the circus tent. Thayne got in the family compartment first and Jacques followed him while talking to Phineas on the earlobe-sized cell phone. "Yes, plug me into it just to listen," he said.

"What is it?" Thayne asked. "Another false alarm?"

"Shhh!" Jacques said, holding one finger to his lips and pressing the other in his ear. Tears started to creep out of the corners of Jacques' eyes as he listened to whatever he was listening to for the ride home.

"What is it?" Thayne again demanded to know.

Jacques didn't talk to Thayne or anyone on the phone for the entire way. The only words he said for the entire trip, whenever Thayne repeated his question, were to whisper, *"Oh, mon dieu!"* Oh, my God!

Thayne knew that this was no false alarm when they came over the last ridge revealing the family's mansion in the valley below. Wyoming State Police and FBI helicopters were landing and taking off. Every security person on staff was walking around with their hands in their coats and their fingers in their ears. But everyone stopped when Thayne's tank halted at the front door to the house.

Phineas Rubino was waiting at the foot of the front steps. As always, Chopsie was waiting at the top of the steps outside the front door. As soon as the car stopped, Thayne jumped out over Jacques and ran up the steps to get Chopsie.

Jacques caught up with him as Phineas walked back up the steps to speak.

"I'm sorry, sir." It was the first time in Thayne's life that Phineas Rubino had ever called him "sir" and he did it with a sarcastic tone. "There's no easy way to say this, but your parents have just been killed."

The horror of the words hit Thayne with a force harder than a truck running over a tomato. He exploded into a piercing, red-faced scream, grabbed hold of Chopsie, and dissolved into a quivering mass of tears. Jacques grabbed hold of both the boy and his dog and just kept repeating, *"Oh, mon dieu!"*

THAYNE GOES IT ALONE

It took quite some time for Thayne to recover from the shock of so suddenly becoming the richest orphan in the world. Without a funeral to attend with family or friends, it was hard to start mourning; and so, it was even harder to stop. There never was a funeral because the bodies of Thayne's mom and dad were nowhere to be found. Apparently, the missile that hit their car carried out Thayne's parents' well known last wishes to be cremated and have their ashes spread over their beloved Wyoming ranch.

During the first week after the explosion, all fifty of the heads of the family's companies came to Wyoming to meet with Thayne, Jacques, and the family's lawyers and hear the reading of the will. Lucius Birch, the senior partner of the family's law firm, summarized the inch-thick document for everyone present in the library.

"Thayne's parents, of course, have left everything they owned, the ranch, the plane, and all of their companies and investments, to Thayne. Not having any relatives or friends more trusted than Mister Marquis, they have appointed him to be Thayne's guardian until he turns eighteen. All of the companies will continue to be run by their own head executives and boards of directors. All of Thayne's other investments and directions for Mister Marquis, as Thayne's guardian, will be managed by a board of five trustees."

"Who will be the trustees?" Jacques asked.

"I will be one trustee," Mister Birch replied. "The other four will be elected from the heads of the family businesses. You, Mister Marquis, will be Thayne's advocate to the board, who will pretty well act as an extended group of parents until Thayne reaches age eighteen; at which time, he will be legally old enough to manage his own affairs."

Thayne sat silently with Chopsie on his lap while Mister Birch spoke. As numb as he was, he couldn't much care. At the end of the meeting, everyone rose one at a time, walked up to Thayne's seat at the end of the conference table, put a hand on Thayne's shoulder, said how sorry they all felt that this had happened, called him "sir," and, thankfully, from Thayne's perspective, left him alone.

For the next month, Thayne did almost nothing but sit with Chopsie's head resting on one side of his lap or walk with Chopsie and four security guards all over the property. Thayne said hardly anything for the month. Every question Jacques or anyone else asked seemed to fall on deaf ears.

At the end of the first month, everyone came back to Wyoming for the first monthly report and the election of the board of trustees. Before the meeting began, Jacques escorted Thayne to sit in his chair at the head of the conference table in the library. He sat down in the chair beside the boy and said, "The managers already have an idea who they want to elect to the board of trustees, but they want to know if there is anyone in particular you want to have elected?" Thayne just sat there with Chopsie on his lap and shrugged his shoulders.

All of the companies' managers arrived, sat down in two rows around the conference table, and reported their monthly results. After the last report was done, forty-six of them got up one at a time, walked to Thayne's seat, and again called him "sir." They repeated how sorry they were and wished that he would get well soon; as if there was any way to get well from being an orphan.

Mister Birch and the four remaining managers gathered at Thayne's end of the table. The family lawyer set down a stack of newspapers and magazines and started to talk to Thayne. "The media are continuing to hound the managers for pictures of their new owner, sir."

"No pictures," Jacques said. "It is going to be hard enough protecting him as it is. He may need to travel in hiding sometime and you cannot travel under an assumed name if everyone in the world knows what you look like. His parents have never allowed anyone to take his picture and I'll be darned if we are going to start now."

"Jacques is right," Thayne said. "I really don't want to be seen by anyone; at least, not for right now."

"Fine," Mister Birch agreed. "A statement then," he suggested.

"No statement either," Thayne said.

"No statement?"

"No statement," Jacques repeated. "What are we supposed to say? His parents were murdered. We don't know who did it yet. And he's still in shock about it." Jacques picked up all of the magazines and newspapers and threw them into the trashcan beside his chair. "Forget the media. They're nothing but a bunch of bloodsucking leeches trying to sell their stuff. So no pictures, no statement, no nothing. No response from anyone who works for the boy. The media will eventually go away. I think I have the support of the rest of the board on this. So call a vote, Mister Birch."

"Don't you think you should let him speak on this?" the lawyer asked, pointing at Thayne.

"Jacques is right on this one too," Thayne said.

"So there," Jacques said. "You heard it from his lips, so go ahead and call a vote on this. No pictures and no statement. No response from anyone who works for him in any way and the media will go away. Am I right on this?" Jacques looked at the other people left around the table and raised his hand, even though, technically, he could not vote. All of the others somewhat reluctantly raised their hands. "Motion carries," Jacques said. "Motion to adjourn?"

"But we haven't discussed the boy's welfare, yet," Mister Birch said, trying to regain some control.

"Thayne and I are taking care of his welfare on a day-to-day basis. If anything big comes up that we need to ask you folks about, then we will give you a call. Other than that…" Jacques raised his hand again and looked back around the table. Everyone but the lawyer raised his hand. "Good. Meeting adjourned."

Mister Birch and all the trustees came up one at a time

and told Thayne, if there was anything that he needed, then he should give them a call and, if not, then they would see him in a month.

After everyone had left, Thayne whispered to Jacques, "Thanks."

"You're welcome," Jacques said.

"No more meetings here, okay? We don't need them."

"Don't you want to stay up on what everyone is doing for you?"

"If I want to know something, then we will fly out and get it or figure it out by virmail. Other than that, I don't want to go anywhere or do anything but work on figuring out who killed my parents." Thayne looked toward the door and then back at Jacques. "Have they made any progress on finding out who killed them?"

"Not really," Jacques said. "Phineas says that several radical, anti-American, anti-imperialist terrorist groups have claimed responsibility for it, but no one has been able to prove who did it, yet."

Thayne sank deeper into his chair and started to well up as tears began to roll down his cheeks. "Why did they do it?" Thayne asked, he starting to cry a very little bit.

Jacques reached over, put a hand on Thayne's shoulder, and waited a second for him to calm down. "We won't know why until we find out whom; but it isn't going to matter, because it won't bring them back."

"I just want to know who and why," Thayne said. "And then I want to kill whoever did it."

"I know you do, Thayne. It's only natural that you would. But you and I both know that you can't take these matters into your own hands. Your folks wouldn't like it."

"I know, but they're dead and I want to find their killers

and kill them," Thayne argued.

Jacques and Thayne went back and forth over this point a few times, until Thayne tired out and went to his room, with Chopsie skittering through the door, as it swung closed behind them.

* * *

Very little changed for Thayne for most of the first year after the explosion. Neither Phineas, the local police, nor the state nor federal bureaus of investigation made any progress on finding out who murdered Thayne's parents or why. Phineas, however, convinced the board of trustees that they should not let Thayne off the ranch until they knew what had happened.

As the time for his fourteenth birthday and the anniversary of his parents' death rolled around, Jacques asked him what he wanted to do about either one.

"I don't care if I ever celebrate another birthday again," Thayne answered. "The last party I had killed my parents."

"Oh, Thayne, that isn't true and you know it."

"If we wouldn't have had the party, then they wouldn't have gotten blown up," Thayne argued.

"You know that's not true," Jacques said. "So don't make yourself responsible for it because your parents wouldn't like it." Jacques had taken up the habit of justifying everything he corrected Thayne about with, "So don't be like that because your parents wouldn't like it."

"Well, I'll tell you something else I want to do, which they wouldn't like," Thayne said.

"What's that?"

"I want to go to a real high school."

"You what?" Jacques asked alarmedly. "Thayne, you've

read almost every book that there is to read. You know more stuff about more stuff than most college professors combined. What can you possibly learn from going to high school? If you want to go to a school, then go to a university."

"No," Thayne explained. "I want to learn the one thing you told me I could never learn from a book. I want to learn how to be a part of the world, instead of being apart from it. I'm tired of living my life all alone with people older than me and I want to go to school with some kids my own age."

Jacques looked a little bit hurt. "No offense intended," Thayne apologized. "You know what I mean."

"None taken," Jacques assured him.

"I want to go out in the world and make some friends. I want to talk about whatever is going on out there with people my own age. I want to play sports and be part of a team and win at something sometime. Heck, even losing would be okay, as long as I got to play with someone else."

"Your folks and I didn't raise a loser, Thayne," Jacques corrected him. "You know they wouldn't like that."

"Well, that's what I am going to do," Thayne informed him.

Jacques smiled slightly. He knew that he was beaten on this idea and there was no way that either he or the Board or Phineas Rubino could keep Thayne locked up on the ranch, if Thayne didn't want them to.

"I'm going to have to talk to the board of trustees about this," Jacques said. "They won't like me letting you do something like this without their okay and it won't be an easy thing to convince them about."

"Do we have to involve the board on this?" Thayne asked.

"Well, you're going to have to do something to either get

the board and Phineas to go along with it or find some way to work around them."

"Well, I've thought a lot about this and I think I have a good plan that will work. If I can get rid of Phineas Rubino and replace him with you, then, without Phineas being on top of me all the time, I can work around the board of trustees."

Thayne looked at Jacques and then told him, "Call the lawyer and have him call a meeting. I'll explain to them what I think they need to know. But at just the right time, you have to make them vote on it, okay?"

"I'll try," Jacques said, resigning himself to being Thayne's co-conspirator.

"We can't just try, you know."

"Why not?" Jacques asked.

Thayne smiled. "Because my parents wouldn't like it."

* * *

Jacques had not warned Phineas nor any of the trustees about what Thayne was going to ask them to let him do during the meeting. They had not lived with Thayne since he was born. They did not understand the true price the boy had paid, being the poor, lonely rich kid that he had been forced to be all of his life.

As Jacques and Thayne finished laying out Thayne's request, Phineas yelled, "Jacques, you cannot be serious!"

"Why, not?" Jacques retorted. "The boy wants to get out more, meet some people, and live a little."

"Because from a security standpoint, it is the stupidest idea I have ever heard," Phineas argued. "We're just a year after his parents were killed, we still don't know who did it or why, we don't know if they'd like to kill him next, and there is absolutely no way to protect him in an unsecured environment like a high school."

Jacques ignored the first part of Phineas's argument. "That depends on where he wants to go."

"Why does he want to go to a high school in the first place?" Phineas asked. "He already has everything he could possibly want here and at the companies."

"Because, as we all know, Phineas, you want to spread your wings a little as you're growing up. You grow, you evolve, and you mature into a man. He wants to be able to do that, normally, with people his own age."

Phineas would not stop. "But he could still get killed!"

"So what if I do!" Thayne yelled at him.

"What?" Phineas asked.

"So what if I do?" Thayne stood up and took control. "So what if I do get killed, Mister Rubino, so what if I do?" Thayne walked around the table where everyone was sitting. "We all agree that even though I'm only fourteen years old, because of the learning abilities given to me by my parents, I'm still the smartest person in this room." Thayne continued to walk around the table and circled his finger at all of them. "Maybe smarter than all of you combined. And, obviously, because of the fortune heaped upon me by my parents, I'm also the richest person in this room and probably richer than all of you combined. But even with all of that knowledge and money, what good is it to me without some family and friends to share it with. Now, I don't have any family …"

Thayne stopped behind Jacques and put his hands on Jacques shoulders. "Except for my Dutch Great Uncle Jacques here; and I don't have any friends …" Thayne paused and looked around the table. "Except all of you. But, let's face it; that's not a normal group of friendships. So, I ask you this, What kind of a life is that?" Thayne repeated himself. "I ask you, What kind of a life is that?"

Phineas banged the tabletop in front of him. "It's a live life is what it is."

"Mister Rubino, I know you are the only person here who will lose his job if I die."

"What?" Phineas asked.

"I know that according to my parents' will, if I die without an heir, then all of my companies will go to whoever is employed in them. Unfortunately for you, you don't work for any of those companies. I also know, while I'm still alive, your job is to keep me that way; and you won't have the job you do now if I end up dead. So naturally, I know you want to keep me locked up here under your security services as long as you can."

"You don't understand, sir," Phineas interrupted. "It is my security services that have probably kept you alive this long."

"And it is the failure of those services, Mister Rubino, that is probably the reason my parents are dead."

"Your parents insisted on driving to your party alone!" Phineas argued, looking at Jacques. "I have explained that to you enough times already."

"Regardless," Thayne continued. "Now, I have also read my parents' will and while, until I turn eighteen, this board is able to run my companies and investments, my guardian and I have full control over the hiring and firing of the personal household staff." Thayne pointed his finger at Phineas. "You, Mister Rubino, are part of that personal household staff and, as of this minute, you are now fired." Thayne pointed toward the door. "Jacques, in addition to being my guardian, you are now in charge of my personal security. Tell the guards to escort Mister Rubino from the grounds." Thayne walked around to his chair again and sat down as Jacques nodded to the two security men at the other end of the room.

Phineas stood up and yelled. "No need to throw me out, Jacques! I am glad to go! Goodbye and good riddance!" He walked out of the room mumbling and then began yelling, as he was escorted down the hall, "You will rue the day you did this, sir. You will rue the day!"

A quiet settled across the room as Phineas' voice trailed off in the distance.

Thayne looked at the faces of the remaining members of the board of trustees left sitting around the table. "As for the rest of you," Thayne continued. "If any of you have the idea of trying to keep me locked up in this mausoleum any longer, then please remember, in four more years, I will have the unfettered right to fire you as well." Thayne sat down and pulled his chair up to the table.

Mister Birch started to say, "Sir, I just don't think –"

Jacques cleared his throat. "Well, then," he said, putting his hand up in the air. "All those in favor of letting the boy go to school when and where he wants signify by raising your right hands." All four of the company trustees shot their palms up. "Motion carries!" Jacques said. "Motion to adjourn?"

* * *

That evening, Thayne told Jacques the next step in his plan.

Jacques asked, "So where do you want to go to high school?"

"Well, it needs to be a pretty big school, where I won't stick out like a sore thumb," Thayne said. "And it needs to be a pretty hard school, so it won't be too easy for me."

"I suppose you've already done some virnet reading on this as usual."

"Yes, and I've narrowed it down to two places. The first place is the Scorsos International Academy and University in Wilmington, Delaware."

"Why there?"

"Well, it's run by Gregory Scorsos, who's an international businessman, just like my dad was. They are very big and accept only the best students in the world, so I should be able to blend in."

"And the other place?"

"The other place is on the island that Mom and Dad were always talking about, Demeverde. There's an international school there, but it doesn't seem on its virtour to focus as much on business. It's more of a liberal arts kind of place. It's run by a guy called Unius."

"Did your folks ever tell you anything specific about Demeverde?" Jacques asked.

"No, just the stories about how I was their little souvenir from there and how they met this man named Unius, who helped them have me while they were down there. My parents always told me, if I ever needed to go learn something somewhere, Demeverde would be the best place to do it."

"So, do you want to take a little vacation there and check the place out?"

"No. I don't want to go there as Thayne Davidson Miller, the third, and have any more people than absolutely necessary associate me with that name."

"So what do you want to do?"

"I want you to make contact with the head of the school, this Unius. Tell only him who I am, what's happened to my parents, what I want to do, and why I am thinking about going there under a new name. Don't tell anyone else but Unius who I am or what I am thinking about."

Jacques did not like the idea of Thayne being so far away from Wyoming. Nonetheless, he knew from experience, once Thayne wanted to do something, he usually found a way to do it. "Whatever you say, sir," Jacques acquiesced. "Whatever you say."

* * *

Jacques was curious about the ease with which he was able to make contact with Unius without telling anyone who he was representing. He grew even more alarmed when the first virmail to Unius saying that he was the guardian for an anonymous prospective student was answered by a virmail directly from Unius himself. An interesting looking fellow's head stretched up from the virtual screen and said,

> Greetings. I know who you are and whom you represent. Rest assured that I have told no one else. I look forward to your coming to visit me in person at your earliest convenience. Greetings."

GODEAU, DEMEVERDE

As the Milmart jet circled Isla Principal, the main island of Demeverde, Jacques took in the panoramic view. Reddish mountains surrounded pleasantly planned and developed green valleys and blue lagoons. Thayne's emissary surveyed what looked like a normal diverse civilization below. Several interesting landmarks caught his attention. The top of the tallest mountain appeared to have been sculpted into a flattened ring with steps winding around it down to the ground.

Thayne had insisted Jacques take a company plane instead of his family jet because the cover story for the visit was that he was researching an idea of Thayne's about expanding Milmart, the largest retailer in the world, into the mid-Atlantic islands. Finally seeing it in person for the very first time, he told himself, "No wonder they fell in love with the place."

The plane landed and taxied to a stop in front of a hangar, next to a thin, olive-skinned man waiting alone.

"Welcome to Godeau, Demeverde, Mister Marquis," the man said. "I am Chose. Unius asked me to escort you."

They walked a few feet and Chose stepped onto one of a row of clear, one-inch thick by two-foot wide, plastic-looking discs.

"What's this?" Jacques asked.

"A SlipDisc," Chose answered. "Better than a moving walkway, because it can take you wherever you need to go. If you haven't used one before, then please allow me to instruct you."

"Never seen such a thing in my life; so, please, go ahead."

Chose pointed his left foot forward and put his right foot a shoulder's width behind it pointing to the side. "You would do well to take a T-stance like this." Jacques did the same thing. Chose nodded his approval.

"Bend your knees." Chose looked down at the front of the SlipDisc and said, "Parking lot, space two one four seven, please."

A soft pleasant female voice answered back from a glowing spot on the front of the SlipDisc, "My pleasure."

Intrigued by the new technology, Jacques stepped on one of the clear manhole covers, gave it the same instructions, and received the same response.

As he caught up with Chose, Jacques asked, "What do

these things run on?"

Jacques did not understand much of what Chose said during the next three minutes, while they exited the tarmac and traveled through the parking lot. Something about diffusion of water vapor in the air, separation of hydrogen and oxygen atoms, refusion of the gases, production of energy, Bernoulli's law, creation of wind streams, and a variety of other things, which Chose rattled through much too quickly for Jacques to catch it all. He understood some and came to learn more by experience; the relatively transparent disc seemed to float, accelerate, decelerate, and navigate on a slip of air.

The SlipDisc came to a stop in front of what looked like a car-sized, oval bubble made of the same material that the SlipDisc was. The etching on the rear of it read, "SlipStream 2020." Underneath the name was the statement, "Pure guarantium."

Chose pushed a spot set in the side and the door slid open. "After you," he said.

Jacques got in and sat down on the bench, which was as clear as the car's body. The craft looked and worked like an overgrown SlipDisc with seats.

"Godeau Mountain steps, please," Chose said to the glowing disc on the inside of the front of the bubble. "My pleasure," the disc replied, as the car started to accelerate and turned, following the road out of the parking lot.

Within minutes, they were at the base of the huge mountain with the carved top, which Jacques had spied from the air. A simple sign stood in front of the mass indicating it was Godeau Mountain. Chose pushed the spot to open the door.

"Why are we getting out here?" Jacques asked, while

getting out, looking around, and seeing no sign of civilization at the foot of the mountain.

"The SlipStream 2020 does not do steps," Chose answered, pointing to the perfectly cut rectangles of rock leading up and away, arching out of sight around the side of the mountain.

"A car that uses nothing for fuel and floats on a stream of air can't do steps?"

Chose shrugged. "What can I say? It's a five-year-old model."

"How many steps is that?" Jacques asked, nodding at the many flights of fifteen steps, each leading to a long landing, which was followed by the next level.

"An even one thousand," Chose said, starting up the seemingly unending stairs.

"My goodness," Jacques complained, following closely behind him. "Unius owns and runs the largest and most technologically advanced company and school in the world and he doesn't even have an elevator?"

"Oh, we have them," Chose said.

"Good, then let's go use one." Jacques turned around and started back down the ten or so steps he had already climbed.

"We just don't have one here," Chose explained, pausing and turning to call back to the portly man, who was turning around to climb back up and catch up with him.

Jacques trudged up the first level of hewn rock rectangles noting his displeasure, "Heck of a way to run a railroad."

"We're not a railroad," Chose replied.

About halfway up the side of the mountain, Jacques asked, "Does everyone who wants to see Unius have to make this trek?"

"Yes, but he does not see many."

Jacques boasted, "Yes, well, he is seeing me."

"Only because you represent someone who apparently is very special."

"I think so."

"Who is it?" Chose inquired.

"Did Unius tell you, when he asked you to pick me up?"

"No."

"Then why should I?"

"Because you are not Unius."

"Neither are you."

The two of them walked in an agreed upon silence for the final twenty levels of steps. When they reached the top of the mountain, Chose led Jacques through the one doorway cut in the ridge. They entered into a vast expanse of a room, which Jacques estimated was a little over ninety feet in diameter. The chamber appeared to have been carved out of the top twenty feet of the mountain. The continuous, circular wall of the room was about two feet thick. It was fenestrated with thirty-six, evenly spaced, four-foot wide windows, each beginning about four feet off the floor and continuing up for about twelve feet, where they were capped with about four more feet of the rim of the mountain.

At the far end of the room, perched on top of the rim wall, balanced upside down on the pinkie finger of his right hand, stood, if you can call such a position standing, a very thin, but well-muscled, man with receding, long, brown hair coming down, or up as it were, to the level of his short, brown beard.

Jacques rubbed his eyes and looked back at the man on the wall, trying to figure out why his tunic was staying down, or, rather, up, around his ankles, instead of falling around his head, like his hair should have also been doing.

"Ahem," Jacques cleared his throat trying to get the man's attention.

"Shhh," Chose rebuked him. "When he's ready," he advised.

Jacques rolled his eyes at Chose. "Ahem!" he cleared his throat again, a little more loudly this time.

"Shhh!" Chose corrected him again. "When he is ready."

Jacques rolled his eyes at Chose again and breathed in for a really loud throat clearing.

"I heard you, Mister Marquis," a voice softly said from behind him.

Jacques looked behind him only to see that no one was there and then looked back at the man on the wall.

The man began to descend from his perch. First, he came off of his right pinkie onto the rest of his right hand. He then put down his left hand and lowered himself partway, to balance on his forearms, on the top of the rim over the opening beneath him. His feet stuck straight out behind him into the center of the round room. Next, he lowered and separated his sandal-shod feet to brace one against each side of the inside of the top of the window. Then he slid down the inside of the window, until his feet touched the bottom of it. Finally, he stepped back to the floor.

Jacques rubbed his eyes again. When he opened them, the man had come all the way across the cavernous room and was right in front of him.

"Yes?" the man asked Chose.

"Unius, let me present Mister Jacques Marquis. Mister Marquis, Unius."

"Thank you," Unius said, reaching out with his left index finger and almost touched Chose on the forehead. A bright spark arced between Unius's finger and Chose's forehead, before it spread out and disappeared evenly over Chose's entire body.

Chose closed his eyes, smiled with closed lips as he absorbed the energy just shared with him, and then opened his eyes again about a second later. "My pleasure," Chose said, turning and walking out the door in the rim wall and straight off the side of the landing. He simply disappeared from view, instead of taking the steps that went back down the side of the mountain.

The sight of the man literally walking off the cliff shocked Jacques. "Whoa!" he gasped, reaching out to somehow help Chose from twenty feet away.

"He'll be fine," Unius said. "Come, sit down." He pushed Jacques in the back and guided him toward the table and chairs, which looked as though they were cut from the mountain itself, while still attached to it.

Jacques stopped short and said, "Uh-but," looking at the landing where Chose had just walked off and "Uh, how did you do that?" pointing to the opening down which Unius had just slid.

"Easily," Unius said, smiling again urging Jacques toward the table.

"And what's with the spark of light thing?"

"Oh, this?" Unius held up his finger and emitted another spark of light. "Just a T-I-P tip."

"A what?"

"A Thanks In Photons tip," Unius explained. "Chose used some of his energy, by bringing you here for me; so I shared a bit of my energy with him to thank him."

"Oh."

"But enough about that," Unius said, handing Jacques one of two glasses of thick brownish-green liquid that were sitting on the table. "Let's have lunch."

Jacques smelled the drink and then turned up his nose. "What's this?" he asked.

Unius was already half done with his glass in short order. "A balanced blend of juices made from local fruits, vegetables, legumes, and grasses. Three glasses of this a day is about all I eat."

"One glass of this a day and I would curl up and die," Jacques said, setting the glass on the table.

"Suit yourself," Unius said. "But I am older than you are and I only look half your age."

Jacques picked up his glass and choked down the first sip. "Not bad," he said, before having some more. "It kind of grows on you."

"Good," Unius said. "Now, I understand that you have some news about some friends of mine."

"Bad news I'm afraid. My gentleman and lady are dead."

"I know. I saw."

"Yes, it was on the news."

"Of course."

"But their son is fine."

"I know. I saw."

Jacques scrunched his face with a question. "But his son hasn't been on the news."

"Of course."

"So how could you have seen?"

Unius avoided the question. "How is the boy?"

"He's fine, except now he wants to reclaim his childhood

and go to high school."

"Excellent!" Unius exclaimed. "We happen to have a very good high school right here in Godeau. My company's developmental high school, the Global Optimum Development Academy."

"I know, Unius. That is why I'm here. His father always told him, if there was anything he ever needed to learn, then he should come here to learn it. But he wants to consider other places as well. He's been thinking about some other schools, like the one he virtoured in Delaware, Scorsos Academy."

"Scorsos!" Unius sounded alarmed. "Never! Their virtual tour is nothing but lies."

"What lies? They say it's the Scorsos International Academy, founded by Gregory Scorsos, the intercontinental currency-trading billionaire, to promote worldwide cultural, business, and economic exchanges, much like your school does here."

"Scorsos?" Unius shook his head. "It is nothing like my school because I am nothing like Gregory Scorsos. He is a liar, a cheat, and a thief, who was thrown out of the European Union, after he was accused of being involved with criminals. Apparently, he made his first hundred million having unsavory associates kill his competitors. I would not be surprised if he was somehow involved with the deaths of your employers. They were competitors, you know, in several different businesses."

"No," Jacques said with surprise. "I've known Mister Miller for all of his life and he never mentioned being in competition with Scorsos."

"That's because Scorsos hides most of his deeds through a thick haze of false companies. How insulting that you should even compare the two of us."

"I'm sorry," Jacques apologized. "I didn't mean to insult you. We'll look into Mister Scorsos, as soon as I return to Philmont."

"Not just me, but by even comparing us to Scorsos you've insulted everyone else here in Godeau." Unius opened his arms wide. "We improve on people's ideas and make them available to the world. Scorsos just steals them and keeps them for his own enrichment."

"Come now."

"He has not had an original or creative thought in his life. Why the very idea to even have a school, he stole from me. Besides, he will accept any student who will pay his exorbitant tuition, unless he learns we want them, in which case he takes them for free like we do. We, on the other hand, take only gifted students and share our knowledge with them for free, while taking care of all of their basic needs."

Unius paused for some response, but got none because Jacques appeared to be thinking. Unius summed up simply. "Besides, he belongs here with us."

"Why?"

"Do you have any idea what we do here in Godeau?" Unius asked.

"I have some clue," Jacques answered.

"Did his parents ever talk about it with you?"

"Not a word, but I've done some research on the virnet."

"Did you know that they shared here a while?"

"Yes," Jacques said. "But they never talked about it with me.

"Yes, the year before their son was born," Unius said. "But they only stayed here for four months."

"They told me that they were taking a second honeymoon." Jacques chuckled a little bit, almost to himself. "It was apparently a success."

"In a manner of speaking," Unius agreed. "They could have shared more had they stayed longer."

"Why didn't they?" Jacques asked.

"They'd accomplished what they wanted to do and thought it was time for them to go."

"How did they do it?" Jacques asked.

"Do what?"

"You know," Jacques asked. "How did they finally get a baby here when they couldn't before?"

"I can't say."

"Or won't," Jacques argued.

"Or won't," Unius firmly replied.

The look on Unius's face told Jacques that persistence would be futile on this point. "So," he asked, "what do you guys do here, after all?"

"We share our precious life's resources to achieve the global optimum development of people, places, things, and ideas." Unius began to explain. "When I first came here seventy-five years ago, this entire island was hardly inhabited. The local Demeverdans only amounted to at most ten thousand people. They lived a very advanced lifestyle, but on the simplest of terms, on the eastern side of the main island here. I noticed, however, that they were an incredibly well-educated people and superbly inventive at making little devices to do whatever it was they wanted to do. They always found ways to do something better or more efficiently than they had done it the last time. Naturally, I figured that it would be a great place to put a new research laboratory. So first, I built the company, Global Optimum Development

Enterprises."

"Um-hmm," Jacques hummed, nodding his head.

Unius continued, "After we got up to about ten thousand employees here on Demeverde, we got so busy that we couldn't find enough local talent to come work for us. We first tried getting families with children to move here, but most of the adults were not as gifted at development as the Demeverdans were. So then, we just started focusing on working with children who have a variety of gifts. We decided to educate them ourselves at our own high school, the Global Optimum Development Academy. After a few more years, we needed a college; so we started Global Optimum Development University."

"And what's so special about your schools?" Jacques asked.

"Well, first, we only take those children who, by the eighth grade, have shown themselves to be gifted in some special way."

"And then?"

"And then, we share with them ways they can develop their gifts, far beyond any level they could possibly conceive."

"And how do you do that?"

"We basically share with them how to put their minds over matter."

"Their minds over matter?"

"Yes, their minds over matter."

"How's that?"

"It's very difficult to explain," Unius said. "If you aren't ready to believe it, then I doubt you will be able to understand it."

"I'm a skeptic," Jacques challenged him. "But try to

explain it anyway."

"Fine," Unius said. "How much of your mind believes I am right here beside you right now?"

"All of it, I guess."

"And if I used all of my mind and body to convince you I was talking to you from this side of the table?" Unius asked, instantly seated on the opposite side of the twenty-foot diameter slab of mountain between them. "How much would you believe it?"

"None," Jacques answered with a stammer. "I think."

"And, how about now?" Unius was again right beside him.

"I'm not exactly sure."

"So you have just seen a use of mind over matter," Unius said.

"So what does that have to do with the optimal development of the mind and body thing?"

"Well, I was able to use my mind and body to do either one of two things."

"Which were?"

"Either my body was able to move to the other side of the table faster than you could see it."

"Or?"

"Or my mind so thoroughly clouded yours that I was able to make you think I had moved all the way over there when I was still right here." Unius smiled broadly at Jacques.

"So which was it?" Jacques asked.

"Which would you rather believe?"

"Neither."

Unius pointed to the precipice over which Chose had earlier disappeared. "And what if I said I could drop you off this mountain, like Chose just did, and stop you, before you hit the ground?"

"I'd say you were a raving lunatic."

"Well!" Unius appeared tired of trying. "Then nothing else I can tell you will change your mind."

Jacques thought to himself for a minute. "So then, assuming the boy decides he doesn't like Scorsos, when does school begin here?"

Unius slightly furrowed his brow and spoke in a somewhat deeper tone. "Forget about Scorsos. The boy belongs here."

"But, then again, we could just forget about Scorsos, because I have a feeling the boy belongs here."

"Of course, he does," Unius agreed, unwrinkling his forehead. "The next session begins on the first Monday in August. We will make arrangements for him to fly in with the rest of the new students from the states then."

"Fine … and one more thing," Jacques said. "He wants to come under an assumed name. We still don't know who killed his folks or why or whether they want to kill him next. His parents never allowed any pictures of him, so no one knows what he looks like. But he needs a new name. Any ideas?

"What do you want to call him?"

"Well, I had a best friend when I was a kid and I always thought, if I ever had a boy, then I would name it after him."

"What was your friend's name?"

"John Arnold Carver," Jacques said. "But we always called him Arnie."

Unius did not appear to care about what they called Thayne as much as he cared that the boy should come back to Demeverde. "Arnie Carver sounds fine to me."

"And don't let anyone know who he is, okay?"

"No one will know any more than he shares," Unius said. "His secrets will stay safe as long as he keeps them to himself."

"Good then," Jacques said. "My work seems to be done here, so I will be getting on." He got up and walked to the landing at the top of the stairs.

"Come and I'll show you the way down," Unius said, pushing Jacques over the edge of the mountain.

"AAAAAAAAAAAAAAAAAAAAAAAAAAAAAA AAAYYYYYYYYYYYYYYY!!!!!!!!" Jacques screamed incessantly as he fell. Half his life passed before his eyes, as he thought he was about to die from being thrown all the way down the mountain. Suddenly, he stopped and found himself hanging, horizontally in the air, five feet from the ground, at the bottom of the mountain, balanced on his chin on Unius's outstretched forefinger, and staring Unius in the face.

Unius asked him, "So which was it? Did you just fall off a mountain or I did just make you think you did."

"Don't ever do that again, okay?" Jacques shakily said, leaning back off of Unius's finger.

"Chose will take you back to the transit port now," Unius said, rotating Jacques to put his feet on the ground. "Enjoy your flight."

"Lunatic!" Jacques said, just loudly enough for Unius to overhear him. He walked toward Chose and the SlipStream he had left a few hours before.

"Nonsharers," Unius gruffed, kneeling deeply and then jumping back up the mountain.

Chose smiled as Jacques approached him. Pushing the spot to open the door to the SlipStream, he asked, "Did you have a pleasant visit?"

"Just fine," Jacques said mockingly, "if you don't count

the thousand-step climb up and the six-hundred-foot drop to get back down."

The two of them found their places in the SlipStream.

"This is a very bizarre place," Jacques said.

"Not once you get to know it well," Chose replied.

"I know it well enough." Jacques got in the oval bubble. "I virtoured it before I came."

"Virtual tours don't do it justice." Chose got in with him and closed the door. "Would you like to have a real tour? Unius asked me to make you as comfortable as possible and learn all that there is about you and your ward."

"He said he wasn't going to tell anyone."

Chose wrinkled his forehead toward the right and stared intently into Jacques eyes. "He didn't; you will."

"I may as well see it all while I am here and I'll tell you what I can."

"Good then! Let me share Demeverde with you." Chose turned back around to the glowing disc on the front. "Full island tour, please."

"My pleasure," replied the soft woman's voice from the disc, as the SlipStream began to move.

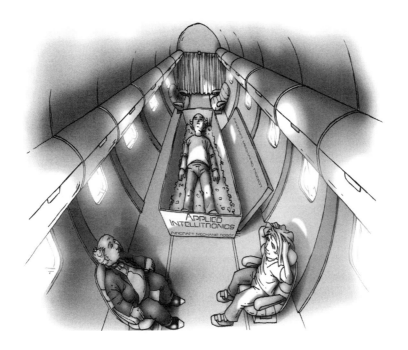

THE FIRST DAY OF THE REST OF YOUR LIFE

Thayne eagerly waited for the last seconds of the Milmart jet's roll to a stop at the airstrip behind Miller Manor. "So what did you find out?" he asked Jacques, as the old man came off the plane. "Any more than the virtour showed?"

"More than you could possibly imagine," Jacques said. He seemed a bit more sunburned, but a lot more relaxed, than when he had left the day before.

The two of them and Chopsie walked past two security guards standing at the end of the sidewalk between the house and the middle of the airplane taxiway behind them.

Once they were out of earshot of the guards, Jacques said, "Scorsos Academy is definitely out and GODA is definitely the place for you."

"Good," Thayne said. "I'm not happy with the idea of going to Scorsos anyway. The more I studied them on the virnet, the more I didn't like them."

"There's more to them than meets the eye on a virtour." Jacques advised him.

"How so?"

"According to Unius, Gregory Scorsos is some kind of silent competitor of many of the Miller companies."

"Oh, really?"

"Unius says that, based on his reputation for killing off competitors in Europe, he wouldn't be surprised if Scorsos had something to do with your parents death."

Thayne's mouth gaped open for a moment, until he regained his composure. "Then let's get someone looking into it immediately."

"Yes, sir."

Thayne pointed to the front of Jacques' red, balding head. "It seems like you enjoyed a little bit too much of the tropical sun while you were there."

"Clear cars, no shade, long tour," Jacques replied, wiping across his brow.

Jacques continued to review the trip and all that he had seen and experienced. Chose and Unius, SlipDiscs and SlipStreams, steps and drops, bad looking, but good tasting, fruit and vegetable drinks, and everything else that Chose had shown him on the full island tour.

"And now for the bad part," Thayne said, with a low tone to soften the words and show the seriousness of the issue.

"Which is?"

"I'm going to have to go there alone."

"I figured you were going to say that."

"Until we find out who killed my parents and what their intentions are toward me, I need to go into hiding; and showing up at a school in Demeverde, with my own security guards and a gentleman's gentleman, is not exactly that."

"So?"

"So, while I go off to school in Demeverde with the rest of the people coming from the states, the guards, Chopsie, and you are going to have to stay here and be the ready for whoever tries anything. You are going to have a decoy going to school for me here in Philmont."

"And who's going to be the decoy for you?"

"I've already arranged for that," Thayne explained. "While you were off at Demeverde, I virmailed Claude Raines at the Applied Intellitronics plant. I had him to start very secretly on an Intellitron that will look and act just like me. We took the download from the last year of all of the security cameras on the ranch here and he is going to use it to program the thing."

"Do you think that it will be a good enough decoy to fool everyone?"

"I know what it does, Jacques," Thayne reminded him. "I helped with the self-teaching neuraltronic circuitry, on the two-point-two version, three years ago. We made Intellitrons able to explore their surroundings and convert the analog and digital input to virtual informatics. It's gotten even better since then."

"I hope so, sir."

"It will give the perfect impression of being me. You wouldn't believe the latest things Claude has made them do in the past year. Now, it eats and chews and even goes to the bathroom a few times a day. Of course, it doesn't digest anything. It just flushes down the toilet exactly what it chews up. But it's good enough to fool anyone who may be watching too closely." Thayne paused, chuckled, and said, "I guess it's even good enough to do-do anything that I do, then."

Jacques tried not to laugh, but couldn't keep a stifled chuckle from getting out.

"Do you think it is a good idea for Claude to know there is an Intellitron for you out here?" Jacques asked, with a concerned look.

"I told him we are going to use it for some security scenarios to train the guys and we're going to make the scenarios so tough that it was going to be destroyed in the drills."

"Good," Jacques said. "So now I see why you were so insistent about going away under an assumed name. If we're going to have the Intellitron here for you as a decoy, then it only makes sense. But why let Unius know who you really are?"

"Because, I am going to have to trust someone there and he already sent the virmail saying he knows," Thayne explained. "So I need to decide on what I want to be called. I've always wondered who I would be, if I wasn't Thayne Davidson Miller, the third."

Jacques shook his head back and forth twice. "How your great-grandfather ever tagged your grandfather with that moniker I will never know, but I am glad you are getting to change it."

"So, what should we call me, Jacques?" Thayne asked. "How about something very American like George Washington Jefferson or something like that?"

"Too old and dusty sounding, if you ask me."

"Well then, how about something like Steve or Bill or —?"

"Well, Unius and I picked you a new name. If you like it, then we can keep it and if you don't, then we can pick another one."

"So, what is it?"

"Well, I was thinking," Jacques began. "Do you know how I was always calling you Arnie when your folks weren't listening?"

"Yeah, I just thought you were picking on me."

"Well, Arnie was the name of my best friend growing up; and we always said, if we ever had any boys of our own, then we would name them after each other."

"And you want to name me after your best childhood friend?" Thayne asked.

"Well-ll-l," Jacques said slowly. He was a little embarrassed by the whole thing, now that he said it.

"So, what was his real name?"

"John Arnold Carver," Jacques told him, "but we always called him by his nickname, Arnie."

"John Arnold Carver." Thayne tilted his head back and forth and repeated it to himself. "John Arnold Carver." He looked in the mirror on the wall and stuck out his right hand. "Hi, I'm John Arnold Carver." He waved to himself. "John Arnold Carver here!" And then he shortened it and stuck his hand out again. "Hi, I'm Arnie Carver." Thayne looked in the mirror and added a line that he had often heard his father say to his mother. "*Comment allez vous, mon petit chou?*" He batted his eyebrows at his target in the mirror.

He turned back to Jacques and smiled. "I guess I like it, Jacques. I'd be happy to be your childhood friend growing up." He stuck out his hand to shake with Jacques. "Hi, I'm Arnie Carver."

Jacques took his hand and pulled him into a big bear hug. He had a bit of a tear in his eye and sniffed a little to dry up his nose. "Arnie," he said, "I love you just like you were my very own Dutch grandnephew."

* * *

A few weeks later, Thayne sent the plane to the Applied Intellitronics plant in Japan. "Just pick up the maintenance mechanic Intellitron and come back here," he told the pilot. "You can take it to the repair hanger at the Chicago airport the day after tomorrow. Check into the airport hotel after you land and get some rest. The Miller Av-Services people will pick it up, do the thousand-hour service on the plane, and have it ready for you after you get some sleep."

The plane got back late the next night. Long after the pilot had left, Thayne and Jacques told the two security guards at the back door of the house that they were just going to check on the box on the plane and walked down to the hangar.

A coffin-like crate was sitting in the aisle. The box was labeled, "Applied Intellitronics" in big letters. A small row beneath the company name read, "Aircraft maintenance robot." Jacques could not believe his eyes when he popped the lid off the container. An exact replica of the boy he had come to know and love appeared to be peacefully sleeping inside.

"Goodness! It looks just like you. They even got your hair all gooed back straight. It would even fool me, if I didn't know you were the real one."

"That reminds me," Thayne said. He opened the plane's lavatory door, stepped in, and turned on the water.

Jacques sat down on the seat beside the crate. "Now, before I take him out of here, we need to talk about a few things."

Thayne came out with his curly hair freed of the cream and sat down across the aisle from Jacques. "Are we about to have the 'sending the kid off to camp talk'?"

"Something like that," Jacques said. "Now, you and I know there is nothing from a book that I can teach you."

"If you say so." Thayne did not like saying he was smarter than Jacques.

"But there is a lot about making friends your own age you have not had to deal with."

"Like not being an almost-know-it-all and always having to be right?" Thayne asked, with a sheepish grin.

"That would be a good start," Jacques said through a smile. "But mostly, what you want to do is just relax, help everyone else around you, and always champion the underdog."

"Champion the underdog?" Thayne asked.

"Yes," Jacques explained. "Whenever it seems like someone has the deck stacked against them, that's the person you want to help the most."

"Why?"

"Because I was the underdog when your grandfather helped me and it is the greatest lesson I ever learned from him."

"Okay, don't be an almost-know-it-all, don't tell everyone that I am always right, even though I probably will be, relax, help everyone around me, and champion the underdog. Anything else that I should know?"

"No, nothing. Except as soon as you get there, try to find Chose. He's the only person I know there, besides Unius, and he knows Unius believes you're someone special. He and I got to be great friends during my tour of the island. He should be able to help you out of any jam you get yourself in."

Thayne sat in silence for a minute with a sad look on his face. Jacques could see that the almost-know-it-all was troubled by something. "What is it, Thayne?"

"I don't know," Thayne answered. "Just the thought of leaving you and Chopsie and the ranch and everything. It seemed like a fun thing to do on my birthday, but now it's kind of scary."

"Don't worry, Arnie." Jacques used Thayne's new name for some practice. "You're going to do fine." Jacques got up and stepped across the aisle to sit beside him. "Chopsie and I will find a way to come out and see you in a couple of months. Now do you have everything that I gave you?"

"Yes."

"Satellite phone just in case?"

Thayne touched his right pants pocket. "Check."

"Money?"

Thayne touched his left pocket. "Check."

"You know how to get from the repair hangar to the Global Optimum Airways gate?"

"Memorized the entire airport off the virnet and prenavigated the route off of a virtour."

"Good. Now remember, contact Chose as soon as you can, after you get there."

"Okay."

"Good." Jacques gave him one last hug around the shoulder and pointed toward the pilot's cabin. "Now you get up there behind the curtain of the galley in the front while I get the new Thayne here up and running and inside the house.

Get back in the crate when we are gone. Have a good night's sleep and you'll wake up when they take off for Chicago in the morning. Stay in the box until all is quiet after you land and head over to the Global gate. Okay?"

"Okay."

"You don't have to worry about any baggage because I already sent it to the airport in Chicago. It's checked through to Godeau under John Arnold Carver; so it should be there with everyone else's when you get there. Okay?"

"Okay." Thayne gave his Dutch great-uncle a kiss on the cheek, something that he had never done before. "Thanks, Jacques, for taking care of all of the details as usual." He teared up a little. "I'll miss you a lot."

Jacques rubbed his cheek. "Aw, we'll find a way to come see you in two months. Now get behind the curtain and get back in the box when we are gone." Thayne moved as Jacques stood over the Intellitron in the crate. "You'll never guess where they hid the on-off switch," Jacques said, removing and reading a note attached to the Intellitron's head. He lifted back the simulated kid's left eyelid and pushed up.

A few seconds later Thayne's double opened its eyes and looked up at Jacques. "Why am I in this box?" the double asked standing up.

"I don't know, Thayne," Jacques answered. "But it's time to go in the house and go to bed." Jacques helped the decoy out.

Chopsie barked and sniffed the shoe and pant cuffs of his friend getting out of the box. Thayne's idea to send Claude some clothes that he had worn seemed to be fooling the dog.

"Chopsie!" the decoy asked. "How is my puppy?"

Jacques looked back and winked at the real Thayne as he

followed the decoy down the steps of the plane.

* * *

The next morning Thayne heard the pilot get on the plane. He stayed in the crate until about an hour after he felt the plane land and park in the maintenance hangar in Chicago. He rolled over on his stomach and peeked out of a hole in the end of the box, but he couldn't see anything except the front aisle of the plane. He scrunched himself up like a pretzel and peeked out the hole in the other end. All he saw was an empty plane and an opened door.

He took a deep breath and whispered to himself, "Here you go, Arnie Carver. Today is literally the first day of the rest of your life."

ARNIE CARVER'S FIRST FRIENDS

For the alter ego of a billionaire genius, Arnie Carver was very unsure of himself walking around the Chicago International Airport. He had never been anywhere without his parents, Jacques, or at least a few security guards accompanying him. He had never carried money for himself and now felt extremely uncomfortable with a huge wad of cash bulging in his pocket. He thought someone might try to take it from him any minute. Sure, he could always call Jacques on the satellite phone in his pocket, but that was only for emergencies. Of course, getting robbed in the Chicago Airport would qualify as an emergency, but he was determined to make it in life from then on all by himself as Arnie Carver; just a plain old kid like everyone else.

Arnie's first order of business was to scope out the Global Optimum Airways gate and get some breakfast. The rumbling in his stomach was starting to get serious.

As he walked to the tram stop in front of the maintenance facility, Arnie realized that he had never taken a tram before. Usually, when he had traveled with his parents, he simply climbed into the tank that would be lowered from the cargo hold of the plane and a guard drove them wherever they needed to go. Arnie had such a good time riding the tram, he rode it twice for the entire loop around the airport, before his stomach rumbled again and reminded him of his real mission.

Getting off at the Global Optimum Airlines terminal, Arnie had no problem finding gate number one. A food court was right next to the gate. "Time for breakfast," he thought to himself.

The curly-headed kid walked around all of the eateries in the court. He recalled all of the various companies' virsites that he had clicked on during his virtour of the airport days before. He stopped at the McDonalds. "Two hundred billion sold" read the sign that was printed beneath the golden arches.

"May as well make it two hundred billion and one," he said walking up to the counter.

Six cashiers were all talking to the air in front of them asking to take people's orders. Arnie walked up to the one that seemed to be talking to him. "Hi, I'm Arnie Carver," he said, nervously trying out his new name for the first time out loud in public.

"Hi, Arnie Carver," the lady said. "May I take your order,

please?"

"That's short for John Arnold Carver."

"That's nice," the lady replied. "May I take your order please?"

"I'm fourteen years old and I'm here from Wyoming."

"That's nice, too," the lady said under her breath. "May I take your order, please?"

The man behind him told Arnie to hurry up and tell her what he wanted or the man would go ahead of him.

Arnie studied the menu. "May I please have a famous Big Mac, fries, and a cola?"

The lady repeated his order. "That will be fourteen ninety-five," she informed him.

Arnie very carefully reached in and pulled off only one of the bills from the wad in his pocket. He handed her the thousand-dollar bill.

"We can't take that," the lady said.

"Why not? It's legal tender for all debts public and private," Arnie told her, reading the statement from the bill itself.

"I don't have enough change in my drawer."

It dawned on Arnie that he had no real concept of what anything cost. Someone else had always paid for anything that he ever wanted. He felt embarrassed not to have thought about the fact that the difference between the fourteen ninety-five printed on the menu board and a thousand dollars was going to be a hefty chunk of change.

"I'm sorry. I don't have anything smaller," he apologized.

The man behind him grew impatient. "Hurry up," he grumbled.

The lady shot the rude man a nasty look and told Arnie,

"You'll have to go to the currency exchange booth in the main concourse, get change, and come back."

As he made is way to the main terminal and back, Arnie reminded himself to say something to Jacques about sending him out in the world with just thousand dollar bills, even if it was a hundred of them. Arnie didn't have a clue about these things, but Jacques should have known better. Arnie came back with a wad of ninety-nine one thousand bills in one pocket and another wad of one hundred ten dollar bills in the other. He would just have to remember which pocket to reach into to avoid the embarrassment of his riches again.

Fifteen minutes after he had left, Arnie made it back in line in front of the same lady. "Well, if it isn't Arnie Carver, the rich kid from Wyoming," she said.

"Shhh," Arnie blushed. "Let's not talk about that." Arnie suddenly realized that giving up too much information about himself could come back to haunt him. "Do you still have my order?"

The lady reached under the counter and brought up his tray. "Fourteen ninety-five, please."

Arnie paid with two of the ten-dollar bills, took his change, and sat down at the only available table to eat the first fast food he had ever had. He had never seen a double-decker hamburger before and playfully opened and closed the edge of it a few times before devouring it in eight bites. Not feeling full, he got back in line in front of his favorite server and bought two more with more appropriate bills.

After his second bite of the second burger, a girl holding her own tray walked up to the table. "This seems to be the only seat available," she said, looking all around the crowded food court. "Do you mind if I sit down?"

Arnie looked up and saw the most beautiful person that

he had ever seen. "Sure! Go ahead," he said, moving the chair across from him out from under the table with his foot.

"Thanks." She put her tray down, sat in the chair, and stuck out her hand. "Hi. I'm Bernadette Rogers," she introduced herself.

Arnie shook her hand. "Hi. I'm Tha—Arnie," he stuttered. "John Arnold Carver, actually, but you can call me Arnie."

"It's nice to meet you, Arnie," she replied, letting go of his hand. "And how are you today?"

"I'm fine," he replied. Not knowing what to say for small talk, he batted his eyebrows and said the first thing that came into his head. "*Comment allez vous, mon petit chou?*"

Bernadette cackled a quick laugh at Arnie's expense, before she smiled, and asked, "Why did you just call me your little cabbage?"

Arnie's face flushed. "I don't know," he answered. "I just heard my father say it to my mother a lot."

"Well, learn what you're saying, before you start talking to a girl in French. You could end up married awfully young, doing something like that." She giggled again at him.

The boy blushed and decided to put the conversation ball back in her court. "So, who are you and where are you from and stuff like that?" he asked.

Arnie munched his French fries and continued to gaze at his first new friend. She had long, red, curly hair and clear skin with just a few little-bitty freckles on her cheeks. And white teeth peeking through red lips, which would not quit smiling, as she loquaciously told him her entire life's story in one long breath.

"I'm a south central California coastal native, whose mother has made sure that I've been in every stage of beauty pageant competition in the states since I was three years old, a straight-A student at the hardest private school in my town, and team captain of every sports team in my school, except for football, because they would only let me play as the kicker, though I did get to be the quarterback at least once a season for some trick play on punts and extra points, which usually meant that all of the guys on my team would try to not make it look like they were trying to let all of the guys on the other team through the line just to get me, which they never did, because I was too fast and smart for them and . . ." on and on and on until Arnie had run out of fries and started to pick up his hamburger again.

"Oh, my gosh!" She pointed to his hamburger. "Please tell me that you are not going to eat that."

"Why not?" he asked, while offering her the third one he had bought. "Do you want one?

"No, thanks," she replied pointing to her own tray. "I'm strictly a grilled Portobello kind of girl, but I grew up on Big Macs. Do you know what's in them?"

"Sure," Arnie said. "two all-beef patties, a three-piece sesame seed Big Mac bun, pasteurized process American cheese, Big Mac sauce, lettuce, pickle slices, dehydrated onions, and grill seasoning; all of which comes to five hundred and sixty calories total; of which two hundred and seventy calories are from thirty grams or forty-seven percent of a normal day's intake of fat, of which twelve grams are saturated fat; eighty milligrams of cholesterol, one thousand and ten milligrams of sodium, forty-two grams of carbohydrates, three grams of dietary fiber, eight grams of sugar, and twenty-five grams of protein; all of which is two percent of the recommended daily allowance, the RDA, for vitamin A, two percent of vitamin C, sixteen percent of calcium, and fifteen percent of iron."

Bernadette's mouth fell open as Arnie rattled off the ingredients. "Oh, my gosh! How did you know that?" she asked.

"I read it off of their virnet site when I virtoured the airport."

"Oh, my gosh! And you remembered it all? How did you do it?"

"I guess I am just good with remembering everything I see."

"And what happens," she started to say, "if we replace your meat patty with my tasty grilled Portobello mushroom?"

Arnie rocked his head back and recalculated the numbers. "That leaves two hundred eighteen calories, of which fifty are from three-point-seven grams of fat, less than eleven milligrams of cholesterol, only three hundred twenty grams of sodium, thirty-one grams of carbohydrates, but five grams of dietary fiber, still eight grams of sugar, but only twelve grams of protein, still six, ten and four percent of the RDA for vitamins A and C and calcium, but only one percent of the RDA for iron."

"But, more importantly," she explained, unwrapping her version of the sandwich, "you can eat over two for one of them for the same number of calories." She smiled, pointing at her own abdomen. "That's how I keep this girlish figure," she whispered.

Arnie whined, "But, I like Big Macs," defending his new found favorite food.

Bernadette looked at her watch. "Oh, my gosh!"

"What?"

"Here," she said pushing her plate toward his. "Want the rest of my tofu salad? I have to go check in for my flight to Demeverde."

"Are you going to GODA, too?" Arnie asked.

Bernadette realized that they were about to be schoolmates. "Oh, my gosh! You, too?" She picked up both of their trays and turned toward the trashcan nearby. "Then you better hurry or we'll both be late."

Arnie grabbed his last hamburger off the tray, before Bernadette threw it out. "I'll scarf this on the way."

"Suit yourself," Bernadette said, as the two of them gathered their belongings.

Arnie munched down the rest of his burgers, walking with Bernadette toward the counter at the Global Optimum Airlines gate, just in time to hear the announcement of the first boarding call for the flight. They waited in line to check in at the counter. A clear piece of glass hanging in the air projected "Welcome Global Optimum Development Academy Sharers," in shimmering silvery-white letters, which looked like foam on the surface of blue sea water.

While they were waiting, Bernadette turned to Arnie and asked, "So, Arnie, what's your gift?"

Arnie didn't want to discuss his learning advantages, so he acted like he didn't know what she was talking about. "I didn't bring one," he said. "Should I go back to the gift shop and buy one?"

Bernadette laughed at him. "No, silly," she said, "not that kind of gift. What kind of gift do you have that got you into the academy?"

"You tell me yours, first; and then, I'll tell you mine."

"Well, one," Bernadette started, "I'm a winner. I win at almost everything I do. Two, I am a team leader. Almost everything I do with other people, they somehow naturally pick me to be the team leader. Three, I am able to learn things very quickly and I made straight A's all the way through school. But, four, which I guess is my greatest gift of all, is the ability to somehow sense exactly what it is anyone around me wants or needs and then convince them that I can help them get it."

"Oh, really?" Arnie said. "That's all nice and everything, but it doesn't seem to make you appear very gifted."

"Oh, really? Well, let's just see." Bernadette proposed. "We've only known each other for about twenty minutes, right?"

"Right."

"So let's just see how I am sensing you." She closed her eyes for a second and then started to talk again with her eyes closed. "You have had a recent horrific emotional trauma in your life. This is your first time away from home and your parents." Arnie's mouth fell open. "You feel very awkward, because you are smart as a dickens, but not very sure of how to use it, and you really want to fit in and be well liked at school." Bernadette opened her eyes and reached over and closed his mouth saying, "So, how'd I do?"

Arnie's eyes were still as wide as saucers. "Oh, my gosh!" he said, "You're a psychic."

"Not really." Bernadette flipped her fingers through her hair. "It's not like I can tell the past or the future exactly or anything, but I can sense what people are feeling and help them get what they want." She touched him on the cheek. "But don't worry, Arnie Carver, because I am going to take good care of you and make sure everybody likes you."

Arnie was a little suspicious. "Why would you do that?"

"Because I like you, silly." She shook her head. "So, what's your gift?"

"I guess it's that I can remember everything I see so

well." Arnie tried to think of something else to say. "It's not like I got straight A's in school or anything because my parents homeschooled me."

"So how smart are you?" Bernadette asked.

"Well, let's just say that I'm sure I'm smart enough for high school, even at GODA."

"I'm sensing false modesty," she said. "I like that in a man."

No one had ever called Arnie a man before and he was not quite sure how to respond. Luckily he didn't have to, because the lady behind the counter was now talking to Bernadette. "Name please?"

"Rogers, Bernadette P."

"Yes, ma'am." The lady looked at her list on the piece of glass she had in front of her and touched it. Bernadette's name changed from red to blue. "Go ahead, ma'am."

"Thank you," Bernadette said.

"My pleasure," said the lady, looking at Arnie. "Name, please." she requested.

"Carver, John A."

"Yes, sir," the lady said, while changing the color of his name on the glass. "Go ahead, sir."

Arnie thanked her and she replied again that it was her pleasure. Arnie figured that she must be required to say that to everyone.

Bernadette disappeared to somewhere while Arnie was checking in, because she was nowhere to be found when he was done. "She must have gone to the restroom," he thought, walking over and sitting down next to a rather large boy, who was trying to put back together his pocket VirtuComp game, which he had for some reason taken apart.

"What are you doing there?" Arnie asked him.

The guy did not look up, but he did answer Arnie. "I'm trying to see if I can enhance the display of this pocket virtual experience computer, by reversing the holographic generator to have the images show up life-sized in three dimensions, instead of looking like little, three-dimensional figures, right on top of the screen."

Arnie had never thought to try doing that when he was over at the VirtuComp development center in Italy. Of course, he couldn't very well tell the other kid that. Nonetheless, he was curious to see how the fellow was trying to do it. If it turned out, then he would somehow get the information back to the developers at VirtuComp.

"How are you doing that?" Arnie asked.

The guy looked up at Arnie and then held up two pieces of blue and red glass. "Well, first, I cut and ground down the other half of each of these lenses that came with these three-dimensional glasses. Then I mounted them on top of the holographic generator that this thing uses for a screen and then I reversed the polarity of the generation." The guy was having some trouble getting the VirtuComp case back closed. "But now the whole thing is too thick to get back in the case." He held the wobbly mess out to Arnie and demanded, "Hold this with one hand on top and one hand on the bottom for a second."

Arnie did what he was told, while the inventor dug in his backpack and took out a roll of duct tape. The guy tore off a long piece and rolled it into a pliable rod, approximately equal to the circumference of the machine Arnie was holding. He stuck it in the crack that the stack of lenses made between the two halves of the case. Then he cut another long piece of duct tape and covered the rod and enough of the two halves of the case with it to hold everything all together.

"There, that should do it." He took the VirtuComp back and said, "Thanks. Let's see how it runs." The kid pushed the red button on the back of the VirtuComp and the big V of the manufacturer's logo rose up about five feet from the screen. "Pretty cool, huh?"

"Yeah." Arnie was impressed, until the name "VirtuComp" showed up under the logo incorrectly. "Except that all of the letters seem to be backwards."

The large boy noticed it, but he did not seem to care. "That's okay. I'll work that out later. What matters is that the fight scenes of the game now come out at you in life-sized virtual reality so it really seems much more in your face." Several figures started hitting each other and shooting guns everywhere within the six-foot cube of holographic glow. "What do you think?"

Arnie could not tell him all that he knew about the game. "I think you need to send that idea to the company that makes those things. I bet you they would pay you good money for it."

"Do you think so?"

"Sure they would," Arnie said, sticking out his hand. "Hi. I'm Arnie Carver."

The guy shook his hand. "Hi. I'm Steven Schocken, but everyone just calls me 'Tinker'." He held up the VirtuComp as one good guy paused in the middle of a strike and was about to kill a bad guy. "Guess you can see why, huh?"

"Where did you learn how to do that?" Arnie asked.

"Three generations of picking up broken stuff, fixing it or making it better, and selling it, I guess."

"What?"

"My great, great, grandfather was a junkman when he came to America from Europe. He used to pick up, repair,

ARNIE CARVER'S FIRST FRIENDS

and resell broken things that everyone threw away. My great grandfather did the same thing, but he focused more on sales and got other people to do the picking up and repairing. My uncle just got new stuff made for his company and became a massive retailer of it all. Maybe you've heard of their stores, Schockenstores."

"Yes." Arnie said, not mentioning that Schockenstores was a retailer of a lot of VirtuComp's sales in the United States and Canada."

"Good," Tinker continued. "My dad didn't do as well as the rest of the family, though. He just likes inventing stuff and getting companies to make it and sell it. Anyway, he's the one who taught me to take stuff apart and make it work better."

"Well, you just made that VirtuComp even cooler than it already was, so you must be pretty good at it."

"It's a gift, I guess."

"So is that why you are going to GODA?"

"Yeah. My dad says that if I do well at Global Optimum Development Academy, then I may be able to go on after high school to Global Optimum Development University. If I do well there, then I might get to work at Global Optimum Development Enterprises on some really cool stuff someday."

A pleasantly familiar voice came from behind Arnie, "And I am sure that you will, too," Bernadette encouraged him.

"Bernadette!" Arnie said excitedly, turning around in his chair. "Come sit down." He pointed to the chair beside him. As she was cutting between them, he introduced her. "Bernadette Rogers, this is Steven Schocken. He's loosely related to the Schockenstores family." Arnie thought he

◁   77   ▷

would name drop for Tinker a little bit. "Tinker, this is Bernadette Rogers."

"Pleased to meet you," Tinker said, disappearing back into his VirtuComp game. Tinker apparently had no use for or interest in girls; or, at least, Bernadette. Arnie and she picked up their conversation where they had left off.

"So have you been to Demeverde before?" Arnie asked.

"Yes. My parents took me there for vacation last summer and, while we were there, they found out about the Academy and everything."

"Everything? Like what?"

"Like it is the coolest place in the world to go for a vacation. Demeverde is a group of islands and one of them, Isla Principal, the main island, is devoted to a huge vacation theme park called Global World with about four or five other parks in it. It takes up about a quarter of the whole island. About another quarter of the island is GODA and GODU. A big hunk of the island is off limits to tourists, because that's Global Optimum Development Enterprises' research and executive facility. The rest of the main island is where everybody lives." She paused for a second. "I'll have to tell you all about it on the plane because I think that it's about time for the second boarding call." She stood up to lead the way and directed, "We better go find our seats."

As Arnie got Tinker's attention and the three of them started to gather up their belongings, a polite male voice announced on the intercom that it was the second boarding call for the flight to Godeau, Demeverde and that all passengers in the terminal should please make their way to the plane and find a seat.

The three of them made their way down the gateway, paying attention to a flight attendant speaking over the overhead virtual displays. "Today you will be flying on a GOAL plane, a Global Optimum Airlines Luxuryliner, especially designed for long trips and longer conversations." A projection of a wide-bodied craft eased into the air. "Unlike the seats on most airplanes," the flight attendant on the preflight virtual video in the gateway explained, "the seats on a GOAL plane are 'Cheds,' a Global Optimum Development Enterprises exclusive combination recliner that are especially designed and manufactured to serve as both a chair and bed."

The virtual attendant explained and demonstrated, "Each ched can incrementally shift from a full upright to a fully reclined position by merely pushing against it. For dining, working, or recreational use, a fully adjustable table is easily extendable from the underside to the top." The image of the plane began to land on an open plain. "In the unlikely event of an unscheduled descent into terrain, the tabletop can be used as a SlipDisc for individual transportation. Simply remove the table top from its holder and its guarantium elemental structure will begin to generate the energy required to create a slip of air on which the SlipDisc will ride. Simply stand on the SlipDisc to use it like a motorized skateboard to travel to the nearest safe location." The projection of the plane took off again, only to land smoothly in an ocean and the virtual flight attendant slipped what looked like a large rubber band around the edge of the table top. "In the unlikely event of an unscheduled descent into water, an attachable shroud can be used to transform the SlipDisc into a SlipHover for individual aquatic transportation."

Bernadette led Arnie and Tinker onto the plane. The cheds were arranged in twenty U-shaped groups of seven on each side of the center aisle. The last two groups closest to the door of the plane had some vacant seats. A dark-skinned boy and a modestly dressed, dark-skinned girl occupied two cheds near the windows behind the group on the right side of the aisle. Bernadette pushed the trio toward them.

As Bernadette slid into the horseshoe of seats, Steven Schocken pulled Arnie's arm back a little bit and pleaded, "Please sit between me and any girls. I'm not too comfortable around them."

"Sure," Arnie said, thinking to himself, "at least you've been around girls." The only time that Arnie could remember being around any girls his own age was when he was with four of them at his birthday party the previous year. He started to well up inside at the memory.

Bernadette stopped and turned around. "What's wrong, Arnie? Homesick already?" She pulled him toward the other boy and girl. "Let's meet these other kids and you'll forget all about it." She stuck out her hand to the dark-skinned girl. "Hi, I'm Bernadette Rogers and this is my good friend, Arnie Carver, and his friend, Steven Schocken."

As the girl let go of Bernadette and shook Arnie's and Steven's hands she said, "Hello, I'm Roberta Rivers and this is my twin brother, Robert."

Robert shook hands with the three of them, and said, "Nice to meet you," to each one. Bernadette took the seat at the bottom end of the U with her back to the windows. Arnie and Tinker took the next two seats.

"So where are you from and what do your parents do?" Bernadette asked them while pulling on Arnie's arm again to keep him in the conversation.

Roberta explained, "We're from Atlanta, Georgia, and our parents are both doctors of science in social work, who run a struggling, non-profit Muslim civil rights foundation."

"That's fascinating," Bernadette said. "I have lots of Muslim friends in California, but I've never really had the chance to learn much about the religion. What's it all about?"

As Bernadette and the Rivers twins segued into a discussion of comparative religions, Arnie looked away and watched a muscular boy with very white skin sit down on the other side of Tinker. The fellow, who was taller, but leaner, than Tinker, stuck out his hand, which Tinker did not notice because he was investigating the way the ched was put together.

"Hi, I'm Alex Shelikhov," he said, with a light Russian accent.

"Steven Schocken," Tinker said, kneeling back on his feet in front of his ched. He pointed around the rest of the group. "Arnie Carver, Bernadette Rogers, Robert Rivers, and his twin sister, Roberta."

Alex waved to them all and repeated his name to each of them as he settled his belongings under his seat. He started to listen to Tinker tell him about how the cheds were made.

"Each of these cheds has a chain mail outer body, with adjusting wires running through the links of the chain mail at right angles attached to an integrated motor. The motor appears to sense pressure and strain and then adjusts the tension of the wires in the desired direction to adapt the seat to the size and shape of its occupant and the desired amount of reclination."

Bernadette interrupted Tinker with an excited squeal, as she saw a very well-dressed girl with shoulder length, straight blond hair standing at the open end of their grouping of seats with four bodyguards around her.

"Oh-my-gosh!" she said, looking at the girl with her

mouth wide open. "You're Amanda Purvis!"

"I'm afraid so," the girl said. She looked at her bodyguards and said, "Thanks, guys," at which time, they all turned around and sat down in the four seats nearest the middle of the plane in the group of cheds on the other side of the aisle.

"Folks," Bernadette said, grabbing Arnie and Robert's arms. "The President's daughter is going to GODA with us. Did you know that her father is the only person to serve as a congressman, a senator, the Vice-President, and the President of the United States?"

"That's the former president's daughter," Amanda corrected her. "And he did most of that, thankfully, before I was born. I only had to live through one term as the daughter of the Vice-President and two terms as the First Kid." She pointed her thumb back over her shoulder. "Imagine living your entire life with four of these guys keeping you from doing anything with hardly anybody."

"Don't I know it," Arnie whispered to himself.

"What?" Bernadette asked him.

"Nothing."

"So, Amanda, what is it that is taking you to GODA?" Bernadette asked.

"First, it is the only place where my father agreed to let me go without these guys tagging along."

"They are still here," Roberta corrected her.

"But they won't be, a few weeks after I get to Demeverde. It has the strongest security force and system in the world and they have assured my father that the secret service will be a waste of the government's money there."

A virtual image of a lady in uniform eased forward out of the overhead displays in the aisle, which were facing each group of seats. "This is the captain from the flight deck here. I hate to interrupt your conversations, but I just want to ask everyone to make sure that your ched is in its full and upright position and snugly adjusted at the hips and shoulders for take off." The plane started to back away from the gate. "We're next in line to get underway and we will soon be accelerating to a takeoff speed of two hundred and fifty miles per hour."

Alex whistled and said, "That's fast."

The captain continued, "We'll continue a slow acceleration up to just under three times the speed of sound or about two thousand miles per hour." As the plane moved onto the runway, the captain proceeded, as well. "With acceleration and deceleration times, we should be making the three thousand two hundred and sixty mile trip in approximately three hours and fifteen minutes." The engines began to rev. The passengers could feel the plane strain against its brakes holding the colossal craft in place, while the captain finished up her announcements. "And by the way, if you have any satellite phones or other electronic devices with you, feel free to use them at any time, because we are Global Optimum Airlines . . ." The plane began to swoosh down the airstrip. "And nothing bothers us."

"Cool!" Tinker said, struggling against the force of the plane pushing him back into his ched. He bent over, pulled up a small duffle bag from under his seat, and took out the duct-taped VirtuComp game.

Once their takeoff was complete, Bernadette asked Amanda, "And so, Miss Purvis, what is your gift?"

"Just call me Amanda, please," she replied and continued. "I can integrate any spoken or written language in as long as it takes me to read a dictionary including grammar rules and hear the pronunciation of a good representative group of the words."

"Wow!" Bernadette said.

"That, plus I am a whiz at computers and programming. What about you guys?"

"She's a psychic," Arnie blurted out.

"Pfft, not hardly," Bernadette corrected him. "Just very empathetic with well developed leadership and teambuilding skills," she explained apologetically. "Arnie here has a photographic memory and he tells me that Tinker there can take anything apart and put it back together better than it originally was. And I don't know about the rest of us." She looked at Robert and Roberta Rivers. "What are your gifts, guys?"

"We're sibling sympaths," Roberta answered her.

"What's that?" Tinker asked.

"We feel each others thoughts, emotions, and sensations in stressful periods."

"Wow! Way cool," Tinker said. He turned to Alex and asked, "And what's your gift, my Scandinavian friend."

"I am not Scandinavian!" Alex loudly informed him. "My ancestors were Russian who once lived in Alaska and moved back to Russia during the Revolution. My parents then moved back to Alaska before I was born, so, while I may not sound like it or look like it, I am as American as anyone else here."

"Geez! I'm sorry," Tinker apologized. "I didn't mean to offend you. So what's your gift?"

Alex studied Tinker for a second before responding. "Near perfect sensory perception."

"Like how perfect?" Tinker asked.

"I can see to almost any horizon with almost perfect resolution. I can hear and resonate to the limits of any hearing range known to man or animals. I can feel the slightest of air currents on my skin. And I can smell and taste anything with a unique odor or flavor to a dilution of approximately one part per billion."

"Wow!" Tinker agreed with him. "That's pretty perfect."

Bernadette took back control of the discussion. "So, how many of us have been to Demeverde before?" she asked raising up her hand. "I vacationed there last year."

Robert raised his and Roberta's hands. "We traveled there with our parents to study the Demeverdan social system three years ago."

Amanda raised her own hand and said, "I've been there lots of times for international economic conferences with my father."

"Never been there," Tinker chimed in.

"Me neither," Alex concluded.

A flight attendant came down the aisle with a rolling cooler of drink bottles in every color of the rainbow. "Doctor Ginger's?" she asked.

"Oh, my gosh! Arnie, Tinker, Alex," Bernadette said, getting up and tugging each one of them in turn by the hands. "You have to try some of this. Amanda, Robert, and Roberta will agree, if they've had them, these things are great."

"What is it?" Arnie asked.

"Doctor Ginger's Naturally Carbonated Fruit-Flavored Drinks," Roberta informed them, while helping Bernadette by picking up two bottles with each hand. "Three hundred and sixty-five different fruit blends bottled with Demeverde's naturally carbonated water from Bicarbonate Springs." She gave one to each of them and twisted off the cap from one for herself. "A different flavor every day of the year," she read off of the label, "and a positive thought printed in the top of every cap."

Arnie read the inside of his cap out loud. "Do something new everyday."

"Sounds good to me," Bernadette said. "How about yours, Alex?"

Alex looked in his cap. "You can do well doing good," he read.

Tinker looked at his cap and smiled. "Let's see how good your eyesight really is," he said, walking all the way up the aisle of the plane reading his cap. He balanced the cap on its side facing the back of the plane on the top of the ledge of the doorway to the pilot's cabin. After he ran back to the rear of the plane, Tinker asked, "So what does that say?"

Alex stood in the middle of the aisle and focused his eyes on the cap. "Challenge yourself with every deed."

"Wow!" Tinker gasped. "That's some pair of peepers you got there, Alex."

"Not really," Alex admitted. "I read the big print while you were looking at it going down the aisle."

Amanda looked up and said, "Aw! No fair!"

Alex looked a little harder at the top and continued, "But the little bitty print around the inside of the rim says, 'Send us your positive thoughts. If we like them, we'll print them here.'"

Arnie and Tinker looked at the inside of Arnie's cap. "Man!" Arnie exclaimed, while Tinker added, "Awesome!"

Bernadette passed out a Doctor Ginger's to everyone else in the group and sat down.

As they enjoyed the sweet drinks, Robert asked the entire group, "If we are going to be traveling at three times the speed of sound, which is about seven hundred and sixty miles an hour times three or two thousand two hundred and eighty miles an hour and, the distance is only thirty-three hundred miles, why is it taking us three hours to get from Chicago to Demeverde?"

Everyone around the group shook their heads and said that they did not know, except for Arnie.

"Because you are missing several parts of the problem," Arnie advised him.

"So enlighten us, O aeronautical master," Robert challenged.

"Well, first, you have to account for the fact that you are calculating based on the speed of sound at sea level instead of at a cruising altitude of about sixty thousand feet. Your speed of sound up there will only be six hundred and sixty miles and hour, three times which will only equal nineteen hundred and eighty miles per hour. Plus, you have to account for take off and acceleration times to warm the plane up slowly and then deceleration times, and that it why it takes so long."

Everyone looked at Arnie while he continued telling them all about supersonic aircraft until Bernadette interrupted and asked with a sly smile, "And so how can you calculate how long is it going to take for us to get served lunch on this thing?"

Arnie started to think for a second and then began to answer. "Okay, there are twenty rows of groups of these cheds on each side of the plane, equals a hundred and forty per side, times two sides, equals two hundred and eighty cheds. Now, I've counted six flight attendants; so assuming that …."

ORIENTATION

Three hours and fifteen minutes after takeoff, the GOAL plane landed at the Godeau, Demeverde transit port. Being the last ones on the plane and having the seats nearest the door, Arnie and his new friends were the first ones to get off.

Bernadette suggested, "Let's all stay together, seeing as to how we've already gotten to know each other so well. Okay?"

Two of Amanda Purvis's security guards led the way in front of Amanda and the other two fell in behind her.

Alex looked at Arnie and commented, "It must be really

convenient to have a phalanx of armed guards clearing the way for you."

"Yeah, right," Arnie said, with an incredulous tone.

When they reached the customs and immigration booths, a uniformed agent was standing under a sign that read, "Welcome to Demeverde." Under the greeting, the sign also read the national motto, which Arnie remembered from his virtour, "Peace and satisfaction for all."

The agent instructed them, "Please put your palms on the scanner, look at the camera, and say your full name into the microphone at the same time to be formally registered for entry into Demeverde."

The first Secret Service agent complied with the command and started through the line's body scanner. His gun set off an alarm and the group's progress came to a screeching halt, as a pair of clear gates closed off his exit from the scanner.

"Nothing that could be used as an offensive weapon is allowed in Demeverde," the customs agent said.

Amanda's agents all held up their identifications and badges as the one trapped in the scanner explained, "We are the United States Secret Service protection detail for the First Daughter of the President of the United States."

The customs agent just shook his head, "Not even for the United States Secret Service." He tsked three times and argued on, "And, besides, President Purvis is no longer in office and he was specifically informed that your weapons would not be allowed on Demeverde."

Despite the explanations as to who they were and whom they were protecting, the customs agent informed them that he was not going to change his mind. Three other flights had come in simultaneously and the immigration and customs area was suddenly full with about one thousand international young teenagers who were all about to start high school at the Global Optimum Development Academy.

Bernadette moved up next to Amanda. "Unless they can be convinced to turn over their weapons, no one else in this line is going to get to go anywhere." She looked at Amanda squarely in the eyes and suggested, "Go assert yourself here."

Amanda Purvis turned around to convince the agents to turn over their guns. "Look, guys," she instructed them, "you four are the protection detail assigned by the former President of the United States, who knows full well that no offensive weapons of any type are allowed on Demeverde. So just consider the order from this nice customs agent, who is only doing his job, to be an order from my father and put your guns in the plastic bags like this guy is telling you to do and let's get on with this. Okay?"

The agents continued to protest, but, eventually, they did as they were instructed. With a relieved smile, the customs agent repeated his instructions. "Thank you, gentlemen. Just put your hands on the palm scanner, look at the camera, and say your full name to identify your confiscated goods. You can pick them up on your departure."

Once they cleared the Immigration and Customs Department, all of the new students proceeded to the next set of booths in their lines. A white-clad nurse informed them. "You will all be required to have a vaccination against any viruses that you may be bringing with you or that are already present on Demeverde. Please pay attention to the explanation screens above you."

On the screens, a very pleasant, motherly-looking lady, whose identification tag read "Health Department," held up something that looked like a cosmic ray gun in her hand and explained what was about to happen. "These vaccination guns will blow a fast-acting, short-duration local anesthetic into the injection site with air and then inject you once simultaneously in each arm with ten small shallow needles. A third vaccination gun will be used to inject specific vaccinations for spinal meningeal diseases in the meaty part of your neck right beneath the bony knob on the back of your head."

Once they had all been cleared by the medical assistants, the group found themselves at the SlipDisc demonstration center, where another virtual display explained how the main method of individual transportation on Demeverde worked. "Simply stand on a SlipDisc and tell it where you want to go." A short virtual clip showed a person saying, "Transit port SlipStream stand, please," and being whooshed away. The display then requested, "Please select a SlipDisc and ride it to the SlipStream stand."

As everyone stepped onto their SlipDiscs Bernadette added to the instructions, "Remember to stay together."

An overhead sign reading, "SlipStream Stand" came into view under the awning outside the transit port. As everyone in the group stepped off of their SlipDiscs under the sign, the SlipDiscs flowed back into a long line of them that seemed to completely cover the sidewalks for as far as the eye could see. Rows of large SlipStream Dozenberths, each capable of seating twelve, hovered idling two inches above the ground.

Arnie turned to Bernadette and sarcastically asked, "Now what, dear, great, fearless leader?"

Bernadette looked around and then back at the group. "I guess we just need to get in one and see what happens next," she answered. She leaned over to Amanda, who was standing beside her, looked into her eyes, and whispered, "Why don't you have your guys run along outside this thing on those SlipDiscs."

The seven of them got in the Dozenberth nearest them and sat down. Amanda turned to the Secret Service agents and suggested, "Why don't you guys just ride along beside this thing on those SlipDiscs."

As the agents stepped on some SlipDiscs going by, another girl with a healthy tan, long brunette hair, and the number 10 in a circle pinned to her chest led three other students onto the Dozenberth. "*Bonjour, mes amis,*" she said in French, before switching to English with a bright French accent. "My name is Émilie Chanel. I am from Paris, France, and I am a T-T-P from last year's freshman sharers class. Part of my responsibility is to serve as your T-T-P until the end of your first session of your freshman year. Any questions yet?"

Émilie waited for a response, but received none, and so, she continued, "Good. First, does everyone here know each other?"

"Yes," Bernadette answered her. "We all came in together from the United States this morning."

"Okay," Émilie said, "then let me introduce the last three of your deca. First …" Émilie pointed to an obviously Eurasian featured girl, "representing the Pacific Rim countries, we have Ahn Min-su from the Republic of North Korea."

Min-su said, "Hello" in English with a Korean accent.

"And representing the African continent, Aurelia Musyoka, from South Africa."

Aurelia also said, "Hello," in English with an African intonation.

"And last but not least, from South America, Hugo
Guelar, from Argentina."

Hugo added his, "Hello," in English as well, but in a
deep Latin voice.

Émilie made her way to the seat in the front of the
Dozenberth and turned around to face the group. She looked
worried about something. "We don't usually like having this
many Americans in a deca. It's usually better to have a more
representative international group."

Tinker chimed in, "Well, Alex here is kind of Russian."

"I'm not Russian!" Alex protested. "My parents are
Russian."

"Oh well, that's a little better, I guess," Émilie said. "Oh,
well, as Unius might say, 'If fate has seen fit to bring you
together like this, who are we to impose our will on it?' So,
I guess you're a deca. Any questions?"

"Yeah," Alex asked, "What's a deca?"

"A deca is a group of ten sharers," Émilie answered him.
"You ten sharers are a deca now. You arrived here together
and you will pretty much stay together for the rest of high
school here at GODA. Unless, of course, some really good
reason comes up for changing your composition. The idea
is to take people from all over the globe and bring them
together to share their thoughts, knowledge, and ideas with
each other, in order to have a more optimal development of
the world."

Robert Rivers asked, "Sort of like a United Nations High
School?"

"As if the UN could do anything as well as we can at
GODA," Émilie scoffed. "But, yeah, you could almost say
that. Any other questions?"

Bernadette inquired, "What's a T-T-P? And how can I

become one?"

"A T-T-P is a Top Ten Percenter. At the end of your first session, you will appoint one person from your deca to be your Top Ten Percenter. He or she will be your representative on the Class Council to help discuss any problems that you may have or solutions to others' problems that you may want to share."

"Share?" Aurelia asked.

"Yes, share," Émilie answered. "You see, here at GODA, people neither teach nor learn. Everyone just shares. Teachers share with students and each other. Students share with teachers and each other. Almost everyone is very big on mutual respect and understanding."

"Oh," Aurelia said.

Everyone else took in what Émilie had just explained and nodded in agreement.

"Where was I?" Émilie asked herself. "Oh, yeah. At the end of the first year, each Class Council picks from their own class, the T-O-P's, that's Top One Percenters, who then make up the entire GODA Student Council with the T-O-P's from the other three classes. Each class's T-O-P's then pick their own Number One, who is the class representative on the Unius Council. The Number Ones meet once a year with Unius and Mrs. Liedgarten for continuous quality improvement to make school better the following year."

"Who is Mrs. Liedgarten?" Hugo asked.

"Mrs. L?" Émilie repeated. "She's the headmistress of the high school. Everyone's mother away from home; unless you make her mad." Émilie pointed and wagged her finger at the group and faked a Viennese accent. "So do not test her!" she joked. No one laughed and everyone had a puzzled look on his or her face. "You'll understand that better after you meet her." Émilie looked at the control disc on the front dash of the Dozenberth and then back at the rest of the group. "If there are no more questions?" She paused for a second and heard none. "Good, then." She turned back to the control disc on the Dozenberth's front dashboard. "If you please, Madame, the full island tour and a final stop at the GODA S-U."

A pleasant female voice came from the disc and replied, "My pleasure." The Dozenberth moved slowly at first and then accelerated out of the loading area and merged into a line of tens of other transports passing under a sign pointing an arrow toward the word "SlipRail". Another sign that read "SlipRail entrance" appeared. The SlipRail was an elevated highway made out of what looked like very big and thick clear glass that ran along the ring of hills around the island. As the line of Dozenberths on the SlipRail moved up a hill to the south of the transit port, the beaches, resort area, and Global World came into view.

"I'll show you the fun parts of Demeverde, first, and then show you where and how the local Demeverdans live. After that, we will travel past never-never land and the university; and then, we will finally end up at the GODA Student Union."

Émilie told them about all of the leisure activities that were available on the island. "You won't have much time for leisure for at least the next four months of your first term," she informed them. "But, the weekend after mid-term exams is dedicated to doing nothing but enjoying all of the tourist traps on the beaches, the food shops, and the stores. Not to mention that, for the first twenty-four hours after exams are over, all GODA sharers get into Global World for free. So, at least you have that to look forward to."

The transport made a turn to the left, heading north. "Over the next hill . . .," Émilie started to say, directing the group past a forest to the west going up a ridge toward the center of the island. "You will see four small mountains and a valley covered with homes, apartment buildings, and commercial areas to the east. The local residential area opens to the ocean to the east through the gap between the two easternmost mountains."

Next, they turned northwest continuing to circle the island over the hills sloping down toward the valley below. "Looking back to the left again, this is Valle Central Grande, which Hugo will tell you means the Big Central Valley in Spanish. The south central valley is used for farming to feed the entire island and the north central valley is never-never land, which means that you never, never go there uninvited."

Émilie pointed to a massive complex of buildings, hangars, launching towers, and other structures, all of which were surrounded by a pair of rivers that started at the base of Godeau Mountain and split around the industrial complex. "Those are the research, development, and executive offices of Global Optimum Development Enterprises, which is the goose that lays every golden egg on the whole island and pays for your education here at GODA. So nobody does anything to make the people at GODEnt mad for any reason, got it?"

No one really responded, so Émilie expounded for them. "This is really serious stuff here, guys. A lot of the things that they do there are very dangerous and they take their security very seriously. So I am supposed to make sure that all of you understand that you are not to go beyond the Paired Rivers without permission from GODEnt. Understand?"

Everyone nodded their head, but that was not enough for Émilie. "I am supposed to hear you all say that you understand this," she emphasized.

Everyone said in unison a mixed chorus of, "Right," "Sure," "Got it," "Yes," "Affirmative," "Jal," "Yep," "Si," "Uh-huh," and "Okay." Bernadette summed up the deca's consensus for Émilie, "We all understand."

A while later, they turned south on the west side of the island and entered the north side of the university. Émilie explained, "After you finish at GODA, you'll be invited here to the university." She pointed to a large collection of utilitarian-looking buildings. "Of course, their campus is not as pretty as ours."

Past the university, the SlipRail dipped just above the coast and beneath the western base of Godeau Mountain. Émilie pointed to the mountain and said "That's Godeau Mountain, where Unius lives and works."

Arnie noticed the beginning of the steps going up the south quarter of the mountain and remembered Jacques's description of climbing them. "A thousand steps," he said quietly, thinking he felt something subconsciously pulling him up them.

It may have been, however, just Bernadette pulling on the shoulder of his shirt. "You okay over there?" she asked.

Arnie snapped back to reality. "Yeah, sure," he answered.

The group's Dozenberth passed a huge three-story rectangular building with a four-story round section attached to each corner. A huge Global Optimum Development Academy logo and the words "Student Union" were hung on all four sides. Everyone heard and felt a swoosh of air generating under the transport as it slid off the SlipRail and descended to come to a rest in front of one of the round towers. Amanda Purvis's security guards, looking quite the worse for the trip, followed the Dozenberth on their SlipDiscs.

Émilie pushed a spot on the dashboard and the door beside her seat slid open. She instructed them, "Okay, everybody, get out quickly so that this Dozenberth can get out of the way of the others." She thanked the disc as she stepped out and was acknowledged with a "My pleasure" from it. Everyone else made the same exchange of greetings on the way off the transport.

Alex asked Émilie, "What's with all of this 'my pleasure' stuff?"

"It's just a Demeverdan kind of thing," Émilie explained. "The locals are all a real gracious bunch of people and they basically say, 'My pleasure,' almost every time that someone says, 'thank you' to them. I guess it just gets programmed into everything after a while." She looked around to count noses and then looked back at Alex. "You'll probably start saying it yourself sometime. It's kind of contagious."

Émilie started walking backwards and talking to the group at the same time. "Please stay together and let's go inside." She pointed behind herself with both thumbs over her shoulders. "This is the freshman quarter of the Academy Student Union, where you will be spending a minimum of three hours every day, at least four days a week, Mondays through Thursdays, for the next four years."

"All right!" Tinker exclaimed. "Three-day weekends!"

"You wish," Émilie corrected him. "Fridays, Saturdays, and Sundays are reserved. On one of those days you can enjoy whatever Sabbath your particular religion, if you have one, requires you to observe. On the second of those days you will have a leisure day. And on the third of those days you will have a 'think day'."

"What is a think day?" Arnie asked.

"It's exactly what it sounds like," Émilie answered him. "While you are in school here, you are going to be learning so much information, so much faster and so much longer than most people are used to, that you are going to feel as though you never have time simply to sit and think about things. Your think day is the one day of each week that you do just that, merely sit and think."

"Man," Alex asked, "how am I going to just sit and think for a whole day?"

"You don't start off thinking for a whole day. You start off with about an hour at a time a couple of times per think day, but don't worry about that now. A mental perfect will help you with that later this week."

"What's a mental perfect?" Min-su asked.

"A perfect is the school's master of whatever his or her particular discipline is. There are mental perfects and physical perfects and sensory perfects."

"Like Alex here," Tinker said.

"Are you sensorially gifted?" Émilie asked Alex.

"Just a little," Alex admitted.

"Well, after about twenty more years at it," Émilie said, "you might be near to being a perfect in it." Émilie looked at her watch. "Now look, folks, enough questions for right now. We really have to get inside. Mrs. L is going to start speaking in fifteen minutes and we need to get in and seated, because, as you will soon come to learn ..." Émilie wagged her finger at them again, "you do not want to test her."

Émilie walked up to the entrance of the round section on the corner of the Student Union building. She led the group to a long row of individual eight-foot high, one-piece, rotating doors set into the otherwise solid clear wall. Each revolving door was three-quarters of a round tube standing on its end, with an eight-inch push flange sticking in toward the middle of the tube about halfway into the tube from each of its two long edges.

Émilie started to explain their operation. "The doors in this place are designed for maximum security and energy efficiency, but their use and operation can be a little tricky for new sharers."

Tinker walked up toward a door and asked Émilie, "What could be so tricky about it? It's a door, man." The door swung its opening toward him and he stepped inside and pushed on the flange, in an attempt to move it around him. The door stayed still in its outside position. "Hey! It's locked," he called back from inside it.

"Exactly," Émilie explained. "Here are the door rules. They sense that you are approaching them and will turn their open side toward you if no one else is in them or closer to them on the other side. They only let one person through at a time. They will only let you through if you are authorized to be in that space. They will only let you in if you push your palm flat on one of the push flanges, look up at the disc in the middle of the top of the door, and say your name. If your facial scan, palm print, and voice print do not match what you gave Customs and Immigration when you registered earlier today, then you are not going to go through any of the secured doors on this whole island."

Émilie stepped into the door next to the one that Tinker was in, pushed on a flange, looked up, and said her name. The door rotated around her to move the open quarter of the tube from the outside to the inside of the wall. She stepped in, turned around, and repeated the demonstration to come back out to the group.

She joked, "So if someone tries to cut off your hand to try to get in, they need to bring your head and voice with them at the same time." She turned around into the door again. "Follow me inside, everyone."

One-by-one the group made its way through the row of doors in the wall. They regrouped in a huge cavernous lobby with a variety of stairs, escalators, and a huge rotating corkscrew connecting the four levels of the building. Several small, medium, and large gathering places stuck out into the airspace of the open four-story round section suspended by steel cables from the ceiling or steel girders coming out from the walls.

The entire group seemed fairly impressed with the overall appearance of the facility. Robert Rivers asked, "Do all of the four classes have the same type of accommodations?"

Émilie informed them all, "Each class has a separate quarter of the building, all of which are basically identical, except that some of the smaller classrooms and laboratories on the third floor have different equipment. Any sharer from any class can travel to any quarter and classroom to audit higher classes in any free time that he or she may have, which won't be much."

Émilie led the group over to the corkscrew and explained, "This is a SlipScrew. If you want to use a SlipDisc and still go up or down levels, then you simply ride over to these things that look like a big threaded screw running the height of the lobby with these D-shaped clamps sticking out of it. The clamps will lock onto your SlipDisc and take you up to the level where you want to get off. Hold onto another D-clamp for safety. To get off, just push away from the pole and the clamps will let you go."

Tinker looked at the SlipScrew and said, "I can make that thing go a lot faster if you want me to."

"That could be fun," Alex said with a grin.

"Until the centrifugal force throws you off," Arnie cautioned.

"Regardless," Émilie said, cutting off their conversation. "We need to go get seats for Mrs. L's orientation, because we …"

Everyone caught onto the joke and they all wagged their fingers back at her saying in unison, "We know. We don't want to test her!"

Émilie smiled and nodded slightly in satisfaction. "Follow me," she said, leading them up an escalator. The deca flowed off the disappearing steps in front of another row of revolving tube doors in a clear wall at the top and rear of a lecture hall that was shaped like a fourth of a pie. The hall took up a quarter of the interior of the building and slanted from its back, on the second floor of the building, down to its front, where the lecturer stood, on the ground floor. The arched rows of rolling chairs and tables started out with forty across in the back row and decreased incrementally to five across on the front two rows. The aisles running down the sides of various sections of the seating in the hall continuously sloped down to the front in one long gradual glide with no steps. The tables appeared to be made out of some opaque material and the chairs were all covered in satiny, light silver colored cloth.

It took five minutes of complex negotiations for the group to decide where they wanted to be seated. Bernadette started their first argument as a deca. "We need to pick where we are going to sit."

"Why does it matter?" Aurelia asked.

Bernadette explained. "Where you sit the first time you gather somewhere usually determines where you sit for the rest of time you go there. And location in a classroom can affect your grades. I believe that we need to be grouped on the left side of the front few rows because statistics have shown that that area is where most teachers focus the majority of their attention and the students there get better grades."

Arnie argued. "I want to sit in the back third of the room so that we can blend in the easiest."

Robert added his desires, pointing to his sister and himself simultaneously. "We've been told to sit somewhere where we could make a clear message of our presence in the class."

Amanda sighed. "I don't care where we sit, except that I would prefer that it not be in the very back."

Tinker and Alex whispered between themselves and then Tinker said, "We want the very back row so we can sneak in and out of class."

"That won't work," Émilie informed them. "The doors will not open during class times except in cases of emergency."

Min-su said, "I like Bernadette's idea."

"I'm with Arnie," Hugo said. "The back third sounds best."

"I'm with Amanda," Aurelia said. "I don't even care."

Finally, they all agreed, with the help of Bernadette's diplomatic skills. "Fine, everybody's had a say on this. Now, let's just go down and take the first row that has ten chairs all the way across. It's near enough to the front, the third row, to get plenty of the teacher's attention. It's far enough back for Arnie to blend in. It'll allow us all to set a clear presence taking up the first row available for an entire deca and it isn't on the very last row. The only people who aren't going to be happy are Alex and Tinker and their sole reasons are moot because these tube-thingie doors won't let us out or back in during class."

Everyone followed Bernadette down the long gradual ramp to the third row of the lecture hall. Émilie stood in the aisle beside the group, until the rest of the lecture hall started to fill up. "I have to be going now," she told them. "I have my own lecture to go to, but we can regroup later. When Mrs. L is done speaking, the rest of the classes will greet you and then we will group up at five back here. Okay?"

"That'll be fine," Bernadette said for the deca.

As Émilie walked to the back of the hall, the lights began to dim. The door at the front of the lecturer's pit opened and out stepped a brass-haired woman with pale but tight, smooth, almost porcelain skin in a classic ankle-length natural linen dress and jacket. She tapped on the microphone a few times to quieten the crowd and then said, in a thick Viennese accented English, "The next time that anyone walks into a room to share with you, you should please be quiet and stand up as a sign of basic respect and decency." The woman turned and walked out of the same door through which she had entered.

A moment later the same woman came back through the door. The entire class immediately became quiet and stood up. "Please be seated," the woman began again, "My name is Mrs. Liedgarten. I am not a perfect in any discipline, but I am the headmistress of this academy and I do expect perfect discipline from each and every one of you and ...," Mrs. L wagged her finger at them, "You would be very wise to never test me on this."

Mrs. L continued. "You have been selected to attend the

Global Optimum Development Academy because you have shown in the first eight years of your education that you are well ahead of those children with whom you have previously gone to school. In addition to whatever special gifts that you may or may not have, you are all straight-A students. Rest assured, however, that you are now truly among your peers and any ideas that you may or may not have about just sliding through this academy with as little work as you have had to put forth before should all now be set aside and ..." Mrs. L wagged her finger at them again. "You would be very wise to never test me on this."

The stern lady proceeded to tell them many more things on which they should never test her. She pushed a button on the lectern in front of her and commenced an audio-visual presentation that began as a virtual projection of scenes from around the campus on the screen above and behind her.

"It is my responsibility to make sure that all of your classes run on time and that everything that can be done for, to, and about you for the next four years is done as well as it can be. You will have classes in subjects and be taught in ways far different from what you have experienced before."

The virtual images spread from the front screen across the ceiling, floor, and walls until it appeared as though the entire class was sitting in the Roman Colosseum. Many "ooh's" and "aah's" escaped the children's lips. The table tops appeared to become white marble slabs and the chairs looked like marble benches.

"Instead of history, civics, language, arts, and literature, for the next eight four-month sessions you will participate in the GODA Heritage Program, which will allow you to simultaneously explore and experience, either directly or virtually, the development of all aspects of the entire world's civilization in all disciplines, from the beginning of recorded history to the present time." The virtual scene changed to a series of complex laboratories, amid a hubbub of additional exclamations. "Instead of limiting yourselves to math, biology, chemistry, and physics, you will participate in the GODA Science and Technology Development Program and experience, either directly or virtually, the actual discoveries and refinements of science and technology as they have occurred in the past and will be occurring in the future." The scene changed again to the interior of the Library of Congress. "Finally, you will also be schooled in a variety of seminars called Basic Secular Knowledge, which are essentially everything that can be shared about anything that does not fit in our Heritage or Science and Technology programs."

A collective "phew" wisped around the room as the images disappeared and the lights brightened. A short applause broke out, only to be stifled by Mrs. L curtly zipping a short imaginary zipper in the air, with a flick of her wrist.

"In addition to these classical fields of study," Mrs. L informed them, "you will also be trained by perfects, in as many disciplines as will be appropriate to each of you, in classes that will be individually designed to result in the constant improvement of your unique mental, physical, and sensory gifts, to the highest level that you could possibly attain."

"Man!" Robert whispered to his sister.

"Uhm-hmm," she agreed.

Mrs. L continued, "After four years of sharing at the Global Optimum Development Academy, you will be ready to either continue another four years at the Global Optimum Development University or return to your homes or wherever else you may choose to go and be fully capable of doing your share to help bring about the optimal development of ideas, people, places, and things around the globe."

"Is it too late to go back home now?" Alex asked Tinker.

"In addition to studies, however," Mrs. L told them, pushing another button on the lectern. The virtual display around the room jumped back to life with a screen of kids running around throwing, dribbling, and kicking two different types of balls at and to each other. "Recreational sports are an important part of both school and life. The most popular recreational game on Demeverde is coco, which has been played for thousands of years by the local Demeverdans, whose ancestors thought that it would be a considerable amount of fun to fill each others' caves in the mountainsides with coconuts."

The walls, floor, and ceiling showed a historical montage of apparently early Demeverdans chunking coconuts at each other. "We have modernized and improved the game quite a bit from its original form," Mrs. L said, "so that it maintains various aspects of all of the sports with which most of you are familiar including basketball, soccer or futbol, for those of you who are not from America, and hockey." Several seconds of the game footage played across the screen. "All students are required to play coco on the intramural level and tournaments will be held at the end of each year."

Mrs. L explained several other things to them. Finally, she appeared to be wrapping up. "I understand that you are probably getting hungry and want to meet the other students in the academy, including the more senior classes. So ..."

Mrs. L paused as the walls on either side of lecture hall began to rise up into the ceiling, revealing that the corresponding walls in all three of the other lecture halls making up the rest of the Student Union had already been raised. Three display screens were set up facing each lecture hall behind Mrs. L. Apparently, all of the other classes had been waiting for the end of the freshmen's orientation.

"Prepare to be greeted by all three higher years of your peers," she concluded, as the other classes began clapping their hands in unison while the three other display screens recessed into the floor. "Relax, discuss, and enjoy a wonderful lunch in the many eating courts available on levels one and two," Mrs. L said loudly over the noise, "for tomorrow you begin your own optimal development."

At that point, pandemonium broke out, as the three thousand upper class members began coming across the entire building to mingle and mix with the one thousand new kids in the school. The deca attempted to keep their group together, but trying to keep ten relative strangers united in a pulsing mass of nine hundred ninety other children being pulled in all directions by three thousand upperclassmen was an impossible goal.

Arnie was taken aside and asked several questions about himself and his background over and over again by at least a dozen different people in the next thirty minutes.

"Hi, I'm Choi Guihah," a Chinese girl said as several others looked on. "Who are you and where are you from?"

Arnie was a little bit shell-shocked, but then he tried to give as many vague answers as he could. Mostly, he stuck with the plain story, which Jacques and he had talked about over the prior week. "Hi, I'm Arnie Carver from Wyoming."

A British sounding boy introduced himself, "Charles Winston Churchill." He quickly shook Arnie's hand. "Where did you go to school?"

"Any relation to the former P.M.?" Arnie asked him.

"None whatsoever."

"My parents home schooled me," Arnie answered his question. He tried to steer to conversation back away from himself. "So, what do people call you? Charles, Winston, or Churchill?"

"Well, my good friends call me Winnie," he replied with a smile, "but you can call me Charles."

"Fair enough."

"So, what's your gift?" Winnie asked.

"Just a very good memory for things I've seen."

"That's it?" Guihah asked.

"Afraid so," Arnie replied.

"That's not much," she retorted.

"And what's yours?" Arnie asked, trying to put the spotlight on someone else.

"Physical concentration."

"What does that mean?"

"Guihah has the uncanny ability to do things with her muscles that are almost beyond belief. She's currently up to a twenty-foot vertical leap."

Arnie's head rocked back at the thought. "How far can you jump down?"

"I can presently make a soft landing from sixty feet."

"My goodness," Arnie said. "That's almost as tall as this building."

"It is as tall as the main section," Guihah said.

"And yours?" Arnie asked Winnie.

"Persuasive debate."

"You're kidding, right?"

"Not at all," Winnie defended himself.

Guihah interjected, "He can argue any side of any point

absolutely convincingly."

"My ancestors are nothing but solicitors and politicians," Winnie said. "So I can lie equally well from either side of my mouth." He muffled a laugh at his own expense.

Fearful that they might ask a question for which he was not prepared, Arnie excused himself. "Well, I have to go mingle." He stuck out his hand to the girl. "Guihah." As she shook his hand, Arnie gave hers a prolonged, firm squeeze and looked her square in the eye, with a challenging smile on his face.

Guihah pressed down a very little bit. "I could," she said, "but then you'd need a cast for a month."

Arnie relaxed his grip and turned toward Winnie. "Mister Churchill."

The boys shook hands. "I was just kidding about the Charles thing. You can call me Winnie like everyone else."

"Winnie, then,"

Arnie escaped to the main entry halls and backed up to a wall in a medium-sized gathering area, off the second floor of the sophomore class's four-story lobby.

A sophomore named H.M. Crist, who also had a Top Ten Percenter "10" pin on the collar of his shirt, had drawn several members of his own freshman deca into the conversation pit, on the other side of the gathering space. Arnie began to eavesdrop on what the guy from Émilie's class was saying.

"Let me give you the real inside story on how to get ahead of your classmates here at GODA," he said. "There's a secret pecking order that the various higher level sharers and perfects all eventually develop for the entire class and you want to make sure that you get yourself pecked in at the top instead of the bottom."

He obviously had his deca enthralled. "So, H.M.," one of

them asked him, "how do we do that?"

"Well, first, help no one but yourself," he replied. "And if you feel like you have to help someone for whatever reason, then at least don't help anyone who is not in your own deca."

H.M. eventually brought the conversation around to how he could help them move up in the school, but that they would have to be beholden to him if he did. "For example," he said, "freshmen sharers are not really allowed in the sophomore tower, which always has better food and virtual games, but if you ever want to come over, then just tell anyone who asks you what you are doing there that you are looking for me and I'll take care of whoever dares to give someone from my adopted deca a hard time. Okay?"

After a few minutes of watching H.M. Crist glorify himself, Arnie started feeling lonely. He quietly moved along the wall to the second floor hallway and walked back to the freshman lecture hall to rejoin his own deca.

Bernadette was the first one to notice him arriving. "Where have you been? The rest of us have been worried about you."

Arnie felt good that there were at least some people in the world who were concerned about him, but he couldn't tell them so. "Sorry," he said to them all.

He looked at Émilie and said, "Hi."

"*Bonjour*, Arnie," she replied.

Arnie asked Émilie, "Who is H.M. Crist and how did he get to be a T-T-P?"

"Well, that all depends on who you ask."

"What?" Arnie asked.

"Well, if you ask H.M. Crist, then he will tell you he is God's gift to the rest of us here at GODA, because he has looks, physical greatness, brains, talent, and money all in the same package; so he always knows what's best."

"And if you ask the rest of the world?" Min-su asked.

"Then they would tell you that he is an egotistical boaster who doesn't deserve the time of day, even if his father is, as he is constantly reminding everyone every chance that he gets, currently serving his fourth term as the governor of Delaware, which, if you ask me, is one of the best reasons for term limits that I have ever seen."

"And how did he get to be his deca's T-T-P?" Roberta joined in.

"H.M. bribed five of his decamates to let him have it by buying them almost everything they wanted during the mid-semester break. Which goes to show that some of us here at GODA are just as corruptible as the rest of the world." Émilie sighed. "All of you should know that T-T-P's should be picked on overall merit and who you think will most fairly represent you all, individually and collectively, on the council, on the T-O-P's, and with Mrs. L and Unius. If you can't agree on it unanimously, then you don't have the right person."

"Speaking of Unius," Alex asked, "when do we get to see him?"

Émilie chuckled at the question, but no one in the deca seemed to understand why. "Hardly anyone ever sees Unius in person, but you will hear from him almost everyday on a virscreen with some sort of a message for us."

"Why don't we get to see him in person?" Alex asked.

"Because he is busy running a trillion dollar company, which spans the globe, at the same time he is serving as the dean of the university. Plus, he simply exists on such a higher plane than we do, that most of us don't really feel entitled to bother him. And those who do couldn't reach him uninvited even if they wanted to."

"Why not?" Alex continued to probe.

"Because he lives alone like a meditative owl on the top of Godeau Mountain and he likes it that way. Trust me, however, if Unius wants to see you for something, you will get the call." Émilie looked at her watch and started leading them toward the exit. "We need to get over to the freshman dorm and get you all settled into your deca's apartment."

Once they got outside the Student Union's doors, Émilie stood beside a line of SlipDiscs slowly moving alongside the sidewalk. "Just in case any of you have not gotten the concept of using these things, just step on one, take a stable stance and tell it where to take you. In this case, you want to tell it 'Freshman Dorm, Tower Two,' and it will take you there the shortest, fastest, and easiest way." Émilie put her foot on one of the SlipDiscs and continued, "SlipDiscs are convenient, four times faster than the average walk, and just plain fun. And for those of you who are worried about exercising, the isometrics done to stay balanced on these things equals walking a fifteen-minute mile. So, everyone get on one and let's go."

The decamates each walked up to a SlipDisc, got on, and asked for the Freshman Dorm, Tower Two. Amanda's agents noted the number of the SlipDisc that she had mounted and told theirs to converge on hers and track it. After a pleasant chorus of "my pleasures," they were all on their way.

The SlipDiscs deposited the entire group, complete with escorts, in front of the freshman dorms. Four, twenty-seven story, round towers were attached, one each, to the corners of the two-story, square building.

Émilie advised them, "Keep one foot resting on your

SlipDiscs because you're still going to need them."

"Are all of the dorms like this?" Amanda asked.

"Yes," Émilie answered, looking up approvingly. "Twenty-seven stories of shimmering one-way translucent guarantium, the strongest translucent material known to man. Mined from the ocean floor, bonded and machined over at GODEnt, and erected here with the ability to withstand the strongest hurricane in the history of the Atlantic Ocean."

"Why do we still need the SlipDiscs?" Arnie asked.

"Because when things are real busy like this, with everyone trying to get into the dorms at the same time, it is much faster to stay on a SlipDisc and ride a screw up to your floor and get off than it is to wait on the elevators to go up and stop on this floor and that floor and come back down."

They watched several people ride their SlipDiscs through the rotating tube doors and clip into a SlipScrew.

"This is a good opportunity to practice self directed SlipDiscing," Émilie said lifting her second foot back onto her ride. "I know you rode some of these a little earlier at the transit port, but you need to work on maneuvering now." She demonstrated some close-quarter moves. "Just lean in the direction that you want to go and the SlipDisc will move that way. Lean more to go faster."

The ten freshmen drivers started moving around a few feet in random directions.

"Note that you cannot accidentally run into anything," Émilie said, heading toward Roberta and then acting like she was not paying attention to where she was going. The SlipDisc flattened its pitch as she got near her target. "As you get near anything at all, the SlipDisc will adjust its course to pass it safely." Then, she intentionally pushed the front of her SlipDisc back down again and tapped Roberta a little bit out of balance. "But you can override the safety feature and intentionally slip right into something if you really want to, which is how you get into a door or clip onto an elevator screw."

Everyone practiced intentionally bumping each other for a few seconds, until Émilie told them that it was time to go in.

The eleven of them made it through the tube doors without too much bumping around, negotiating staying upright, pushing a hand flange, looking up to have a facial scan, and saying their names all at the same time. "You are assigned to tower two, floor twelve," their T-T-P informed them. The ride around twelve revolutions of the SlipScrew was almost a relief after bumping around in the tube doors.

Émilie showed them to their apartment, then stepped off of her SlipDisc, and led the way in. The SlipDisc headed away on its own back toward the SlipScrew. Everyone else stepped off of their SlipDiscs and let them go before going through the apartment's rotating tube door.

As she spun around to point to the entire apartment at once, she began to sound like a saleslady. "Your home away from home is composed of a large, round central gathering area furnished with a semi-circular sectional pit of small cheds arranged round this small table in the middle." She then began pointing to a series of ten rotating tube doors, which protruded equally spaced around the back wall of the room. "Each of those doors has a different one of your names displayed next to it. All of your rooms are essentially the same, so, everyone go check them out all at once and then come back out here."

Arnie, like all of the others, stepped into his tube, looked up and said his name to the disc above him, and pushed the flange to rotate the opening around his body. He stepped into his room, which was a section of the semi-circular ring surrounding the central area measuring about fifteen feet by fifteen feet. A set of cabinets ran along one wall and a ched was positioned on the other side of the room. As he stuck his head into the private bathroom, he nodded approvingly at the small shower, toilet, and sink. He popped himself back through the door to see everyone else arriving again at about the same time.

"Well, guys," Émilie said, "that's about it for orientation." She started to walk toward the door of the apartment. "Your stuff is already in your rooms. Unpack, shower, shave, and whatever and try to get to bed by a decent hour because tomorrow is the first of three days of introductory large group classes in the main lecture hall. Classes start at eight o'clock. The union opens for breakfast at six."

Émilie left followed by two of Amanda's agents, who took up positions on either side of the door in the hall. The other two took up similar positions on the inside.

After Émilie left, everyone went to and came back from their rooms a few times and talked to each other in the central room. Arnie started to yawn first and the yawns became progressively more infectious until everyone ended up going to their rooms and not coming out again for the rest of the night.

Arnie noticed that the ceiling had begun to glow less and less as he sat on his ched in his room. He also noticed that, even though there was a solid sheet of translucent guarantium on the outside wall of his room, he could apparently hear the sounds of the surf on the beach in the distance coming through it. It was a calming sound and he stretched his legs out in front of him as the ched automatically adjusted to his position. The regular, gifted boy, who had started the night before as the richest orphan in the world, pushed back into a flatter laying down position and the ched adjusted some more. The longer he stayed still on the ched, the dimmer the ceiling became. The sounds of the surf lulled him to sleep as he dreamed about what the next day might bring.

CHOSE KNOWS

$\mathcal{A}$rnie awoke from his sleep and looked at the time. The wall clock read five thirty-two. He noticed that the ceiling of his room had begun to glow brighter. The surf sounded as though it was hitting the shore louder and louder. Strangely, a sunrise was developing on the horizon of the ocean, which seemed almost impossible, because his room was on the western side of Isla Principal when he went to sleep. The perspective from which he was watching the sun come up seemed to be as if he was on the beach. Shrugging off the geographic incongruity, Arnie pushed his feet down and sat up as the ched adjusted itself from a flat bed into the shape of a chair.

The ceiling glowed in nearly full brightness and a crawler of letters began to scroll across the window wall. The message read, "Good morning, John Arnold Carver. Uniforms are mandatory. Check your cabinets."

Arnie realized that he had not unpacked his suitcase, which was open on the floor beside his ched. He picked up a stack of clothes from the suitcase and opened the largest cabinet on the wall across from him.

Half of the cabinet was empty and had a label across the top that read "For the clothes that you brought from home." Arnie put the stack of clothes on the middle shelf of the empty half of the cabinet.

The other half of the cabinet was full of clothes arranged in an organized manner and had a label across the top that suggestively read "For the clothes that you are going to want to wear at GODA."

A paper-thin sheet of what looked like clear plastic was attached to the second shelf and displayed a note.

> This year's GODA uniform wardrobe has been carefully coordinated by last year's T-O-P's and approved by Mrs. L and Unius. All items are new designs, which are made of all natural fibers with natural dyes derived from plants found in Demeverde. All sharers have the option to mix and match the coordinated separates as they see fit.

Arnie ran his hands over the neatly folded underwear, socks, shirts, shorts, pants, sweaters, sports clothes, shoes, boots, and sandals. Every piece of clothing, including the socks, had his name neatly printed on an inside surface.

Arnie finished unpacking his suitcase onto the right side of the cabinet and then chose some clothes from the left side containing the uniforms. "Better to blend in with the crowd," he thought. "Besides, uniforms are mandatory." Dressed for the day, Arnie pushed on the flange of his room's tube door, looked up, and said his name.

Several other members of the deca were already in the central gathering area talking and comparing wardrobe choices. Only one of Amanda's agents was standing at attention inside the apartment door. Arnie walked over to Amanda and asked her about the absence of the rest of the team.

"I had them call Daddy last night and tell him that they really weren't needed around here. We compromised on having them follow me one at a time until I can convince him to get rid of them altogether. They're all rotating out of an apartment on the local side of the island."

"Congratulations," Arnie said. He more than knew exactly how she felt. If he weren't living under an assumed name at the time, he would have been feeling the same way himself.

"You don't know the half of it," Amanda assured him. "It's been like living in a glass cage for my entire life. I'm really looking forward to living like a normal person here in Demeverde."

"I know how you feel," Arnie commiserated with her.

A tone and a beam of light came from the disc above the door to the central hall outside the apartment.

"What?" Amanda asked.

"Nothing," Arnie replied, heading for the door.

A picture of Émilie was visible on the disc.

"How do you answer these doors?" Arnie asked the agent standing by the door.

"Just say 'Come in' out loud and it will release for her,"

he replied.

"Thanks."

"No problem." The agent smiled for a second before reassuming his blank stare into the room.

"Come in," Arnie said to Émilie's face on the disc above the door. The tube slid around to reveal the rest of Émilie on a SlipDisc.

"*Bonjour, mes amis!*" Émilie said, clapping her hands to some music playing in her earplug. "Are you ready to do the workout on the way to breakfast? I so very much love to get my exercise by doing calisthenics on my SlipDisc, as I ride around the campus each day."

The rest of the deca filtered out of their tube doors dressed in a variety of pieces of the uniform ensemble.

"How did whoever picked our uniforms for us know the right sizes?" Roberta asked.

Émilie explained, "Your body shapes were scanned as you registered through Customs and Immigration. A computer cut and sewed your clothes to match your dimensions and an Intellistaffer robot delivered your clothes to your cabinets during orientation."

"Cool," Tinker said. "They have robots working here?"

"Just a few hundred Intellitrons for the staff," Émilie replied, counting heads. "Now that everyone is here," she said, "let's do the workout on the way to breakfast! Just follow me and do what I do."

Everyone pushed through the apartment's tube door and followed Émilie's pulsing body over to the SlipScrew. "Just step on a SlipDisc as it comes by," she said, clipping onto the screw.

Everyone stepped onto a SlipDisc and followed Émilie to the Student Union. Some of them tried to imitate Émilie's exercises, but mostly they tried to concentrate on staying on their SlipDiscs for the ride. Bernadette, however, followed Émilie's every movement and exuberantly sang "Heads, shoulders, knees and toes, knees and toes!" and other cadences in French as Émilie and she did the workout.

As they had done for lunch the day before, the numerous food service stations in the Student Union served up a huge variety of foods for breakfast, including a global selection of ethnic, ethical-social, and religious restricted diets. After everyone had heaped food on their trays, they rejoined Émilie at a large, round table.

"I'll be in classes myself all day," Émilie said. "But I'll see you again this evening to answer any questions you might have. If you need me, then send me a virmail and I will try to respond as soon as I can."

At exactly eight o'clock, according to the display at the front of the lecture hall, the tube doors swung their openings closed. The class hushed in anticipation of who might come through the door of the lecturer's pit. The lights over the seats grew dimmer as a single cone of light beamed down behind the lectern centered in the pit. The tube door began to rotate from open to closed and the entire class stood up to receive whoever might be coming through it at the next moment.

The door revolved back open and out stepped a moderately short, thin man dressed in a soft but rough off-white shirt and matching pants, both of which were covered by a knee-length coat of the same material.

"Please feel free to be seated," the thin man said, stepping into the cone of light behind the lectern. The noise of five thousand wheels beneath one thousand chairs rolling the students up to their tables was soft, but very audible. The sound gave Arnie the feeling that he was part of some wave coming to a shore.

The strong, focused lighting from above cast shadows beneath the speaker's deep-set eyes. The darkened triangles beneath his nose and chin gave him an almost eerie appearance.

"I see that Mrs. L has stated her preference that you all rise when a more senior sharer comes into the room," he said. The voice, though deep and full, did not seem to match the ominousness of the shadowed face. "Rest assured, however, that many of us who live and work higher on Godeau Mountain have no need for such formalities. Therefore, when I approach you, you should feel free to stay just the way you are any time I come by." He tilted his head thoughtfully. "Mind you, however, that many senior sharers still desire the approbation and you should still stand for anyone else much more senior to you, until instructed otherwise." He shifted to a high-pitched voice, sounding like Mrs. L, and wagged his finger at the class, adding, "And you would do well …" The class tittered so much at his imitation of Mrs. L that he felt no need to complete it.

His voice then dipped back to the depth that it had in the beginning. "But, I am not one of those." The man looked up at the back row of students, which put his face more directly in the cone of light and revealed a tight-lipped, but wide, smile and inviting eyes. "I am Chose," he said.

"Wow!" Arnie whispered in awe to Bernadette, who was seated right beside him.

Chose shot his right hand above his head and waved it back and forth a few times. Each time that he moved it, the ceiling became brighter and brighter, until after the third or fourth wave, the room was fully aglow in a soft, even light.

"More wow!" Bernadette whispered back.

"I am one of several assistants to Unius," Chose began. "He wishes that he could have come down here in person to greet you on your first day at the Global Optimum Development Academy, but he is unavoidably involved in a growing crisis elsewhere in the world. He has sent me and a virtual rendition of himself in his place."

"I wonder what the crisis is," Arnie whispered again.

"Don't worry about the crisis," Chose assured them, "as Unius and those who share with him are more than capable of resolving it." Chose touched the top of the lectern in front of him and the entire wall behind him displayed the island group of Demeverde. "In the meantime," he said, "let me share with you more of what we do here at GODA and what will be expected of you for at least the next four years."

Chose spent the next several minutes displaying images on the wall behind him and discussing, in what seemed like one continuous breath, what a GODA education was all about.

"Individual countries, competing with each other and subjugating each other at various times throughout history, have had a retarding effect on the optimum development of the world as a whole. Unius, through GODA, GODU, and GODEnt, has proposed to bring about a global-centered world where all peoples can come together in a more peaceful and more satisfied existence, by freely sharing all thoughts and ideas with all people around the Earth. This should allow everyone on the entire globe the same opportunities to have a longer and more fulfilling life."

Chose pushed a spot on the lectern and the room again became alive with a virtual globe of the Earth spinning slowly on its axis. Multiple brief virtual projections of scenes simultaneously popped up at several points on the world for several seconds. Each scene then triggered another scene in another part of the planet.

During this display, Chose continued. "It is vitally important to learn about the development of the entire world as a whole, instead of limiting oneself, as most countries' educational systems do, to learning about the development of just one country or the development of the world in relation to that one country."

"Interesting idea," Bernadette whispered to Arnie.

"It is only by studying the entire heritage of all peoples," Chose explained, "and seeing how the errors and omissions of all of the various countries, developing and using their science and technology, have had such a devastating impact on other countries around the world. Doing this, we can see how to change things in the future, in order to not repeat those same mistakes."

Chose pushed another spot on the lectern and the lights began to dim again. "And now," Chose began to speak slower with a deeper voice, "the moment for which I am sure you have all been waiting, in order to give you a fuller understanding of your role in global optimum development, I give you . . . " He pushed another spot on the lectern. "Unius."

The lights in the room dimmed until the only light came from the glow of the front display spanning from wall to wall and from the ceiling to right above Chose, who had stepped to the side wall. Unius's thin face pushed forward into the lecturer's pit in a virtual projection. He began to speak in a plain tone that belied the knowledge and power of the wealthiest and supposedly one of the wisest men on Earth.

"To whom all these presents may come, greetings," he said. "I am Unius."

"Hmmm," Arnie wondered just barely out loud.

"What?" Bernadette whispered very quickly.

"He's not at all like I imagined," Arnie replied very softly.

Unius continued, "Before anything else, I want to thank you for agreeing to spend at least the next four years of your lives sharing your precious life's resources with all of us here in Godeau and, hopefully, the rest of the world."

Robert Rivers, sitting on the other side of Arnie, whispered, "I wonder why he is thanking us. He's the one paying for everything."

"I want to thank you first," Unius said, "because without your willingness to leave your homes and loved ones and share with us your life's vital resources of your self, time, effort, energy, emotion, and intellect, we would have no chance of bringing about the globally optimum development of the world."

"Well, there you go," Arnie said to Robert.

"You wonderfully and variously gifted children from around the world are about to embark on a journey to greatness. On that journey you will learn how to share with others your gifts and their gifts and work together as one people on one planet seeking our unified and globally optimum development.

"Once we have reached that condition, the entire world will be able to enjoy a peaceful and relaxed state of mind, knowing that everyone is using perception, planning, preparation, practice, persistence, and patience to create, use, and recreate their life's precious resources of self, time, effort, energy, emotion, intellect, property, and people to transform their vision into an attainable mission to do the right thing, which is the best thing for the optimal balance of the highest priority and largest number of those to whom and for whom our values make us responsible. You are the ones who can, and hopefully will, help the world reach its global optimum development. You are the ones whom we hope, over the next four years, will become leaders of your world's nations. You each already have your own unique gifts, which you can use to do this. We only wish to show you what, when, where, why, and how to do it."

"That's a tall order," Arnie whispered to Bernadette.

Unius continued. "While that may be a tall order, we are delighted to have you come with us on this journey to greatness and we all wish each and every one of you the most success in sharing with us."

"Whoa!" Bernadette quietly said to Arnie. "This guy is awesome."

"In closing," Unius said, "there is just one code by which we operate here in Godeau and that is, 'we do not impose ourselves on others nor appreciate those who do.' Remember this code in all you do and you will get along fine in the world. Until I see you again, greetings."

Unius's image receded back into the wall display and the room went dark for a moment as his voice seemed to reverberate in the air. Chose waved his hand up over his head a few times, stepping back behind the lectern.

"That is it for this morning," he said, pushing a spot on the lectern. The tube doors in the back of the hall swung their openings toward the inside of the room. "Go and have some lunch. Discuss amongst yourself what Unius and I have shared with you until now. We will meet back here at one o'clock for the introduction of the perfects and their disciplines."

Almost everyone streamed out of the hall and toward the four-story, round gathering gallery.

Arnie stopped short of the doors and said to Bernadette and Robert, "I'll catch up with you guys later. I want to ask Chose a question."

Alex overheard him and asked, "Trying to get ahead already?" He walked by Bernadette and Arnie without waiting for an answer.

"No," Arnie defended himself to Bernadette, who was now the only member of the deca still on their side of the doors. "I just want to ask him something."

"Go ahead," Bernadette said, pointing to the growing line of people who must have had the same idea. "But you may have to wait a while."

"I don't mind," Arnie said. "I'll see you later."

"You, too," Bernadette said, turning and disappearing into a revolving door.

Arnie waited at the back of the line, as first one person and then another walked up and asked questions or made comments. Chose answered them so softly that no one other than the person right in front of him could possibly hear. Each time someone else got in line behind him, Arnie came up with some excuse to lose his place in line, so that he could go last.

Finally, the last person in the hall other than Arnie and Chose turned away from the lectern and Chose politely waited for Arnie to step up. Arnie looked at Chose and then checked back to see if the last person had made it through a tube door to the other side. Turning back to Chose he started to say, "Mister Chose …"

"Just Chose," the man corrected him.

"Sorry," Arnie apologized. "My parents won't let me call someone older than me by their first name. They taught me that it's not polite."

"That's okay, Mister Carver," Chose said. "But Chose is the only name that I am used to."

"Okay," Arnie acquiesced. "But, then please call me Arnie."

"Very well."

It dawned on Arnie that Chose already knew his name. "How did you know my name?"

"I review the names and faces of all sharers who come through Demeverde," Chose answered.

"That is a lot of names!" Arnie said. "How do you learn them all?"

"Like you, Arnie," Chose answered him, "I have a photographic memory."

"Cool," Arnie said. "What else can you do?"

"I don't know."

"You don't know?"

"No," Chose explained. "I haven't done everything that I am ever going to do yet, so I don't know what else I can do."

Arnie thought about the logic of Chose's statement for a moment then clarified his question. "What I meant was, what else can you do that you have done already?"

"It's best left unsaid."

"Why?"

"Because people should not share everything about their own gifts," Chose said. "First, it seems like you are bragging, if you tell everyone everything that you can do. Second, it destroys the allure of the unknown. If you know everything that there is to know about someone, then there's no excitement in the relationship, no moving power to find out new things. And, finally, third, there may be people who will attempt to use their knowledge of your gifts against you."

Arnie took in Chose's ideas for a moment. "How did you know that I have a good memory?"

"Your 'Dutch great uncle,'" Chose grinned as he said it, "Jacques Marquis, told me much about you, as we toured the island when he was here."

"Then you know why I am here?"

"I know pretty much all there is to know about you, Arnie. Unius says that you are special to him."

"Special?" Arnie was puzzled. "How could I be special to Unius?"

"He has not shared exactly all of that with me, yet."

"How long have you known Unius?" Arnie asked.

"All of my life."

"How did you meet?"

Chose closed his eyes in frustration. "Too many questions about too many things, Arnie Carver." He shooed Arnie back from the lectern. "You will have at least four years to learn all you want to know. Don't try to do it all on your second day." Chose gently pointed to the back of the hall. "Go, sit with your deca, talk, but more importantly, listen. Then, think about all that you learn and try to use it for the greater things of your destiny."

Arnie realized that he was being dismissed. "Yes, sir, Mister Chose." Arnie said, turning and walking toward the inclined rows of chairs.

"Just Chose," Chose reminded him.

Arnie paused and turned his head and shoulders to the lecture pit just in time to see the tube door slide around

Chose. "Yes, Chose," he answered softly.

* * *

Unius's face pushed forward out of the wall that separated the lecture hall from the hallway behind the lecturer's pit. "A very interesting, inquisitive boy," Unius said to Chose.

"Yes, he is, Unius. Very interesting and very inquisitive indeed." Chose began to walk and the virjection moved along the wall with him. "Any progress on the young French child?"

"Medical is watching her carefully, but we can't do much else."

"Any idea what exactly is plaguing her?"

"Some new neurological disease. Medical is being asked to work on it."

PARADE OF THE PERFECTS

By the time Arnie found them in the Student Union's gathering place, the rest of the deca was polishing off the last of their bottles of Doctor Ginger's. Alex appeared to be leading the Americans in directing questions to the other members of the deca.

"Some say that I have an exceptional way with animals," Min-su said.

"Like you talk to them and they talk back?" Alex asked.

"Not exactly," Min-su explained. "It's more like I gaze into their eyes and they gaze into mine and we see into each other's …" Min-su appeared worried that what she was about to say would not be taken correctly. "We see into each other's heart or mind or soul or something like that."

"But you don't know how you do what you do?" Alex asked.

"No," Min-su answered.

"Of course, that's not unusual," Bernadette defended her. "I don't know how I get what I feel from people. So I'd be willing to bet that it's kind of like the same thing."

"Whatever." Alex turned to Aurelia. "So Aurelia, what's a nice girl like you from South Africa doing in a place like this?"

"I run," she answered.

"You what?"

"I run," Aurelia repeated.

"So do I," Alex taunted her. "A six-minute mile. So what's the big deal?"

"I run a lot."

"How much is a lot? A marathon?"

"Four marathons."

"You've run four marathons?" Alex asked.

"In a day," Aurelia said.

"Oh, my gosh!" Bernadette said. "That's over a hundred miles."

"My longest run though is a two hundred K."

"That's over a hundred and twenty miles," Arnie said. "How do you do it?"

"Like Min-su said, I don't really know. I just start out running and then disconnect my mind from my body and it just keeps on moving until I get where I want to stop."

Robert broke in. "So when you say that you are going to go for a run around the island you really mean that you are going to run 'around' the island." He laughed at his own joke, as did everyone else.

The deca settled back down from the laughter and Alex continued the questioning, "So, how about you, Hugo, what's your gift?"

"Biofeedback," Hugo answered.

"Like how?"

"Like …" Hugo held out his hand, "hold my hand."

Alex took his hand like he was shaking it and said, "Wow! It's like you are burning up with a fever."

"No, I'm not," Hugo said. "Touch my head."

Alex touched Hugo's forehead and looked at the others around in dismay. "Cold as a cucumber."

"And how do you do it?" Roberta asked.

"Unlike most of you, I think that I understand it."

Arnie joined in the questioning. "And 'it' is?"

"Purposeful thought," Hugo answered. "An old Argentinean man taught me to focus my attention on a part of my body and tell it to do what I want it to do. If it is physiologically possible, then I can train myself to do it."

"Cool." Arnie said. Everyone else seemed to collectively nod in agreement.

At just that time, H.M. Crist walked through their gathering area loudly calling for attention. "Petition for change!" he said. "Petition for change!"

"What's this?" Bernadette asked, to no one in particular.

H.M. walked over to the group in the gathering space next to the deca, where he began talking and gesticulating wildly at some paper that he had on a clipboard. He gave them a pen and each of them signed the paper. While the other group was signing, Bernadette said, "Don't forget what Émilie said about this guy."

H.M. walked over to them. "How would you all like to sign my petition to change the way we elect members of student government?"

"No, thanks," Bernadette said, serving as the self-appointed speaker for the group. "We're pretty much in favor of the status quo."

Tinker decided to speak for himself. "Unless you can show us a good reason to change," he added, staking his own position. "Change can be good, I sometimes say."

"I like the way you think," H.M. replied, winking at Tinker. "What's your name?"

"Schocken," he said. "Steven Schocken." Tinker shook H.M.'s hand. "But most people call me 'Tinker' because I'm always changing things."

"So how about changing the way that we elect student government? Sign my petition for direct, at-large elections of the student council."

"And why should we do that?" Bernadette asked.

"Because now, if you are in a deca that you don't like…" H.M. looked around the room and then added "or doesn't like you, then you can never get a chance to be on the council."

"But if you can't get along with those who know you best and get their support, then why should the rest of us vote for you?"

"Because you should get to make up your own mind about things." H.M. pushed his clipboard into the group and asked, "So sign my petition for change and you can decide for yourself."

"No, thanks," Bernadette repeated, looking around the deca for nods of support.

"How about you, Tinker?" H.M. pushed the clipboard at him.

"No, thanks," he said. "I usually like to see how things work first before I tinker with them."

"Your choice," H.M. said with an exasperated sigh. "But when you want something from me, and you will, just remember that you told me no first."

H.M. shoved his pen back into the clip of the clipboard and walked onto the next gathering space.

Roberta held her nose in disgust. "Phew! That guy has a stinking attitude. Where was he last year when Unius was telling everyone the code about not imposing ourselves on others nor appreciating those who do?"

I have an idea," Bernadette said. "We need to meet some more people in the class. So why don't we all go meet at least one person who is not in our deca and come back to report on who they met at lunch?"

Everyone except Tinker nodded their heads and said, "Okay."

"Look," he explained. "I'm just not a people person, okay?" Tinker picked up a SlipDisc that he had been holding in place for a while with his foot. "Besides," he said, turning it over, "I want to fiddle around with this thing and see how it works."

"Fine, then you'll save our place here," Bernadette said.

The rest of the deca dispersed and fanned out into the mass of other sharers from their class spread out through the four levels of the tower.

Two hours later, Arnie returned to the deca's gathering space carrying a tray piled high with food. Setting the buffet down in front of Tinker, he said "I brought enough for the both of us. I figured that you wouldn't get up to go feed yourself." As he sat down at the circular table, Arnie pointed to the SlipDisc turned upside down in front of Tinker. "So have you figured it out yet?"

Tinker kept touching a spot on the opalescent bottom, which kept changing colors in a wavy pattern. Quickly withdrawing his singed finger after every touch, he cooled it in his mouth. "Not quite," he said. "Sometimes this spot burns hot and milliseconds later it burns cold." Tinker tried to push the SlipDisc bottom side down onto the tabletop, but he could not force it all the way down to the surface. "When I hold it like this," he said, "it creates a breeze that comes out opposite the direction that the thing moves."

It moved across the table away from the tray of food leaving a slight breeze in its wake. "Well, stop it," Arnie said. "You're making our lunch get cold."

"Okay." Tinker let go of the SlipDisc and it slid across the table, until it fell off and then righted itself and skittered across the floor, to merge into a row of other ones hovering against the wall. "What did you bring me?"

Arnie and Tinker reviewed the large variety of fruits, vegetables and mushrooms in front of them. "Have you noticed that the food here tastes better than it does elsewhere?" Arnie asked.

Tinker agreed. "Someone told me that it is all organically grown here on the island."

"Yeah, but some of the species are different as well." Arnie picked up a large grilled mushroom and put it on the bottom of a sliced bun. "Have you ever seen a mushroom that looks, feels, and tastes like a hamburger patty?" He piled veggies and condiments high on the open sandwich. "Even Bernadette was impressed last night and she's a vegetarian."

"Just an ovo-lacto vegetarian," Bernadette corrected him. "I do eat eggs and dairy products."

Arnie turned around to see Bernadette with Aurelia, Hugo, and Amanda standing behind her, and Min-su bringing up the rear.

Amanda asked Bernadette, "So, you don't mind exploiting the poor little animals as long as none of them get killed in the process?"

"Something like that," Bernadette replied.

"Hi," Arnie said the others. "So what do you think about all this stuff?"

The five of them sat down opposite Arnie and Tinker and then scooted around to the back of the pit to make room for Robert and Roberta, who also arrived.

"I don't know," Bernadette said. "I haven't had a chance to eat everything yet. But what I have had has certainly been different."

"Sorry," Alex chimed in, arriving and sitting down, "but I still prefer my meat." He cut a piece from a chicken fried steak that he had smothered in milk gravy. He looked straight at Bernadette, who gave him a sickened look and then looked at Arnie.

"Dead cows notwithstanding," Arnie said.

"Please excuse our Alaskan friend," Roberta apologized to Bernadette. "What he lacks in manners he makes up for with his insensitivity." She put a fork full of salad in her mouth.

"So you're a vegetarian as well?" Arnie asked.

"Yes," she replied, glaring at Alex, "and I would appreciate it if you did not slake your carnivorous urges when we are around." She looked at Bernadette. "As I suppose Unius might say, 'That which is offensive to others, don't impose by doing it in front of them.'"

Bernadette toasted Roberta with her Doctor Ginger's

bottle. "Thank you, my sister," Bernadette said. "Now, enough about the food, let's report our explorations of the rest of the class."

The conversation for the next thirty minutes confirmed that most of the rest of the class was pretty much just like them. People from all around the world, with straight A's in school and various other gifts, had been requested to attend GODA for free.

Amanda waited to go last in reporting her meeting. "I encountered a most interesting girl from Italy. Her name is Karmen Speranza and she has a voice that won't quit."

"How so?" Arnie asked.

"She can go from as low as a fog horn to so high that you can't even hear it."

"I could probably hear it," Alex said.

"Anyway," Amanda continued. "Her mother's family is somehow connected to organized crime in Italy, but her mother rebelled against Karmen's grandfather and married an old gelato maker's son."

"Interesting," Arnie said. "Did they have lots of ice cream at the wedding?"

"Beats me," Amanda pushed on. "But the real interesting part is that her grandfather, the mafia man, tried to convince Karmen to go to Scorsos International Academy to learn about business and prepaid her tuition. When Scorsos contacted her mother, the lady got all angry about the old man trying to pull her daughter into his clutches; so then, she started looking around for a place far away from Italy to send her daughter."

"Scorsos is a horrible place," Min-su said.

"Several people who I met here said they had also been accepted there," Bernadette said.

"A horrible place," Min-su repeated. "The focus is on nothing but money, money, money, money, money. One of the classes in their bulletin was literally titled 'Success at all costs'."

"How do you know so much about it?" Robert asked.

"They recruited me right after GODA did," Min-su replied. "I virtoured their school and just decided that it was not for me."

"Interesting," Arnie said. He didn't tell them that he had once considered applying to the Scorsos school himself.

At exactly one o'clock, the tube doors to the lecture hall rotated to their locked positions. The class quieted to a hush of one or two people still finishing their conversations in whispers. Most of the talking was about the notebook-sized slabs of what appeared to be plastic or durable glass on the desks in front of them. Arnie picked his up and inspected it. Etched into the bottom edge was the word, "GLADAASS," and the statement, "Pure guarantium."

The tube door in the lecturer's pit rotated closed and the class stood up in anticipation of who might come next. The longer they stood still the dimmer the lights got. Mrs. L stepped out of the opening as it rotated back around. She waved her hand in the air a few times and the ceiling brightened again. No one gasped this time like they had earlier in the morning.

"Not as impressive as when Chose does it, is it?" She laughed just a little. "Please be seated," she instructed them.

As everyone sat down, the ceiling brightened a little more.

"I'll bet you all thought turning on the lights was some

kind of gift that only the perfects like Chose can do." She stood in front of the lectern. "If you have not figured it out by now, the lights on Demeverde are all controlled by sound and motion sensors." She waved her hand again. "The more movement or noise in a room, the brighter the lights will get." The motherly woman made a very uncharacteristically loud screeching sound and the ceiling luminesced even more and the Gladaass on the lectern began to flash and project the words, "Sound spike alarm – Freshman lecture hall." Mrs. L explained, "And if you get too loud, then I will know about it." She pushed a spot on the lectern and the room went dark except for the cone of light shining down on her. "We can also manually control them." She pushed another spot and the room brightened again. "See, no gifts of the perfects involved. Just science and technology, which you will find is the case in most things."

Everyone remained silent as Mrs. L put her palm on her own notebook-sized piece of whatever it was.

"Good afternoon, class," she greeted them.

The class responded as a whole, except for one person toward the back of the room who waited until the end and then tacked on, "Good afternooooooooooooooooon, Mrs. LLLLLLLLLLL!"

Arnie and several others in the front of the room turned around to see who it was. A freckle-faced, red-haired boy, the obvious culprit, slunk lower in his chair.

"Avramel Kimvelevitch," Bernadette whispered to Arnie quickly but quietly, while she still looked straight forward. "Born in Brooklyn, New York, and now lives in Tel Aviv, Israel. Thinks he's a wonderful comedian and entertainer. I met him at the break. It wasn't a pretty sight."

Mrs. L looked at Bernadette as she was whispering. "Do

you have something of interest, Miss Rogers?"

"Ma'am, no, ma'am," Bernadette responded with a military tone.

"I thought not," Mrs. L replied. "This …" She picked up her own notebook-sized slab identical to the one in front of everybody else, "is a Gladaass Device." She looked to the very back of the room. "The spelling is G-L-A-D-A-A-S-S. I will leave you to spell 'device' on your own." She paused to see if anyone would laugh at her wit. No one dared.

"The emphasis is on the first syllable," Mrs. L continued. "The proper pronunciation is GLAD-aass and not Glad-AASS, as someone like Mister Kimvelevitch might like to say it."

Avramel slunk even lower in his chair as Mrs. L glared at him. Several others in the class snickered.

Mrs. L then wagged her finger at them all and added, "And you would do very well for yourselves not to test me on this."

Arnie, Bernadette, and Robert each said the last few words of her warning with her under their breaths.

"G-L-A-D-A-A-S-S stands for Guarantium Loose Alpha Data Acquisition, Assimilation, Storage, and Sharing device."

Mrs. L paused again, while several people said to their neighbors, "A what?"

She continued. "This Gladaass device is the latest and greatest improvement by Global Optimum Development Enterprises over the legacy hardware and software still being sold in the rest of the world. In an effort to bring you the most satisfying educational experience here at GODA, you are being offered the chance to use this new technology long before anyone else in the outside world."

"Cool," Tinker whispered from a few seats away, poking on the thing. "But how do you turn it on?"

"Now, if you will all place your full palm in the middle of your Gladaass, it will automatically register you as the owner and download your personal information from the Gladaass server in the admissions and administration offices."

Everyone did as Mrs. L instructed them and all of the slabs changed from dull slabs of guarantium to full-screen, borderless displays, with light softly emitting from the bottom, the top, and all four sides.

"This Gladaass will replace your notebook, your textbook, your pens and pencils, your personal digital assistant, your legacy tablet or desktop computer, your video camera or player, and almost anything else that you could or would ever use for acquiring, assimilating, storing, or sharing data obtainable through all five of your senses of sight, smell, hearing, taste, or proprioception."

Many people were enjoying playing with the cursor, which followed their fingers dancing across the screen.

"You may use either your finger or any hard object as a stylus to enter data or move the cursor or you may also use the simulated flat or ergonomically designed holographic keyboard."

Mrs. L was obviously enamored with the new technology and could have talked about it for hours, but the door to the lecturer's pit rotated away from her. "I would love to tell you more about this, but obviously it is time for the Parade of the Perfects, so please review the onboard tutorial for the rest of the operational instructions."

Mrs. L stepped back and to the side of the tube door and demanded, "Please rise."

The tube door rotated open and Chose quickly moved

from the opening to the lectern. "Thank you, Mrs. L," he said, all but ignoring her, as he looked at the students. "That will be all."

"My pleasure, Chose," Mrs. L said, stepping into the opening of the tube door, looked up, said her name and pushed the flange.

Alex mimicked her very quietly, but just loud enough for those immediately around him to hear. "My pleasure," he repeated with a disquieting tone. "Paradisial parrots."

Chose shot Alex a look, and then made eye contact with Arnie before looking back at Alex. Then he looked at the rest of the class. "Please," he said, shooing the sharers back into their chairs several times with the backs of his fingers, instructing them, "sit, sit, sit."

Everyone reoccupied their chairs and rolled them back up to their tables.

"This lecture has been called by prior sharers as the Parade of the Perfects," Chose began. "Like any other parade, the idea is merely to introduce you to the disciplines of the mind, body, and senses and the masters of those disciplines."

Chose pulled his own Gladaass out of his coat and set it down on the lectern. "If ever you desire to have a closer look at any of the virjections that I will be presenting, feel free to do so, on your own Gladaass device." Chose pushed a spot on his Gladaass and a virjection of a square-faced man with a short, scraggly beard emitted from both the Gladaass on the lectern and the full-sized wall display behind Chose.

"The first of three perfects with whom you will be sharing this session is Perfect Aryeh Dan, who is a perfect of the mental discipline." Chose went on to explain, "Mental perfects come in a combination of one or more of empaths, analypaths, and extropaths. Empaths range from unintentional recipients to intentional harvesters of the thoughts of others. Analypaths are able to assimilate, integrate, and analyze any thoughts or information gained by them by either sensory or extrasensory perception. Extropaths are able to convey their mental thoughts to others at will. Almost all of the sharers in Godeau are at the very least high level analypaths, though they are not able to completely utilize their gifts without many years of practice."

Chose pushed another spot on his Gladaass and a second virjection of a very pleasant, though not beautiful, woman moved from his Gladaass to the wall display. "The next perfect who will share with you this session is Perfect Sandrahartha Vinhathasarghi" Several of the sharers gasped at the complexity of the name.

The woman, dressed similarly to Chose's standard outfit of a soft, textured shirt, pants, and long coat, was sitting on a stool, with one leg apparently tucked under her because only one leg was sticking out of the bottom of her coat. Her hands were crossed in her lap and apparently hidden in the cuffs of her opposite sleeves.

"Of course, she will probably spare you the burden of saying her name too many times and ask you to call her what the rest of us do, which is Perfect Sandra Vin."

The woman raised her right hand from inside her left, twinkled her fingers at the air in front of them, and replaced her hand back in her sleeve.

"Perfect Sandra Vin is a master of the physical discipline, which means that she can do things with her body that are probably much beyond your wildest imaginations at this time." Chose went on to explain, "Physical perfects can make their bodies do anything they want, up to the point that they may even appear to defy some laws of science.

Many people at Godeau appear to be moving along a path to physical perfection."

Chose pushed another spot on his Gladaass and continued to explain, as a virtual projection showed a man laying facedown on a floor. "One example of physical perfection is the ability to meditate indefinitely while standing on the fifth digit of one hand. This is a gradually acquired ability, which begins by first learning how to lie facedown on the floor."

The sharers erupted into a brief spate of laughter, before Chose shushed them and proceeded to explain what was happening on the display wall. "From a position of resting on one's palms, forearms, abdomen, hips, and toes, a physical perfect can proceed through stages of arching their backs to get their feet and then hips off the ground and then extend their shoulders to rest on their head, palms, and forearms." The figure assumed a headstand position and then pushed himself up to a handstand. "Next they can develop the ability to do handstands for hours, while maintaining blood perfusion to their toes. After this, they can learn single-handed handstands; first, on their palms and then the palmar aspects of the four lateral digits, the pads of the four digits, the tips of the four digits, the tips of the three lateral digits, the tips of the two lateral digits and, finally, the tip of the most lateral fifth digit." Finally, the man was balanced on the tip of his right pinkie.

Pushing another spot to begin another virjection, Chose looked at Arnie briefly and then scanned the rest of the room. "Another physical perfect ability is what appears to be phenomenal strength. This is actually, however, only the ability to focus the entirety of the musculature to move in a given direction at one time. This ability is useful for moving the body over great distances; moving great weights over short distances; or moving directly inversely related, lesser weights over longer distances or with more force or speed." A woman on the display wall appeared to be jumping from rooftop to rooftop among several school buildings. "Sometimes physical perfects can move objects at speeds beyond their ability to dissipate heat gain from air friction, at which point the objects appear to self-destruct or disappear." The woman rubbed a steel rod until it glowed bright orange and wilted.

"Another physical ability that many physical perfects possess," Chose expounded, "is the ability to shift fluid between interstitial spaces in their bodies to rapidly cool burned areas and focus metabolic energy and blood flow to heat cooled areas."

Chose pushed another spot and a third virjection of a very sweet looking, grandmotherly woman took Perfect Sandra Vin's place on the Gladaasses and the wall display.

"The third perfect who will share with you this term," Chose went on to say, "is Perfect Givernie Waterlily, who is a master of the sensory disciplines."

Chose elucidated some more. "These perfects are complete sensory savants of nature and have tremendous acuity due to the hyperplasia or hypersensitivity of their physical receptors. Sensory perfection is not something that can be taught. One either has the hyperplastic or hypersensitive receptors for one or more of the five senses or one does not. Being taught how to recognize that one has these receptors and how to use them, however, is the key to being a sensory perfect."

Chose pushed a spot on his Gladaass to make the virjection of Perfect Givernie Waterlily dissipate and waved his hand in the air a few times to brighten the room. "And that, my friends," Chose paused and looked at the audience, "and, yes, you are all my friends, is the Parade of the Perfects for this term. Any questions?"

No one in the room had any idea of what question would be appropriate at the time, so no one raised a hand.

"Good," Chose said, pushing another spot on his Gladaass to rotate the tube door openings in the back of the hall to the inside. "In that case, one more thing. There are some advantages to being freshmen sharers at GODA. One advantage is that, to encourage you to play and practice coco as much as possible, freshman have priority rights to any coco valley on campus for the first session of the year. Therefore, feel free to impose this one little bit and get as much coco playing time in as possible by kicking off whatever upperclassmen you find playing in the valleys at any time."

Chose stopped talking, but no one moved. "That's all," he said. Still no one moved, so Chose shooed them away with his fingertips again, encouraging them to leave by softly saying. "Go, go, go."

As the deca moved toward the exits, Alex commented, "I liked most of the physical perfect stuff, except for the meditation foolishness. What good is it to be able to stand on your pinkie?"

Bernadette responded, "Oh, Alex. You have to expand your mind and go with the flow. Try it, first, before you knock it. My yoga meditation has been very enlightening for me."

Amanda agreed, "I'd like to learn how to stand on my pinkie."

"That's the spirit, girlfriend," Bernadette rejoined, sticking out her right pinkie toward Amanda. "Give me some pinkie power, right there!"

The two of them locked pinkies as Amanda said, "My pleasure."

"My pleasure, my pleasure," Alex mocked them, disappearing through a tube door. "Paradisial parrots."

COCO

*A*fter the Parade of the Perfects, everyone in the deca regrouped and sat around a large, round table, on the rooftop garden of the Student Union to learn how to use their Gladaasses and watch the late afternoon sun make orange paintings in the clouds on the western horizon. All at the same time, everyone's Gladaass had a virmail logo descend along the right border of their devices and insert itself into an envelope in the bottom right corner.

"Incoming virmail," Aurelia said.

"Me, too," Min-su concurred.

"Us, too," said the Rivers twins, simultaneously, with

several others responding the same way close behind them.

One-by- one, after they all tapped twice on the envelope, Émilie's face lifted up out of the screen and said, *"Bonjour, mes amis!* I am supposed to introduce you all to the pains and pleasures of coco this afternoon. So, go put on your coco shirts, shorts, socks, and sneakers and meet me outside of freshman tower two at six o'clock. See you there."

As fast as their SlipDiscs would take them, the deca went to their apartment and changed into the green-colored clothes that were on a shelf in their cabinets labeled, "Coco uniform, deca two-twelve." They were SlipDiscing in front of their dorm as Émilie arrived.

"Bonjour, mes amis!" Émilie yelled, capping the small hill in front of the dorm. "Well, if it isn't the Green Apple Army. You can see those shirts from a mile away." She rode past them without stopping. "Follow me!" she said excitedly, leading the way east toward several big gray dots on some hills, below the canyons and small mountains in the distance. As she rode along, Émilie juggled a big, greenish thing, about the size and shape of a rugby ball; a rough, brown thing about the size of a softball; another green ball about the size of a soccer ball; and a brown ball about the size of a baseball.

As they approached the mountains, the gray dots came into better view and turned out to be huge concrete bowls built into the ground. Bernadette scooted up to Arnie and leaned toward him. "This would be a great place to rollerblade," she said, while they all lined up on the edge of one of the valleys.

Émilie started to speak while still juggling the four things that she had with her. "This," she said, while pointing to the paved hole in the ground with her nose, "is a coco valley. I know it looks like a one hundred meter cereal bowl, but they call it a coco valley."

Next, Émilie bent forward a little and tucked the big green thing she was juggling behind her neck while she kept moving the other three things. "This," she said, while bobbing her shoulders up and down, "is a coconut. I know it doesn't look like what you think a coconut should look like because this is really a coconut in its shell." She continued to juggle the other three things. "Now, one day, hundreds, maybe thousands, of years ago, some Demeverdan native kids from one cave, way up in the mountains there in front of us, thought it would be really fun to take some coconuts, which had fallen from the trees in the valley down there, and just fill up the cave of some friends of theirs, way up on the other side of the valley." She continued to move the items between her hands. "Don't ask me why they thought this was going to be so much fun because I'll just have to tell you I don't know. But they did and we are glad they did, because, if they wouldn't have, then none of the people on Demeverde, from then until now, would have had anything to do in their spare time, and then Demeverde would have been a really dull place. Is everyone with me so far?"

No one answered because they were too busy being astounded by the demonstration they were watching. Émilie yelled to get their attention. "I SAID, IS EVERYONE WITH ME SO FAR?"

"YES!" They all yelled back.

"Good," she said, straightening up quickly to toss the green coconut off of her back and let it fall onto the ground behind her. "Moving on." She continued to work with the three things she had left. "Now, this," she said, sticking the rough brown thing behind her neck, "is what most of you think a coconut should look like, right?"

Several of the deca nodded their heads, but not with the level of enthusiasm that Émilie was looking for. "I SAID THIS IS WHAT MOST OF YOU THINK A COCONUT SHOULD LOOK LIKE, RIGHT?"

"RIGHT!" Everybody yelled.

"Now you're getting into it." Émilie smiled and continued. "Now, the kids in the cave, way up on the other side of the canyon, started talking among themselves and they said, 'You know, we're getting tired of these kids messing up our caves with their coconuts. So, the next time they try to bring some more coconuts up, let's throw these that they already left here back at them.'" Émilie kept up her juggling. "And so, the next time that the kids from this side of the canyon took some more coconuts to the cave way up on the other side of the canyon, do you know what happened?"

"WHAT?" Everybody yelled.

"NOTHING!" Émilie yelled back. "Because those big green coconuts were too big and too soft to throw hard enough to hurt those marauding, coconut-leaving kids." Émilie juggled with only her left hand for a moment and then only with her right. "So do you know what they did then?"

"WHAT?" the deca asked in unison.

"They said, 'Well then, if that's how the marauding, coconut-leaving kids want to play this game, then we'll show them a thing or two.' And do you know what they did then?"

"WHAT?"

"They took all of those big, green coconuts back. That's what they did."

"AND THEN WHAT HAPPENED?" everyone yelled to

Émilie.

"Wouldn't you like to know?" Émilie teased them, but no one said anything. "I SAID ..." she started to yell, while she continued juggling.

"JUST TELL US WHAT HAPPENED!"

"ALL RIGHT!" Émilie yelled back. "I'LL TELL YOU!" she said, "But prepare yourself, AND – DON'T – BE – SCARED," she added, "because it isn't pretty."

"SO TELL US ALREADY!" They pleaded, mesmerized by Émilie's show.

"Well, the coconut-receiving kids became way too smart for the kids leaving their coconuts because they figured out how to peel a coconut and get this." Émilie took the rough brown thing from behind her neck and tossed it up and down in one hand, while she juggled the green and brown balls in a circle with her other hand. "Yes, this," she said, holding up the rough brown thing, "which we all know is what a coconut is really supposed to look like. Right?"

"RIGHT!"

"Exactly!" Émilie smiled a very big smile, still juggling the remaining two balls in one hand and tossing the peeled coconut up and down with her other. "And do you know what they did next?" she asked.

"WHAT?"

Émilie turned toward the line of the deca standing beside her, still juggling the two balls in her right hand while she tossed the coconut up and down in her left. She stopped tossing the coconut, but kept the other two balls going in a circle, while she wound up for a pitch. "Well, then ..." she said, winding up a little more. "They ..." She paused and then threw the coconut at Arnie, who was closest to her. Arnie, with lightning fast, cat-like reflexes, caught the coconut and then let go of it and shook his aching hand. "They chucked those peeled coconuts as hard as they could at the other kids." Émilie started juggling the remaining two balls with both of her hands.

"AND?" Everyone asked.

"And it hurt like heck. Didn't it, Arnie?" Émilie smiled at Arnie, who was still shaking and blowing on his palm.

"Yes," Arnie admitted.

Émilie kept on juggling the two balls back and forth with her two hands. "And then one thing led to another and the other kids figured out how to peel coconuts and a constant battle went on, with kids from both sides of the canyon stuffing unpeeled coconuts in the caves on the other side of the canyon and getting peppered with peeled coconuts, until it simply became part of the culture of Demeverde. People started going cuckoo for coconuts and that's how the game got started."

Émilie kept on juggling the two balls with her hands.

"YAAAAAAAY" Everyone shouted thinking the explanation was over.

"But wait!" Émilie said. "There's more!"

"AND MORE!" they sarcastically yelled.

"Yes, more," Émilie repeated, still juggling the two balls. "Because, here at GODA, we have improved on the game." She kept on juggling. "To make it safer and more fun," she added. "Do you want to know how?"

"HOW?" Everyone screamed.

"Just wait!" Émilie answered them. "And I'll tell you." She went back to juggling both balls with her right hand and pointed to the paved bowl in front of them. "First, we paved you a valley, one hundred meters wide by three meters deep, so you wouldn't have to run up and down across a real, rough valley and maybe trip and fall and hurt yourself." Émilie paused her speaking, but she kept on juggling.

"AND?"

"And, second …" she said, still juggling with one hand, while she pointed across the coco valley with the other. "Do you see that big one meter by one meter square-front and triangular-sided net with a round bottom pointing down on the other side of the coco valley?"

"YES," they all answered.

"Well, that is a cave," Émilie told them. "Look down and you will see another one right under me."

Everyone looked down and back at Émilie. She kept on juggling the two balls with one hand, still pointing down with the other. "And if you look under the net you will see that it empties into a tube, which is just a little bit bigger than one of these big green balls here." She kept pointing to the green ball and moving her pointing hand as the green ball kept moving up and down in the juggle. Everyone looked down and back up again. "And as tall as ten of these balls." She kept pointing at the ball and added, "With numbers on it from one to ten."

Émilie went back to juggling the two balls with both hands and said, "So you can keep score. Because it wouldn't be a very good game without a way to keep score, would it?"

"NO!" they all answered.

"Right!" Émilie said, still juggling the balls with two hands. "And the first team to chuck ten of these balls in the other team's cave and tube …" Émilie quickly tossed the brown ball way up in the air, leaned way out, dunked the green ball in the net below her, and then caught the brown ball behind her neck. "Wins!"

"YAAAAAAYYYYYYYYYY!" Everyone yelled.

"But wait!" Émilie screamed to them.

"WHAT?" they asked.

Émilie stood up, rolling the brown ball down her back and catching it with one hand without looking. "There's more!"

"MORE?" they all yelled. "MORE!"

Émilie held her arms level, shoulder high, in the shape of a circle, and started rolling the ball inside them. "Yes, more," she said. "Do you see this brown ball here?" Émilie asked.

"YES!" they all answered.

"Well, there are two things you can do with this ball."

"AND THEY ARE?"

"Wouldn't you like to know?" Émilie asked.

"YES!" they all answered again, louder this time.

"You would?" she cajoled them again, smiling.

"YES!"

"Are you sure?"

"YES!" they screamed.

"Then I'll tell you," Émilie said. "First, you can throw it at an opposing player holding a green ball for more than three seconds to make them think twice about trying to leave it in your cave." She caught the ball as it went past her left hand and acted very quickly, pretending to throw it at Arnie, like she had done with the coconut.

Arnie flinched, but then everyone laughed when Émilie revealed that she had let the ball go, in the back of her wind up, and it was really still behind her back, in her right hand. Émilie started to toss the ball up and down in front of her with her right hand again, while she pointed to the bottom of the scoring tube under the cave on the other side of the valley.

"Do you see the nine balls in that tube under the other cave?" Émilie asked.

"YES!" they all yelled.

"And do you see the red and white bull's-eye target at the base of the tube?"

"YES!" they screamed more loudly this time.

"Well, if you chuck this brown ball in the center of that target ..." Émilie grabbed the ball in mid-air with her left hand and threw it at the bull's-eye on the other side of the coco valley. As everyone watched the perfect arch of the ball going all the way across the one-hundred-meter coco valley, Émilie finished saying, "It will release all of the balls then scored in your tube, thus extending the game and giving you more of a chance to ..." Émilie's shot hit the bull's-eye squarely in the middle and all of the balls rolled out of the tube and started rolling down the other side of the valley to settle in the bottom of the bowl. "Win," Émilie finished.

Everyone looked at Émilie with their mouths wide open.

"Any questions about coco?" she asked, but none of them could yet close their mouths. "Okay," she said turning and stepping off of her SlipDisc. She starting to run toward the bottom of the valley. "Last one to the bottom is a rotten egg."

The deca chased Émilie to the bottom of the bowl, where she showed them that all of the loose balls fell down into a pipe with a disc in it, which pushed up one ball at a time.

"The game begins with all of the players standing on the edge of the valley. You can't move until you hear the horn that sounds when the first green ball, which we call a coco, pops up out of this pipe." Émilie tapped her foot on the hole in the bottom of the valley. "Then you run down here and either kick or pick up the coco before the other team gets here first." She then kicked the ball into the air, bounced it off her left and then right knee, and then flipped backwards, kicking the ball behind her, over her head, and into the net on the far side of the bowl, tying the score one to one. "After that," she continued, "it's pretty much anything goes. You can throw the coco." She threw one into a net. "You can hit it with your hand." Émilie tossed a ball in the air and then served it with her fist into the other net. "You can dribble the coco," she said, making a one-bounce shot into the first net. "You can head the coco." She tossed one up and headed it into the next goal. "You can even hold or run with the coco." She tossed a green ball to Arnie and ordered him, "Run, Arnie!"

Arnie took off running with the green coco, while Émilie reached down and picked up one of twenty little brown balls that were stuck in a trough around the pipe. "But, if you are holding or running with the ball ..." She yelled at Arnie, who was halfway to the opposite goal. "Stop, Arnie."

Arnie stopped and turned around. "NOW WHAT?" he yelled back.

"HOLD IT STRAIGHT OUT IN FRONT OF YOU BY THE SIDES," Émilie bellowed.

"If you hold the coco for three seconds or run more than one step while holding the coco ..." Émilie paused while she fired a shot straight at the coco in Arnie's hands. "Then the other team can throw a brown nut at you, to make you let it go."

Émilie's nut hit the coco that Arnie was holding square in the middle, knocking it out of his hands and into his chest, whereupon both balls began rolling back to the bottom of the valley, with Arnie chasing after them.

"Everyone plays the entire game until, one side gets ten cocoes in a cave or three, fifteen-minute periods expire. There are five-minute breaks after each fifteen-minute period." Émilie continued. "There are a myriad of strategies for positioning players and making plays, but that's pretty much all there is to it."

"What about defense?" Bernadette inquired.

"Well," Emily asked, "Do you see that half-circle four feet in front of each cave?"

"Yes," Bernadette answered for everyone.

"That's the outer boundary of the cave and only one defender from each team can be inside that boundary at a time. One of them is defending their team's cave and trying to keep cocoes from being put into it. The other one is defending their team's cocoes already in the opponent's cave and trying to keep anyone from shooting a nut at the bull's-eye and letting all of their cocoes out."

"Cool," Bernadette said.

Émilie continued. "Anyone can attempt to take a coco away from whoever on the other team has it, but you have to be tackling the coco and not the other player," Émilie said. "You can block a shot on the fly, but you cannot reach inside the cave to do so. If you stop in front of an opposing player, they cannot intentionally run through you. Picks and screens are allowed, but not moving ones. There is no offsides, so fast breaks are encouraged."

"What about penalties and referees?" Roberta asked.

"Four referees usually station themselves one per quadrant of the valley," Émilie explained. "Penalties are for unnecessary roughness, which has to be very blatant, nutting a player who is not holding or running with a coco, and goal tending. Penalized players have to sit on the rim for one to five minutes. Goal tending results in a penalty shot, with the original shooter starting from wherever he or she wants, but no closer than his last shot, and the defenders starting in the cave. Everyone else stays behind the shooter until he shoots his penalty shot."

"Is that all there is?" Arnie asked.

Émilie thought for a second, to see if she had left anything out. "Yep," she finally said, "that's about all there is. The rest you just pick up by playing." Émilie picked up two nuts and threw one in each bull's-eye to release all of the cocoes. When all of the cocoes had returned to the pipe, Émilie told them to divide up and play five-on-five while she refereed.

The deca practiced for almost an hour, at which time everyone but Aurelia was winded, and only a few had scored goals. They gathered in a clump and sat down on the ground, above the rim closest to the dorm.

"So tell us," Amanda demanded from Émilie. "How long have you been a physical perfect?"

"Who me?" Émilie asked. "I'm nowhere near being a perfect. Just physically gifted. Though I have been working with Perfect Sandra Vin, since my first week at GODA."

"What's she like?" Bernadette asked.

"Totally cool and laid back," Émilie answered. "She loves music of all kinds and can sing anything published in the past century, if you just give her a few words. But, of all of the kinds of music that there are, she is partial to country and western."

"So are you like the coco champion at GODA or something like that?" Roberta asked.

"No, just the class one-on-one coco champion," Émilie admitted.

"Wow! I'd hate to have to play the other person, if they were competing with you. Who was it?" Bernadette asked.

"H.M. Crist." Émilie shook her head and sighed with exasperation as she said his name. "And he was a real jerk about losing to a girl, after his deca went undefeated in the class intramurals."

Émilie looked at her watch. "Okay, that's all the time I have for today." She got up to mount a SlipDisc. "See you tomorrow."

All of the deca got up to say goodbye. After Émilie sped off into the distance, Arnie looked around at the rest of them and said, "Another game?"

THE PLAGUE OF DEMEVERDE

*A*fter showers, shampoos, and shaves, most of the deca were sitting on the sectional cheds in the central gathering area of the apartment. Robert and Roberta were in their separate rooms, working on communing with each other through the walls. Tinker was continuing his fascination with a SlipDisc that he had taken into his own room. The remaining seven of the deca were sitting in the gathering area doing various things with their Gladaasses.

Alex was fast-forwarding through the VNN International Virnews Roundup, to catch up on what had happened in the world that day. "Boy!" he exclaimed, which naturally got everyone else's attention. "I'd sure hate to be in this guy's shoes."

"Whose?" Aurelia asked.

"This poor little rich kid in Wyoming," Alex answered, virjected the story from the front of his Gladaass.

A correspondent stood in front of a street corner being guarded by a variety of policemen and reported, "This is Geraldo Enquirea and I am standing on the corner of the grounds of the Philmont County High School in Philmont, Wyoming. Thayne Davidson Miller, the third, reported to be the richest orphan in the world, is expected to arrive and begin his first day in Philmont's public high school any minute. It is bedlam here this morning. To give you a better idea of what is going on, let's take you up to our eye in the sky, the VNN IVR Satellite."

The picture zoomed away from the reporter and showed a bird's-eye view of the school being protected by many police cars. A big tent had been set up at the front entrance of the main building. "As you can see, security for young Mister Miller is very tight and the county school board has spared no expense to make sure he can arrive for his first day at his new alma mater in as private a way as possible. The young man, whose parents were killed over a year ago, leaving him a business conglomerate worth over fifty billion dollars, is expected to arrive by armored car and be ushered into school by his private protection team through that security tent. The media has been banned from the school grounds and it will be nigh upon impossible for us to bring you a clear shot of him arriving. Nonetheless, we have arranged to interview the Philmont High School principal, Mister Rufus Spurlock."

The satellite zoomed back in on Geraldo and the principal. "Principal Spurlock, thank you for giving us a few moments of your time. You said you wanted to make a statement."

"No problem, Mister Enquirea, and thank you for keeping your distance from the school." Principal Spurlock turned square to the camera. "As everyone knows, today is the first day of school and it is an especially significant first day this year because, for the first time in his life, young Thayne Davidson Miller, the third, will begin attending public school. As has been reported all summer, Mister Miller was home schooled by his parents, who were tragically killed in a car explosion last year. Not having any other family in the world, he is being cared for by his family's butler, who has decided that he should try to develop as normal a life as he can by beginning to attend public school. We are, of course, delighted to have him here with us at Philmont County High and we are going to do everything in our power to give him as normal an educational experience as we can."

Geraldo interrupted the principal's statement. "If so, Principal Spurlock, then why have all of this extraordinary activity and security? Why not just let the boy come and go like any other child, so we can get a good look at him?"

"As you know, Mister Enquirea, Mister Miller's butler is very security conscious and has requested that we do our best to attempt to ensure the boy's privacy as much as possible. We are asking all of the media, Mister Enquirea, including yourself, to work with us on this as much as possible and just leave the poor boy alone."

"Poor does not quite seem to be the right adjective for Thayne Miller, principal. He is worth over fifty billion dollars. Does his status as the wealthiest orphan in the world have anything to do with your willingness to do whatever he has asked you to?"

"Absolutely not, sir. Mister Miller's butler, Mister

Jacques Marquis, has asked us to treat young Thayne like we would any other child in our school, except for paying special attention to his security needs, and that is exactly what we intend to do."

A motorcade of two police cars, leading an armored car, which was then followed by two more police cars roared by with sirens blaring and pulled into the white canvas tent.

"I'm so sorry, Mister Enquirea, I need to go now," Principal Spurlock explained, rushing off across the school's front lawn and disappeared into the protective awning.

"So there you have it, ladies and gentleman. The first day's arrival at public high school for the world's richest orphan. For VNN IVR news, I am Geraldo Enquirea."

The virjection faded out to nothingness as Alex repeated himself. "I'd sure hate to be that boy."

Arnie swallowed hard and agreed. "Me too."

"You're from Wyoming, Arnie. Did you ever meet this guy?"

Arnie thought for a second to figure out something to say that would not be a lie. "I think I saw him once in my whole life, but I don't think he saw me, because he seemed to have his eyes closed the whole time."

"Uh-oh," Hugo said, which shifted everyone's focus.

"What?" Alex asked.

"I think I found the 'crisis somewhere else in the world' that Unius is working on."

Everyone converged around Hugo and his Gladaass. They all watched as Hugo rewound another VNN virnews article. "I'm Candy Caine," the attractive reporter started, "coming to you for VNN IVR news, directly from the Los Cabos, Argentina, hospital where an Argentinean child has just been diagnosed as the second young victim of juvenile variant Creutzfeldt-Jakob Disease." The reporter faded out to a scene apparently near the Eiffel Tower, but her voice could still be heard. "The first child victim ever reported to have had this terrible disease presented in France six months ago. The only connection between the two cases appears to have been vacation visits to Demeverde three and five years ago. An executive communications spokesman of Global Optimum Development Enterprises, the owners and operators of many interests on Demeverde, have suggested that the similar vacation plans between the two victims is, at the present time, thought to be merely a coincidence. Nonetheless, the spokesman told us all of the resources of Global Optimum Development Enterprises' Medical Division are being made available to the Argentinean and French health authorities to discover whatever information might be available and helpful for diagnosing and treating the two unfortunate victims of this dreadful disease. In the meantime, the spokesman has said, the Demeverde Tourism Department has reported increased bookings for the coming fall vacation season. For VNN IVR news, I am Candy Caine."

"Oh, man," Alex said, as the virjection dissipated.

"Looks nasty to me," Hugo said.

"Poor kids," Aurelia added.

"What's Creu – Creutz – Creutzfeldt-Jakob Disease?" Bernadette asked.

Everyone looked at Arnie.

"What?" he said, trying not to be an almost-know-it-all.

"Well, do you know anything about it?" Bernadette pumped him for information.

"I've read a little bit about it," he said.

"And?" Aurelia pleaded.

"And, let's see," Arnie stalled for a second, not wanting

to show off his instant recall. "Oh, yes. Creutzfeldt-Jakob Disease is a rare, degenerative, invariably fatal brain disorder. Typically, you start to see symptoms in people who are about sixty. There is currently no way to test for it except by a brain biopsy. But, because it is untreatable, most doctors don't do a brain biopsy, unless they need to rule out a treatable disorder. It does not seem to be spread from person to person."

"It's untreatable?" Aurelia needled him.

"I'm afraid so."

"How do they die?" Hugo inquired.

"Most people with it die within a year. At first, they may have failing memory, behavioral changes, lack of coordination, and visual disturbances. Then they develop mental deterioration with pronounced and involuntary movements, blindness, weakness of the extremities, and then, a coma."

"What causes it?" Aurelia continued to grill him.

"About twenty years ago, they thought it was caused by a type of protein called a prion. The harmless and the infectious forms of the prion protein are nearly identical, but the infectious form takes a different folded shape than the normal protein. No one is quite sure how it spreads, but they think eating things that contain infectious prions spreads it."

"Like what?" Bernadette wondered.

"Like meat or animal feed containing infected nervous tissue."

"See!" Bernadette exclaimed. "I told you that being a strict vegetarian could prevent lots of diseases."

"So what's juvenile variant Creuz – whatever it is?" Hugo asked.

"I have no idea," Arnie said. "The virnews story said that these were the first kids ever to have symptoms similar to the adult form of the disease, so I doubt that anyone knows too much about it."

"I wonder if we are going to get it?" Amanda pondered.

"I doubt it," Arnie assured her. "The kids both being here is very probably a coincidence like the GODEnt people said."

"But I still would avoid the animal flesh, if I were you guys," Bernadette added.

* * *

Several weeks passed before any more mention was made of juvenile variant Creutzfeldt-Jakob disease on Demeverde or anywhere else in the world. Arnie's deca and all of the rest of the freshmen were settling into a routine of regular classes, homework, and coco games. Daily messages of encouragement from Unius usually preceded the morning's first lectures. The Heritage Program classes had begun and they were all studying how to use primary sources of history to interpret what really occurred during the time that a particular primary source supposedly originally existed.

At the same time, the Science and Technology Program was using images from the Far Solar Space satellite telescope. The FSS scope was continuing on year fifteen of a fifty year mission shooting pictures of the "big bang" dust cloud moving out in space. The mission was to get bigger, better, brighter, and closer pictures of the "big bang" event and try to interpret the origins of the universe.

After a few large group classes in the lecture hall, the perfects began seeing the decas one at a time for small discussion groups.

CHAPTER TEN

No one privately or publicly thought or said anything about juvenile variant Creutzfeldt-Jakob Disease, until GODEnt decided to expand their help with the diagnosis and treatment of the two little kids who were sick in France and Argentina. They sent each hospital treating the children one of the latest full body, electron microscopic imaging scanners developed by GODEnt's Medical Services Division.

Bernadette read the story in the local GODA virnews to Arnie as they were eating some breakfast in the union. "That's awfully nice of Unius, isn't it?"

"It will come back to haunt them, I'll bet," Arnie replied.

"What do you mean?" Bernadette asked him.

"'No good deed goes unpunished,' my father always said. The media will find some way to turn this around on us, just watch and see."

"Pessimist," Bernadette teased him.

"'It's not what they say,' my father always said, 'It's the way they so thoughtlessly say it that does the worst damage.' And, trust me, GODEnt's good deed in this case will be no different."

* * *

Several days later, as was their habit on any given evening, after a daily afternoon game of coco, most of Arnie's deca were gathered in the central area of their apartment, either studying, playing virgames, or watching virnews or virprograms on their Gladaasses.

"Uh-oh," Hugo said, which usually meant that he had discovered something bad being reported on the virnews. As usual, this brought everyone around his Gladaass to see what he had found.

Sure enough, GODEnt's good deed was receiving the virtual media's unjustified punishment. A virjection of a series of crates being unloaded from a Global Optimum Delivery Express plane appeared under a story headlined:

GODENT SENDS SCANNER TO HELP FIGHT PLAGUE OF DEMEVERDE

"Oh, my gosh!" Bernadette shouted softly. "They're saying there's a plague on Demeverde."

Bernadette's reaction must have been the same as many others. Within hours the corporate spokesperson for GODEnt was on as many virnews sites as possible explaining the situation. "No one thinks there was or is any plague of Demeverde or any connection between the two sick children in Argentina and France and their trips to Demeverde so long ago and two years apart for that matter. No other children have been diagnosed as having the signs and symptoms as the two sick children and, because millions of people have lived in and vacationed in Demeverde for years without showing any evidence of any disease such as this, there could not be any connection between these unfortunate cases and Demeverde."

"So what is GODEnt doing to help with the plague of Demeverde?" the reporter asked, completely ignoring what the spokesperson had just said.

"There is no plague of Demeverde," he repeated. "Nonetheless, GODEnt has committed to doing anything it can to help diagnose and treat the two children. Therefore, we're GODExing each hospital the latest GODEnt total body scanners for free, to make sure the hospitals have the very latest and greatest technology available to do whatever needs to be done. Plus, we are working on this disease nonstop in our own research labs."

"Good for us," Bernadette said to them all. "We're still the good guys, it seems."

Unius's message the next morning repeated the statements of the GODEnt spokesperson. "Rest assured that all of us here in Godeau and on the rest of Demeverde are doing everything we can to help solve the problem of this dreadful disease. Nonetheless, everyone should know we are not downplaying this for our own economic reasons. None of us here at GODEnt would ever do anything that would hurt anyone else or fail to do anything that could help anyone else. It's just the way we are."

Everyone's parents started sending their children virmails asking if everything was all right. Later that night, all of the deca were sitting in their cheds in the gathering space responding to virmails from home with the same story being put out by GODEnt.

As everyone else was reading their responses aloud to each other, Arnie got up to get a snack from the kitchenette, while everyone else answered their virmails by repeating Unius's assurances about the non-existence of a plague on Demeverde. Everyone in the deca seemed to simultaneously notice that Arnie was the only person in the deca who had not received a virmail from home, because they all seemed to look at him at the same time, as he got up.

"Why haven't your parents virmailed you, Arnie?" Bernadette asked him. "Don't they care about you?"

Arnie's face turned completely sullen and his eyes started to moisten. Bernadette sensed that she had touched on something very sad and that she had gone somewhere she shouldn't have.

"I'm sorry, Arnie," she said, reaching over and touching him on the hand. "That was a horrible thing for me to say and I don't know why I said it that way. I didn't mean to say your parents don't care about you. Maybe they just haven't noticed the news, yet?"

"THEY CAN'T NOTICE THE NEWS FOR THE SAME REASONS THEY CAN'T CARE ABOUT ME!" Arnie suddenly screamed, falling back into his ched and starting to cry. All of the ceilings in the gathering space turned their brightest white and began flashing.

"Well, why not?" Bernadette asked, stroking his arm trying to comfort him.

"BECAUSE - THEY - ARE - DEAD!" Arnie yelled. "DEAD! DEAD! DEAD! DEAD!" He repeated over and over again.

Everyone else looked up at the flashing ceiling and then at Bernadette and Arnie. All of their mouths gaped wide open.

"W-w-well, w-what, how?" Bernadette didn't know how to respond. "How did it happen?" was all that came to her mind and out her mouth.

"I DON'T KNOW," Arnie said between sobs. "One minute they were in the car, late, on their way to my birthday party," he managed to say getting some control of himself for a short second. "AND THE NEXT MINUTE THEY WERE DEAD!" Arnie dissolved once again into a blubbering mass of hysteria. He leaned straight back in his ched and then backflipped out the top of it, turned around, stepped to his tube door, pushed the flange, yelled "ARNIE CARVER!" and disappeared into his room.

As well built as the apartment was, everyone else in the deca could hear Arnie sobbing in his room. But no one moved. No one knew what to do.

As the noise in Arnie's room seemed to be subsiding,

Bernadette walked over to the tube door, but it did not rotate to open on her side. "Arnie," she said just loudly enough to be heard, "come out and let's talk."

"Go away!" Arnie yelled back. "And leave me alone."

No one had any idea how to handle the situation. The rest of the deca discussed it in whispers among themselves. They agreed that apparently none of them had been faced with something like this before.

Bernadette looked at Aurelia and said, "Call Mrs. L." She then looked at Hugo and said, "And you call Chose."

Aurelia touched her Gladaass and quickly found the virsite for GODA and navigated to the administration page. A large red bell in a big dot in the bottom left corner was encircled with letters that read, "FOR EMERGENCIES ONLY!"

"Well, if this isn't one, then I don't know what is," Aurelia said, pushing on the button.

Mrs. L's face appeared above the Gladaass. "What's the matter, Miss Musyoka?" Mrs. L seemed to be looking around the room. "I see that there has been a sound spike warning in freshman room two-twelve."

"Yes, ma'am, Mrs. L," Aurelia started to answer.

Mrs. L's face turned to the side as her shoulders moved a little while she was apparently doing something with her hands just out of view. "Why is Arnie Carver screaming and crying in his room?"

"I don't know, Mrs. L," Aurelia seemed a little flustered. "Well, I mean I know, but I don't understand. Well, I mean that I understand, but I ... I...." Aurelia stammered. "What I am trying to say is that he just told us that his parents are dead."

"Oh, my goodness!" Mrs. L said mutedly, but in as much

of an exclamation as anyone had every seen her utter. "I'll be right over."

Hugo had made a similar connection to Chose, who told him that he had been monitoring the apartment since a sound spike warning had just gone off in it and he was simultaneously listening to Aurelia's flustered explanation to Mrs. L. "We are both on our way," Chose said in a calming tone. "Everyone else should just leave him alone."

In just a few moments, which seemed like an eternity, first Mrs. L and then Chose rotated through the tube door of the apartment. "Has he come out yet?" Mrs. L asked.

"No," Bernadette said, still in charge of the situation and acting as the self-appointed spokeswoman for the rest of the deca.

Mrs. L walked over to Arnie's door. "Mister Carver," she said, "It's Mrs. Leidgarten."

"And Chose," Chose added.

"We'd like to come see you, if you wouldn't mind."

After a few seconds the tube door rotated open to the gathering space and Arnie said in a muffled voice, "Just Chose."

"Very well then, Mister Carver," Mrs. L replied, "just Chose." Mrs. L stepped out of the way, directed Chose to the tube with her outstretched palm, and then walked into the central gathering space with the rest of the deca.

Chose stepped in and rotated the tube door opening around him to Arnie's side of the wall. He stuck his head out of the opening and looked to the side of the room where Arnie was laying face down on his ched. "Arnie?" he asked softly. "Arnie Carver, are you all right?"

Arnie pushed his head and chest off his ched and looked over at Chose. "Of course, I'm not all right, Chose." He turned over and sat up as the ched adjusted itself to his new position. "My parents are dead and I don't have anyone to care for me!" Arnie cried softly.

"Oh, come now, Arnie," Chose comforted him, sitting on the arm of the ched, which then flattened out to the side to give him more room. "Jacques Marquis cares for you."

"Yeah," Arnie reluctantly agreed.

"Enough to send you home here to us. And Unius even cares for you."

"He doesn't even know me!" Arnie complained.

"He knows you more than you could imagine," Chose corrected him.

"How do you know?"

"Trust me," Chose said. "What little I know about you, Arnie, Unius knows even more."

"Yeah, sure," Arnie said, unconvinced.

"I'll tell you a secret, if you swear not to tell a soul on pain of death."

"What?"

Chose held his hand out palm up toward Arnie. "Connect with me and swear first."

Arnie put his hand palm down in Chose's and they tightened their hands around each other's. Arnie felt a tingle like his hand was just waking up from being asleep. "I swear not to tell a soul on pain of death," he said.

"Unius watches almost everything that goes on, almost everywhere, almost all of the time."

"Yeah, sure, like he's God or something," Arnie mocked.

"Oh, no," Chose replied. "Not like God. And Unius would not appreciate such a comparison. But Unius does pay attention to almost everything that goes on, almost everywhere, almost all of the time."

"How?"

"Don't ask me how," Chose said. "Just trust me that he does."

"So what if he does?"

"So he has seen you and paid attention to you."

"Not that I have seen."

"No," Chose explained, "because he does not want to call attention to himself or to you."

"Why not?"

"Because attention would not be good for either of you."

"But, still," Arnie argued, "no one cares for me."

"Like I said, Arnie," Chose went on, "Jacques Marquis cares for you, Unius cares for you, and I care for you."

Arnie just stared at Chose.

"And Mrs. L cares for you and your deca cares for you and your class cares for you and, in fact, I would be willing to bet that anyone in this school, on all of Demeverde and probably all of the world, if they knew you and your story like we do, then they would care for you, too."

"My story's not that great," Arnie complained.

"Your story has just barely begun," Chose said. "There is much more that Arnie Carver will show the world before he is done."

"But I still don't have any family," Arnie said.

"Then let all of us be your family," Chose told him. "You can live with us and love with us and fight with us and laugh with us. You can do everything other kids do with all of their own families. If you will just give them a try, the rest of the world will adopt you, Arnie Carver."

"It's not like having a real Mom and Dad."

"No, it is not," Chose agreed. "And there is nothing either of us can do about that, right now."

"I guess not."

"So ...," Chose prompted him.

"So, I guess this is just as good as it's going to get."

"For the time being," Chose said, "I am afraid so."

Arnie looked at Chose and asked. "Chose, who killed my parents and why did they do it?"

"Who says they're dead?" Chose answered his question with a question.

"Why, of course, they're dead. Their tank was blown into smithereens."

"Did you see their bodies?"

"Well, no," Arnie answered. "But there was almost nothing but ashes left from the tank."

Chose poked Arnie in the chest, "Can you still almost feel them still alive right in here?"

Arnie brightened just a bit. "Well, ... yes, ... maybe, I don't know."

"Well, then, while you are looking for who killed them and why, you should never give up hope that maybe somehow they are alive."

Arnie thought for many seconds and then looked Chose in the eye. "Thanks, Chose," he said, squeezing Chose's hand.

"*Ain ba'aya*, man." Chose shook Arnie's hand a little in his own before letting go.

Arnie wonderd what Chose had said, but he did not think to ask him.

Chose closed his eyes for a moment and nodded reassuringly. "Now, Arnie, we have a little crisis management and security work that we have to do."

"Like what?"

"Like you have just announced to your deca, and for all intents and purposes, the rest of the world that your parents died in a car accident on the way to your birthday party."

"And?"

"And that is a pretty rare set of events that may lead someone to figure out who you are."

"Oops," Arnie said, realizing that maybe he had shared just a little too much of his past.

"Now, we can't lie about anything, because that would be an imposition and an honor code violation."

"Yes," Arnie agreed with him, but then asked, "so what can we do?"

"Well," Chose thought for a second. "You have not said your party was in fact on your birthday or which one it was."

"So?"

"So if anyone ever asks you any questions about how your parents were killed or when it happened, just politely tell them it is dreadfully painful for you and you would rather not talk about it ever again. Okay?"

"Okay."

"But, of course, if you ever do need to talk about it ever again with anyone ..."

"Yeah?"

"Then feel free to call me and we can talk about it all you want. Okay?"

"Okay."

Chose gave Arnie a quick hug around the shoulders with one arm. "So, what say we go out and be with the rest of the deca? Okay?"

"Okay."

Chose went out first and waved to the crowd with the palm of his hand facing down to signal that everything was fine. He then put his finger to his lips indicating that everyone should be quiet.

Arnie came out and looked around the room. He smiled just a little and then said, "Sorry for kind of going a little crazy there."

"That's all right," several of the deca said all at once.

"Let's just leave it at that. Okay?"

"Sure," some of them said. "Whatever you say," said some others.

Arnie looked at Mrs. L. "Sorry for getting you all the way out here, Mrs. Leidgarten."

Mrs. L looked at Chose, who just barely, almost imperceptibly, shook his head, and then she said, "Well, that is quite all right, Mister Carver. That's part of why I am here."

Arnie then looked at Chose. "Thank you, too, Chose."

"No problem, Arnie. That's part of what I am here for, too." Chose directed Mrs. L to the door of the apartment, pointing with his whole hand. "Come, Mrs. L," he said. "Let us be away."

The two of them passed one by one through the tube door after which everyone gathered around Arnie for a spontaneous private group hug.

Arnie whispered to Amanda. "Amanda, what language is *ain ba'aya* and what does it mean?"

Amanda thought for a second and whispered back. "Modern Hebrew. It means 'There is no problem.'"

Arnie looked at the tube door, where he had last seen Chose, and smiled.

RUNSUMFORFUN

*A*rnie's existence at GODA became more comfortable after his catharsis about being an orphan. Someone in the deca must have mentioned it to some other sharers because it soon became well known that Arnie Carver was essentially alone in the universe. Several sharers from higher classes virmailed him, just to say "Hello," introduce themselves, say they were sorry to hear of his loss, and offer whatever they could. Even some workers at GODEnt and other places on Demeverde virmailed words of support. Arnie discovered, while he was the only orphan in his class, several other orphans were scattered throughout the other classes in GODA and GODU. But none of them were in the circumstance of not having any family anywhere in the world.

Then, thankfully, the hubbub died down. Arnie didn't want to be known in Demeverde as the poor little orphaned kid. In fact, for security reasons, Arnie would just as well have liked not to be very well known in Demeverde at all.

Mid-term exams were approaching. In the last week of September, Arnie had eight more days until they arrived. He planned to enjoy his favorite hobby on Sunday, study from Monday to Thursday, have a think day on Friday, read quietly on Saturday, enjoy his favorite hobby on the next Sunday as well, and then take his first ever mid-term exam. For a kid who had never even been to a school, much less one that had exams, it was a pretty big deal.

Not that he was worried. Arnie knew he could handle any book-knowledge type of question. And his knowledge of the mental and sensory disciplines was on par with the rest of the class. Luckily, there weren't exams in the perfects' disciplines, because none of it was the kind of stuff one could test. Either you had the gifts and could improve your use of them or you didn't and couldn't. Arnie had no idea how the perfects would know if anyone was really trying or not; but that was the perfects' problem, not his.

Eight days before exams, however, Arnie's particular problem was figuring out how all of the different animal, vegetable, and mineral life on Isla Principal fit in with the taxonomic nomenclature naming system he had learned for the rest of the world. Demeverde held many different kinds of animals and insects that he had never seen or even imagined before. The plant life was simply phenomenal.

Arnie was using the camera feature of his Gladaass to capture images of every form of life on the islands of

Demeverde and add them to his growing virtual catalog. He was quite focused on the task and was understandably disconcerted when Bernadette suddenly called out behind him.

"Fancy finding you here!" she yelled, from about a hundred feet down the trail behind him.

"Yipe!" Arnie shrieked, dropping his Gladaass when she startled him.

Aurelia was walking beside Bernadette. The blank look on her face showed that her mind had separated from her body, like she had explained.

Arnie picked up his Gladaass and inspected it to be sure it wasn't harmed from the fall. As the girls reached Arnie, Bernadette grabbed Aurelia and shook her a little to break her out of her trance. "Let's rest a minute here, girlfriend, and chat with Arnie."

Aurelia noticed Arnie for the first time. "Oh, hi, Arnie," she said. "I was somewhere off in the distance."

"On another planet is more like it," Bernadette corrected her. "We're ten miles into a twenty-five mile hike and she hasn't said one word, since 'Let's be off then,' back at the dorm."

Bernadette watched Arnie, who was still inspecting his Gladaass. "You couldn't hurt it if you tried. Tinker's been trying to take the darned thing apart for the whole six weeks that we've had them, and he hasn't been able to crack it. He even threw the bleeping thing off the roof of the union." She took Arnie's Gladaass out of his hands, wiped the dust off of it with the butt of her pants, and handed it back to him. "If a four-floor fall won't even scratch it, then your fumble fingers couldn't possibly do anything to it."

Arnie took his Gladaass back and erased the seconds of

the scene of Bernadette's butt rubbing against it. "Thank you, very much," he said.

"So, what are you doing way out here, anyway?" Bernadette asked, sitting down on the grass. She pulled Aurelia down beside her and took off her backpack.

"Cataloging."

"Cataloging what?"

"Everything. It's a hobby of mine to collect images of specimens of everything that I see when I'm studying an area. I've cataloged literally every bug, bat, and rattlesnake back home in Wyoming."

"And so now you're cataloging all the life on the islands of Demeverde?" Bernadette shook her head in amazement. She put her hand in the back pack and asked him, "Got time for an ice cold Doctor Ginger's?" She pulled out three screw-capped bottles still covered with frost. "I froze them in liquid nitrogen before we left." She held all three bottles between the fingers of one hand. "I've got a Frapberry Soda, a Cock-a-doodle Dew, which I'm told tastes just like chicken, even though I can't remember what chicken tastes like, and a Banana Split, which is so cute." She wiggled the bottle. "See, the layers stay separate, even as you drink it."

"Sure," Arnie said. "I'll take the Cock-a-doodle Dew. It's been a while since I had some good chicken."

Bernadette gave him his choice and then held the other two out to Aurelia. "Pick," she demanded. Aurelia picked the Frapberry. "Good choice," she said, "because I really wanted the Banana Split."

They each screwed off the tops, took a long drink, and then looked to read the sayings printed on the insides of the caps.

"What does yours say?" Bernadette asked Arnie.

Arnie looked in his cap and written in a circle was one word. Arnie scrunched up his eyebrows and tried to read it for her. "RUNSUMFORFUN."

Bernadette looked at hers, wrinkled her own brow, and said, "Mine, too." She looked back at Arnie. "Wonder what it means."

"Break it down into smaller words and try it again," Aurelia told them.

"Run - sum - for - fun," Arnie read slowly. Then he put it all together, "Run sum for fun!"

"A fitness wish!" Bernadette said, reading it again. "But they spelled 'some' wrong."

"No, they didn't," Aurelia informed her.

"What? They did, too!" Arnie and Bernadette said, one right after the other.

Aurelia smiled very broadly. "It's sooooooo nice to know something that the two of you don't for a change. Rare as that instance may be."

"So what does it mean?" Arnie asked, again with Bernadette saying each word right after him.

"Stop that!" Arnie scolded her. "It creeps me out."

"Sorry," Bernadette said.

"So what does it mean?" Arnie repeated.

"S-U-M is an acronym for Seven Uncharted Miles."

"Which are?" Arnie asked, once again with Bernadette pathing his words.

"I'm warning you," he playfully scolded Bernadette, again.

"So what are the Seven Uncharted Miles?" Bernadette asked.

Aurelia explained, "Seven miles is the distance across Uncharted Island, where Doctor Ginger sponsors a race the

Thursday after each fall session's mid-terms."

"Oh," Arnie said. This time without Bernadette's echo in his ears.

"Of course, the race is never just seven miles long because there is no footpath that runs straight across Uncharted Island."

"Of course not!" Bernadette exclaimed very quickly, as Arnie started to say the same thing. She looked at Arnie and smiled. "Beat you."

"Bah," Arnie said to Bernadette, turning back to Aurelia. "How do you know so much about this?"

Aurelia answered, "Because Robert and Roberta told me they saw it when their parents brought them here a few years ago." She took another drink from her bottle. "Every deca picks one person to run in the race. We were planning to talk to you about it tonight after dinner."

"Why?"

"Because we want you to be our deca's runner."

"What?" Arnie asked. "Why? Probably more than half the deca can run faster than me." He turned to Aurelia. "You're the runner of our bunch."

"But none of them has a photographic memory," Aurelia told him.

"So, what does my memory have to do with running a race?"

"Because it's not speed in the SUM Run that matters."

"It's not?"

"No." Aurelia explained. "The secret to winning the SUM Run is knowing the shortest and most direct path from one side of the island to the other. The footpaths are so numerous, run so many ways, and have so many dead ends, that the whole island is pretty much one gigantic natural maze."

"Cool," Arnie cooed.

"Cool, indeed," Aurelia agreed. "Especially if you memorize the satellite geological map that everyone gets to see right before the race."

"Aha!" Bernadette said, as Arnie finished the last swallow of this chicken soda. "And so, all Arnie has to do is memorize the map, pick the right path, and then get across the Uncharted Island as fast as he can go."

"Exactly," Aurelia concurred. "As long as he keeps up a decent fast walking pace, he should be able to beat anyone running around trying to guess their way through the maze."

"So, Arnie?" Bernadette asked him. "Are you up to at least walking SUM for fun?"

"I figure I'd be branded a traitor if I don't agree; so, I guess I'll have to try to be the deca's runner." Arnie picked up his Gladaass. "But I'll only do it if you go finish your walk, so I can finish cataloging this side of the island."

* * *

The next day, Arnie's deca finally got to have their first small group discussion with Perfect Sandrahartha Vinhathasarghi. Several of the other decas had already had their first encounters with her. They all said it was a tremendous eye-opening experience, but they couldn't talk about it because she had sworn them to secrecy about the details of what they had learned about her.

The deca assembled in a small discussion room on the third floor of the Student Union. At exactly eleven o'clock the tube door rotated to the inside of the room. Everyone stood up briskly.

Perfect Sandra Vin came into the room and immediately said in a British Indian accent, "For goodness sakes, please, sit down." She was still sitting like she had been during the Parade of the Perfects; squatting on the same leg, on the same stool, with her hands in her sleeves. Except, this time, she was doing it while riding a SlipDisc down the aisle in the middle of the small room. "I'm one of the informal ones Chose told you about."

She was wearing an earplug attached to what looked like a small Gladaass about the size of her earlobe and bobbing her head to the beat of some music. The diminutive lady took one hand out of her opposite sleeve, pulled the plug out of her ear, put it in her pocket, and placed her hand back in her sleeve. "Hi, guys," she said. "I am Sandrahartha Vinhathasarghi, but you probably already know that."

Perfect Vin jumped right into her lesson of the day. "The purpose of this class—" She abruptly stopped and snapped, "Very funny! Mister Shelikhov, but yes, I did hear the pin drop."

Alex gulped.

"Now, please, pick it up."

Alex did as he was told.

"It seems silly that someone with sensory gifts such as yours would feel the need to test me like that."

"Sorry, ma'am," Alex said softly. "Won't happen again."

"It seems that with all your sensorial gifts they just left out plain common sense, does it not?"

"Yes, ma'am," Alex muttered, now thoroughly embarrassed by the excessive attention. "Sorry again." He put the pin in his pocket. "Won't happen again."

"That's okay, Mister Shelikhov, there's one in every

freshman deca."

Perfect Vin started over. "Now, as I was saying, the purpose of this class is to school you in the discipline of physical perfection. By the end of this class we will dispel many myths, biases, and prejudices you may consciously or unconsciously harbor. But, before we can do that, I want you to tell me your perception of physical perfection."

One-word answers came from everyone. "Beauty," Min-su started. "Grace," Amanda added. "Strength," Alex boomed. "Power," Tinker boomed even louder and longer. "Form," Bernadette said. "Stamina," Aurelia declared. "Ability," Arnie contributed. "Fitness," Roberta posited. "Suitability," Robert recommended. "Attractiveness," Hugo suggested.

"All simple answers," Perfect Vin said, "but let's see how they hold up." She took her right hand out of her left sleeve and put it inside the left shoulder of her coat. As she pushed the tunic off, she let her right hand fall straight down to allow the coat fall to the floor.

Several gasps in the room could be heard by anyone, with or without Perfect Vin's and Alex's super sensitive hearing. The Physical Perfect Sandrahartha Vinhathasarghi was much less than anatomically perfect. Her left arm was not much longer than her right elbow and the fingers on her left hand were three nubs on the inside and two stumps on the outside. And she was not sitting with her left leg tucked under her like everyone thought. Her left leg was also a stump about half the length of her right thigh.

"Oh, my goodness! What happened?" Aurelia whispered toward Bernadette.

"Thalidomide, Miss Musyoka," Perfect Vin answered. "Thalidomide happened."

Aurelia swallowed hard, realizing that she, too, had been overheard. "I apologize, Perfect Vin. That was horribly insensitive of me."

"Perfectly all right, Miss Musyoka," Perfect Vin assured her. "It is a common reaction."

"What was Thalidomide?" Tinker asked. "An Indian H-bomb?"

"No, Mister Schocken," she answered looking straight at him. "It was not an Indian H-bomb. By the way, it is a myth that the H-bombs caused birth defects." She looked around the classroom. "Anyone else?" she asked, looking at Arnie for a long second.

Arnie just shook his head as if to beg her to not ask him. He knew the answer, but Bernadette had suggested that he not talk so much in class. Arnie was not doing so well heeding Jacques's advice not to be so much of an almost-know-it-all.

"No takers?" Vin asked. "Okay, then I will explain. Thalidomide was a pharmaceutical, a supposedly safe drug, which well-meaning doctors prescribed in the late nineteen fifties to people as a sedative and to help pregnant women who were suffering from morning sickness. Luckily, when people like me started being born with flippers for arms and legs, governments around the world banned it fairly quickly."

"So it was a bad drug?" Amanda asked.

"Well, like most things in life, whether Thalidomide was good or bad is a matter of perspective."

"How so?" Amanda asked.

"Well, about fifty years later, the doctors discovered other uses for Thalidomide. Using it is fine as long as no one taking it is capable of having children again." She paused for a moment and then explained, "So one extra lesson we all can learn from this is that things we think are safe may not always be safe. And another way to say that lesson is that something that has the power to do great good may also have the same power to do great harm."

"And vice versa," Arnie chimed in.

"And vice versa is right, Mister Carver," Perfect Vin replied. "Yes, the opposite is true. Something, or even someone for that matter, having the power to do great harm or great evil may somehow also be transformed to do great good."

"Hmmm," several of the deca said, while considering the thought.

"But we digress," Perfect Vin said. "We were discussing your concepts of physical perfection. I think we have shown that I do not have what you would consider to be perfect beauty or form." She leaned a little and her SlipDisc moved around behind her desk. "What about strength and power?" She took a round rubber ball out of her drawer. "Mister Shelikhov?"

"Yes, ma'am," Alex answered.

"You seem to be the strongest and most powerful member of this deca."

Alex blushed just a little. "Yes, ma'am," he reluctantly confessed, sure that she was about to prove him wrong.

Perfect Vin tossed him the ball and pointed to the back wall of the room. "Take this hollow rubber ball and throw it against the wall as hard as you can so it will stick to that wall."

Alex threw the ball against the wall and it bounced right back to him.

"Oh, come now, Mister Shelikhov. You throw like a

girl." She smiled, as did most of the deca. "Surely you can throw harder than that."

Alex stood up, took a big wind-up with the ball, and threw it so hard that it popped its seam and fell dead.

"Very good, Mister Shelikhov." Perfect Vin took another ball out of her drawer and started bouncing it off of the wall. As she kept dribbling the new orb back and forth against the walls of the room, she continued lecturing. "So we have seen the application of brute strength and power." She ricocheted the ball off two, then three walls, and, finally, the ceiling and a wall, only to have it to come right back to her hand. "What about using some thoughtful, focused, and non-destructive strength and power?" Perfect Vin threw the ball at the top corner of the back of the room, where it instantly became stuck in the corner, having been squeezed and pinched in there by the force and precision of her throw.

"Wow!" Bernadette exclaimed. "Awesome!" Amanda agreed. "Cool!" Tinker called out.

"So we have seen that Mister Shelikhov has brute strength and used it to accomplish the goal of keeping the ball from coming back at him."

Everyone nodded in agreement.

"And we have seen that I do not have his huge muscles and perfect body, but, by using my ability to focus my power and precisely throw things, I was able to accomplish the same goal of keeping the ball from coming back at me."

Everyone nodded even more.

The lady added, "So that proves what the wise man said. 'Some folks have and some have not, but what matters most is what you do with what you've got.'"

"Unius said that?" Arnie asked.

"No," Perfect Vin answered. "The greatest songwriter of

the twentieth century, Kenny Rogers, said that."

Everyone laughed until Perfect Vin took a third ball out of her drawer. "One more lesson and an exercise, and then, I will let you go for the day." She started bouncing the ball very quickly against the wall. "We all have two types of muscles, which are called fast twitch and slow twitch." She speeded up the bouncing of the ball to the point that it became a colorful blur. "Now, Mister Shelikhov has plenty of bulky slow twitch muscles and I have plenty of fast twitch muscles. So he has plenty of strength." She then caught and held the ball, which was now smoking from the heat buildup of being thrown so much. "But what about speed?" she asked, throwing the ball so quickly that no one saw it leave her hand.

They did, however, hear the pop as the ball blew up in the air above them.

"Hey!" several of the deca yelled in surprise, as the explosion showered them with little pieces of hot rubber.

"Which proves that too much speed can kill."

Perfect Vin pulled herself up onto the empty top of the desk. "Now," she continued with the lesson, "if physical perfection is the discipline of putting whatever you have in your body to its optimal use, then how do you learn to do that?"

"Let me guess," Bernadette answered. "Like any good coach says, you're going to tell us, 'Practice, practice, practice.'"

Perfect Vin patiently smiled. "Close, Miss Rogers. I'm going to tell you to focus and practice using the power of balance and meditation." She turned her right side to face the class. "So, everybody, please, lay facedown on the floor and I will direct you through the positions of my meditative ballet."

"Your what?" Alex asked.

"Just do what I do, Mister Shelikhov, and when you cannot do the next position, just sit and watch."

"Yes, ma'am."

Everyone laid face down on the floor. Perfect Vin described the changing positions as she did them. "Now, for position one, support yourselves on your palms, your forearms, your hips, and your toes."

Everyone copied Perfect Vin's position. Alex spoke up from his side of the room. "Not much balance going on here."

"Silence in the class, please!" Perfect Vin demanded. "But it's nice to know, Mister Shelikhov, that you have been able to at least master the first position."

Several sharers in the deca snickered.

"Now, for the second position. Starting at the bottom, contract your toes, the soles of your feet, your calves, your hips, and your buttocks until your legs are arched up in the air."

With several grunts, all of them were able to get most of the fronts of their thighs off the ground, until Perfect Vin added, "And hold them there for one minute," at which time Alex cried "Argh!" and dropped his toes back down. He was followed a few seconds later by Tinker.

"Guess we'll have to practice a lot," Tinker joked softly with Alex, as they assumed a seated position under Perfect Vin's scornful glare.

"For those of you left," Perfect Vin continued, "the third position. Contract your back muscles to pull your feet higher up in the air and your hips off the floor."

Hugo tried, but finally dropped back down to the first

position and then turned over and sat. With a whole lot of effort, Arnie was finally able to get his hips up enough to rock on his arched stomach, but only because he had bent his knees to get his feet back over his hips. The other six of the sharers, all five girls and Robert Rivers, the most nimble boy, were perfectly arched.

"Now for the hard part," Perfect Vin said. "For position four, contract your shoulders, rotate your shoulder joint, and come up to a headstand on your head and your forearms."

Arnie had silently given up halfway through the explanation and was watching those who were left.

"Nope, can't do that," Robert and Roberta both sighed loudly, collapsing back down to positions two and one.

"Me neither," said Aurelia, coming down as well.

Bernadette, Amanda, and Min-su smoothly executed position four. Amanda whispered to the others. "Lucky we all took gymnastics in elementary school, huh, girls?"

"Quiet. For position five," Perfect Vin instructed, "lift up to a hand stand." This was no problem for the three girls. "And then on one hand."

"Nope," Amanda said, losing her balance.

"Me neither," Min-su said, collapsing as well.

Bernadette shifted her shoulders and moved her left hand out in the air slowly and jerkily back and forth, until, finally, she brought it in line with the rest of her body, which was then centered over her right palm.

As Bernadette was teetering to get her balance, Perfect Vin, who had skipped position four and gone straight to a one handed handstand on her right hand, bent her elbow and lowered herself to change to a one handed handstand on the end of her deformed left arm. "It doesn't matter which hand you pick for position five as long as you pick one of them," she joked. "Now, the next to the last position, position six, is to rock up onto the tips of your fingers."

"No way!" Bernadette yelled, trying to roll just a little forward off of her palm before falling in a jumble of arms and legs.

"Way!" Perfect Vin retorted. She rolled up onto the ends of her two left fingers. "And finally, for position seven you just lean to the outside and balance on your little pinkie finger just like ..." she bent her inner finger, "THIS!"

Everyone in the deca applauded for a few seconds along with a chorus of wows, cools, and awesomes.

Perfect Vin opened her eyes and asked, "Not bad for a sixty-six-year-old gimp from India, is it?"

"She doesn't look a day over forty!" Roberta whispered to Aurelia.

"We age differently on Demeverde," Perfect Vin explained. "The longer we live here, the slower we age." She lowered herself slowly back down through the positions to her forearms, head, chest, hips, legs, and toes. Finally, she finished the lesson. "For each position you achieve, practice holding it, for at least one, but, preferably, five minutes, before moving onto the next one." She climbed back down off the desk and onto her stool, picked up her coat with her right hand and put it on, placed her earplug-sized Gladaass back in her ear, and leaned the SlipDisc toward the door. "I will see you again the week before finals. Until then keep focused and practice the ballet. By the way, since you are the last group of freshman I have to share with, you are not sworn to secrecy about this first class."

She entered the tube door singing, "Love your neighbor as yourself. Don't use money to measure wealth. Trust in God, but lock your door. Buy low, sell high and slow dance more."

UNCHARTED ISLAND

The last Friday before mid-term exams was supposed to be Arnie's weekly think day. He had switched it, however, with his usual leisure day on Sunday, so Émilie could tutor him on the SUM Run. Émilie had not competed in last year's race, but she was very reassuring. She greeted him with a hearty *"Bonjour, mon ami,"* as they met in front of the freshman dorm and stepped on some SlipDiscs.

"Let us say my reconnoitering skills leave a lot to be desired," she told him as they rode to SlipHover Beach. "If it weren't for these things' ability to take me places, I would get lost going from my dorm to the Student Union at least three times every day. But I've talked with a lot of the runners from last year and they gave me plenty of pointers. It's really about seeing where you start and where you have to go, and figuring out the best way to get there."

"Great," Arnie said, with some relief in his voice.

"Of course, it doesn't help things that the undergrowth grows so quickly any footpaths anyone makes last less than a day. That makes it impossible to map the place. Hence the name Uncharted Island."

Arnie repeated himself sarcastically, "Grr-eat. I'm still hesitant about the idea of being the deca's runner for this thing. The Seven Uncharted Miles seems to me to be more than I'm up to in a day."

"Don't worry about it, Arnie. Everyone agrees your ability to see and remember the satellite geological map will give you more of an advantage than any physical abilities some of the others might have."

Arriving at the resort area SlipHover Beach, Émilie and Arnie rode through the beach's sunscreen shower and then traded their SlipDiscs for a larger, more seaworthy version, a SlipHover. They cast off from the western shore of Isla Principal and headed north by northwest for the four-mile journey to Uncharted Island. During the trip, the two of them had plenty of time to talk about the tips that last year's runners had given her. By the time they reached the shallow outer reefs surrounding Uncharted Island, Arnie was feeling chafed by his life preserver and sunburned despite using plenty of sunscreen.

Approaching the island, Arnie noticed a good deal of sea spray coming up off the surface of the water a bit off the shore. He took out the binoculars he had brought with him to get a closer look. "What's all that?" he asked.

"That's spray coming up off the outer reefs that surround the island," Émilie answered him. "The water is so shallow that the only things that can cross them are these SlipHovers. Anything else would get stuck on them."

As they hovered over the reefs, Arnie had Émilie slow the craft and steer it more toward the eastern side of the island to get a closer look at something that seemed strange. Several large, bright red-feathered birds were picking at a very large carcass. One of the birds had an orange blaze of mutated feathers on its tail.

"What kind of birds are those over there?" he asked, pointing to them. "I've never seen so large a carnivorous specimen before."

"Scarlet Vultures," Émilie answered. "They keep the reefs and beaches as clean as a whistle. You've never seen them before because they never fly farther than the outer reefs of Uncharted Island."

"What do they eat?"

"Any animals that wash up on the reefs and beaches or end up dead on the island. What is it they're eating now?"

Arnie peered through his binoculars. "If I didn't know any better, I'd say it was a pile of about three or four Texas longhorn beef." Arnie rubbed his eyes with his hand and looked again. "I wonder how those beef got all the way out here?" He looked at the island's horizon. "Where do the vultures nest?"

"Inside the rim of Mile-Wide Volcano," Émilie answered him. "They like the sulfur there for some reason."

"Where's Mile-Wide Volcano?"

"On the west side of Uncharted Island," Émilie answered turning the SlipHover back north. "Let's pull up on South Beach west of Gaping Canyon and I'll draw you a map and show you."

A few minutes later, Émilie drove the SlipHover onto the pristine, smooth, sandy beach. Arnie grabbed a small cooler, hopped over the edge of the SlipHover with Émilie, and they walked to a shady spot under some huge, dense Sobbing Seawillow trees. Arnie took out two Doctor Ginger's and gave one to Émilie.

"Hope you like Mint Twolip Melon," Arnie said.

"One of my favorites," Émilie smiled. "Though the whole fruit is better than what Doctor Ginger's does with it. There is nothing like ripping apart the two halves by their lips and just sucking out the minty juice from the inside."

Émilie downed the first bottle without stopping and then used the neck of the bottle as a stylus. "Okay, here's the layout of Uncharted Island," she said, drawing in the sand. "First, you draw this big, nearly perfect circle, about seven miles wide, no matter which direction you measure."

"Hence the Seven Uncharted Miles," Arnie added.

"Exactly. Then you draw this little circle dead in the middle. That's Omarosa's Point, the highest point on the island. Are you with me so far?"

"Got it," Arnie said. "A seven-mile-wide circle with a dot in the middle."

"Now," Émilie continued, "treating the island like a big clock, draw one line from one o'clock down to Omarosa's Point and then back out to two o'clock and a second line from eight o'clock up to Omarosa's Point and back out to close to ten o'clock. Got it?"

"Still with you," he told her. "A big wedge here from one to the center and back out to two and a bigger wedge here from eight to Omarosa's Point and back out to close to ten."

"Okay, now draw one circle next to the ocean inside each wedge. The circle from one to two is Too Soon Lagoon and the one from eight to ten is Mile-Wide Volcano, which is one of only two active volcanoes in Demeverde. Still with me?"

"Still with you. Move on." Arnie retraced her circles with his finger.

"Good." She continued to make marks in the sand. "Now, draw a line from Omarosa's Point down to about five-thirty."

"Okay."

"Then start about fifteen minutes back up the shore on each side of where that line hits the beach and draw two more lines parallel to it back up to the sides of Omarosa's Point."

"What's this?" Arnie asked.

"The line in the middle is the Tongue River, whose origin is right below Omarosa's Point and Omarosa's Face, and the two outside lines are the ridges of Gaping Canyon."

"None of this seems too uncharted to me," Arnie said.

"This has been the easy part so far," Émilie insisted. "It only gets worse from here."

"How so?"

"See these three ridges?" Émilie asked, pointing to all of the groups of lines she had just drawn coming out from Omarosa's Point.

"Yeah."

"Well, they define the three uncharted valleys of Uncharted Island. They are very dense with vegetation, which grows so thick and so fast even the wild boars can't keep a footpath clear for a day."

"Wow!" Arnie exclaimed. "That's pretty thick."

"Right," Émilie agreed. "Now this valley north of Gaping Canyon and south of Too Soon Lagoon is the Lush Valley. It has the least vegetation, but it also has quicksand pits that seem to come and go from place to place and a vine lattice that climbs up a sheer cliff."

"I thought that this was not supposed to be a physically trying event," Arnie reminded her.

"It's not rigorous," Émilie replied. "It's just tedious."

"Sure," Arnie mocked. "What's next?"

"The Valley from West of Gaping Canyon to the south of Mile-Wide Volcano is the Lusher Valley, which has denser vegetation." Émilie pointed to the forest of Sobbing Seawillow trees right in front of them. "These Sobbing Seawillows hang their branches so low to the ground that you have to push your way through their limbs again and again, moving from tree to tree, in order to get through them."

"More non-rigorous tediousness, I'm sure," Arnie quipped.

"Right," Émilie said. "Until you get to Mud Meadow."

"Soooooo, where's Mud Meadow?" Arnie asked hesitantly.

"Well, the Sobbing Seawillow Forest only goes half way up Lusher Valley. The rest of it, up to Omarosa's Point, is a forty-five degree incline of moist mud. Again, not rigorous, just tedious." She smiled at Arnie, "And good and dirty."

"Great!" Arnie replied. "If I could just learn to slide uphill."

"Yeah," Émilie joked back. "Now the third valley from the north of Mile-Wide Volcano around to the east of Too Soon Lagoon is called Lushest Valley."

"Because it has the most vegetation?"

"Obviously. But it's not very tall. Just a wall-to-wall

carpet of trapfoot vines."

"Trapfoot vines?"

"Yeah, trapfoot vines. These are very low vines that grow layer by layer on top of each other making a fluffy mass of big slippery leaves. Every time you take a step on them your foot slips down inside the layers and gets trapped. Unless, of course, the trapfoot vines have grown over an entrance to one of the Vineveiled Tunnels."

"The Vineveiled Tunnels?"

"Yeah, the Vineveileds are a group of mud-lined tunnels. They happen to be the fastest way to get from Lushest Valley to the bottom of Omarosa's Face, which is the sheer cliff at the origin of the Gaping Canyon and the Tongue River. So if you step in an entrance to a Vineveiled Tunnel, then your foot isn't going to get trapped. Nor is the rest of your body. You are going to fall through the trapfoot vines and into the tunnel and take the ride of your life to the headwaters of the Tongue River. Of course, you don't want to try and take the easy way out and just ride out on the rapids through the Gaping Canyon because no one from GODA has ever been brave enough to make the trip. So, if you do ride the tunnels you are going to have to scale your way back up one of the walls of Gaping Canyon and then run the ridge out to the coast."

"Still more non-rigorous tediousness?"

"Exactly," Émilie smiled. "But enough of this fun, let's hover around the island and I'll show you a few more things and tell you the SUM Run rules."

"Right, coach," Arnie teased her.

Arnie picked up the other bottles of Doctor Ginger's that they had emptied during her "sand talk." After the two of them got back into the SlipHover, Émilie inflated the craft's apron and nudged the craft back off the beach and into the water.

"We'll just circle the island counterclockwise and I'll show you some more stuff." She pointed back to a steep two hundred foot deep chasm cut into the coast of Uncharted Island. "That is the mouth of Gaping Canyon with the Tongue River running out of it." Moving them directly in front of the canyon, Émilie pointed out to the back of the chasm. "We can just see the top half of Omarosa's face, which," she explained, "is a sheer drop where half of the central mountain was blown away in a volcanic eruption thousands of years ago. Legend has it that the Goddess Omarosa was angry about being stood up at the altar by her beloved intended and blew up the island; but she left her own face in the cliffs. If you ever get a chance to cross the Scenic View Rope Bridge, which crosses the canyon, stop in the middle and you can see all of Omarosa's Face."

They hovered around the eastern side of the island for the next ten minutes past Lush Valley. "Like I said, there are quicksand pits that seem to come and go and move around in the back of Lush Valley. So, if you go through there, be very careful where you step. If you have to go this way, then pick your way through it and climb up Omarosa's Locks. That's the lattice of vines going up the sheer cliffs in the back of the Lush Valley. The locks will take you to Omarosa's Point. Don't worry about falling, because there are auto-belays to use. They won't keep you from falling, but they will lower you to the ground to start over if you slip."

"Great," Arnie scoffed. "I may come in last, but at least I won't die."

"Right, whatever," Émilie said with a blasé tone. She turned the SlipHover into a big, one-mile-diameter lagoon with a sheet of waterfalls coming down in the back of it. "Welcome to Too Soon Lagoon."

"Why is it called that?" Arnie inquired.

"Well, there are two explanations. The first is that the reason Omarosa's intended left her standing at the altar is that she had gotten there a day too soon. The waterfall in the back looks like a big bridal train so it is called the Bridal Train Falls."

"What's the other reason that it's called Too Soon Lagoon?"

"Well, do you see those rapids running down the mountain leading back up to Omarosa's Point?"

Arnie looked up above the falls. "Yeah, so?"

"So, those are the Ten-Turn Terraced Rapids that run back and forth and then spill out into the train. The rapids make ten hairpin turns as they run back and forth. All of the hairpin turns have plenty of roots sticking out from the banks to grasp onto and pull yourself out. The ninth hairpin turn is called Last Chance Grasp, because it is your last chance to get out and climb down the ridge running from the edge of the precipice down to the beach north of the lagoon." Émilie pointed to the beach to their right. "You don't want to miss Last Chance Grasp and take the tenth turn, however, because then there is nothing to do at that point but ride the water train over the edge of the cliff."

"So?"

"So if you were to just ride the train down, the undertow at the bottom would suck you under and your life would be over way 'Too Soon.'"

"That would be bad," Arnie deadpanned.

"Very bad," Émilie agreed, "but there are two ways to survive the fall."

"And they are?" Arnie asked. "Just in case." He smiled mischievously.

"Well, the first way is to hang back just a little bit before you go over the edge. Hanging back a second will make you fall through the top of the train and you will end up on the back side of the train and the undertow. Then you have to swim back to the shore and walk around and outside either edge of the train. It's the safe way over, but having to climb around on the rocks back there takes way too long and whoever does it never wins the race."

"And the second way?"

"As you come to the precipice of the top of the train, push off from the lip as hard as you can and dive out as far as you can to get out into the lagoon away from the undertow. If you do it, then you'll overshoot the undertow and catch the express current out to the reef at the mouth of Too Soon Lagoon."

Arnie was shocked. "And the school allows runners to do that?"

"No, silly," Émilie explained. "There's a huge cargo net across the rapids before the top of the falls. If you miss Last Chance Grasp, then the cargo net will catch you. You'll have to climb it, get over to the edge, and walk down to the beach. Once again, you're safe, but no one who has ever had to use the net has ever won the race because it takes so long."

Arnie looked as his watch. "Speaking of taking so long," he informed her, "we need to be heading back to GODA."

"Okay," Émilie said, turning the SlipHover into the express current flowing straight out from the falls.

"Whoa!" Arnie said, feeling them slipping into the speeding water.

"Tell me about it," Émilie replied. "See how fast the

express current flows?"

They exited Too Soon Lagoon and turned northwest. A few minutes later Émilie turned the SlipHover back pointing toward Uncharted Island. The entire Lushest Valley was covered in a medium-green, shiny velvet of growth.

"Those are the Trapfoot Vines of Lushest Valley. Like I said, you want to be very careful where you step because, if you don't, then you will end up in the headwaters of Tongue River."

"That would be bad?"

"No, that would be good, because it is the fastest way out of the Lushest Valley."

"So that would be good?"

"No, that would be bad." Émilie smiled at him. "Because then you have to rock climb back up Omarosa's Face to get to Omarosa's Point."

"Why would anybody do that?"

"Because the SUM Run Rules say that everybody has to cross Omarosa's Point and pick up the bottle of Doctor Ginger's there with their deca's name on it."

Arnie and Émilie traveled a few minutes more around the west side of the island. Arnie noticed steam rising out of Mile-Wide Volcano and more steam rising out of the dark beach below it.

"Why is the beach so dark here?" Arnie asked.

"That's Black Sand Beach. As lava slowly works its way out from Mile-Wide Volcano it hits the water and crystallizes into black sand. If you look closely, you'll see some blow holes, which are tunnels in the lava the surf crashes up through as it hits the beach."

"Cool," Arnie replied, seeing some water shoot up in a fountain. He looked through his binoculars up at the rim and saw several nests of Scarlet Vultures appearing to enjoy skulking in the vapors of sulfur rising around them. "That's a lot of vultures up there."

"Hundreds of them," Émilie explained. "But they never leave Uncharted Island."

Émilie turned the SlipHover out toward the reef surrounding the island. As they crossed over the reefs on the way back to GODA, Arnie noticed some more vultures eating some more beef carcasses snagged by the reef.

"Still, I wonder how those beef got here?" he asked a second time.

"Beeves me," Émilie jokingly answered him.

Arnie laughed and followed her lead. "Very punny."

Émilie asked, "So how's the coco practice coming?"

"Everyone's mastered the basics of the game. We're starting to work on strategies for positioning players around the valley to get the coco to the goal as quickly as possible. We've had a few friendly scrimmages with some other freshman decas and we're holding our own pretty well."

"Good," she said with a smile.

"Except when we got a little cocky and asked a sophomore deca to get out of a valley."

"What happened?" she asked.

"Well, we thought we could just tell the sophomores that we wanted to practice and have priority like Chose said we could."

"But?"

"But H.M. Crist made us play his deca a game first in order to get control of the valley. The fourteen minute ten-to-two drubbing did nothing for our self esteem."

Émilie snarled, "Just like H.M. to pull a stunt like that."

* * *

Arnie got back to the dorm just in time to change for coco practice. After getting cleaned up from another pickup game of coco with some other freshmen, the deca was enjoying its usual early evening jam session in the "Pit," which is what they had come to call the semi-circular grouping of cheds in the gathering space of their apartment. Most everyone would scour the virnews programs from their Gladaasses for good things that had happened in the outside world and Hugo would mock them and balance the joviality, by finding all of the bad things that were going on.

"Uh-oh," Hugo said, in a way that had become all too familiar an indication of his success.

"What now?" several of the deca asked simultaneously.

"Unius, we have a problem," Hugo said, as if he was talking to the big man himself.

"What?" the chorus responded in their familiar ritual.

Hugo read the story from the virnews service. "Dateline – Genoa, Italy. Amid concerns that a number of beef cows from Scorsos International Foods' American beef feeder lots being shipped to Scorsos's European farms have died during transit, governmental health authorities have quarantined the feeder cattle stock of the European farms subsidiary of Scorsos International Foods. The dead cows may have been infected with Mad Cow disease."

"In a related story in Venice, Italy," Hugo continued, "a third child has come down with what is apparently now a world-wide epidemic of juvenile variant Creutzfeldt-Jakob Disease. As have the first two children to be stricken with this disease in Argentina and France, the girl, who is ill with similar signs and symptoms in Venice, recently traveled for a holiday vacation last winter in the tropical vacation resort on Isla Principal, Demeverde."

"In a final related story," Hugo went on, "T.D. Miller Pharmaceuticals has announced progress at reversing the prion folding process thought to be responsible for neurological symptoms in diseases like Creutzfeldt-Jakob disease. Though Miller's research has been limited to young rat-tailed mice, the results are very promising that a cure for the disease can be had in less than ten years."

"My goodness," Roberta said, "GODEnt's public relations are going to have a mad cow themselves when they read this."

"Yes," Robert agreed with his sister. "One kid who had been here is interesting and two is a coincidence, but three is the start of a very bad trend."

"At least someone is trying to do something about it," Tinker added. He looked at Arnie. "Arnie, isn't T.D. Miller the maker of VirtuComp? That's probably why they haven't sent anything back to me on my improvements for their hologame system. They're too busy working on medical stuff."

"I don't know, Tink," Arnie answered. "I haven't been following them very closely for a while. I've been too busy studying here." Arnie tried to show no reaction to the mention of one of his companies.

Bernadette looked straight at him, with a suspicious look on her face and said, "Yeah, way too busy indeed."

* * *

Sure enough, GODEnt's public relations spokespeople were on the story almost as soon as it hit the virnews.

Paula Poundsand, GODEnt's Vice-President of Communications, handled the interview herself. "There is still no clear correlation between these unfortunate children's travels to Demeverde's resorts at separate times, several years apart, and their development of whatever similar signs and symptoms they may be suffering," she claimed in a virtual press conference. "We understand that all of the children were known to be big meat eaters," she explained. "At this point in time, it is just as likely they contracted their diseases from eating contaminated meat from Scorsos International Foods, which controls over half the animal products market worldwide, as it is their disease has anything to do with traveling to Demeverde."

THE TUMBLE IN THE JUNGLE

While they obviously had not taken anyone by surprise, mid-term exams seemed to come too soon at GODA. None of the freshmen sharers could believe that the first eight weeks of their first session was already over.

The Heritage Program mid-term on Monday was one question long, but allowed the equivalent of twenty screens of their Gladaasses to answer. The question read:

> The Heritage Program is designed to encourage you to explore many of the creative works, seminal ideas, pivotal events, and fateful problems that have shaped the human experience from prehistoric times to the present. Why is this important?

Arnie wrote several pages discussing how the perspectives from Europe, Asia, Africa, and the Americas were helping the sharers to define the origins and natures of the heritages of the West, while learning to appreciate cultural diversity and recognize shared humanity.

He added that taking the course made the sharers more able to comprehend the interwoven dynamics driving the world they were inheriting and in which they would soon be working as active participants shaping the future. Arnie explained how the course allowed the sharers to interpret contradictory evidence and conflicting perspectives to understand and defend their own interpretations of past events, wrestle with their own prejudices and biases, and make effective use of an expanded knowledge base that was making the sharers keenly aware of the intricate pattern of events which, when woven together, produced the tapestry of human existence.

Arnie further explained that developing such a historical consciousness was crucial to understanding the achievements, problems, and challenges of the modern world. Only by being able to hear the different voices in history, Arnie surmised, and by appreciating the rival perspectives within the Western tradition and in other traditions around the world, he wrote, would the sharers of GODA, as the next wave of world leaders, be able to heighten their global and multi-cultural awareness.

Finally, Arnie summed up his answer, respecting and embracing the entirety of the world's philosophies and religious aspects challenged the sharers to make value judgments and decisions in a more reflective way, which was crucial to their development as critical thinkers, who would soon be leading peoples around the globe.

Arnie could not have been prouder of his answer, until he discussed it with Bernadette in the pit Monday night. Bernadette said, "I wrote at least twice as much."

Tuesday's Science and Technology midterm was also one question.

> Query: Whether man has made greater scientific and technological progress in times of minimal or maximal protection of intellectual property, such as by legal patents and closely guarded trade secrets? Choose one side of the debate and support it completely.

Arnie explained to Bernadette how he wrote another ten pages arguing that the greatest technological advances were made in an open environment without worrying about intellectual property protection. Bernadette told him that she had written eighteen pages arguing that free markets and the ability to control one's inventions for profit led to the increased speed of advancements so far in the early twenty-first century.

Wednesday's Basic Secular Knowledge midterms covered what was now known to the sharers as "the kitchen sink". Anything that was not covered in Heritage or Science and Technology got lectured on in Basic Secular Knowledge. The midterms for each area were a hundred multiple-choice questions. Arnie didn't mind showing off his photographic memory to Bernadette by recounting each question for their post mortem discussion. Bernadette didn't mind telling Arnie that many of his answers, on topics that he had not bothered reading the class materials about, might have been wrong.

Finally, midterms were over. The next day would be the Seven Uncharted Mile Run. Almost the entire GODA campus had been partying since five o'clock that afternoon, after the last test in Basic Secular Knowledge; except for each deca's designated runners. They were forced by the rest of their decas to go home early to bed. The festivities, however, were almost beyond compare. Dinner and desert had never been so lavish. Then nine-man teams played an intramural double elimination coco tournament, which ended up with the Green Apple Army, coached by Émilie, playing H.M.'s Hummers, coached by her nemesis, H.M. Crist.

"Isn't it just like him," Émilie humpfed, "to name his deca after himself?"

All of the Green Apple Army, except for Arnie, of course, swore to avenge their maiden Émilie's displeasure and hummed the Hummers ten-to-six after two and a half periods. After the coco games, most of the GODA students enjoyed the free admission to Midnight Madness at Global World. Finally, at about three in the morning, everyone went to their dorms and corkscrewed their SlipDiscs back up to their apartments for a few hours of sleep, before the SUM Run's scheduled start, at ten o'clock the next day.

At eight in the morning, a general alarm was played inside and outside of every building on GODA's campus. Avramel Kimvelevitch had set up a Gladaass broadcasting virtual experience, where every Gladaass on Demeverde could receive a live feed of the day's activities emceed by "Avi Kaye" as he called himself.

"GOOOOOOOOOOOOOOOOOOOOOOOOOOOD MORRRRRRRRRRRRRRRRRRNNNNNING!!! DEMEVERRRRRRRRRRRRRRRRDE!!!!" Avi screamed in all of his virjected glory. "Two hours until the SUM Run begins. So get up, get out, put on that sunscreen, strap on those life vests, grab a SlipHover, and get yourself out to your deca's starting point on Uncharted Island."

Except for Arnie, who had slept like a lamb, the rest of

the deca was pretty bleary-eyed. As they left the apartment and stepped onto some SlipDiscs on the SlipScrew, Arnie said again, "I wish you guys would have picked someone else for this, but I'll do the best I can with it."

Alex replied for the rest of them, "As tired as we all are, in our present conditions, no one in the deca would do better than you."

"I told you guys not to stay out all night," Arnie said to them.

At half past eight, everyone began traveling north to Uncharted Island. Everyone but Arnie carried a collection of signs and banners to decorate the deca's SlipHover a bright green apple hue for the day.

"So, this is what you all were doing all night?" Arnie asked them.

"Nah," Hugo answered him. "This is just what we were doing between nine and ten before we went to the park."

They all took turns holding the decorations as everyone went through the sunscreen showers at SlipHover Beach.

At nine o'clock, a virjection of Avi's face and voice, showing him walking around the beaches of Uncharted Island came up loudly out of every Gladaass around, especially loudly from the fifty-foot Gladaasses that had been set up on all of the public beaches around Demeverde.

"HELLLLLLLOOOOOOOOOOOOOOOOOOOOOOOO!!! DEMEVERRRRRRRRRDE!!!!! Avi Kaye here, with the latest and greatest scoop on the Demeverde SUM Run for the Global Optimum Development Academy. We are broadcasting at this moment from Black Sands Beach on Uncharted Island. As you can see, ..." Avi pointed to a row of pairs of flags, one red and one green, stuck in the sandy beach disappearing around the island. "Both the start and the

finish lines surround the entire island. It will be an exciting
event indeed as the champion runner of each deca at GODA
starts at their deca's green flag on one side of Uncharted
Island, travels to Omarosa's Point to pickup their deca's two-
liter bottle of Doctor Ginger's Naturally Carbonated Fruit-
Flavored Drink, and then finishes the race by delivering their
bottle to their deca's bonfire picnic on the exact opposite
side of Uncharted Island from where they began."

A satellite camera raced through several fast-forwarded
trips across the island at different angles, as Avi continued,
"Each race route has been chosen for a particular class of
decas based on that route's level of difficulty. Senior sharers
run level four difficulty routes and so on down to the level one
routes designed for our inexperienced freshman runners."

Someone's hand appeared in the virjection and gave Avi
the wrap it up sign. He began to finish the segment. "Okay,
I am told that we have to go now to our next location, which
will be from Omarosa's Point, right before the race. Until
then, remember, this has been Avi Kaye for G-O-D-A."

Émilie was already waiting for the deca as they emerged
from the sunscreen showers in the resort area. *"Bonjour, mes
amis,"* she called from a hovering craft.

The deca quickly adorned it with their respendent green-
colored decorations. They pushed off from SlipHover Beach
on the eastern side of Demeverde and headed north with
the rest of the four hundred deca's making the same trip.
Arnie asked Émilie, "What's this about having to go over
Omarosa's Point and get a Doctor Ginger's for the deca?"

"Didn't we discuss that last week?" she asked
beguilingly.

"NO!" Arnie said emphatically. He was curious what
else she had left out.

"You must have just forgotten it," she insisted with a wry smile toward the others. "Are you nervous or something?"

"No, … well, … maybe a little."

"Oh, well," Émilie sighed, reaching in the cooler beside her and pulled out a large bottle of green drink. "Then a key point is that you have to cross Omarosa's Point and pick up this two-liter of Doctor Ginger's, which we are all going to autograph for you for good luck."

"Anything else that you failed to mention?"

"Arnie," Émilie said with an exasperated sigh. "I know we talked about all of this. Just relax."

"Anything else?"

"Just the opposite side of the island stuff that Avi Kaye talked about. We will have our pre-SUM Run party at our deca's green flag as soon as we find it. Five minutes before the race, they will broadcast the live satellite view of Uncharted Island for five minutes. When the race starts, the only thing that you will be able to take with you is a miniature Gladaass, which sends your location to the global positioning satellite and shows everyone else's location but yours on the island. Of course, the Gladaass doesn't show any details about the island once the race starts. It just shows the island as a circle, Omarosa's Point as an X and all of the players as little dots running around the circle."

"Well, what good is that?" Arnie asked.

"Well, first of all, your Gladaass transmitting your position is a safety feature so that we can come find you after the race if you don't show up by the end of six hours."

"Well, that would be good," Arnie said.

"Yes," Émilie agreed. "And being able to see how the rest of the runners are doing will help you know how fast or slow you are going. If you look up and see you're close to

Omarosa's Point and not too many other dots are near there, then you know you're ahead of the pack. If a lot of dots are moving away from Omarosa's Point and you haven't made it there yet, then you know you need to really pick up your pace."

"Sounds logical," Arnie said. "Anything else?"

"No, that's about it," Émilie answered.

About fifteen minutes later, Émilie steered them over the reefs surrounding Uncharted Island and turned to circle it to east. Émilie then yelled, "Okay, everyone, stand up and start scanning the beach with your binoculars for the deca's start or finish flag. You're looking for either a red or a green flag that has a big two and a twelve on it."

The looking was good, but the findings were sparse for a long time. With one pair of flags about every three hundred feet of shoreline, it took a while to cover a substantial part of the island.

Finally, Alex, who was not using any binoculars, called out "Flag ho!" from the front of the boat.

"RED OR GREEN?" Émilie yelled over the noise of the wind and the surf, looking directly inland from them.

"RED," Alex yelled back.

Everyone else was scanning the shore right beside them and complaining that they could not see the flag.

"POINT," Émilie demanded.

Alex pointed way off at the farthest point to the north where the beach could be seen bending around the northeast side of the island.

"Oh, no!" Émilie cried out.

"What?" the chorus asked at varying pitches and paces.

"Keep pointing, Alex," Émilie requested, heading the SlipHover around the eastern edge of the island.

Arnie stepped back up beside Émilie. "What is it?" he asked.

"Don't worry, Arnie. We can work around it."

"Work around what?"

Émilie didn't answer him. She just kept moving the SlipHover more to the north and west.

Finally, several more of the deca called out that they saw the flag, too. Arnie trained his binoculars where everyone else was looking and eventually spotted it.

"What's wrong with that?" Arnie asked.

"Just wait, Arnie, and you'll see," Émilie told him. "But don't worry, we can work around it."

They were getting fairly close to the flag when everyone realized they were running out of beach to the west of them.

"Don't worry about what?" Arnie asked. "We can work around what?"

Émilie turned the boat to face straight into the shore so Alex's extended arm was pointing from the front of the boat, right at the red flag. "We can work around that," she said.

Arnie thought that she was talking about having to work around the flag being well off the beach and stuck in a reef bowing out from the shore. "So we have to meet up on a reef, that's not a big deal." Arnie was pointing his hand at the flag like Alex was.

"Not that," Émilie said, moving his hand a few inches higher. "That!"

Arnie readjusted his sight and, finally, and shockingly, realized that his deca's finish flag was planted on the reef squarely in the gate of Too Soon Lagoon and right in the middle of the express current coming from Omarosa's Bridal Train Falls.

"Oh-my-gosh!" Bernadette bellowed. "You have to come out here?"

"Don't worry," Émilie tried to reassure them all. "We can work around this." She turned the craft back parallel to the shore and pushed it to full speed to get them to the exact opposite side of Uncharted Island.

Émilie piloted the SlipHover in silence until they reached the other side. Alex again was the lead bloodhound for the start flag and they found it very quickly this time.

Émilie beached the SlipHover right by their start flag. Everyone looked straight up off the point of the craft and right up the middle of Lusher Valley.

It was nine forty-five. Ten minutes until the viewing of the live satellite geological map of Uncharted Island. Émilie began drawing the same map in the sand that she and Arnie had completed the Friday before, except she was not talking at all and adding a lot more detail this time.

"Arnie!" Émilie called him over. "Put your photographic memory to use over here and let's do a little last minute planning."

"Right, Coach," Arnie said. He was quite a bit more nervous than he was letting on.

Everyone gathered around the two of them to hear Émilie's pep talk.

"Now, here," Émilie started, pointing to the middle of the shore of Lusher Valley, "is where you are going to start." She then looked Arnie in the eye. "Now the computer picked this angle as a level one, so there must be something pretty easy about being right in the bottom of Lusher Valley. I'd be willing to bet that it's going to be something like a boar trail right up the lowest part of the valley straight up to Mud Meadow." Émilie drew a line straight in from the coast up the middle of the valley.

"A boar trail?" Arnie asked.

"Yeah, the wild boars are so low to the ground that they can scoot pretty much right under the lower tips of the Sobbing Seawillow branches. They hate walking off balance, so they probably have a straight shot through the bottom of the valley to the coast. That way, when they are done baking themselves silly in a trough in Mud Meadow, they can just walk down to the coast and wash themselves off."

"Uh, Émilie?" Arnie asked her.

"Yeah?"

"Did we talk about any wild boars last week when we were here?"

Émilie thought for a long second. "Uh, I think so. If not, then I guess it must have slipped my mind."

"Do you have any concern about the fact that there might be a wild boar on that trail right up the middle of Lusher Valley?" Arnie asked.

"No," Émilie retorted, "but, then again, I'm not running this race, am I?"

"So should I be concerned about the fact that there might be a wild boar on that trail right up the middle of Lusher Valley?" Arnie asked.

"You might be," Émilie smiled, "but you shouldn't be."

"Why not?"

"Because they are just wild boars."

"That's just it, Émilie," Bernadette butted in. "They are 'wild' boars."

"Yeah," Émilie smirked, "but just because they are wild doesn't mean that they are hazardous."

"Why not?" Arnie asked.

"Because they are non-carnivorous wild boars. They are

herbiboars, herbivorous boars, and they only eat the redberry truffles that grow around the mossy trunks of the Sobbing Seawillow trees. If you come up on one, then move laterally up the hill and that fat lazy boar will go right on past you."

"Speaking of fat lazy bores," Amanda said from the back of the pack, "here comes one right now."

"What are you talking about?" Roberta asked.

Amanda pointed to her right. "There's H.M. Crist over there at that flag. He's the biggest fat lazy bore I've ever seen in my life."

H.M.'s Hummers were quickly setting up for the start of the race. "Great!" Émilie exclaimed with anger. "What else can go wrong?" She peered over to see what they were doing. "Who's running for the Hummers?"

"Cravath Swainmore," Alex answered, looking across at them. "And from the looks of the diagram that H.M. is drawing on the side of their SlipHover, they are having pretty much the same talk we are."

Émilie turned her attention back to Arnie and the map.

"Look, just be careful of anything that Cravath tells you. If the apple doesn't fall too far from the tree over there, then you can categorize almost anything coming out of Swainmore's mouth as a lie."

"Doesn't that violate the nonimposition code?" Robert asked.

"We are not here to debate ethics at the moment, Robert." Émilie snapped. "We are here to win or at least beat the Hummers." Her attitude had now completely changed.

Before anyone could try to calm Émilie back down, Avi's voice and face popped up out of all of the Gladaasses set up around the beaches on Uncharted Island. "Just here to remind everyone, the satellite geological preview will be in five minutes, which is plenty of time for a Doctor Ginger's Naturally Carbonated Fruit-Flavored Drink."

"Now," Émilie demanded everyone's attention, "if we can get back to business here." She pointed to Omarosa's Point. "Once you get to Omarosa's Point, you are going to have to make a judgment call."

"How so?" Arnie asked.

"If you have a good lead," Émilie expounded, "then take the slow but safe route walking around to the north of Hot Spring Pools which are the headwaters of the Ten-Turn Terraced Rapids and the Bridal Train Falls. If you do that then you will eventually end up on the ridge looking down on Last Chance Grasp. From there you can scale down the rocks to the edge of Lushest Valley, scoot down to the beach, and run out along the reef to meet us in the middle of the gate to Too Soon Lagoon."

Émilie pointed to the area on the map and traced the desired path. "If you are running late, however, then you are going to have to risk running the rapids and get out at Last Chance Grasp. It's faster than walking around on the ridge." Émilie looked back up at Arnie. "Do not forget everything we discussed last Friday about what to do if things go wrong up there. Finish first if all goes well, but at least finish alive if it doesn't. Okay?"

"No argument here," Arnie assured her. "Arriving alive is always a key thing with me."

"Good. Now everybody put a hand in." Émilie stuck her hand in the middle of the grouped deca and everyone put one of his or her hands in on a pile. "Okay, the 'Green Apples Win!' on three. One, two, —"

Bernadette put her hand up and stopped them. "No, wait, wait, wait!"

"What?" Arnied asked.

Bernadette grabbed Arnie's pinkie with her thumb and stuck her own out to Hugo beside her and demanded, "Everyone, grab the next guy's pinkie and make a ring."

Hugo protested, "Oh-my-gosh. Only a girl could—"

Bernadette glared at him. "Shut up and hook up!" she yelled

"Whatever," Hugo relented

Arnie looked at Bernadette and asked, "Are you ready now?"

"Well, 'Green apples win' doesn't really do it for me. Can we yell 'Pinkie-Power!' instead?"

Hugo tried to extricate his thumb from Bernadette's curled pinkie and objected, "NO! I am not saying that."

"Fine. 'Green apples win' on three then," she agreed, looking around and winking at the other girls in the deca, who were spread out every other person around the ring. Before Arnie could say anything, she quickly added, "One, two, three,"

"GREEN APPLES WIN!" Everybody yelled at the top of their lungs.

The girls held their grips on the guys, added, "With pinkie-power!" and then tossed the guys' hands down.

Hugo looked at the girls exasperatedly.

Bernadette cocked her head under the approving glance of her decasisters. "Don't tell us women, no."

"Let's go," Émilie said. She walked over and took the two-liter bottle of Doctor Ginger's Green Apple Cider out of the SlipHover and an indelible pen out of her pocket. She held the bottle up for Arnie to see. The fluorescent green liquid could be seen for a mile. "Just in case it helps, this is the color of Doctor Ginger's that you are going to be looking for on Omarosa's Point. Grab it and don't lose it, because you can't win without it."

"Right, Coach," Arnie said.

"Everyone but Arnie needs to sign the bottle so we can give it to the race workers for delivery to Omarosa's Point," Émilie told them all.

Avi came back on the Gladaasses. "HELLLLOOOOOO! DEMEVERDE! Avi Kaye here for G-O-D-A and the Doctor Ginger's RunSUMForFun Seven Uncharted Miles Race. As we've explained earlier, the object of the SUM Run is ...." Avi explained all of the rules of the game that Émilie had just reviewed with the deca. "Aaaaaannnnnnd now, the moment that everyone has been waiting for. For the next five minutes we will display a live satellite geological survey image of Uncharted Island. Runners, plot your paths and good luck. This should be SUM kind of run."

No one appeared to get Avi's pun, nor did they care to. Émilie and Arnie started going over the map.

"Okay, I've got it memorized," Arnie said.

"That fast?" Émilie asked.

"That fast."

"Okay, so let's go over it for a while, so I can show you some things that you can do with it."

"Okay, Coach," Arnie trumped up some enthusiasm for her.

Émilie pointed to their starting point. "See us here?" She asked.

"Yes."

"Good, start here, and as best you can, make your way low under the tips of the Sobbing Seawillows staying in the bed of the Lusher Valley." She pointed to what looked like a bunch of lines etched in Mud Meadow. "See this stuff that looks like chicken scratch here?"

"Yes."

"Well those are ridges between the mud ponds. Memorize where they run, because they are the hardest rock that is just covered with about one inch of mud. The mud on the ridges cakes and cracks in the sun and the ridges look like this. But," Émilie added, "if it rains a little, like it's forecasted to do around eleven or noon, then the cracks are going to go away and the entire Mud Meadow is going to look just the same. If you walk on the ridges, then you will be able to leave anybody else not following directly behind you, way behind you."

"Right, Coach," Arnie said to her suggestion.

Émilie then pointed to the steep side of the hill leading down from Last Chance Grasp to the edge of Lushest Valley. "See these outcroppings of rock?"

"Yes."

"They are going to look different from the ground than they do here. But if you memorize them, you can just jump the six feet or so down from one to the other and get down to the edge of Lushest Valley faster than mere mortals."

Just then Avi's face and voice came back out of the Gladaass. "Time is up, guys and gals. This is Avi Kaye here again for the Doctor Ginger's SUM Run. ARE YOU READY FOR THE TUMMMMBLLLLLLLLE IN THE JUNGLLLLLLLLE?!!!!!"

Approximately four thousand usually restrained, but now screaming, teenagers yelled, "YES!" all the way around the island.

Avi's head rocked back at the noise, to which he replied, "All right then!" Before anyone could say anything else, he let loose an unexpected and very quiet, "Let's get ready, set, go."

A huge horn set up at Omarosa's Point sounded and the runners started scurrying inland. Everyone else got back on their decorated SlipHovers and headed to set up camp for the lunchtime barbecues that they had planned at their designated finish lines.

Hovering past the rest of Arnie's deca, H.M. Crist yelled over to Émilie, "Your poor little orphan will have his hands full with Cravath Swainmore. I trained him myself. It'll take a lot more than just memorizing the island to beat him."

"Hammond Milo," Émilie started. She knew H.M. hated to be called by his full name. "You couldn't train a man to pour water out of a boot, even if you put the directions on the bottom of the heel."

Everyone in Émilie's SlipHover laughed as H.M. seriously thought about the insult and acted like he was pouring water out of a boot. Finally, he got the joke. "Very funny, Émilie Chanel," he said. "See you at the edge of Too Soon Lagoon."

Arnie started running along the beach away from the starting place of H.M.'s Hummers. He had noticed on the satellite map several slivers of dirt were visible between the bushy Sobbing Seawillows just west of the middle of Lusher Valley. Rather than shoot up the entire middle of the valley on his stomach, like Émilie had suggested, he figured out his first shortcut. He could get a faster start making an end run and threading betwixt and between the trees to the west to end back up in the center of the valley halfway through the Sobbing Seawillow Forest.

Every time that Arnie made a turn around a tree, he stopped and closed his eyes to recall from his memory the satellite map he had only gotten to study for the same five minutes as every one else. The Sobbing Seawillow trees stood about forty feet tall and their limbs began to come off the trunk about a foot off the ground. The lower limbs seemed to grow out horizontally with twists and interlocking turns so that trying to climb through them seemed perilously difficult. The long compound branches at the ends of the limbs held lengthy stems of long, sturdy, and sharp leaves hanging down forming a shell of layers of leaves over the twisted spiny limbs of the interior.

After the fifteenth turn around the outside edge of the first thinner group of trees, closer to the shore and west of the center of the valley, Arnie lost count. Was it the sixteenth turn? Arnie couldn't quite remember. Regardless of which turn it was, Arnie had somewhat lost his bearings. "Come on, Arnie Carver," he whispered out loud to himself. "Relax, don't panic, and work through this." He was on a flat plateau and could not figure out which direction was north toward the top or east toward the middle of Lusher Valley.

He tried to look up the hill to find Omarosa's Point, but all he could see was a wall of Sobbing Seawillow leaves all around him. He looked up in the sky to locate the sun, but the gaps between the trees were too narrow.

Arnie stopped for a minute and looked at his Gladaass while he thought about a way to get his bearings. Many of the dots, representing everyone but him, seemed to be getting closer to the X in the middle than he thought he was. He started talking to himself again. "If I don't figure out which way is north pretty soon and move east to the middle of Lusher Valley, I may as well give up on winning this race." He pondered his situation lost in the Sobbing Seawillows for a moment. "I guess my only choice is to climb inside a tree, feel for the moss, and figure out which is the north side of the tree."

Looking around and hoping for someone else to come walking through, he finally gave in. "Here goes nothing," Arnie said, with a sigh to no one at all, getting down on his belly to scoot under the ends of the branches of leaves hanging down from the outside of the tree. Once he was about halfway inside, the branches thinned in number and thickened in size toward the trunk. It was pretty dark and the only light was some faint sky visible from above.

And then Arnie felt it and smelt it. Hot breath and a sweet dirty smell with a hint of fruitiness. The grunt that came from right in front of his face clinched it for him. Arnie was face to face in the dark with a Demeverdan Wild Boar. His eyes could barely make out the pug-faced visage, which was no more than six inches from his.

"Go on, shoo," he told the boar. But it just stood there and grunted. "Go on, back up, and get out of the way," he said to it, but the boar held its ground.

Arnie tried moving to either side, but he could not because of the snarl of dry thick limbs around him. The boar moved forward and squealed. Arnie couldn't understand the boar any better than it could understand English. He asked it, "So, is that an angry squeal because I'm blocking your way or a friendly squeal because you're looking for company to share a mouthful of redberry truffles." Then he asked it rhetorically, "Where on earth is Min-su when I need her?" The boar began to paw the ground between them. "Well, regardless of whether you're angry or not, I'm not about to stay here to find out." He reached up into the thicket of limbs above him. "If left, right, front, back, and down are out of the question," he told himself, "then the only alternative is to climb up in the branches."

Arnie slowly and carefully reached up and pulled himself up a branch or two, which got him about waist-high up in the tree. He felt, smelt, and just barely saw the boar pass under him. He started to climb back onto the ground, until he heard a few more boars routing around the base of the tree and tearing the moss off the trunk to get to the redberry truffles. "Oh, well," he said, again to no one in particular, because no one else was there, "nothing ventured, nothing gained."

Pulling himself along the limbs of the tree, Arnie felt for larger ones to know that he was still heading for the middle and the trunk. Finally, reaching the trunk, he could faintly make out the snorting boars routing around a few feet below him. He reached down all sides of the trunk to see if any moss was left that could clue him in about which way was north. "Rats!" he whispered to himself. "They picked the trunk clean."

Having no choice now but to get moving and get moving quickly, Arnie decide to climb the Sobbing Seawillow tree and see if he could spot Omarosa's Point. Pulling himself higher and higher into the tree, Arnie started waving with the trunk as the wind and the light both became more pronounced and the trunk became less so. Finally, Arnie was sitting on the last horizontal branch in the top of the tree and he still could not see past the skin of long stems and sharp leaves covering the outside. Slowly and carefully, Arnie pulled his feet up onto the last branch and stood up to poke his head out of the small opening in the dead center of the top of the Sobbing Seawillow. Holding onto the last thin spike of the central trunk of the tree, Arnie yelled "Eureka!" looking over the last half of the forest straight at Omarosa's Point. A split second later, he painfully remembered the first lesson of tree climbing, which his father had taught him in his backyard in

Wyoming many years ago. Never put both feet or both hands on the same limb of a tree.

"YIPE!" he yelled.

SNAP! SWOOSH! WHACK! THUMP! CRACK! SCRATCH! Arnie made these and about twenty other sounds as he fell straight down the side of the trunk and broke off every limb on the entire side between the top and the ground. Every boar routing around the trunk ran out under the bottom branches to get out of the way. THUD! Arnie, once again, proved that gravity still worked well, as he found the ground. Scathed but unbroken, he looked up from lying on his back and saw a clear opening in the tree where he had fallen. Having so clearly marked the side of the tree, Arnie had at least determined Omarosa's Point was pretty much due north and the center of Lusher Valley was to his left.

Arnie rolled over and scooted on his belly under limb after limb, until he felt the ground dip beneath him and start to go up again. He backtracked just a little and turned to his left. "Now," he quietly told himself, "head due north up the middle of Lusher Valley and straight toward Omarosa's Point." Everything was "just peachy," Arnie thought, until he felt something bump up against his feet. He jumped forward and rolled to his right to let what he thought was another wild boar pass. But what crawled up beside him turned out to be a different kind of animal.

"Arnie Carver," Cravath smirked. "Fancy meeting you here." Cravath looked at his own Gladaass to check on everyone else's progress. "It's a shame that our individual Gladaasses show us everybody else's position, but not our own," he said. "You wouldn't want to trade would you? That way when we stop we can compare the two dots holding still and know where we are."

Arnie was naively shocked that a GODA sharer would suggest cheating. Everyone knew it was against the code. "Don't you think that cheating is an imposition on others?" Arnie asked him.

"Okay, never mind," Cravath defended himself. "Don't get yourself all in a twist about it. Besides …" he looked at his Gladaass one last time and put it back in his pocket. "You've apparently been the only dot holding still while we've been talking. So now I know where you are and, hence, I know where I am, but you don't." Cravath started to quickly crawl away from him up the valley. "See you later, sucker!"

Arnie quickly whipped out his own Gladaass and watched it for a dot heading due north up where he estimated the middle of Lusher Valley would be. Assuming that the dot was Cravath, Arnie knew pretty much exactly where he was, too, and took off following behind Cravath. "See you later yourself, sucker!" Arnie scoffed to no one in particular.

As Arnie crawled due north, he felt some drops of water on his back as he moved from under one tree to the next. A small rivulet of silty water started to run down between his hands and knees. Fifteen minutes of belly crawling later, the water was flowing more beneath him. Arnie popped out of the Sobbing Seawillow Forest into a warm Demeverde noontime shower, which was arriving pretty close to its forecasted time.

Several other sharers were well ahead of him going up Mud Meadow, including Cravath Swainmore. Arnie's first inclination was to charge up the hill after him straight towards Omarosa's Point directly ahead. But then Arnie noticed Cravath and a few others step off of the ridges, which then, being wet, looked like the mud pits on the surface. As Cravath and the group stepped off of each ridge, they fell straight into the mud pits and sank up to their hips. He started walking along the edge of the forest behind him to locate the first ridge to the east leading up the hill.

Arnie then turned north, counted paces, and turned again. Picking his way through the terrain, he passed all of the others stuck in the mud pits. When he reached Cravath, he looked down and reminded him, "Cheaters never prosper."

Cravath pulled himself out of the mud pit he was in, quickly started to follow Arnie, and, very soon, was right behind him. Several other sharers fell in line right behind them. Soon, Arnie was leading a trail up the side of Mud Meadow. If they didn't have a photographic memory to remember the location of the ridges, at least they were smart enough to recognize he did and use the opportunity presented to them to follow him.

Arnie checked his Gladaass and realized that his ants and he were closer to the top than anyone else. He turned back over his shoulder and taunted Cravath. "I'm halfway tempted to lead you all on a wild goose chase all over Mud Meadow, but I want to reach Omarosa's Point as quickly as everyone else does."

Cravath scowled. "Mighty nice of you, map boy," he said. "But be careful you don't get trampled by us, once you get us out of here."

Leading the procession snaking up the top of Mud Meadow, Arnie could see the huge display screen set up on the crest of Omarosa's Point and hear Avi doing commentary on their progress from his broadcasting stand.

"And the ants go marching one-by-one, hurrah, hurrah," Avi chanted.

Arnie climbed over the rock rim of Omarosa's Point and could hear yelling and screaming from all sides of the island.

Arnie and his ants were the first sharers to reach Omarosa's point.

"Now, let's see, guys and gals," Avi said to his fans, "how quickly each of them can find their two-liter bottle of Doctor Ginger's Naturally Carbonated Fruit-Flavored Drink and begin their second leg of Doctor Ginger's SUM Run."

As the platoon of runners broke ranks and jostled him, while making a frenzied dash past him, Arnie looked ahead at a four-foot deep pool twenty feet across that had four hundred two-liter bottles of Doctor Ginger's bobbing around on the surface. Arnie tried running around looking for the bottle filled with fluorescent green and thought he saw it near the edge. He jumped into the pool and snagged the prize, but it turned out to be "Limeberry Elixir" instead of "Green Apple Cider." Several people started jumping into the pool to look at the bottles in the middle. Whoops and hollers soon followed as more and more people found their bottles and climbed out heading for Hot Springs Pools. Several other contestants started to arrive as well.

Arnie looked around and was at least glad to see that Cravath Swainmore was not having any better luck than he was. They both kept looking. A few minutes later Cravath thundered "GOT IT!" and splashed past Arnie on his way to the edge of the tank nearest Hot Springs Pools. "See you later, sucker!" Cravath sneered at Arnie.

Arnie noticed a bulge in Cravath's back and had a hunch what it was. He reached out, grabbed Cravath by the back of his shirt and ripped it as hard as he could. As the strip ripped out of the middle, out fell the bottle of Doctor Ginger's Green Apple Cider.

Cravath looked at the evidence and then at Arnie. He grabbed Arnie's bottle and flung it to the far side of the pool.

"OOPS!" Cravath yelled. "How did that get back there?" Arnie sloshed hard after his bottle and flipped himself out of the western edge of the pool as he grabbed it. He looked over the pool in the direction of his finish point, just in time to see Cravath Swainmore go over the rock rim of Omarosa's Point, heading in the direction of the Hot Springs Pools and the headwaters of the Ten-Turn Terraced Rapids.

Arnie took off after him. Cravath started to head for the rim to the north of the rapids, but then looked back and saw Arnie pop over the rock rim about a hundred feet behind him. Throwing caution to the wind, Cravath jumped off the rim and into the first turn of the rapids. Arnie quickly closed the distance between them and got in the water about fifty feet behind Cravath. Arnie started swimming in the first long straightaway of the rapids, using the bottle like a torpedo and kicking fiercely with his legs. He closed the distance between him and Cravath just a little more.

Swimming hard through each successive chute, he continued to close the distance between them. Coming through the ninth hairpin turn, Arnie saw Cravath hanging by his legs from a root in the side of the bank above Last Chance Grasp. Cravath reached down and pulled the root closest to the water up and out of Arnie's reach. Cravath ridiculed Arnie, as the boy floated by desperately kicking his legs to get higher in the water and trying to make his arms stretch longer. "Sorry, sucker!" Cravath said. "You seem to have missed your Last Chance Grasp." As Arnie headed toward the tenth turn, Cravath added, "It will take you forever to climb up that cargo net."

Arnie could not remember a time when he had been more angry at someone. He was absolutely livid and out of control. Not thinking about the danger or even caring if he lived, Arnie came around the tenth turn at full speed. He put the bottle of Doctor Gingers straight out in front of him and held it pointed at the cargo net with both hands. Then he took one big gulp of air, held his breath, and pointed the bottle, his arms, and the rest of his body down deep into the water.

Heading toward the net at the water's full speed, Arnie was amazed at how clear the water was, rushing through the squares of rope under the surface. Twisting and turning his legs like a rudder, Arnie aimed the bottle and his arms for the dead center of a square made by the ropes of the cargo net. His aim was almost perfect and he shot through the cargo net with just a little bit of scraping. Looking down at the bed under the last bit of the rapids below him, Arnie then pulled his knees and his arms to his chest and tucked himself into a tight ball. Just as the last bit of rock came underneath his face Arnie planted his feet and then exploded his hands and his legs straight out to make himself as straight as an arrow.

Avi's virvideo cameras shooting from the ridges of Too Soon Lagoon could not have framed the shot any better. Arnie popped out of the crest and rode the airwave caused by Omarosa's Bridal Train Falls all the way out and splashed down about twenty feet away from where the falls hit the water. Arnie could hear people yelling from the ridges on both sides of the Lagoon. He treaded water for a moment, looked up to the north, and saw Cravath, his tattered shirt flopping behind him, running the ridge and about to turn down the face of the cliffs to the north.

Arnie felt too exhausted to move, much less swim and go faster than the express current, which was pushing him toward the reef at the mouth of the lagoon. He closed his eyes for a second and saw a vision of his mother encouraging him in a swimming pool race against his father. "Never give up," he heard his mother say to him in his mind, like she had done all his life. He wanted to swim on ahead, but he couldn't let go of the bottle, which kept pulling his arms below the surface of the water. Thinking as best he could, Arnie rolled over on his back, screwed off the top of the Doctor Gingers and gulped down half of it to give the bottle more lift. Then he screwed the top back on tightly, hugged the bottle, now half-filled with air, to his chest as a life-preserver and kicked as hard as he could to drive himself home.

Avi was commenting on the split screen showing Cravath running from the base of the cliffs and Arnie kicking in the express current, both of them less than a hundred yards from their finish flags. As soon as Arnie felt the first piece of reef scratch him on the back he flipped over, jumped up, and started running with the half-empty bottle of Doctor Ginger's toward his flag. Throwing the bottle like a football to Bernadette, Arnie dove the last ten feet to grab his flag just a second before Cravath Swainmore made it to his.

The fifty-foot Gladaasses replayed the last twenty feet of Arnie's run over and over again. The perfect spiral of the half-empty bottle of Doctor Ginger's would probably go into some commercial. Everyone was yelling and screaming. Bernadette opened the bottle of Doctor Ginger's and started passing it around for everyone to have a celebratory swig.

Then H.M. Crist, Cravath Swainmore, and the rest of H.M.'s Hummers started running over to the officials, who had come to congratulate Arnie and his deca. "FOUL! FOUL!" H.M. was yelling to the officials.

"What foul?" the head official asked.

"The rules say that you have to deliver the whole bottle of Doctor Ginger's to the finish flag and he only delivered a half-empty bottle." The fifty-foot Gladaass was replaying the toss to Bernadette again and H.M. pointed at it for evidence. "H.M.'S HUMMERS WIN OFF THE FOUL!"

Arnie walked over to H.M. and Cravath and yelled, "I HAVE THE OTHER HALF OF THE BOTTLE RIGHT HERE AND MY DECA IS MORE THAN HAPPY TO SHARE IT WITH YOURS!" Arnie then swallowed a big gulp of air, leaned back and burped up a huge fluorescent green shower that sprayed, not only H.M. and Cravath, but pretty well covered the rest of H.M.'s Hummers with a green sticky goo.

The officials blew their whistles a second time and the head official yelled. "THAT'S IT. FINAL DECISION. Arnie Carver of deca freshman two-twelve wins this year's Doctor Ginger's Seven Uncharted Miles Run!"

Cheering could be heard from all over the ridge of Too Soon Lagoon.

Bernadette walked over to Arnie with the rest of the deca behind her and presented him with the now empty bottle.

"You might want to keep this as the first trophy with our deca's new name."

Arnie took the bottle and read the label where the rest of the deca had signed it in indelible pen earlier that day.

It read:

IF FOUND PLEASE RETURN TO
ARNIE'S GREEN APPLE ARMY.

CHOCOEARLY-COVERED WRINKLED BERRIES AND EIFFEL'S CAFÉ ET BEIGNETS

One of the greatest pleasures of being the winner of Doctor Ginger's Seven Uncharted Miles Run, aside from getting to intentionally barf all over Cravath Swainmore, H.M. Crist, and the rest of his H.M.'s Hummers, was that Arnie got to take all of his Green Apple Army out for an all night dinner and dessert extravaganza at Vegestaurant, Doctor Ginger's vegetarian gourmet bistro, and eat anything any of them wanted on the menu.

Everyone in the restaurant was still talking about the finish and the controversy. "Man!" One kid on vacation was saying to another, "I have never seen someone puke such a beautiful color green."

Finishing a fine twelve-course tasting menu of the most intricate and delicious vegetarian food any of them had ever had, Arnie and his army were enjoying their seventh round of iced cold Doctor Ginger's in a variety of flavors. Finally, Doctor Ginger herself came out from the kitchen to present them with a dessert item she had prepared. She put down in the middle of the table a big tray of about fifty little cups each with a different color of what looked like raisins.

"What are these?" Arnie asked. "I've never seen anything like them."

Bernadette quipped, "And he's cataloged the entire island of animals, minerals, and vegetables since he's been here."

"Wrinkled berries," Doctor Ginger answered in a very thick French accent. "I have been working with GODEnt's Horticultural Research Group to develop this line of fruit and vegetable hybrids. They taste very good." She pointed to the colored bits and listed off their flavors, as everyone picked some up, one flavor at a time, and popped them in their mouths. Doctor Ginger continued, "We have red raspberry, cherry, strawberry, red bell pepper, tomato ---"

"HHHHHHHHHHHHHHHOT!" Hugo started to yell, quickly guzzling the last half of his bottle of Doctor Ginger's. "HOT! HOT! HOT! HOT! HOT! HOT! HOT!"

"Habanero peppers," Doctor Ginger continued, nonchalantly handing Hugo the butter plate. "Here, eat some butter. It will help with the burning." She moved to the green colored berries, "We also have green apple, which I am sure will be a big seller now, along with celery and avocado."

"These all taste so much sweeter than the fruits and vegetables themselves," Roberta remarked.

"The berries have less water than the fruits and vegetables

that they were engineered from, so the flavors are much sweeter and stronger," Doctor Ginger explained.

"Cool!" Tinker said, noticing a bowl of brown sauce in the middle of the assortment of berries. "What's this goo?" he asked.

"Chocoearly sauce," Doctor Ginger informed him. "Like chocolate, but made with an inverted sugar, so we call it the opposite. Instead of choco-late, we call it Chocoearly."

Arnie had tasted almost every flavor of wrinkled berry in front of him and was then pouring chocoearly sauce over a plate full of assorted ones. "Do you have any other deserts?" he asked.

Doctor Ginger clapped her hands and yelled back toward the kitchen, "The more desserts they want, the more desserts they get!" A procession of cooks and servers began bringing out plate after plate of sweet, tasty vegetarian delights.

As the procession ended and everyone was nearly completely stuffed, Arnie was breaking the wrinkled berries out of the Chocoearly sauce that had hardened on the plate. He started tossing them up in the air and catching them one by one in his mouth. After chewing each one, he guessed to Doctor Ginger the flavor of each. The rest of the kids around the table followed Arnie's example. Soon all of them were catching tidbits like seals at a circus.

"Well, Arnie," Doctor Ginger said, "it looks like you have discovered a new Doctor Ginger's treat. In honor of your winning my race, I will name them after you. Arnie Carver's Chocoearly-Covered Wrinkled Berries. We will have to start making them that way and selling them at the store."

"Arnie," Bernadette leaned over and whispered in his ear, "you are going to be famous."

Doctor Ginger walked around the table to stand beside Arnie. "And, now," she said to the entire deca, "the hour is getting late and I have a personal favor to ask of *Monsieur* Arnie. Can the rest of you find your way home without him?"

Several nudges, winks, and comments about older French women later, the rest of the deca had headed home. Doctor Ginger and Arnie were sitting at the table in the empty restaurant.

"What can I do for you, Doctor Ginger?" Arnie asked.

Doctor Ginger blushed with embarrassment. "*Monsieur* Arnie, I am ashamed to ask you this, but a nice man has just opened a coffee and French doughnut shop next door to me."

"And?"

"And he seems very nice to me."

"And?"

"And, when he saw on the Gladaass that you had won my race today, he asked if I could possibly arrange it for him to meet you after dinner tonight."

"And you want me to go have coffee and doughnuts with you, so I can meet him and you can, too?" Arnie asked, catching onto what she wanted.

"Understand, it is for him and not for me," Doctor Ginger replied trying to repair her dignity. "Though he is very nice and I would love to make him very happy."

Arnie smiled very broadly. "Sure, Doctor Ginger, I would love to help you make him very happy."

Doctor Ginger took Arnie by the arm and walked him to the shop next door. As they walked through the door, a short, fat, balding, salt and pepper haired man with a week's growth of beard was standing in front of the serving counter, under a sign reading

Eiffel's Café et Beignets
Jack Marx, Proprietor

Arnie fainted and fell to the floor.

He woke up a few minutes later, lying on his back with his feet up on a chair. He felt a cold, wet rag sitting across his forehead as Doctor Ginger took his pulse. His eyes fluttered open and closed and open again, as he heard Doctor Ginger say, "There, he is coming around."

The man was standing over him behind Doctor Ginger, who was kneeling beside him. He held his finger to his mouth, as if to silence Arnie, saying out loud, "Why, it must have been all the excitement today. I hope you're feeling better, young man."

"This is not the kind of introduction I would have hoped for, *Monsieur* Marx," Doctor Ginger began in her most French accent. "But allow me to present Mister Arnie Carver."

The man helped Arnie up into a chair and then introduced himself. "Well, Mister Arnie Carver, it's my pleasure to meet you." He added with a wink, "My name is Jack Marx."

Jack Marx served the three of them coffee and fried little rectangles of sweet, airy pastry dough covered in white powdered sugar. Arnie tried to amuse himself blowing the white powdered sugar off the doughnuts into the air as Doctor Ginger made small talk with the man that she would love to make very happy.

After the fifth plate of powder-covered rectangles, Jack Marx suggested, "Why don't we walk Doctor Ginger back to her apartment over her bistro? And then I can walk you back to your dorm, Mister Carver."

As soon as they had escorted Doctor Ginger to her apartment and walked a few feet down the deserted street, Arnie looked around to see if anyone was nearby. Then he threw himself around the man's neck and whispered, "Jacques, I don't know how or why you are here, but I am so glad you came."

After Jacques let Arnie hug him for a brief moment, he pulled him off his neck to have a look at him, "Aw, Arnie," he said. "I told you that I would come see you in a few months." Jacques started to usher Arnie back to Eiffel's. "Come up to my apartment above the shop. I have something to show you."

Closing the front door of the apartment behind them, Jacques whistled. Arnie heard the sounds of dogtags rattling and toenails clicking down the hall. He saw what was making the noise, held out his arms, and squealed, "CHOPSIE!"

The boy and his dog rolled around the apartment floor for a long time before Jacques was able to get them both calmed down enough to talk.

"So," Arnie asked. "What are you doing here?"

"Well," Jacques answered, "the Intellitron for you has been working perfectly. Everybody is completely fooled by it."

"Yes! Good."

"But it's just not the same and I got lonely for you. So I had Claude make one up for me and for Chopsie here so we could come down and be with you." Chopsie ran over to Jacques when he heard him say his name. "We would have been here a month ago, but Claude had a problem with the Intellitron for Chopsie here. Do you know how hard it is to program logic for a dog?"

"No," Arnie answered.

"Well, darn near impossible, according to him."

Jacques sat down on one of two easy chairs in the den. He picked up a remote control and turned on a soft symphony. "So, quite a race you won today."

"Yeah," Arnie said, grinning sheepishly and sitting down on the matching chair. "I don't know what happened out there, but it kind of felt like Mom and Dad were talking to me the whole way." Arnie closed his eyes, swallowed hard for a second, and gripped the arms of the chair.

"Well, wherever they are, Arnie," Jacques assured him, reaching over and resting his hand on the boy's forearm, "I'm sure they're watching you every moment." He let go of Arnie and rubbed his hands together. "And they've been some interesting moments from what I've seen."

"From what you've seen? How have you seen me?"

"Oh, Chose has sent me virmails of you almost every day."

Arnie was surprised. "He never told me he was doing that."

"We didn't want you to get homesick, so we kept it our secret."

"Oh."

"You seem to be fitting in nicely and making lots of friends."

"Yes," Arnie said, lost in thought, wondering what all Jacques had seen over the past two months.

"That Bernadette Rogers seems like a wonderful girl."

"She's a good friend, but she can be very bossy."

"Women often are," Jacques commiserated with him. "But, those other boys, Hugo, Alex, Robert, and …what's his name?"

"Tinker."

"No, his real name."

"Steven, Steven Schocken."

"Yes, him. He seems like a very inquisitive fellow."

"He is," Arnie said. "But, enough about here, what's going on at home in Philmont."

"Well, 'Thayne' is doing well in school."

"I saw a glimpse of his arrival the first day on VNN."

"Yes. That pesky Geraldo Enquirea has been trying to snap your picture and find out as much about you as he can."

"Not me, it," Arnie corrected him.

"You … it. I get it confused." Jacques paused. "It's all the same, even though it's so obviously different."

"Hopefully, 'it's' not too obviously different."

"What, the Intellitron?"

"Yes."

"No," Jacques assured him. "It's just like you. No one on the ranch even has a clue. It even thinks it's you. And I've given it your memories. While it powers down at night, I've loaded it with every A-V log that we've ever made that has you in it. Almost the only thing that I haven't been able to give it is your thoughts and dreams."

"Good. It probably wouldn't like my dreams anyway." Arnie changed the subject. "Any luck finding out anything about the murders."

"An absolute dead end, so far."

"Darn."

"The FBI is trying to trace the ordnance that was used, but they still haven't been able to pinpoint it. It was some pretty advanced stuff, which the military says doesn't even exist yet."

"Well, keep everybody that you can working on it. I still

want to find the killers and kill them."

"Now, Arnie—"

Chopsie squirmed in Arnie's lap. "So an Intellitron for you" Arnie said, cutting Jacques off. "And my little friend here, too." He muzzled the puppy's snout with his hand and shook it. "What on earth gave you that idea?"

"Hey, even though it looks like you, walks like you, talks like you, and thinks like you, it isn't you, and I got lonely for you."

"Thanks," Arnie said with a smile.

"So, I figured, if it worked so well for you, I'd sneak one in for Chopsie and me and we'd come be out here for a while as well."

"And who's watching the fort in Wyoming?"

"Oh, I am." Jacques stood up and walked to a secretary cabinet standing against the wall. "I check in all the time using this," he said, swnging open the two doors on the top and folding out the cover of the desk, revealing a computer with six different displays. "Anything that goes on anywhere we have A-V inputs, I can see it and hear it like I was standing right there."

"Interesting."

Jacques touched a few commands on a display. "See, here's you in the manor, playing around in your room." He flicked another screen. "At that same time we are watching Claude, getting to work in Japan."

"Do they know we're watching?"

"Not exactly. Everyone knows that the A-V inputs are working in all the plants and offices and at the ranch and everywhere else that we can put them."

Arnie nodded his head.

Jacques continued, "But most people just forget about

them after a while and no one ever knows exactly who's watching what when."

"Very useful."

"And, there's an A-V and data link to the Intellitrons, as well." He poked another display and the toy Thayne was playing with could be seen in his hands. "Here's the Thayne view." He pushed another spot. "And my view." He touched another place and a pair of feet appeared on a rug. "And, you can even get Chopsie's perspective on things."

"Nice!"

"You can even control them, if you want." Jacques pushed several buttons on one of the displays and picked up a wireless controller. "Just like you used to play with your little you doll." The Chopsie view showed an extreme close-up of Thayne's left foot. "Watch me make Chopsie lick you on your toes. You know you hate that." Jacques snickered, picking a routine choice with the control. "And, now, I'll make Thayne get him." He pushed the button labeled "Mic" on the control with one thumb and moved a mini-joystick with his other thumb. "Chopsie, stop that!" he barked at the device.

Thayne reached down and grabbed the Chopsie doll by the head and rolled him gently to the side. "Chopsie, stop that!"

"Oh, man!" Arnie said, reaching toward Jacques's hands. "You have to let me try it."

Jacques handed him the controller and Arnie did not put it down for almost an hour. Jacques went to the kitchen, made himself a cup of tea, came back, sat down, and watched his young ward play. He noticed that his own Intellitron was in Thayne's room, at the hoop mounted on one wall, playing basketball with Thayne.

"His shot is a lot better than yours," Arnie teased.

"As is Thayne's, relative to yours."

"We're finally going to beat the snot out of the security guys!" Arnie exclaimed.

"It would be wise if we didn't raise too much suspicion," Jacques cautioned him, taking the control away and returning all of the Intellitron's to automatic mode.

Arnie and Jacques stayed up late into the night talking about mundane things that Arnie had been doing for the past two months at GODA and the even more boring things that Thayne had been doing in Philmont. The discussion finally rolled around to Jacques's newfound love life.

"So tell me about Doctor Ginger," Arnie demanded. "Is she a real doctor?"

"Yes," Jacques answered. "She's the local family doctor here in Godeau by day and owner of the vegetarian bistro and many other enterprises by night."

"She likes you a lot, Jacques," Arnie teased him. "She just told me tonight that she would love to make you very happy."

"She is a lovely, isn't she?"

Arnie yawned long and loudly. "I need to get back to my dorm. I can't wait to tell everybody you're here."

"Think about that, Arnie. Just for a second. What are you going to tell them?"

"Great point," Arnie said, realizing how stupid he was about to have been. "I guess I just got kind of carried away in the excitement of seeing you and everything."

"Let's just tell them you had a nice time meeting a new, old man in town who owns a café next to Doctor Ginger's bistro."

"Okay," Arnie agreed. "We won't tell anyone about any

connection between us."

"Good idea," Jacques assured him.

"But you have to let us come eat all of the coffee and doughnuts we want anytime, for free."

"It would be my pleasure." Jacques smiled.

"I see you've already picked up on the local lingo. But you're too formal. All they say around here is just, 'My pleasure.'"

"We all have our own style," Jacques replied, leading Arnie to the door. "Now, let us away."

On the walk home, the conversation shifted to a more serious tone. Jacques caught Arnie up to date on what all of his companies were doing and how they were doing it. When they got around to T.D. Miller Pharmaceuticals, Arnie specifically asked about how they were coming on the work for curing Creutzfeldt-Jakob Disease.

"They are getting a better understanding of how the kids are getting sick, but they aren't close to finding a cure yet," Jacques told him.

"Tell the company to spare no time or expense figuring it out as soon as humanly possible. Have them put every person on it and every moment into it until they do."

* * *

The next day was the first day of the midterm break weekend. All of the deca decided to go to Global World to celebrate Arnie's victory and their survival of their first exams at GODA. Arnie had decided to skip his think day that week. Even Robert and Roberta Rivers, who normally were very strict about attending midday prayers on Fridays as their Sabbath day, decided, just this once, they would go along with the deca.

They all stood on SlipDiscs at the park entrance and looked at the gigantic virtual display of the Earth being virjected in the center of the main plaza. The planet was being held up by ten children, standing in a circle, with their hands over their heads.

"My goodness," Arnie said. "This place sure seems a lot bigger from down here than it does on its virtour." He slowly spun around looking at the bigger-than-life-sized virjections representing real-time scenes of each of the world's nations lining the sidewalks of the plaza. "Man!" he exclaimed to Tinker, "Even with your help, I'll bet you that VirtuComp couldn't top this."

Tinker was also in awe. "You said it there."

"Okay," Bernadette said, breaking into her leader mode and pointing to one of the several small SlipRails running overhead. Let's catch a SlipSkyway and get an overview of the park."

All of the decamates who had never been to Global World before were simply amazed by it. Bernadette, Amanda, Robert, and Roberta were much less impressed.

Arnie and Tinker kept a dialogue going for the entire trip around the park on the SlipSkyway Express. From the air, they could see the park was laid out like a globe map spread flat. Each continent had a Wonders of the World exhibit, each of which was made up of several virtual rides. One in China allowed SlipDiscing along the Great Wall. Moving west, another ride invited them to scale Kilimanjaro.

"Been there, walked that," Aurelia said matter-of-factly. "Got the t-shirt."

Bernadette demanded that everyone follow her lead as they passed over the middle of the Atlantic Ocean. "Wave to us down there in Demeverde."

Once they had finished the tour, Bernadette directed them through a day-long journey around the world riding almost every ride that was available. Everyone had an outstanding time. While they were there, Alex discovered that the Doctor Ginger's stands all over the park were already selling Arnie Carver's Chocoearly-Covered Wrinkled Berries. They quickly became the snack food of the day.

It was a mostly wonderful day. The only bad thing to happen was an unexpected event. While they were walking under a SlipSkyway ride, something messy fell out of a SlipSkyway car and onto Robert's face.

"ARGH!" Robert screamed, wiping his cheek and coughing out the foul tasting stuff. "What the heck was that!"

Arnie looked up and saw just a glimpse of what he thought was a big red and orange balloon going behind a SlipSkyway car moving along a SlipRail in the air.

Amanda suggested, "Someone must have dropped some ice cream from up there." She pointed to the SlipSkyway car.

Robert continued to spit the white stuff out of his mouth. "That was some awfully bad tasting ice cream."

Roberta kept rinsing her own mouth out with the bottle of Doctor Ginger's she was holding.

The rest of that Friday, however, was a memory that each of them would be able to share forever.

The next day, Arnie enjoyed his next rest day, staying in the apartment and reading as he usually did on the day of the week that he chose for his own personal Sabbath. On Sunday, his Think Day, he spent half the day practicing Perfect Sandra Vin's Meditative Ballet. He was finally able to hold the second position with his feet high in the air for almost five minutes.

On Monday, the deca was back in its regular routine of classes, coco games, early evening virnews reviews, and studying in the pit until bedtime. As usual, Hugo was able to find something in a virnews program to worry the rest of the deca.

"Uh-oh," Hugo said. "Unius, we still have a problem."

"What now?" Everyone asked.

Hugo read the story. "Dateline – Wilmington, Delaware. Phineas Rubino, spokesman for Gregory Scorsos, President of Scorsos Enterprises International, announced today that Scorsos has offered the services of its attorneys to assist all present and any possible future victims of the Demeverde Plague."

The name shocked him. "Phineas Rubino!" Arnie asked.

"Unius is going to have a heart attack!" Bernadette exclaimed. She looked at Arnie and asked, "Who's Phineas Rubino?"

"No one," Arnie said, recovering his composure. "It just seems like a strange name."

"What else does the story say?" Min-su asked.

"It's too long to read it all, but I'll summarize. Blah, blah, blah, it talks about the kid in Argentina, the kid in France and the kid in Italy," Hugo continued. "Blah, blah, blah, it says that Scorsos believes that there is a closer connection to the kids' illnesses and their trips to Demeverde than GODEnt and the Demeverde Department of Tourism is willing to admit."

Hugo went on. "Blah, blah, blah. Oh! Well, at least it discusses how Scorsos Enterprises International and GODEnt have been rival companies for years and that many people think Scorsos has an ulterior motive for offering his company's attorneys to attack Demeverde."

"And in a related story," Hugo added, "T.D. Miller Pharmaceutical continues to announce progress in its rat-tailed mice experiments with inducing and reversing prion folding to cause and then relieve symptoms similar to those being seen in what is being called juvenile variant Creutzfeldt-Jakob Disease. The company's spokesperson says they are only able to reverse the prion folding by using an antibody made from the specific substance that causes particular prions to fold, but they are continuing to work on a more general antibody."

"Well, at least they're making progress," Amanda stated.

Arnie silently smiled with pride knowing that one of his companies was working so hard to stop this terrible disease. He would have loved to have said something about it, but he knew he could not risk sharing anything about his true identity with anybody, as long as the people who might have killed his parents were still out there. Not even with those who had become his first and closest friends.

GODEnt responded to the story almost immediately at its own press conference. "Yes, indeed, there is a long-running rivalry between Scorsos Enterprises International and GODEnt," Paula Poundsand explained. "If Gregory Scorsos, one of the most greedy and selfish businessmen on the face of the Earth, wants to deflect attention from his own vile history by sending his own lawyers to create lies about connections of unfortunate sick people where no connections exist, then there is not much we at GODEnt can do about it but redouble our efforts to seek to prove how these wonderful children became ill and how to make them well again. Therefore, effective immediately, GODEnt's Medical Services Division is entering into a joint venture arrangement with T.D. Miller Pharmaceuticals in order to provide them with any resources of GODEnt they may need to continue their vital research."

"Greedy, selfish, and vile?" a reporter asked. "Aren't those some pretty harsh words to use?"

"Hey, if the shoe fits, kick with it," Paula retorted. "And besides, we're Global Optimum and nobody messes with us."

ROBERT'S FOUL BALLS

Life was going well for Arnie's deca, two weeks into the second half of the session. They were running a few moments late for breakfast on the second Monday morning, however, because Robert kept grounding his SlipDisc during their calisthenics exercises on the trip from the dorm to the student union.

After the third time he dug the lip of his SlipDisc into the ground and caused the line of the rest of the deca following him to go awry, Bernadette moved from the rear of the line up to where Robert was. "What's wrong, Robert?" she asked. "Having a problem staying level?"

Robert pounded his hip with his fist. "I don't know. It's like my leg has some stupid twitch in it this morning."

"Well, let's let Arnie take the lead from behind you and we'll take up the rear."

"Aw, man!" Arnie complained. "I hate being the leader. Everyone always laughs at my lack of rhythm."

"Too bad," Bernadette told him. "Lead for a while, whether you like it or not."

Arnie jerkily put the deca through its paces and topped the routine off with a trip up the corkscrew in the union to the freshman food court. Everyone finished picking their breakfast and regrouped to head to their favorite spot, a table at the end of a catwalk sticking out into the air, on the second level of the four-story entrance atrium.

Alex tapped Arnie on the shoulder with his tray and asked, "What is Cravath doing sitting at our table?"

As Arnie brought the deca to a halt at their destination, he asked, "Excuse me, Cravath, but I think you're in our space, friend."

"I am not your friend and this is not your space," Cravath informed him with a dagger-eyed look.

"Sure it is, Swainmore," Alex said over Arnie's shoulder. "We've sat here for every meal since the beginning of the session."

Several of Cravath's decamates began to push past the line of the Green Apple Army and began to place their trays on the contested territory. "H.M.'s Hummers are claiming this space as first come, first served. I was here first this morning and we've got the table."

Tinker moved up into the action. "I don't think so, barf breath. You know we've been sitting here all the time and you are just trying to impose yourself to be a pain."

"It's no pain for us. Is it, guys?" Cravath asked, looking around at his friends.

Roberta crowded into the argument. "Look, fellas, there's no need causing a fight about this. Let's just move to another table and sit down."

"No," Arnie insisted. "It's our spot. We've had it all year. They're just trying to cause problems."

Bernadette sliced up to the front of the line, stared Cravath in the eyes, and started to reason with him. "Now, Cravath. You know you don't want to cause a problem here."

"Oh, I know I don't want to cause a problem here."

"Good—" she started to say.

"And you can forget about trying your suggestive prowess on us, because H.M. has already taught us a way to neutralize it. So just take your cheating champion and the rest of your friends and find somewhere else to sit."

Arnie asked, "So that's what all this is about? You're still sore because I beat you at the SUM Run, and you think that beating us to our table is going to make it better?"

"H.M. says we need to take you guys down a few pegs in the pecking order around here, seeing as to how you all think that you're better than the rest of us."

Roberta stepped back in. "We don't think that we are better than anyone else," she said, in a conciliatory tone.

Alex nudged her aside. "Nope, we don't think it," he agreed. "We know it. We're better than you and we can prove it."

Roberta moved her tray in front of Alex to pull him back. "And we can prove it by letting you have your petty victory and keep the blooming table, if you want it that bad."

"The heck we will," Alex said, reaching over and putting his tray down in the middle of the disputed table. "We can prove it by just tossing you guys right over the rail here." He started to move toward the biggest boy from the Hummers, Ambrosius Ansgar, a sharer from Sweden, about twice his size.

A loud voice barked from behind them all. "Touch one of my Hummers," H.M. Crist yelled, making his way out the catwalk, "and I'll have you in front of the honor council in a heartbeat." He pushed himself between Alex and the Swede.

"What honor council?" Alex asked.

"My honor council," replied H.M. "I've just been appointed chairman last week by Chose and Mrs. L."

"Based on what?" Arnie asked. "Did you buy them presents like you bought your deca?"

H.M. sneered at Arnie. "Based on my perfect scores in the last mid-terms. I'm now tops in my class, I'll have you know."

"You're a T-O-P?"

"Nah," H.M. corrected him. "Not a T-O-P. I wouldn't serve for them, even if they'd elect me."

Amanda interjected, "Which they never would, if they're smart."

"But, based on the last scores, I'm tops in my class and that entitles me to be chairman of your class's honor council. So, if you want to get thrown out of GODA, go ahead and impose your big, beefy self on one of my Hummers and we'll see how you like an honor code violation."

"Not so fast, Hammond Milo!" Émilie called from the beginning of the catwalk. "*Bonjour, mes amis!*" she said to her deca, before she turned to stare H.M. in the face. "I just knew you wouldn't be able to wait to throw your new weight around."

"I've told you, no one calls me that, but my mother."

"And, if she was here to see you bullying around with your newfound power, then she'd be doing so, I'm sure." Émilie walked purposefully out to the table. She moved between Alex and Ambrosius and stared Alex in the eyes. "Pick up your tray, Alex."

As Alex caved in and did what he was told, Émilie talked to the rest of them. "All of my deca, please, walk off of here and we will go find another table."

"Yeah," H.M. taunted them, as they all turned with their trays and began to walk away. "Do what your green apple den mother says. She obviously doesn't want to see her little army drummed out of the corps."

Émilie stopped short and glared at H.M. "Hammond Milo Crist, you are just trying to provoke my deca into misbehaving, aren't you?"

"Hey, if they can't control themselves in the presence of their betters, who am I to stop them."

"Well, we'll just have to see who's better than whom." Émilie moved back towards H.M.

"You suggesting what I think you're suggesting?" H.M. asked, puffing out his chest.

"Exactly," she replied, arching her back.

"Just like last year?"

"Just like last year," Émilie said, turning to her adopted deca. "*Mes amis*, you have been challenged to a grand coco grudge match."

"Great!" Arnie said to Cravath. "We'll beat you fair and square. Winners get the table for the rest of the year."

"Oh, no," Cravath said, "we're way past that now."

"So name the stakes," Bernadette pushed herself forward and demanded.

"The winners get to burn the losers' jerseys at a bonfire after the game, while the losers have to watch."

"That's a stupid thing to do," Bernadette told him.

"Chicken?"

"Nope," she said. "You can be as stupid as you want and let us burn your shirts all night long for all I care."

Émilie looked back at H.M. and asked, "Usual rules?"

"Usual rules," H.M. responded.

"Thursday at six, the lighted valley?"

"Be there."

"You bring your two refs and I'll bring mine."

"No problem, but eleventh graders or older. We don't want any claims of favorites."

"No problem," Émilie agreed, gathering her flock. "*Mes amis*, let us go."

* * *

Practice was especially serious that week, with Émilie figuring out how the deca had been progressing on its own and then drilling them on fundamentals during Monday's and Tuesday's practices. As the deca huddled with Émilie before Wednesday's practice, she asked, "So who do you think is doing what well, Arnie?"

Arnie moved to the front of the pack of kids. "Well, Robert has become a deadly accurate nutter. He's the only player on the team who can consistently hit the bull's-eye from more than a hundred feet away. When he points with his front hand, takes a big wind up, and lets the nut sail, it flies straight as an arrow, right into the bull's-eye."

Bernadette moved up beside Arnie to add her perspective. "Robert's not only precise with the stationary target. He's also deadly accurate and strong at knocking a coco out of a runner's hands. Our opponents have no choice when Robert sees them – they have to either punt, pass, or dribble the coco or risk Robert throwing a nut at them. If they don't get rid of the coco somehow, then they have three choices after Robert throws a nut at them – use the coco to block the nut, which usually results in Robert's nut knocking the coco out of their hands; make a sharp turn and dodge to the side, where someone else on the team, who may have been a little slower than Robert can get a shot at them; or lower the coco and take the shock of Robert's nut raising a nice round welt on the their chest, the pain of which usually results in losing the nut in the end."

Arnie took control back from Bernadette the best way that he had learned how – by talking about her. "Bernadette has become the offensive striker. She's found more ways to get the coco into the cave than anyone has ever seen before. She doesn't yet have your physical strength, Émilie, but, whatever she lacks in distance, she definitely makes up for in finesse."

"Good," Émilie said. "She'll get more strength as she works with Perfect Vin.

"Well, so far, defenders are regularly outfoxed by her slyness. Just when the other guys think they have figured out which way she's going to go and flinch ever so slightly, showing that they've taken the bait of her fake, Bernadette zooms past them with the coco so fast it literally make their heads spin and, sometimes, their feet and everything in between as well."

"Enough about me," Bernadette said. "Alex and Tinker are our close-in defenders. They're fast at reacting, but unfortunately, they have no long distance speed or stamina. Alex's best trick is to turn his back on an offensive player and wait until he hears the grunt and fells the exhale that most players make when they shoot. Then, he turns around and either catches the shot, right before it gets to the cave, or at least bats it away, before it crosses the front of the net."

"Neat trick," Émilie said, "but don't try to use it too often or everyone will catch on pretty quickly."

Arnie shouldered himself back upstage. "Aurelia and Min-su have developed into a terrifying twosome because they complement each other well. Min-su is all speed and jumping dexterity, and she can score a goal from almost any angle within fifty feet of the cave. Aurelia is pure endurance and absolutely never tires when it comes to running after or with the ball."

"Okay," Émilie said.

Bernadette jumped back in. "If someone is dribbling the ball with their feet, Aurelia will catch them and run right beside them until they leave her the shortest opportunity to stick her toe in and steal the coco. If they try to bend down and pick up the ball, she immediately beans them with the nut in her hand as soon as they touched the coco with their hands and take one step. Once she get the coco, she'll dribble it with her feet all the way back toward our deca's cave, where she then turns up to the rim and moves the ball all the way around half the valley, until whoever was defending her finally falls away."

Arnie moved back ahead of Bernadette again. "By the time Aurelia gets close to the opponent's cave, she catches the ball between her feet and flips it up in the air to Min-su who's waiting about ten feet out from the goal. As soon as Aurelia sets the shot, Min-su jumps, flips, twists, and kicks the ball into the opponent's cave."

Émilie looked at Min-su and smiled. "The gymnastics

comes in handy, doesn't it?"

Min-su nodded, but didn't get a chance to say anything before Bernadette broke back in.

"Hugo and Amanda are our midfield defenders, which takes advantage of their speed, power, aim, and endurance. There's a lot of wide open valley to cover in the middle, and Hugo and Amanda are constantly on the move getting to the coco to chip it over the opponent's defenders to get it to Aurelia, Min-su, or me."

Arnie again tried to position himself ahead of Bernadette. "Roberta is the Army's starting kicker. following every goal, after we all get lined up on the rim of the valley, alternating one player from each team, Roberta lines up either just to the right or the left of our cave. As soon as the horn blows to start a new point, she takes off on an unstoppable and unbeatable full speed run to kick the coco off the top of the tube and almost always over halfway to the opponent's cave."

Émilie gave Roberta a thumbs up. "You should be able to chip it all the way to the cave by the end of the year."

Bernadette echoed Émilie's high sign to Roberta and then started talking again. "Arnie's the Army's offensive center. For each kickoff, he starts immediately next to our opponent's cave and jogs halfway down the valley, arriving just in time to receive the kickoff from Roberta and, hopefully, feed it back to Min-su for a quick score. If she's not available, then he gives the coco a long kick to wherever either Aurelia is running high on the rim of the valley or I have managed to get open."

"Cool," Émilie said, looking up to see another group of sharers coming up the slope leading up to their valley. "I've arranged a scrimage with my deca, so you can get a chance to bring out your A-game." She waved to her decamates.

"Bonjour, mes amis. Get ready and we will show them how it's really done."

Émilie's deca began to warm up by chipping the coco back and forth across a circle they made taking up about half of the valley.

Hugo touched Alex on the arm to get his attention. "Whoa!" he said to Alex and the rest. "These guys mean business."

Émilie smiled proudly. "If you get good enough to keep up with us, then you should have no problem with H.M.'s Hummers."

With the increase in number of shots being taken and intensity of their practice, everyone on the team started worrying that Robert might be cracking under the strain of the challenge. The first inkling of trouble came during the second-period of the scrimmage. When Émilie's deca got up on the Army three cocoes to none, Robert missed with a nut that he shot at the bull's-eye. Not only did he not hit the bull's-eye, Robert didn't even hit the target. The nut hit the wall of the valley with a WHACK! and then rolled all the way back down the valley to the trough.

"Sorry!" Robert yelled across the valley to his team. "My fault."

"That's all right, Robert," Arnie cheered him on. "Everyone misses one every now and then."

Toward the end of the second period of the scrimmage Émilie's team was still ahead five to two. One of Émilie's deca had the coco and was trying to run it straight at Robert. Robert pointed, wound up, and let his nut sail. The nut missed the coco, missed the player holding the coco, and caught Arnie unaware and clocked him square in the head, staggering him to his knees. Everyone started running toward

Arnie.

"Awwwww, fungus!" Robert yelled at himself, running towards Arnie. "I'm sorry, Arnie!"

Émilie called off the rest of the game and waved around to the rest of her own deca. "That's it for today! *Merci beaucoup, mes amis. Au revoir.*"

As her decamates gathered up to leave, one of them, Demetrios Giannopolous, a black-haired, Greek Adonis, leaned over to Émilie and said, "You'd better get some control on that one, before he really hurts somebody."

"I'm really sorry, Arnie," Robert repeated, helping him stand back up.

"No problem," Arnie assured him, shaking the stars away from in front of his eyes. "I've always wondered what it felt like to take a shot from you. No wonder everyone blocks it with their coco."

"What's wrong with you, Robert?" Bernadette asked.

"I don't know, Bernadette," Robert tried to defend himself. "It's like, one second I'm wound up and then I just see a flash of light and my hand twitches as I release the nut."

"Are you having any other problems?" Arnie asked.

"Not playing coco," Robert said. "But I am finding that I have to study the same material over and over again, and, when it comes to reciting something I've memorized for class, I just can't remember it. Plus, I've been getting angry very easily. Why, the other day, I yelled at Roberta, for the first time in our lives."

Émilie herded all of them toward the rim of the valley. "Well, let's all go home and get a good night's rest. It's probably just the pressure of the game coming up."

* * *

Early the next evening, H.M.'s Hummers squared off against Arnie's Green Apple Army to avenge what the Hummer's called Arnie's wrongful victory over Cravath Swainmore in the SUM Run and settle who was going to sit at the contested table for the rest of the year. More important than all of that, however, jerseys were at stake and so was their pride.

Avramel Kimvelevitch had been broadcasting a virmercial on his Gladaass station G-O-D-A to be sure everyone in GODA had an opportunity to go watch the event. The aspiring broadcaster hired everyone in his deca to bring their own Gladaasses and use them as cameras transmitting back to him. He then passed the images using his Gladaass as a mixing board to run the game in broadcast mode with an all angle view. Even though anyone in Demeverde could watch the grudge match on their own Gladaass, a huge crowd surrounded the well-lit main practice coco valley, right below the mountains, just outside the campus.

"GOOOOD EEEEEEEEVENING, GODA sharers!" Avramel began his coverage of the game. "Avi Kaye here for G-O-D-A. This evening we have the grudge match between H.M.'s Hummers and Arnie's Green Apple Army to settle a variety of scores between these two longstanding rival decas." Hype was never beyond Avi Kaye.

The crowd began to applaud, which only egged him on some more. "Are you ready for the RALLYYYYYYYYYYY IN THE VALLEEEEEEEEEY?"

The crowd was now in full frenzy; yelling, screaming, making waves around the stands overlooking the valley.

"And now for the introduction of this evening's referees, let's go down to the pipe."

Four of Avramel's decamates were standing with their

backs to each other at the bottom of the bowl and pointing their Gladaasses at the four officials selected by H.M. and Émilie. Each side's supporters appropriately cheered and booed as each name was called out while Avi broadcast the entire proceeding in a quadra-split screen. All of the players from each deca then lined up in alternating order on the rim.

"Okay, this is Avi Kaye and I'll be providing your commentary for the rest of the game. We all know the players and the players know all the rules, so let's dispense with the formalities and just START THIS GAME!"

Avi had not sounded the horn for more than a millisecond before Roberta was off to the pipe for the kickoff. Avi began to describe the action. "Roberta Rivers is speeding to the pipe and all of the Hummers are making a beeline for the it as well. Roberta beats them to the ball, kicks straight through it, and keeps on running between two Hummers. But wait! The Hummers are continuing to run to the pipe." As all of the Army's opponents converged at the bottom of the valley, Robert, Alex, Tinker, and Hugo shrugged their shoulders wondering what was up. "This is something that none of us has ever seen before. The Hummers have each picked up two of the twenty nuts sitting in the trough, which leaves none for Robert to use to bean them."

"Go, Hummers!" H.M. yelled from the side of the rim.

"Well, that's one way to nix a nutter!" Avi yelled to the crowd, as all of the Hummers ran to their positions.

The Hummers were too late, however, to prevent Roberta's kickoff from bouncing up in the air next to Min-su about thirty feet from the Hummer's cave. Min-su went up in the air to chase the coco with her feet and snap-kicked the coco into the cave.

Avi added, "But posting no defense has cost the Hummers the first goal."

After everyone was stationed back on the rim, the lead referee restarted the match. "The Hummers still have all of the nuts," Avi noted, "and their not runing to the pipe for the second kickoff. Apparently, they're electing instead to use a good defense as their best offense. But let's see how they play just using their feet to handle the coco."

Roberta ran at her usual breakneck speed and chipped the coco two thirds of the way to the Hummer's cave where Min-su was again ready to kick it. Avi continued, "Ahn Min-su sets up to shoot what should be another long easy point."

Cravath tossed his nuts over his back and into the Hummer's own cave. "But, hold on!" Avi exclaimed. "Cravath Swainmore seems to have another idea as he jumps up to grab the coco out of the air right from in front of Min-su's foot and takes off running for the Army's cave."

Avi continued providing the color for Cravath's moves and game strategy for his program. "Once a player is running with the coco, there are very few things that an opposing player can do to stop him. The defender cannot tackle the runner, because a defensive player has to be going to tackle the coco and not the player. He can try to strip the coco out of the runner's hands with his own hands or feet. Someone can try to block the runner and make him either shoot or pass the coco if he can't get by; but the most effective tool to stop a runner is a nut in the hand, and, right now, the Hummers seem to have all of the nuts in the valley."

All of the Army players, except for Aurelia, took up defensive positions on all of the Hummers, except for Cravath. Aurelia caught up with Cravath and began running step for step beside him.

"Let's see how the Robert Rivers does with no nuts in his hands this time," Avi suggested. "Cravath is already two-thirds of the way to the Army's cave. He's coming right up to the empty handed Robert and, look at that, he's almost faked the boy out of his shoes going by."

Cravath continued across the valley, as Avi went on, "The only Army player between Cravath and the Army's cave is Alex Shelikhov. Alex steps up to block Cravath. Looks like he's hoping to get Cravath to make an intentional roughness penalty if he goes straight through Alex for the shot. But Cravath changes directions just a little! Alex reacts, but Cravath just drives right past him and slams the coco into the Army's cave!"

The evenly split crowd cheered and booed respectively. In the meantime, Arnie had run down the two nuts that finally fell through the Hummer's cave net. "Well, Arnie Carver has found some ammo for Rivers to use and he's tossed them to him. But, wait!" Robert missed catching the nuts. "Rivers seems to be having a problem getting hold of his nuts."

The crowd guffawed as Robert began to chase the nuts down, before they rolled all the way down to the trough. He finally got them and jogged toward the rim of the valley to set up for the third kickoff.

"And the score is tied one to one by the Hummers!" Avi egged on the crowd.

"Roberta!" Bernadette yelled, to get her attention. "If they don't come hard for the coco, then dribble off."

Roberta took off again for the pipe. Avi painted the picture for those watching. "The Hummers are sticking with their strategy of starting off with a strong evenly spread defense. Roberta stops suddenly, just short of the pipe, and dribbles the ball with her foot to Amanda, who is coming up behind her. Amanda chips the ball to Bernadette, who bounces the ball with her hands like a basketball, slips past a defender, and maneuvers close enough to the Hummer's cave. She shoots!" Avi waited for the coco to hit the back wall of the cave. "And she scores to put the Army up two to one."

The crowd released a chorus of ooh's, ahh's, and aw's. "And the Army takes a commanding lead!" Avi screamed, never missing the chance to make a big overstatement.

"Swede!" H.M. called down to Ambrosius Ansgar, the huge golden-haired Hummer, pointing at Roberta. "Take it to her."

At the next horn, Avi picked up his patter. "Ambrosius takes off running for the pipe. Roberta should be able to beat him, but it will be close. She kicks the ball at full speed, just as Ambrosius tries to pull a Lucy and slide tackle the coco off the pipe to make her whiff it." Ambrosius' foot caught Roberta's ankle from the side and she went down in a heap. "Ohhh! And down goes the Army's kicker."

Both Arnie and Hugo looked at Émilie's referee and yelled, "Hey! How about an unnecessary roughness call there?"

"Just going for the coco," the referee yelled. "Play on."

Possession of the coco passed back and forth several times over the next few minutes. At one point, Amanda was dribbling the ball with Robert running with her on the right. Both of them saw Ambrosius running toward them.

"Quick!" Robert yelled over at Amanda, "chip it to the Swede."

"What!" Amanda asked with suprise.

"Just do it!" Robert demanded.

"What's going on here?" Avi asked, as Amanda did what

Robert had told her and chipped the big green ball up in the air right above Ambrosius's head. "The Army's Amanda Purvis sends the ball right past the Hummer's Ambrosius Ansgar, who reaches up and catches the ball on the fly." Ambrosius made the mistake of taking a step with the coco over his head. "Whoa! It looks like a sucker play and ..." Robert let loose a nut and caught the Swede, right in the solar plexus, and the blonde giant fell to the ground, gasping for air. "The Swede bit on it hook, line, and sinker."

While Amanda was distracted by what had just happened in front of her and Robert was facetiously apologizing to Ambrosius, Ricadonna Romia, the Hummer's version of Bernadette, tipped the coco into the air and scored another point for the Hummers.

Avi shifted back to the action. "But another Hummer takes the coco home to the Army's cave for the score!"

A referee from H.M.'s deca blew his whistle. He pointed at Robert and jerked a thumb toward the valley's rim. "You're out! Two-minute penalty for unnecessary roughness."

Arnie ran down to argue for Robert, who was uncharacteristically angrily running at the ref. "BAD CALL!" Arnie yelled, blocking his decamate.

"He has to throw the nut at the ball!" the ref said. "Two minutes on the rim."

"I just missed where I was throwing!" Robert defended himself.

"You never miss," the ref retorted. "We've watched you before."

"Yeah!" Robert yelled back. "Well, I missed this time because I was aiming for his fat head!"

"Get up on the rim!" the ref told him.

Robert walked past Ambrosius on his way to the rim and

said, "Hit my sister again and I'll aim somewhere else."

Robert apologized to Arnie as he headed to the rim. "Honest, Arnie, my aim was off. I really was aiming for his head."

As Robert was walking all the way up to the rim, Avi jazzed up the crowd. "It's tied at two and the HUMMERS ARE ON A POWERPLAAAAAAAAAAY!!!!"

The Hummers spread the coco amongst all of their players around the valley a few times and scored. They took the lead within the first minute of the penalty. Then, Bernadette picked up her pace a bit and beat both Roberta and the Hummer's kicker, Michio Takafuku. She sent a perfect kickoff from the pipe over everyone's head and straight into the Hummer's cave to retie the game at three apiece.

Avi blandly stated, "Well, that was a short point."

"Yes!" Roberta yelled, throwing her hands up in a V as Bernadette's shot landed in the Hummer's cave. "You have to show me how to do that!"

"No problem, girlfriend," Bernadette replied, sticking out her right pinkie. "Gimme one!"

Roberta hooked Bernadettes's pinkie with hers and the two then pulled on each other's fingers before breaking apart, yelling to each other, "Pinkie power!"

Robert's penalty expired and he shakily got to his feet. He stood up on the rim for the next kickoff, but the horn sounded to end the first period before anyone could run for the pipe.

Bernadette called everyone into a huddle. "Robert, you have to nut our bull's-eye to build us a lead."

"I know," Robert agreed. "But Cravath has been keeping his fat butt in front of our cave protecting their cocoes and I can't get a clear shot at it."

"Then we will just have to make him an offer that he can't refuse," Bernadette schemed. "Amanda?"

"Yes?"

"You and Hugo each split to both sides of our cave with Cravath between you. I'll kick the coco to whichever of you is open to look like we are setting up a drive. Whoever gets the coco, chip it to the other person right across the mouth of the cave very high, almost to the top bar, but kick it nice and easy."

"What?" Hugo asked. "It'll be a sitting duck."

"Exactly," Bernadette explained. "Cravath will have to jump up and take a shot at it to dunk it back in our cave. When he goes up for the coco, Robert, you take the shot at our bull's-eye and pour out their cocoes."

Everyone finished downing some water and mounted the valley's rim for the start of the second half. At the sound of the horn, Cravath dropped down off of the rim and parked himself right in front of the Hummers' bull's-eye holding their three cocoes in the Army's cave. Bernadette stood on one side of the Hummer's cave and looked at Ambrosius, who was standing on the rim by the cave waiting for the kickoff.

Ambrosius mocked her, "In case you didn't notice, you are looking at the wrong cave for the kick off."

"You play your game," Bernadette replied, winking at Robert, who was on the other side of the Hummer's cave. "And we'll play ours."

"How's that chest?" Robert asked Ambrosius, acting like he was tossing a nut up and down. "If you ever get another chance, don't pick up the coco."

Ambrosius walked over and put his face close to Robert's. "Pick up yourself," the Swede said, plastering him square in the jaw with a close right hook.

Avi continued with his colorful commentary. "Whoa! Look at that! And the referees cannot call a penalty because not a one saw it live. Shame they can't use an instant Gladaass replay."

Just as the horn sounded, Bernadette and Ambrosius were off to the races. Distracted by Robert's nut tossing and the short melee that followed, Ambrosius was two steps behind Bernadette from the start. Bernadette chipped the coco to Hugo on the left of the Army's cave. Hugo chipped the coco back over to Amanda on the right with a hang time that was just too much for Cravath to pass up.

Cravath jumped up as high as he could. As the coco passed just out of his reach at the top of his leap, Cravath looked back out to see Robert popping out from behind Bernadette pointing at the bull's-eye below his feet and realized that he had been hoodwinked.

"Nooooooo!" Cravath screamed.

Robert wound up and let the nut fly before Cravath could fall back down in front of the target, but it did not matter. His shot missed the bull's-eye. It missed the entire target. In fact, Robert's shot missed the entire valley, as everyone watched it disappear way up over the rim and off into the distance.

Someone in the crowd yelled, "LOOK!" and pointed to the bowl. By the time that anyone looked back at Robert, he was facedown on the floor of the valley jerking uncontrollably.

Everyone from both teams quickly gathered in a circle around Robert. Some gawked. Several people from Robert's deca glared at Ambrosius.

"I swear," he tried to defend himself, "I didn't hit him that hard."

Roberta's neck began to twitch. She held the front right

side of her head and painfully cried out, "AAAAG!"

"What is it?" Amanda asked her.

"'It's killing him!' he says," Roberta exclaimed, slumping down onto the valley's floor.

Bernadette jumped beneath Roberta as she went down and caught the girl's head in her lap. Arnie got down on both knees right beside Robert and leaned his face down to his fallen friend's to try to see what was the matter.

Alex started to try to roll Robert over, but Arnie stopped him. "No! Don't move his neck," Arnie instructed. "Not until we get a brace on it."

Several people in the crowd pushed the emergency contact spots on their Gladaasses to call Mrs. L and Chose. Doctor Ginger, who was watching the game, came down from the stands, ran over, and pushed herself through the crowd of kids.

"*Exactement!*" the doctor agreed.

A SlipStream Dozenberth outfitted as an ambulance arrived a few minutes later and Doctor Ginger had the twitching twins transported to the hospital.

As the ambulance pulled away, everyone looked back at Ambrosius who was now sitting on the rim of the valley.

"I swear," he repeated again, "I didn't hit him that hard."

CHAPTER SIXTEEN

THE ORANGE-TAILED SCARLET VULTURE

People seldom get very sick in Demeverde and, even when they fall ill, they don't usually do it as publicly as the Rivers twins did. Roberta was back up and around with a screaming headache within hours of reaching the hospital. Robert, however, was a completely different patient. His failure to wake up from the coma after the seizures subsided cast a pall over the entire island. The Doctors Rivers flew in from Atlanta and set up housekeeping in an apartment as near to the small Godeau Hospital as possible. After two days of no improvement, people all over the island started wearing buttons reading, "Wake up, Robert Rivers."

Ambrosius felt more horrible than anyone else on the island. Like the rest of the Hummers, he wanted to avenge his deca's dishonor, but he never intended to hurt Robert by hitting him when they argued on the rim of the coco valley. Unius did not sanction him for striking a fellow sharer in anger, but he did announce a rule change for coco, saying penalties could be assessed for unnecessary roughness using Gladaass instant replay in the future.

The deca stopped by the hospital every morning, on the way to breakfast; every afternoon, on the way to coco practice or games; and every evening, on the way back to the dorm after supper. For the entire first week, Doctor Ginger was cautiously optimistic that patience and conservative treatment were the best approaches to take. When a second week passed with no improvement, however, she started looking in earnest for a different cause of Robert's unconsciousness.

During a visit by Arnie and the rest of the deca, Doctor Ginger revealed her suspicions. "I no longer think this is related to a concussion caused by Ambrosius's hit."

"Why not?" Arnie asked.

She handed Arnie a light. "Look at this." She reached over with her gloved hands, opened Robert's mouth and rolled back his lips. Everyone crowded around Arnie's shoulders. Robert had many white lines running all over the inside of his lips, which looked like someone had drawn a roadmap on the inside of his cheeks with a white ink pen. All of them gasped at about the same time, while looking at Robert's mouth.

"He has had this since the day of the game and it has not responded to any antibiotic that we've tried," Doctor Ginger explained. "I am now thinking it must be some kind of a virus."

"Doctor Ginger, I don't like what I'm about to suggest, but I feel like I have to."

"Yes, Arnie."

"I mean, it's not like I'm a doctor or anything, though I've read a lot of medicine books."

"That's okay, Arnie. Any good doctor is never afraid to listen to a suggestion."

"Well, did any of the other kids who are sick have a mouth rash like that?"

"We don't have any other kids who are sick like this here, Arnie."

"Not here," Arnie explained, "the kids in Argentina, France, and Italy."

Hugo asked, "What?"

Amanda added, "Are you serious?"

Doctor Ginger thought long and hard about what Arnie was proposing.

Hugo asked, in a cracking voice, "Do you really think there might be such a thing as the Demeverde Plague?"

"It is highly unlikely," Doctor Ginger assured them. "Robert and Roberta are both vegetarians and the type of disease the other children have appears to be similar to the adult type, which is supposedly caused by eating bad meat."

"Unless, of course," Arnie argued with her, "what the other kids have isn't what they think it is and there is something in common between them and poor Robert here."

Doctor Ginger tilted her head a little and thought. "Your suggestion may have at least an inkling of merit," she said. "I hope it won't lead anywhere bad, but I'll talk to the researchers at GODEnt Medical, who are following those cases, and see what they say."

"Let us know as soon as you find out something," Arnie said.

Bernadette reached across the bed and hooked her thumb around Robert's pinkie. "All right," she directed, "everybody hook up and let's go."

Arnie stuck his own pinkie in the crook of Robert's thumb and stretched his thumb out for Roberta to reach over and grab. Everyone else in the deca hooked a pinkie with him and finished out the circle.

Roberta leaned over and whispered, "Pinkie power, man," in her brother's ear to give him some luck.

"Pinkie power," everyone, including Hugo, softly repeated.

* * *

The next night in the pit, Arnie accepted a conversation request and Doctor Ginger's face and voice rose up out of his Gladaass.

"Well, Mister Carver," Doctor Ginger's virjection said, "or Doctor Carver I should call you. I checked with the GODEnt Medical researchers and it seems as though you were right. Each of the other three children had the same mouth rash and it has not yet responded to any antibiotic they have tried."

Arnie replied, "Well, it's not good news, but at least we're getting somewhere."

"Yes, Doctor Carver!" yelled several of his friends.

"We tested Mister Rivers today," Doctor Ginger continued, "and he is having the same prion folding that the other three are having."

"Oh, my goodness!" Amanda exclaimed. "Then there is

a Plague of Demeverde!"

"Shhh," Arnie demanded, turning back to Doctor Ginger's visage. "So what do we do now?"

Roberta began to tear up softly. "My brother's going to die," she muttered to herself.

"Is not," Arnie assured her. "If there's anything we can do about it."

Doctor Ginger continued, "The T.D. Miller people in France think they can reverse the folding, but only if they can find out exactly what antigen is causing it. You nine have been with Mister Rivers the most. Do you know how anything may have gotten into his system to make him sick?"

Arnie answered, "We haven't thought about it in that way, so far."

"Well, do your best to figure it out and contact me if you have any ideas."

Arnie assured her, "Will do, Doctor Ginger."

The virtual image disappeared from above Arnie's Gladaass.

"All right," Bernadette began, as soon as the doctor disappeared. "Starting immediately, we need to discuss everything that we have done, eaten, drank, smelled, been in, been on, or been around, and everyone we have done anything with, covering every second, minute, hour, day, week, and month, since we all got on the plane from Chicago, the first Sunday in August."

Alex asked, "You're kidding, right?"

Bernadette tilted her head in Roberta's direction. "Ask Roberta if I'm kidding, Alex." She looked at Arnie and began. "Now, the twins were already on the plane when we got on."

The entire deca, minus Robert, of course, retraced all of the things they could remember that happened over the ten weeks between the start of the session and when Ambrosius hit Robert. None of them, however, was able to think of anything that Robert had done that at least one other of them had not done as well. After an hour of discussing everything they had done, they were no closer to finding an answer than when they began.

"Look, we're not making any progress," Arnie reasoned. "Let's all agree to continue to think about the question and sing out if anyone comes up with anything at all."

"Fine," Bernadette exasperatedly consented for them all.

The decamates went back to reading the virnews programs on their Gladaasses. A few minutes later Hugo made his usual call for attention. "Uh-oh."

"What now?" Most of the deca responded as usual.

"Unius," Hugo said, "we have a leak in security."

"What?" Tinker asked.

"Apparently someone has said something about Robert Rivers to Scorsos," Hugo explained.

"How do you know?" Tinker inquired.

"Dateline – Wilmington, Delaware," Hugo started to read. "Phineas Rubino, spokesman for Gregory Scorsos, who is assisting the international victims suffering from the Demeverde Plague, announced today that he has received information that irrefutably links the illnesses of the current victims of child variant Creutzfeldt-Jakob disease with a similar case of a student at Global Optimum Development Academy in Godeau, Demeverde."

"Oh, my gosh!" Bernadette said. "We are bound to hear from our parents on this one."

"What else does it say?" Tinker asked.

"Scorsos's spokesman would not release the details of what the connection is. All they have done when asked is to tell the reporters to direct questions to GODEnt's Medical Research Division about a patient with the same mouth rash the three current victims all have."

"Well, they got everything except Robert Rivers' name," Alex said.

"Which means that they don't really have as much as they want everyone to think," Arnie said.

Everyone turned to Arnie.

"What do you mean?" Alex asked Arnie.

"All they have is that someone from GODEnt called the doctors about whether the sick kids had a mouth rash," Arnie explained. "The doctors must have told Scorsos's people. They are just assuming that GODEnt would not be asking such a specific question without a good reason." Arnie looked around at the others. "I wonder why Scorsos is doing this."

"Well, here's the reason why," Hugo said.

"Why?" Everyone asked.

Hugo continued, "In a related story, representatives of Scorsos Resorts International, a new vacation division of Scorsos Enterprises International, announced they would honor any vacation package prices offered by any resort in Demeverde for all travelers who feel the need to change their winter vacation plans due to any fears of the Plague of Demeverde."

"Aha!" Amanda shouted. "The truth finally comes out."

Paula Poundsand wasted no time pointing out the truth with her own virtual press conference. From the first question asked, she admitted there was a sick GODA student at Godeau Hospital. "The illness is an isolated case in Demeverde. While there are similarities in the illnesses, there is no known connection between the sick child at GODA and any of the other of the children being discussed in the news. Scorsos Resorts International should be severely chastised for improperly using the other sick children for their own benefit by playing on their illnesses to scare vacationers away from Demeverde and to Scorsos's new resorts."

A reporter asked a followup question. "Candy Caine, VNN IVR News. Could it be true that Scorsos is merely trying to help those people caught in this bad situation?"

"Let's call this duck a duck, okay. Scorsos is not now, nor has it ever been, interested in anything other than the success of Scorsos's various enterprises around the world. It continues to be as likely all of the children suffering from this disease got it by eating Scorsos's tainted food products as they somehow picked up some virus here on Demeverde."

"Isn't the ill child on Demeverde a vegetarian?"

Paula coolly responded, "We are currently investigating a variety of possibilities."

"Still, do any of them point directly at Scorsos?"

"Meats are not the only food that Scorsos produces."

"Still, you don't know of any of Scorsos's brands that are under suspicion."

"We are still investigating all of the possible causes of the disease and we are not going to limit ourselves just to looking at Scorsos's foods at this time." Paula looked at her watch and back at Gladaass broadcasting her. "I have a meeting to attend," she said, concluding the virtual conference.

* * *

The deca spent pretty much every waking moment outside

of class for the next several days thinking and talking about what could have infected Robert. On Thursday, at lunch, Hugo was trying to lead the deca back through the past two months, "Let's reason this out."

"Go right ahead," Bernadette said.

"We've exhausted all the other possibilities, so let's discuss how Robert could have eaten some contaminated beef."

Arnie took a bite of a mushroom patty and mumbled, "Okay."

Hugo looked at Roberta and asked, "Is there any chance that Robert wasn't always a true vegetarian?"

Roberta dropped her hand holding her fork to the table with a loud sigh. "Robert?" she asked, somewhat offended.

"Is it possible?" Hugo repeated. "Just playing the devil's advocate here."

"No," Robert's twin sister defended him. "Don't you know the disciplined life we lead?"

"Hey," Hugo said, defending his approach, "you guys are Muslim, not Hindu. There's plenty of halal meat around GODA. They're sensitive about everyone's religion. Is it possible that Robert could have slipped himself a hamburger somewhere, sometime?"

"Look, I know the bad beef idea is GODEnt's alternative theory for what's causing the other kid's illnesses, but, if Robert did sneak a burger somewhere like you say, why aren't any other sharers laying ill in the hospital?"

Arnie took Roberta's side. "It has to be something else."

Nothing was allowed to interfere with the deca trying to figure out what happened to their friend. They were even talking during their think days, which they almost never did.

Arnie was spending his think day that Friday meditating on the problem, while he was practicing Perfect Vin's ballet on the ledge of the roof of the Student Union. He was finally able to hold the third position for five minutes at a time.

Amanda saw Arnie's head sticking out over the ledge as she rode a SlipDisc toward the entrance of the union and decided to go up and share an idea about the problem. She approached Arnie, who was deep in a meditative thought while he was holding the third position.

"Hey! Arnie," Amanda called, walking across the roof toward him. "Maybe some prion containing bone meal got used as fertilizer?"

As Amanda sat down on the ledge beside him, Arnie did not break his trance or change his position. She sat quietly, waiting for Arnie to come out of his trance, until something whitish-gray softly went "SPLAT" right beside her.

"ARGH!" Amanda shouted, looking over at the whitish-gray wet stuff and then looked up in the sky. "Birdie, birdie in the sky. Why'd you whitewash in my eye?" Amanda smiled and rhymed. "Gee, aren't you glad cows don't fly?"

"THAT'S IT!" Arnie cried out, suddenly coming out of his trance. "Amanda! That's it!"

"What's it?"

"Bird poop is what's it! Scarlet and orange bird poop!"

"Arnie Carver, what on earth are you talking about?" Amanda asked him again.

"When Émilie and I went to scope out Uncharted Island, I saw a Scarlet Vulture with orange tail feathers eating some dead cows that had washed up on the outer reef."

"So?" Amanda asked.

"So when we were in the park on midterm break and

Robert thought someone from a SlipSkyway dropped ice cream on his face and he got some in his mouth ...”

“Arnie, you are not making any sense.”

“It wasn’t a balloon.”

“What wasn’t a balloon?”

“When the stuff fell on Robert, I looked up and thought I saw a red and orange balloon go behind the SlipSkyway car.”

“So?”

“But it wasn’t a balloon,” Arnie continued. “I just had a flashback of it again in my trance as you were saying your rhyme and this time it was the same Scarlet Vulture with the orange tail feathers.”

“So the bird ate the bad meat off the dead cow, somehow caught a virus from it, and then gave the virus to Robert by pooping on him.”

“Exactly,” Arnie agreed with her. “Nothing probably would have happened to Robert, if he hadn’t been in the wrong place at the wrong time like that.”

“So what do we do now?” Amanda asked.

“We have to go find and catch the orange-tailed Scarlet Vulture alive, so GODEnt Medical can isolate the antigen and make an antibody for it.”

“And how do we do that?”

“We’re going to have to go back to Uncharted Island.”

* * *

Amanda and Arnie virmailed the rest of the deca and told them to get back to the apartment. When everyone arrived, Arnie told them everything that Amanda and he had figured out.

“So,” Arnie summed up, “that’s what’s making Robert

sick and all we need to do is go back to Uncharted Island and capture the orange-tailed Scarlet Vulture alive."

After Arnie had explained everything, Roberta asked, "Isn't tomorrow your Sabbath day, Arnie?"

"Yes," he replied, "but don't worry about it."

"Robert wouldn't want you to break your Sabbath. If we had not broken ours to go to the park on that Friday, then none of this would have happened."

Arnie looked at Roberta and then the others in his deca. "Look, guys. We all know I'm not religious. My folks didn't much care for any religion and I hadn't even thought about one until I came here. I just picked Saturday for a Sabbath because we have to take one day for it and Saturday seemed like the best middle of the road choice. So, certainly, to save Robert's life, I'm willing to forego my Sabbath."

All of his friends silently looked at Arnie, apparently not knowing what to say next.

Hugo broke the ice for them. "So that settles it then," he said. "Tomorrow, we all go to Uncharted Island."

BIRD WATCHING ON UNCHARTED ISLAND

As the rest of the deca followed Arnie on their SlipDiscs to SlipHover Beach, he told them, "Once again, guys, you all don't have to go do this with me."

"Robert is our friend, too, Arnie," Tinker reminded him.

"Not to mention he is my brother," Roberta stated emphatically.

"Exactly," Tinker agreed, nodding in Roberta's direction. "We are all in this deca together. So, if you go …"

"WE ALL GO!" Everyone yelled.

"Works for me," Arnie relented. "But if anything bad happens, remember I said you didn't have to go."

Seconds later, Alex asked, "Why aren't we using the SlipHover Beach by the resort?"

Arnie explained, "Because the one north of the GODU campus is much less busy and we shouldn't have to wait."

The deca, minus one, traveled in silence the rest of the way, until they reached the Global Optimum Development University Campus. It was larger and more spacious than GODA's campus, but more austere in its architecture and furnishings.

"So this is how the other half lives," Amanda said, not sure whether she would like doing without all the comforts of GODA.

Bernadette looked around at the sparse surroundings. "I guess they are more interested in their studies than where they are studying."

No one else expressed a comment, though all of them craned their necks back and forth while traveling across the GODU campus.

Reaching the GODU SlipHover Beach on the north side of the island, Arnie tried to dissuade them all from joining him again. "Once more, you guys ..." he started.

"WE KNOW ALREADY," they all thundered back at him. "WE DON'T HAVE TO GO WITH YOU."

Tinker clapped him on the back. "Guess you're just stuck with us on this one, buddy,"

They went to the checkout counter where the grass met the sand on the beach to request an access code for a SlipHover.

"One SlipHover, please," Arnie politely asked the middle-aged attendant.

The attendant looked up, recognized Arnie, and broke out in a broad grin. "Hey, aren't you Arnie Carver?"

"Yes," Arnie admitted. He looked at his friends and apologized. "I've gotten this a lot since the SUM Run." He looked back at the man. "I'm afraid so."

"I saw you win Doctor Ginger's SUM Run," the man said. "Beautiful dive off the Bridal Train Falls."

"It just kind of happened," Arnie said, seeming embarrassed by the attention. "So can we have an access code for a SlipHover?"

"Sure you can, Mister Carver," the attendant replied while pushing some spots on his Gladaass on the counter. "Destination?"

"Uncharted Island."

"Purpose of the trip?" the attendant asked. "Going back to show them how you won the race?"

"Just bird watching," Arnie answered, not wanting to violate the nonimposition code by lying. "Maybe bring back a pet."

"Pets are discouraged on Demeverde," the attendant informed him. "Imposing a claim on another living object of nature is unfair to the animal."

"Well, we're not going to keep it," Arnie defended their plan. "We're all naturalists at heart," he assured him. "We are just going to study it and then we'll put it right back."

The attendant acted like he was thinking about not giving them a SlipHover. Bernadette stepped up beside Arnie.

"The purpose of our trip doesn't matter," Bernadette said authoritatively looking the attendant square in the eyes.

"Oh, well," agreed the attendant, "the purpose of the trip doesn't really matter."

"So just give us the access code, please," Bernadette instructed him.

The man pushed a spot on his Gladaass. "So here's your

code." He read the numbers to them. "SlipHover twelve twenty-five. The code is six thirteen."

"Thank you," Bernadette said. "We'll just go have a nice trip now. Okay?"

"My pleasure," the man said. "Have a nice trip now. Okay?"

They all turned away and started walking toward where the surf hit the beach.

"Whew!" Arnie said looking at Bernadette. "I thought he would never let us go."

"Sometimes you just have to assert yourself with some people," Bernadette explained.

Once they embarked from SlipHover Beach, Arnie began telling them everything that he knew about Uncharted Island. "Most of this I learned from Émilie, but I picked up a few things by myself."

"How are we going to know where to look for this bird?" Aurelia asked. "When we were here for the SUM Run, I saw Scarlet Vultures all over the island."

"Well, they all seem to nest in the rim of Mile-Wide Volcano," Arnie explained. "So we should probably start looking up there first."

"And if we don't find it there?" Hugo asked.

"And if we don't find it there," Arnie responded, "then we will just have to look all over the island."

"Arnie," Tinker said, "at seven miles wide that's a whole lot of island."

"Well, a lot of it should be easy to search from afar," Arnie said. He pointed to Alex. "That's what we have old 'Eagle Eyes' here for."

"What?" Alex asked.

"I want to hover around the whole island once and let

you give it a good once over to look for the vultures in their nests and resting places," Arnie explained. "We may get lucky and see the orange tail on the first pass."

"And what if I don't see it from the SlipHover?" Alex asked.

"Then we will have to go up to Omarosa's Point and see if we can see it from there," Arnie replied.

"And if we still don't see it?" Hugo asked.

"Then we will just have to look a little harder," Arnie retorted. "Don't worry guys," he reassured them. "We will find this bird." Arnie looked forward and slowed the SlipHover, which was approaching the outer reef. "We have to make a stop here by this mass of coral, first," he said.

Arnie stopped the SlipHover and hopped over the edge of the open rear cabin to land in the shin-deep water, which was breaking over the reef.

"This is the way that Émilie brought me out here and I remember the vulture eating some beef by this huge piece of coral sticking up." He reached down, grabbed a horn sticking up out of the reef, and brought up the skull of the cow that was still attached to it. "I think this is the cow I saw the orange-tail eating."

Arnie took a big thick plastic bag out of his pocket and started putting it over the bull's head. "Tinker and Alex," he called to them watching him from the deck, "get down here and help me get this thing."

"What would we want that for?" Alex asked. "We're not going to feed it to the bird are we?"

"No," Arnie explained, as Tinker and Alex jumped over the deck and landed beside him. "We are going to see if there is enough tissue left in the skull for GODEnt Medical to use for anything. If we can't find the bird, then maybe they can find the antigen in the cow's brain tissue."

"Why doesn't this thing smell?" Alex asked as the three of them broke the skull off from the neck.

Tinker explained. "Salt water kind of acts like a natural preservative. It's kept any aerobic bacteria from putrefying the brain."

Everyone looked at Tinker suspiciously. "What?" he asked defending himself. "I know how things work."

"Exactly," Arnie confirmed.

They wrestled the skull and horns into the bag and onto the deck. "Pour some water in there," Arnie instructed, "to keep it preserved."

"And not smelly," Amanda added.

Arnie stood back up at the controls and turned the SlipHover northwest. "Next stop, Mile-Wide Volcano."

Heading for the vultures' nesting grounds, everyone but Arnie and Alex looked through their binoculars and searched the sky over Uncharted Island looking for the orange-tailed Scarlet Vulture. Alex searched the area unaided and saw all three of the Scarlet Vultures that everyone else saw. But, of course, he saw them minutes before anyone else did. None of them, however, had orange tail feathers.

After slowing the SlipHover off the coast of the middle of Black Sand Beach, Arnie turned the bow around and pointed it straight into the mouth of Mile-Wide Volcano. "Legend has it, the western third of the rim of the volcano was blown away during a major eruption eons ago, leaving a panoramic view of the remaining two-thirds. We can best see it from here."

"It is beautiful," Bernadette agreed. "But we aren't here for sightseeing."

"All right, Alex," Arnie requested, pointing to the

remains of the crater, "give it a good look."

Alex started scanning the northern rim of the crater and moved fairly steadily and quickly along the entire rim to the south. After less than two minutes under the unblinking gaze of the eight others in the SlipHover, Alex announced, "Two hundred fifty-seven Scarlet Vultures all sitting in their nests and I can't see one tail among them, orange or not."

"But it has to be there," Roberta stomped her foot and pleaded with a strained voice. "All of the birds nest there."

"Relax, Roberta," Alex tried to calm her, "I said I couldn't see it, not I don't see it."

"Why can't you?" Roberta begged for an explanation.

"Because I only have perfect visual acuity," he explained, "not x-ray vision. Their tails are all down under the rims of their nests." Alex turned back to Arnie. "Sorry, Arnie, we are going to have to look at them from the top of the volcano."

Arnie 'tsked' in disappointment and shook his head. "It was a good idea, anyway." He turned the SlipHover back to the north and picked up some speed. "We'll finish the loop of the island and then beach up on the south side near the mouth of the Tongue River."

On the other side of the island, Arnie stopped at the reef gate to Too Soon Lagoon and had Alex take a look there as well. While they had by then seen thirteen Scarlet Vulture tails, none of them had the coveted orange blaze.

"We'll just have to find it the hard way," Arnie said, pointing the SlipHover back south and heading for the mouth of the Tongue River.

"Which is?" Bernadette asked.

"We are just going to have to go hunt for it." Arnie kept a stern face as he steered the SlipHover around the rest of the island and beached it on the eastern side of Gaping Canyon.

While his friends rested with a bottle of Doctor Ginger's, Arnie used a piece of driftwood to draw the same map Émilie had drawn for him six weeks before. "To me," Arnie expounded, "the easiest way to the top is to work up the west edge of Lush Valley and climb Omarosa's Locks to the rim of Omarosa's Point."

"What about the moving quicksand pits?" Hugo asked.

"We will just have to go very carefully and keep each other from getting caught in a moving pit," Arnie assured him.

"How are we going to do that?" Hugo asked.

"With this," Arnie said, wiggling the stick in his hand. He then reached in his pocket and pulled out a fishing reel, "and this reel of two-hundred-pound deep sea line."

Bernadette interjected, "And some thoughtful, focused, non-destructive power, like Perfect Vin taught us."

"Not exactly," Arnie replied. "Just some good, old, American ingenuity."

"You're going to hook us and reel us out?" Hugo asked in jest, which made everybody else laugh.

"Close," Arnie said, "but not exactly that, either. I'll explain as we go." Arnie started to lead the group up the beach and along the woods at the foot of the ridge bordering the Gaping Canyon. He tied the stick he had been holding to the end of the fishing line, passed it back to Hugo right behind him, and picked up another thick stick as he proceeded deeper inland.

"What you have to understand is that quicksand is not really what most people think it is," Arnie began.

"You mean it's not deep pits of wet sand and stuff that will suck us down if we fall in?" Aurelia asked.

"No," Arnie replied, "not at all." He tied the second stick

to the line and handed it to Hugo. "Pass yours back," he said. Arnie picked up another stick as he kept walking and talking.

"As I was saying," Arnie loudly continued, "there are a lot of myths about quicksand. We aren't going to find roiling pits of dangerous quicksand around every bend in the trail in here and even if we do find one it is not going to suck any of us down like a vacuum cleaner."

"Good," Aurelia called out from the back of the line. "I so much would hate to get sucked down into a pit."

"In fact," Arnie continued, "most patches of quicksand are just a few inches to a few feet deep." Arnie tied off the stick in his hand passed it back down the line, let out another few feet of line and picked up another stick. "Quicksand is just the result of water flowing through sand, clay, or other material and lifting and separating small grains of stuff dissolved in the water."

"Hmm," Hugo said, as Arnie handed him the next stick and picked up another.

"Ordinarily," Arnie went on, "this sand, clay, and junk are shoved up against each other and held together by just a little bit of water. But, sometimes, this stuff can be packed together on a big puddle of water and, if something disturbs the puddle of water, then the material on top gets loose and becomes what people call 'quicksand.'"

Arnie tied off another stick, reeled out some more line, and yelled, "Pass it back." The group each passed their stick to the next person in line.

"Now," Arnie kept on talking, "another way quicksand can form is when something disturbs the packed sand; like a vibration, an earthquake, or a subsurface spring. When that happens, instead of staying all packed together, the grains of sand sift and shift until the whole patch behaves like a liquid."

The train of fish on the line continued to walk along behind Arnie, listening to him continuing the lesson. "The heavier the stuff is packed together, the more powerful the vibration or subsurface spring has to be. But even light stuff can get soupy, in the right conditions."

Arnie kept tying and passing sticks back as hc kcpt on teaching. "Quicksand can be found wherever water and sand or clay come together--creek beds and ocean coasts, prairies, and mountains. One good place to find it is in hilly country, with lots of caves and underground springs just like we have here on Uncharted Island."

Arnie stopped as they came out of the inland side of the trees in Lush Valley and let everyone come up beside him. A huge expanse of sandy, dried-up-looking swamp spread out in front of them for about a mile and appeared to run into the sheer cliffs running east to west across the island. The cliffs nearest them were covered by a lattice of vines.

"What we have in front of us is an old bed of rock perforated by underground springs," Arnie stated. "On top of the rock are eons of dirt, sand, and other detritus."

Aurelia turned around and asked Tinker, "Detritus?"

"That's 'Arnie-speak' for 'stuff'," he told her.

Arnie continued, "When one of the springs gets strong enough to pop through the dirt, sand, and stuff, we get a little patch of quicksand."

"So what are we going to do to get across it?" Hugo asked

"It probably won't be a big patch all at once. So we are going to walk across this plain all spaced out holding onto this." He held up the reel of fishing line attached to everyone's stick. "If you stumble into a quicksand patch, it probably won't reach above your knees. But even if it's deeper, you'll float quite nicely. Just go absolutely limp and hold onto your stick. The rest of us will keep on walking. We will pull you to terra firma and you can get back on your feet."

Everyone spread out, as far as their stick on the fishing line would let them, and started walking from the Lush Valley Forest across the plain to Omarosa's Locks. Arnie's idea worked like a charm. Every time one of them hit a patch of quicksand, the others just kept on going and dragged the fallen one on until he or she could stand up again. Thirty minutes after they left the forest, they found themselves heavily caked with mud from the waist down, but still standing together in front of Omarosa's Locks.

Everyone looked up the side of the vine-covered cliff from the bottom.

"Are you sure this is the easiest way up to Omarosa's Point?" Bernadette asked.

"That has to be a mile high up there," Amanda stated.

"Only two tenths," Arnie corrected her. "About a thousand feet."

"Are you sure this is the easiest way up to Omarosa's Point?" Bernadette repeated her question.

"Trust me, Bernadette," Arnie assured her, "you wouldn't like the last way I got there any better."

Arnie started digging his hands into the leafy growth covering the fist-sized thick vines.

"So how are we going to get up there safely?" Tinker asked. "We can't all climb up on one, two-hundred-pound line."

"Yes!" Arnie said triumphantly pulling out a wire rock-climbing harness attached to a cable going up over the vines and under the leaves. "We're going to climb using these autobelays, which Émilie told me about." Arnie yanked the harness and cable out from the vines, freeing up about twenty feet of cable from the leaves barely holding it down. He pulled the harness down to the ground and started to put his feet in the two loops. "Just find one of these about every four feet apart and put them on like a pair of pants."

Everyone else started feeling around in the vines until they had also found a harness and cable.

"Will these keep us from falling off the vines?" Roberta asked.

"No," Arnie answered.

"No?" several of them quickly and excitedly asked together.

"No," Arnie repeated. "But in the unlikely event that you do lose your grip, it will slow you significantly all the way down."

"Great!" Tinker mocked him. "Nothing like falling slowly to our deaths."

Arnie snapped his harness shut around his waist and started to climb up a few feet. He looked back and saw that everyone else was snapped in as well. "So stay here if you want, you big weenie," Arnie scoffed at Tinker.

"Nope, O great, fearless leader," Tinker retorted. "If you go …"

"WE ALL GO!" Everyone else yelled, stepping up into the vines.

The first three hundred feet only took them about fifteen minutes to climb.

Not all of them were in the best of shape. Tinker, who was covered in sweat, vine leaves, and dirt, breathed heavily, looked over at Arnie, and demanded, "I've gotta have some rest."

"All right," Arnie called over to all of them. "Let's hold up a minute and catch a breath."

Stopping to rest, Hugo started to lean back in his harness to see if it would support him. He felt it slide down a little and thought better of the idea.

"This harness doesn't seem to be stopping me here, Arnie," Hugo advised him and everyone else at the same time.

"It won't start to brake until you begin to fall pretty quickly," Arnie explained. "The ball that acts as the brake won't move up until you fall the first few feet. Then it will slowly lower you all the way down."

Several of the climbers started looking at each other; then, up at the cliff above them; and then, down at the cliff below them.

"And speaking of down," Arnie started to say. "It would be best if you didn't look ----"

"AYYYYIPE!" Amanda screamed, from the middle of the line.

"What?" Arnie yelled. "Did you slip?"

"I forgot!" Amanda squealed back. "I am deathly afraid of heights!" Amanda grabbed the vines in front of her tightly with both arms.

"Nice time to think of that, Amanda!" Tinker yelled at her.

"I knew that I shouldn't have talked Daddy into getting rid of the agents," Amanda whined. "They never would have let me do this."

Tinker, who was climbing right next to Arnie on the end, leaned over to talk to him. "Well, what do we do now, Arnie? If one of us falls, you know that all of us will have to go back and get whoever it is."

Arnie thought for a minute. He reached back into his pocket and pulled out his fishing reel. Wrapping his arm through a loop of vine to support himself, he held the reel with one hand, pulled some line out with his free hand, and threaded it into the lap of his harness. Then he pulled the end of the line through and held it out to Tinker.

"Take this and do what I just did," Arnie told him. As Tinker threaded the end through one side of his harness, left it in his lap, changed hands, and pulled it out to hand it over to Roberta, Arnie yelled down the line. "Look, everybody! Here is what we are going to do. Watch Roberta and do what she does."

Tinker held the end of the line out to Roberta. "Roberta," Arnie yelled, "hold your cable with your right hand and take the line from Tinker with your left." Roberta did as she was told. Arnie continued. "Now put it through this side of your harness and hold it in your lap." Roberta complied. "Now change your grip hand, reach through the right side of your harness, pull the line out of your lap, and hand it over to Aurelia."

Aurelia already had her left hand extended. She did what Roberta did and handed the line to Hugo, who repeated the task and held the line out to Amanda.

Amanda, however, was not about to let go of the vines she was clutched around.

"Take the line, Amanda," Hugo said, holding it out to her.

"No!" Amanda yelled, burying her face in the vines.

"Yes!" Hugo yelled back, while he straightened his legs to free up his cable going up a distance and shifting as much as he could toward Amanda, whose harness was now just a foot out of his reach. "Take the darned line!" Hugo hissed loudly.

"No!" Amanda yelled, burying her face in deeper.

Hugo was red in the face with anger. He brought his legs up and hooked them in the vines in front of him, let go of the cable with his left hand, leaned sideways in his harness and stuffed the line in his hand through the left side of Amanda's harness and held it in her lap. "Bernadette!" Hugo yelled. "Do what I'm doing and reach in and get this darned thing!"

Bernadette tried to reach over to meet Hugo's hand, but she came up about a foot short.

"Hand it to her!" Hugo yelled at Amanda.

"No!"

"Hugo, shut up!" Bernadette yelled.

"Shutting up," Hugo relented, still leaning horizontal with his hand in Amanda's lap.

"Amanda," Bernadette said, looking up at Amanda from her horizontal position. "You can look at my face."

"I can look at your face," Amanda said, glancing a little at Bernadette.

"Good," Bernadette praised her. "Now you can hold on very tightly with your left arm and still not fall."

"Don't say fall," Hugo interrupted.

"Shut up, Hugo," Bernadette hissed. "Do you want to do this?"

"Shutting up," Hugo whispered.

"Amanda," Bernadette calmly instructed her, "you can let go with your right hand." Amanda unclenched her right arm a little. "You can reach through your harness."

Amanda said to herself through gritted teeth, "I can reach through my harness," as she did so.

"You can hand me that line," Bernadette told her.

"I can …" Amanda grabbed the line out of her lap and, without looking anywhere but at the vine in front of her, shot her arm out straight beside her. "Hand you that line."

Bernadette took the line from Amanda's hand and flipped herself back up straight. "Good girl, Amanda," she encouraged her. "Now, relax so we can get up this darn mountain."

Amanda seemed to unwind a bit. Bernadette looped the line through her lap and passed it on down to Min-su, who passed to Alex.

When he had made his last knot, Alex yelled back, "All tied off here."

"All right, Amanda," Arnie called down to her. "That is a two-hundred-pound line running through your harness. If one of us falls, then the two people beside him will simply hold on and catch him. Do you believe me?"

"No!" Amanda called back, looking up at the top of the cliff.

"Roberta!" Arnie called to her. "Hang on tight."

She cinched up her hold on the cable.

"Watch," Arnie said, "Tinker's going to let go …"

"I'm what?" Tinker yelled, looking straight at Arnie.

"And Roberta and I are going to catch him," Arnie finished. "Just let go, Tinker." Arnie assured him. "It's a new two-hundred-pound line. It will hold any one of us easily."

"If I die," Tinker said letting go, which made the fishing line tighten all the way across to Alex taking up the slack. "I will never forgive you."

"See, Amanda," Arnie said, "You couldn't fall now if you tried."

Amanda loosened her grip on the vine somewhat and

kept her eyes fixed on the rim of the cliff above her.

"Come on, Amanda," Arnie called to her. "Look over here at Tinker."

"Don't make me look anywhere but up, Arnie." Amanda demanded. "Let's just go and get me off this mountain."

"Okay, Tinker," Arnie called him back up. "Alright, Amanda, you take the lead and we'll go at whatever pace you pick." Amanda lifted one leg and everyone else did the same. "And remember," Arnie added, "If you go …"

"WE ALL GO!" Everyone else yelled.

While on the way up, they had plenty of time to talk about whatever they wanted. Every few feet or so, Amanda paused and Alex turned around and looked at the Scarlet Vultures, which were flying around after being disturbed from their resting places in the vines by the large group of noisy climbers.

"None of them has orange tail feathers," Alex said at one point, "which is a good thing, because I have no idea how we would go catch it from here."

Min-su asked, "How are we going to catch this thing anyway, Arnie?"

"I have a fishing net in the pocket of my cargo pants," Arnie answered. "We're going to spread it out, tie some rocks around it for weights, sneak up on the vulture and throw the net over it."

"Great!" Alex jeered in a thick Russian accent to break the strain of the climb. "Net fishing for vultures. What a country!"

Approaching the crest of the cliff, Arnie cheered them over. "Great! We've made it."

Amanda curled herself over the top and pulled her legs up beside her. "Thank God!" she said, glaring at Arnie. "Don't ever ask me to do that again!"

After they all got over the top of Omarosa's Point, everyone unsnapped from their harnesses and collapsed on the hard, scalding hot rock ground. All of their clothes were completely drenched in sweat, however; so no one seemed to mind that they could have fried themselves on the rock had they not had their clothes on.

"Thanks, Amanda," Tinker teased her. "You're a great tour guide in the sky."

"As smart as we are," Amanda inquired, ignoring Tinker's remark about her less than stellar performance on the climb, "why didn't any of us remember to bring any water?"

Several of them groaned in agreement.

"Arnie," Hugo asked. "Where's that swimming pool of Doctor Ginger's that you told us about?"

"Good idea, Hugo." Arnie said. "Follow me."

Everyone else liked Hugo's idea better than dying of thirst, so they all went and leaned over into the pool, which was still half full of water.

"Ee-yew," Amanda whined. "It has all the dirt from four hundred runners settled in the bottom."

"Yes," Hugo explained, dipping his cupped hands into the pool, "but what's on the top is at least relatively clean and it's still better than nothing."

Min-su was standing beside the pool, with her eyes closed and her hand on its rim. "No! Wait!" she shouted, opening her eyes. "Some big birds have been here."

Hugo argued, "What? Now you can feel auras left behind by animals, in addition to looking into their hearts and minds?"

"Well," Min-su said, hesitantly, pointing to the ground, "yeah, plus I can see these big bird pellets left on the ground."

"So? Birds don't make in the water," Hugo said. He looked at Tinker and asked, "Do they?"

Tinker shrugged his shoulders. "I don't know. What are you asking me for?"

"Hey," Hugo took on a mocking tone, "you know how things work."

Min-su continued to argue, "If we're thinking that some virus is coming from bird feces, then we may want to be careful about drinking any possibly contaminated water, don't you think?"

Arnie agreed, "She has a very good point. At least one of us is thinking because I sure wasn't. I'm just as thirsty as Hugo." He looked at Alex. "Alex, don't touch any of it, but, very carefully, smell some of those pellets to get their scent and then see if you can smell the same odor in this water here."

Alex kneeled down on the ground and sniffed a small pile of the feces. Then he stood up and bent over to get his nose near the water. After a long inhale, he said, "Hugo, I'd go wash my hands if I were you." Standing up, he nodded toward Min-su. "She was right. It's got the same stuff in it."

"Okay," Bernadette said, looking around them. "Where is a source of fresh water up here?"

Arnie glanced around and then pointed to the east. "The Hot Springs Pools, right over that ridge."

Hugo won the race to the bubbling natural geothermal pools and aggressively washed his hands in one of them. "Better not be drinking out of this one," he warned.

All of them began to pick up handfuls of hot water from the other pools and drink it. After some good long drinks and five minutes of rest, the deca, less their friend and brother, was ready for the trek back west across the Flat Top Plateau to the rim of One-Mile Volcano.

"Just two more miles and we are there," Arnie urged everyone on.

The nine of them trudged across the hot, rocky-topped plateau, chittering and chatting for the next thirty minutes. They walked all the way around to the end of the south rim and spread out looking down into the nests with their binoculars, except for Alex, of course.

"Pee-yew!" Amanda complained. "Alex, what's that rotten-egg smell?"

"Sulfur from the volcano vents," he explained.

"Forget the smell," Arnie demanded. "And go look for the orange-tail." He pointed to the edge of the volcano. "To make an even coverage of the entire rim, one of you start looking here, while the next one of you moves down some and begins looking on the next section. Keep moving out along the rim. As you get through with one section, run on down to the end of the line and start wherever the end of the line is at the time."

As each person on the far left end of the line completed a section, they would run to the right end of the line and start looking down again. The group continued to leap frog each other that way all the way around the rim. Not seeing the orange-tailed bird, however, everyone started to get more tired, thirstier, and more depressed as they made their way around the rim.

Having exhaustively searched every nest under the rim of Mile-Wide Volcano, the nine of them sat down facing Lushest Valley to try and figure out where to look next.

Tinker asked, "What about working down through Mud

Meadow and the Sobbing Seawillows? There have to be some dead animals in there for the vultures to eat."

"No," Arnie said. "Alex can see all of Mud Meadow from over the ridge of the Flat Top and the vultures would never go into the Seawillow Forest, because it's too thick."

"How about going over to the Scenic View Rope Bridge and checking out Gaping Canyon."

"It's possible," Arnie said, hanging his chin toward his chest, "but I so much thought that it would be here."

Suddenly, Alex started to smile.

Arnie noticed his grin and asked, "What, Alex?"

"Arnie," Alex said, "have you ever found something you'd been looking for when you're not even looking for it?"

"Yeah," Arnie said. "Sometimes, I guess."

Alex pointed to a red speck of feathers way off on the other side of Lushest Valley. "Well, there's a Scarlet Vulture laying on its side in the middle of that hill over there." Everyone started training their binoculars where Alex was pointing. "You can't see it's tail feathers," Alex explained, "because they're under a big leaf, but I'll bet you dinner and doughnuts, by the way he's twitching, that's our vulture, because he looks just as sick as Robert."

Roberta found it first, after Alex. "I see it!" she squealed and started to get up. "Come on, everybody. Let's go get it."

Refreshed by the possibility of finally catching their prey, everyone jogged back across the plateau to Omarosa's Point. Alex kept a watch on the bird between watching his steps on the rocky ridge. They were ready to start charging down Lushest Valley, when Arnie stopped them. "Hold on a second, everybody," he called. "Let's slow down a bit and do this thing right."

"Let's just go get the bird, Arnie," Tinker said. "You said last night that we need to get it to the researchers alive and it looks like it's dying, so let's hurry up."

"Well, let's talk about what's in there, before we just go busting across the valley. Okay?"

"Okay," Hugo humored him. "Tell us what's in there."

"Well, it's kind of like the quicksand," Arnie said. "What looks like a solid carpet of green trapfoot vine leaves is actually covering a labyrinth of twisting and turning tunnels that pour out into the headwaters of the Tongue River coming out of the bottom of Omarosa's Face back there." Arnie pointed out over the rim to the south. "If anyone falls off in one of those, then he is going to find himself swimming back to the boat in the middle of the river. Neither the tunnel ride, the fall in the water, nor the ride out to the ocean will kill you, but if we all fall in before we get to the bird, then we will have wasted the day." Arnie reached back into his pocket and brought back out the reel of line. "So I think that we ought to do the same thing that we did this morning. Everyone find a stick and tie onto the line. Let's stretch it tight and drag anyone who needs across the valley."

Everyone quickly found a stick and the trick worked as well as it had before. A few of them slipped down in some holes, but their tight grip on the taut line kept them steadily moving along to the downed Scarlet Vulture. Finally closing in, thinking the entire hard day's work was going to work out, Arnie's heart sank as he realized the bird jerking on its side in front of them did not have any orange tail feathers.

"That's not the bird," Arnie quietly said. "It doesn't have the orange feathers."

"So what if it doesn't?" Tinker asked still holding his

stick even though they were all bunched up around Arnie who was standing over the bird. "Look at the way that it's shaking. It's shaking just like Robert was in the valley."

"So are we going to take it or not," Amanda demanded. "Because I sure didn't climb the face of that mountain to go back home empty-handed.

Roberta pleaded with him. "Arnie, you said we need to take it alive." She pointed to the shivering bunch of feathers. "This guy is dying and we need to get going."

Finally, Arnie stuck the reel of line in his pocket and tucked his stick in his belt, so he was still tied to everyone by the line. Once his hands were empty, he took the net out of his pocket, took two steps closer to the bird and dropped the net over the vulture, which only flapped its wings weakly a time or two.

Arnie stood back up with the bird, half his size, in his arms and took one step back toward the group. "Okay, I've got it," he said. "It's weak, bu-----"

"Swoosh!" was the only other sound they heard as Arnie and the bird disappeared beneath the velvet green leaves of the trapfoot vines. Then a "Snap!" as the line attached to the stick that Tinker was instinctively gripping firmly went taut. Followed by a "Ping!" as it broke, a "Zing!" as the end flew threw the air, and an "Owww!" as the line came back and popped Tinker in the face.

Everyone left standing around the hole where Arnie and the bird had just disappeared was in a state of shock. No one knew what to say.

Then, Tinker started mocking Arnie, "Yeah, Tinker, let go of the vine a thousand feet up in the air. It's a new two-hundred-pound line and it will catch you if you fall." Tinker looked around at the rest of the group, holding his stick tied to the line firmly in his hand. "Well, if you go ..." Tinker said, jumping into the hole.

"WE ALL GO!" Everyone else yelled together, before each disappeared down into the hole, one after the other.

The express route back down to the Tongue River was better than any waterslide or roller coaster ride any of them had ever encountered. The slippery slime from the trapfoot vine leaves above and the pitch-black darkness kept them from keeping track of where they were going. One minute they were all standing together in Lushest Valley and for the next three minutes they were slipping and sliding down a mile of the guts of a volcanic mountain. Finally, they popped out, one after the other, each still holding their sticks on the fishing line, for a twenty foot free fall from the top of a cave to the tepid water flowing out of Omarosa's Mouth that was the Tongue River.

The current slowed down the closer they got to the ocean, but no matter at what speed they went, the group of them was still about one hundred feet upstream from Arnie. Arnie had flipped over on his back trying to keep the vulture from drowning. As the river grew wider and quieter nearing the ocean, Arnie kicked himself with the vulture on his chest over to the bank. By the time that the others caught up with him on the bank, Arnie had taken the net off of the bird and stuffed it back in the pocket of his wet cargo pants. He was sitting by the bird, his eyes brimming with tears, when they walked up.

The Scarlet Vulture had stopped jerking. In fact, it was not moving at all.

Arnie looked up at Roberta and sniffled. "It looks like I killed it," he said.

Roberta sat down beside him and looked at the bird. "It

was all but dead when you picked it up, Arnie. It wasn't your fault."

Tinker picked up the dead bird and started walking back toward the SlipHover, which was still beached where they had left it that morning, just to the east of Gaping Canyon.

A somber mood covered them all as they pushed off from the beach. Arnie set the SlipHover's autopilot, requested a destination of North SlipHover Beach, and got a "my pleasure" in return. He then joined the rest of the nine, seated around the dead vulture on the open back deck, for the long, sad ride home.

The SlipHover slowed on autopilot to scoot over the outer reef. As it did, Bernadette, who had lost her will to look at the dead bird anymore, tried to disturb Arnie, who had not.

"Arnie?" she asked.

"Not now, Bernadette."

"Arnie?"

"Not now!" he said again.

"Arnie!" Bernadette demandingly said.

"What?" Arnie finally relented.

She pointed over the edge of the SlipHover and said, "I may not have old Eagle Eye's vision, but we happen to be passing your favorite bird."

Arnie jumped up, looked at where she was pointing, and yelled "STOP AND REVERSE" at the disc in the front of the SlipHover, which answered, "My pleasure." He quickly yanked the net out of his pocket and threaded a loop of fishing line from his reel through and around the edge of the net. Just as the SlipHover reversed past the orange-tailed Scarlet Vulture, which was eating some carcass on the outer reef, Arnie tossed the net like he had seen some local fishermen do for the past three months.

The net sailed wide open for the twenty feet throw to the bird. As the net started its descent, the vulture took flight over the bow of the craft.

"Darn it! I missed!" Arnie yelled, yanking the net back onto the deck. He turned back toward the front of the craft. "STOP and RESUME COURSE!"

"My pleasure."

"EXPRESS!"

"My pleasure," the disc answered again.

"Where could that guy be going?" Arnie asked no one in particular.

"What do you mean?" Bernadette inquired.

"Scarlet Vultures all live in One-Mile Volcano," Arnie answered her. "They like the sulfur from the fumes." He thought for a moment and repeated the question. "Where could that guy be going?" The orange-tailed Scarlet Vulture turned toward the east of Demeverde. "That's it!" Arnie exclaimed

He yelled back at the disc, "Change course! La Paya del Local!"

"My pleasure."

"The local's beach?" Amanda asked Arnie. "Why there?"

"It's the beach right below the Enojado volcano," Arnie explained. "It's the only other active volcano on Demeverde."

The bird was pulling away from them. "Alex," Arnie called, "please don't lose sight of him."

"For as long as I can," Alex replied even though he had been watching already.

Arnie stuffed the net and fishing reel back in his pants

pocket. Beaching the SlipHover on La Paya del Local, Arnie jumped out off the deck and yelled, "COME ON!"

They all piled into an empty SlipStream Dozenberth and Arnie sat in the front seat. "Lookout on the Enojado volcano, please."

"My pleasure."

"Express, please."

"My pleasure," the disc responded as the Dozenberth picked up speed.

"Emergency speed, please."

"Please state the nature of the emergency," the voice from the disc politely requested.

"Threat to human life," Arnie said.

"My pleasure," the disc responded as the Dozenberth sped up the road spiraling around the volcano to the lookout rim.

Chose's face and voice rose from a small Gladaass beside the disc. "Arnie Carver! Why are you operating a Dozenberth and why have you requested emergency mode."

"Tell Doctor Ginger that we are chasing the index carrier that we think infected Robert Rivers!"

Chose did not argue, but Arnie could tell by the moving background behind him that Chose had picked up his Gladaass and started to move. "What is it?" Chose asked.

"An orange-tailed Scarlet Vulture, which we think lives in the Enojado volcano." Arnie quickly relayed the details about Robert getting hit with the bird's mess. "Just call Doctor Ginger and the GODEnt Medical Research people and tell them to get ready to isolate the index."

The Dozenberth pulled up at the lookout directly above the small active site of the Enojado volcano.

"I've lost him over the rim, Arnie," Alex said excitedly.

"But I haven't seen him fly back out."

The sulfur smell was not as concentrated as it was at Mile-Wide Volcano, but it was acrid enough to water everyone's eyes. Arnie ran to the edge of the lookout booth hanging inside over the rim. As he expected, the orange-tailed Scarlet Vulture was resting in the middle of a nest attached to the side of the rim right below them.

Arnie took the net and reel from his pocket, tossed the reel to his feet, put one foot on it, and swung open the lattice. He leaned out over the edge of the lookout and threw the web just as he had done before. The vulture tried to take flight just as the snare reached the nest and it became hung in full extended span in the trap.

The loop of fishing line around the edge of the net tightened and formed the mesh into a large loose bag with the vulture inside. The whole contraption, net, line, and most importantly the vulture was now swinging back and forth over the edge of the lookout. Arnie carefully bent down and took the fishing reel from under his foot. Alex and Tinker controlled the bird as it came up over the edge of the rail.

"WE GOT IT!" Arnie yelled, sitting down beside the flapping bird in the bag of fishing net. Sirens could be heard coming up the spiral road around the volcano as everyone else sat down around Arnie, Alex, Tinker, and the bird. "We got it!" Arnie repeated.

FIRST, THE BAD AND THEN, THE GOOD

The euphoria of GODA's role in perfecting the vaccine for child variant Creutzfeldt-Jakob disease lasted a very short time. Gathered in the pit, a few nights after they delivered the vulture to GODEnt Medical, the deca began to discuss how to answer all the questions they were being asked.

Arnie suggested a strategy. "The best way to spin this will be to say that we couldn't have captured the bird without the help of a whole lot of people at GODA."

Hugo raised his eyebrows as he broke in, "So it won't look like we went off on a wild adventure all by our little young selves?"

"Something like that," Arnie replied. "Did everyone get the virmail telling us to show up at Mrs. L's office tomorrow?"

Tinker answered, "I did and all the others that I've talked to did as well." Everyone around the pit nodded in agreement. "We have to be sure to tell them Doctor Ginger told us to figure out how the virus got into Robert."

Amanda rejected the idea. "I don't think what we did was what she had in mind when she said if we got any ideas we should contact her."

Aurelia asked, "Did anyone else hear that Chose was going to be there, too? At least he likes us. Mrs. L will just kill us. Do they still allow you to eat people on Demeverde?"

"Not since the early nineteen hundreds," Hugo advised.

Roberta rose up out of her ched. "Look, all we need to say is that we were simply trying to save my brother's life and the lives of three other kids, and avert an economic disaster for GODEnt and the rest of Demeverde. It'll justify anything that we did. What did we do wrong, anyway?"

"Oh, I don't know," Hugo said. "Taking a SlipHover under false pretenses after hypnotizing the SlipHover worker."

"I didn't hypnotize him," Bernadette defended herself.

"Taking an unauthorized and unsupervised trip to Uncharted Island."

"No one's ever told us we couldn't go there," Bernadette argued back.

"Driving a Dozenberth without a license."

"Okay," Bernadette relented, "that may have been just plain illegal."

"At an excessive rate of speed," Hugo continued.

"Extenuating circumstances," Bernadette added. "Hot

pursuit of a fleeing vulture."

Roberta repeated her argument. "The ends justified all of the means."

Arnie sighed loudly. "Okay, the ends and the extenuating circumstances justified everything we did. That's our final stand."

The next day in Mrs. L's office, she was not her usual calm self. She stood them in a line and yelled her questions at them, while Chose looked on from the far corner of the room. "Who was leading your deca in this delinquency?" she loudly demanded.

Arnie leaned forward from the line. "It was all my idea, Mrs. L. I told them that I needed to go get the vulture from Uncharted Island."

Alex quickly interrupted. "Not exactly, Mrs. L. He told us he was going to do it alone and that we should stay behind. We all insisted on going with him, whether he liked it or not."

"Regardless of the danger to yourselves or to others?" Mrs. L responded.

Roberta stated her argument. "We were trying to save lives, Mrs. L. The ends justified the means."

Mrs. L started to reply, hesitated for a moment, and then continued. "Only because you were under the strain of worrying about your twin brother, Miss Rivers, am I willing to overlook your involvement in this matter."

Arnie reasoned, "Not to belittle their sibling relationship, but my deca is the closest thing I have to a family anymore. These guys, and Robert, are as close as I have to any brothers and sisters."

Mrs. L stammered, looking for a rebuttal. "Even your unfortunate status, Mister Carver, cannot justify every wrong you do."

Bernadette assumed a diplomatic tone. "What wrong did we do, Mrs. L?"

"You know everything you did was all wrong, Miss Rogers. Otherwise, you would have asked for permission before you did it."

"All we did is what Unius and GODA is teaching us to do."

"You have no idea what you are talking about, young lady."

"Look, Mrs. L, Unius invited us here because he thought we were leaders."

"Don't presume to know what Unius thinks," Mrs. L shot back.

"Regardless of who thought it, Mrs. L, we were recruited to be here to be the next group of leaders."

"And?" Mrs. L. queried.

"And leaders lead, Mrs. L. Our deca is nothing but leaders and leaders lead. So if you want to punish us for taking the lead and saving the lives we saved, then go ahead and do it."

The rest of the deca stood silent, as Mrs. L inspected them one by one. "Do any of the rest of you have anything to say for yourselves?"

After a long moment's pause, Min-su broke the silence. "We acted as one, we've argued as one, we'll take the punishment as one."

The furious wind had blown out of Mrs. L's sails. She looked at Chose. "Do you have anything that you want to say to these … these …?"

"You seem to have them in your usually capable hands," Chose said.

If Mrs. L was looking for exuberant support, then Chose obviously wasn't going to give it. "Fine," she began, "for misappropriation of a SlipHover, one week's detention. You'll go nowhere but to classes and meals and spend the rest of your time in your suite."

The deca continued to stand silent. Mrs. L continued, "For an extremely dangerous trip to Uncharted Island, a second week's detention."

The deca still stood resolute. "And for driving a Dozenberth without a license at a high rate of speed, a third week of detention. I think that gets us to the end of the session, which I hope will be enough to teach you ..." She turned squarely to them and waggled her right index finger. "Not to test me like this again." Mrs. L looked again at Chose. "Do you have anything you want to add?"

Chose slightly shook his head no.

"You may all now return to your rooms." Mrs. L dismissed them with a final point of her finger to the door.

That same evening, Chose arrived unannounced at the deca's apartment. After the nine sharers assembled in the pit, Chose began to speak.

"You should all understand that I share Mrs. L's opinion that what you nine did was very dangerous."

Hugo replied, "We know."

Chose looked at him skeptically. "What you don't know, however, I am sure, is that I also share Unius' opinion that it was also very brave."

Everyone of them sat a bit straighter and smiled, half proud and half embarrassed by knowing about Unius' attention, except for Hugo, who continued to talk. "So why are we under house arrest?"

"Well, publicly, Unius has appointed Mrs. L to run

GODA's daily operations and he can't very well undercut her authority. What you did was very dangerous and neither she nor Unius can have sharers running off and doing such reckless things without some repercussions."

Arnie asked, "And privately?"

"And privately, after your punishment is complete, Unius plans to recognize you at the final dismissal."

"Coooool," Tinker said.

The others nodded their heads in agreement.

Arnie thought about making a plea for leniency. "But we still have to serve out the punishment?"

"I'm afraid so."

"Oh, well. Can't blame a guy for trying."

"Nonetheless," Chose said, as the got ready to leave, "I just wanted you to know that Unius and I and many others are justifiably proud of what you have done and how you have done it. Just don't tell anybody I said so."

"No problem," Arnie said. "It was our pleasure."

Alex snapped at Arnie in jest, "Please stop using that phrase, you paradisial parrot."

"It wasn't your pleasure, Mister Shelikhov?" Chose asked.

"Oh, sure, it was, Chose," Alex replied. "But I just hate the way everyone on Demeverde mindlessly says that."

"Maybe it's not as mindless as you think," Chose said, disappearing through the revolving tube door.

Arnie and the rest of the deca, still minus Robert, served their "apartment arrest" until the end of the session's final exams. Other than getting to go to classes and meals, the nine of them stayed confined to their apartment. Though they all would have preferred an afternoon coco practice to being locked up inside, the time spent together gave them more chances to talk and share with each other and watch the virnews programs from around the world.

The Monday final for the Heritage Program had been particularly stressful for them all because their minds were with Robert, who was still not home yet. The Tuesday final for Science and Technology was a little easier after they all received a single hour's reprieve from Mrs. L to visit the missing member of their deca. Wednesday's final in Basic Secular Knowledge was almost a breeze after Robert virmailed them all Tuesday night to say he was getting out of the hospital the next day.

Doctor and Doctor Rivers brought Robert back to the apartment to sleep in his own ched for his last night on campus before his parents took him and Roberta back to Atlanta for the two-month intersession break. Everyone was very tearful at the reunion. Robert finally convinced his parents to go back to their own temporary apartment to pack and get ready to go home the next day.

After the Doctors Rivers left, the entire deca, now complete again for the first time in almost eight weeks, sat on their cheds in the pit reviewing the day's virnews on their Gladaasses like almost nothing different had happened recently.

"Uh-oh," Hugo said.

"What?" almost everybody else asked.

"Scorsos," Hugo deadpanned, "you have a problem."

"Finally!" Amanda cried out in joy. "Couldn't happen to a nicer person. What?"

"Dateline - Wilmington, Delaware. Phineas Rubino, spokesman for Gregory Scorsos of Scorsos Foods International, refused comment today on allegations that they have been dumping downer feed lot calves at sea while being transported from Scorsos's U.S. operations to its European and South American farms and ranches. The extent of the dumping has grown as a result of DNA mapping by Demeverdan health authorities of dozens of beef carcasses, which are believed to have been hung up on the outer reefs of Demeverde's Uncharted Island for the past several years. The DNA registration of the animals found on the reefs have all been traced back through the International Food Livestock Registry Program to herds belonging to Scorsos Foods International. The Demeverde health, tourism, and legal authorities have asked the United States Department of Justice and the European Union to aid them in an investigation of whether the dumping of the diseased cows was an intentional act on Scorsos's part to destroy Demeverde's tourism industry as a competitor of Scorsos's Resorts International."

"No mention of us," Alex scoffed.

"Wait," Hugo told him, "there's more."

"More!" the rest of the deca cheered.

"In a related story, all four of the children in Argentina, France, Italy, and Demeverde have completely responded to the antibody and vaccine injections jointly developed by T.D. Miller Pharmaceuticals and GODEnt Medical Research. Paula Poundsand, GODEnt's public relations spokesperson, expressed great gratitude that all of the children have fully recovered. 'While we did not initially believe that the so-called Plague of Demeverde was a natural phenomena of our little bit of paradise, as soon as we discovered that the disease had actually been planted here by Scorsos Enterprises International, several people took all of the actions necessary to discover the carriers of the disease and GODEnt Medical and T.D. Miller Pharmaceuticals have been able to develop an antibody and vaccine that has been one hundred percent successful in treating the disease.'"

"Still no mention of us directly!" Alex complained.

"Relax, Alex," Arnie tried to calm him. "Some of us might not want the attention."

"What do you mean?"

"I just don't want to be in the virnews." Arnie said. "I like my privacy, thank you very much."

Bernadette changed the subject. "I wonder what Unius will say at the session end assembly?"

"I heard that he's going to welcome Robert back from the dead," Aurelia joked.

"Very funny!" Robert replied.

"Have you prepared any words of wisdom for the moment?" Aurelia egged him on some more.

"I'll let you know tomorrow," Robert scowled.

"On another matter," Min-su began, "we have to announce our first Top Ten Percenter tomorrow and I nominate Arnie."

"Forget it!" Arnie protested. "Like I said, I don't like the public eye." He smiled at Bernadette. "Bernadette's a much better choice for leader."

Bernadette looked at Arnie with a glint of disappointment in her expression. "You have to know when to listen to the public, Arnie."

"All those in favor," Min-su persisted, "signify by saying 'Aye.'"

"Aye," everyone but Arnie responded.

"Looks like you're the first T-T-P, buddy," Hugo advised him. "Sorry."

"Not as sorry as we'll all probably be," Arnie groused.

* * *

The next morning, at the session end assembly, all four classes were seated in the Student Union lecture halls. The walls were all up, so the entire four thousand sharers of GODA were all together for the meeting. The quadra-array of virtual displays made an X in the center of the floor so that all of the classes could see the speakers equally well. A round disc on the floor on the freshman class's side of where the four lecture pits came together irised open and Chose and Mrs. L rose up from the hole left by the disc. All of the sharers in the room snapped up out of their chairs.

Mrs. L leaned over to the lectern microphone and said, "Thank you for standing."

Chose flicked his fingers at all of the sharers around the room and said, "Sit, sit, sit, already."

Mrs. L spoke for a few moments about how the current session had ended, noting that it was the first session for some in the room and the next to the last for some others. She welcomed back Robert Rivers and asked him to come down to share a few words of what he had learned from the entire ordeal.

Robert walked down the incline aisle from his chair. He stood beside Mrs. L and looked all the way around the room, before he broke into a broad smile and said, "Don't eat bird poop!"

It took Mrs. L a full two minutes to get all of the sharers back under control. Of course, Robert egged everyone on to continue the laughing, every time it quietened a little.

"Now," Mrs. L said, staring perturbedly at Robert. "Though none of you have yet been afflicted with, ahem, the Plague of Demeverde, Doctor Ginger has assured me that twelve ounces of prevention will definitely be worth a pound of cure." Mrs. L reached inside her long coat and pulled out a bottle of Doctor Ginger's containing a scarlet red layer on top and a familiar fluorescent green on the bottom.

"Each of you will find under your chairs," Mrs. L continued, "a bottle of Doctor Ginger's new flavor, Scarletberry-Apple, which, in this inaugural bottling, contains the vaccine for the disease that hurt Mister Rivers. All of you will now be required to completely consume the entire bottle as we sit here in the next minute."

Mrs. L unscrewed the top of her bottle, tipped it bottoms up, and held it there until all twelve ounces had flowed down her throat. She leaned back over to the lectern and said, "No belching when you are done ..." She wagged her finger at them. "And you would all do very well to not test me on that." She looked in her cap to read the message and mentioned to the sharers, "You will note that each bottle cap is redeemable for one order of free beignets at Doctor Ginger's neighbor, Eiffel's Café et Beignets, courtesy of T.D. Miller Pharmaceuticals, the maker of the vaccine."

Arnie leaked a sliver of a smile as she mentioned the coupon.

"And, now, Chose," Mrs. L introduced him in his preferred understated manner.

Chose began circling the lectern to talk to all of the classes at once as Mrs. L stepped back.

"A Chinese curse comes to mind," Chose began, "that says, 'May you live in interesting times.'" Chose chuckled a little to himself, which was still barely audible to the sharers. Most of the room chuckled as well in response. "And this session has certainly been an interesting time," he continued. "An interesting time indeed."

Chose looked directly at Robert and said, "In all of our history at GODA, we have never lost of a sharer. The near loss of you, Mister Rivers, is as close as we wish to come to that and we certainly hope you continue for many years to come to avoid bird - 'byproducts' - as well."

Robert turned four shades of reddish-brown as almost everyone in the room laughed at Chose's joke.

The disc behind Chose slid back open again. "I had more remarks to say, but won't now." The room grew quiet. "Please rise," Chose instructed as three-quarters of the hall had already started standing, "for Unius."

Unius rose from the hole and appeared to float from it to the lectern.

"Oh, my gosh!" Bernadette exclaimed. "He's really here."

"I thought he'd be bigger," Alex whispered down the row.

"Please, feel free to be seated," Unius said.

"Oh, my gosh!" Bernadette squealed in excitement. "He wants us to sit down."

"Please control yourself, Bernadette." Arnie snapped at her.

"To all whom these presents may come, greetings."

Unius pulled a bottle of Doctor Ginger's Scarletberry-Apple drink from the inside of his own long coat. He unscrewed the top and read the message in the top. He nodded at the message with approval and put the top in his pocket before turning up the bottle and draining it to share in the vaccination ritual of the day.

"First, the bad, then, the good," Unius began. Everyone seemed to have a puzzled look on their faces at his cryptic introduction. "For most of our existence," he continued, "we have been subject to attack, from without and from within, by that which attempts to turn us to the bad from our good."

Unius paused a moment and started speaking again. "Seven weeks ago, we had something occur on a coco valley that has never occurred there before." Unius's gaze fell on Ambrosius Ansgar. "One of our sharers struck another in anger. And, while it did not turn out to be the blow that caused the other's illness, it still was a tremendous departure from our one code."

Ambrosius sank low in his chair as Unius continued. "The forceful dominance of one over another, in any extreme, from a fist to the head to global nuclear war, is always a violation of our singular code. We do not impose ourselves on others nor do we appreciate those who do."

Ambrosius' eyes began to brim at being the object of what was now universal scorn. "Rise now, Mister Ansgar, and go receive Mister Rivers' forgiveness."

Ambrosius stood and walked over to where Robert Rivers was seated on the aisle of the deca's row and shook his hand. Robert stood up and embraced Ambrosius around the shoulders to a thunderous applause. Robert sat back down as Ambrosius returned to his chair.

"So much for the bad," Unius continued. "And, now, for the good." Unius looked at the row of Arnie and his friends. "Would deca freshman two-twelve please rise?" The entire row rose. "It has come to my attention," Unius continued, "that your deca is significantly responsible for saving not just our school but all of Demeverde from one of the most heinous threats to our lives that could ever be imagined." Everyone applauded until Unius raised his hand to quiet them. "And while your last trip to the Uncharted Island was completely unauthorized and is not to be repeated without consultation of Mrs. L or Chose, it has also come to my attention that some honorable mention is in order both collectively and individually."

The deca shifted nervously. "To the deca as a whole, for showing exceptional teamwork, drawing on each others' strengths and supporting each others' weaknesses, please accept the thanks of not only those of us here in Godeau, but also the thanks of all of Demeverde and the three other children around the world."

The deca bowed their heads as everyone in the room applauded wildly.

Unius led the applause for a moment and continued. "To Miss Amanda Purvis," Unius said as Amanda raised her eyes to his, "for having the right rhyme at the right time and learning to climb …" Unius paused as many people chuckled. "Please accept the thanks of your fellow sharers."

Everyone laughed and applauded at the same time.

"Miss Bernadette Rogers, for your calm persuasion at all stressful times …"

"Like now," Bernadette whispered to Arnie.

"Please accept the thanks of your fellow sharers."

Bernadette bowed her head a little and smiled.

"For the rest of your decamates, all of whose contributions to the effort are too numerous to list …" The classes all began to applaud. "Please accept the thanks of your fellow sharers." The clapping continued for a good minute as the sharers took bows and waved to their friends. Unius raised one hand for a second and the noise subsided.

"And now could Mister Arnie Carver come forward?" Unius asked.

"Aw, man!" Arnie protested to Bernadette beside him.

"Go on," Bernadette said, pushing him into the aisle.

Arnie walked down to be next to Unius, Mrs. L, and Chose. "For sharing with your deca and all of us, your knowledge, your bravery, and your persistent refusal to never, never, never give up ..." The applause started loud and then got much louder. "Please accept the thanks of your fellow sharers."

Unius let the applause wash over Arnie for quite a long time and then quieted the crowd. "Mister Carver," Unius said, while pointing the microphone in Arnie's direction, "I give you the honor of having the last words for the session and I wish you all a good intersession. Greetings." Unius backed away from the lectern with a wave to the sharers.

Arnie stepped up to the lectern and turned around to survey the entire hall full of people. "Mister Unius ---"

"Just Unius," he corrected him.

Arnie shook his head and he started again. "Unius," Arnie said. "On behalf of us all ..." Arnie turned around with his arms extended to include everyone in the room. He looked straight at Alex and said, "It was our pleasure."

The crowd clapped long and loud.

"Paradisial parrot," Alex seethed under his breath.

Arnie smiled very broadly. He raised his hands and brought them down again to quiet everyone and then yelled "Let's go home!"

* * *

A while after the festivities, Bernadette found Arnie, sitting in a gathering space, off the second floor of the freshman tower of the union.

"What are you going to do for the intersession?" Arnie asked her, sitting down beside him.

"I'm going back to California to be with my folks." Bernadette put her hand on his arm. "What about you?"

"I've got a job here working at Eiffel's," Arnie told her.

"Really? That's good." She said. "That Jack Marx seems very nice." Then she added patting his stomach. "I've noticed you have been spending a lot of time eating beignets there."

"I like him, and them, a lot," Arnie admitted, patting his own belly as well. "He's kind of adopted me I guess, because he's willing to give me all of the beignets I want for free."

"Well," Bernadette said getting up, "virmail me everyday and I'll see you back in two months." She kissed him on the cheek.

Arnie blushed at getting his first kiss from a girl. He rubbed his cheek. "Why'd you do that?" Arnie asked.

"I don't know," Bernadette said, walking away toward the SlipScrew. "'Cause I like you, I guess."

Uncharted Island

GO

GODA

Isla
Principal

Godeau
Mountain

Slip Hover
Beach

Globa
Reso